RANDOM HOUSE

LARGE PRINT

THE PROPHETS

THE
PROPHETS

A NOVEL

ROBERT JONES, JR.

R A N D O M　H O U S E
LARGE PRINT

All rights reserved.
Published in the United States of America by
Random House Large Print in association with G. P. Putnam's
Sons, an imprint of Penguin Random House LLC.

Copyright © 2021 by Robert Jones, Jr.

Cover design by Vi-An Nguyen
Photograph of the author © Alberto Vargas

The Library of Congress has established a
Cataloging-in-Publication record for this title.

ISBN: 978-0-593-29550-2

www.penguinrandomhouse.com/large-print-format-books

FIRST LARGE PRINT EDITION

Printed in the United States of America

10   9   8   7   6   5   4   3   2   1

This Large Print edition published in accord
with the standards of the N.A.V.H.

For my grandmothers Corrine and Ruby,
my grandfathers Alfred and George,
my great-uncles Milton, Charles, Cephas,
and Herbert, my father Robert,
my cousins Trebor, Tracey, and
Daishawn, my godparents Delores Marie
and Daniel Lee, Mother Morrison and
Father Baldwin, and all of my elders and
relatives who have passed on over,
who are now with the ancestors,
who are now, themselves, ancestors,
guiding and protecting me, whispering
to me so that I, too, might share
the testimony.

THE PROPHETS

JUDGES

You do not yet know us.

You do not yet understand.

We who are from the dark, speaking in the seven voices. Because seven is the only divine number. Because that is who we are and who we have always been.

And this is law.

By the end, you will know. And you will ask why we did not tell you sooner. Do you think you are the first to have asked that question?

You are not.

There is, however, an answer. There is always an answer. But you have not yet earned it. You do not know who you are. How could you possibly reckon with who **we** are?

You are not lost so much as you are betrayed by fools who mistook glimmer for power. They gave away all the symbols that hold sway. The penance for this is lasting. Your blood will have long been diluted by the time reason finally takes hold. Or the world itself will have been reduced to ash, making memory beside the point. But yes, you have been wronged. And you will do wrong. Again. And again. And again. Until finally, you wake. Which is why we are here, speaking with you now.

A story is coming.

Your story is coming.

It is the whole purpose of your being. Being (t)here. The first time you arrived you were not in chains. You were greeted warmly and exchanged food, art, and purpose with those who knew that neither people nor land should be owned. Our responsibility is to tell you the truth. But since you were never told the truth, you will believe it a lie. Lies are more affectionate than truth and embrace with both arms. Prying you loose is our punishment.

Yes, we too have been punished. We all have. Because there are no innocents. Innocence, we have discovered, is the most serious atrocity of all. It is what separates the living from the dead.

Eh?

A what this now?

Haha.
Forgive our laughter.
You thought **you** were the living and **we** were the dead?
Haha.

PROVERBS

On my knees, in the dark, I talk to them.

It's hard, sometimes, to understand what they saying. They been gone so long and they still use the old words that are half beat out of me. And it don't help that they whisper. Or maybe they really screaming and just so far away that it sound like a whisper to me. Could be that. Who can know?

Anyway, I dig in the spot they told me to and I bury the shiny sea stone just like they ask. But maybe I do something wrong because Massa Jacob still sell you off even after he say I a part of his family. Is this what toubab do to they family? Snatch them out they mother's arms and load them up on a wagon like harvest? Had me begging. In front of my man, had me begging until the only man I ever love can't even look at me right no more. His eyes make me feel like it's my wrong instead of they's.

I ask them, the old dark voices, about you. They say you right proud. On your way to becoming a man yourself. Got a lot of your people in you, but don't know it yet. And quick, maybe too quick for your own good. I surprised you still living. I ask them, I say, "Can you take a message to him? Tell him I remember every curl on his head and every fold on his body down to the creases between his toes. Tell him not even the whip can remedy that." They don't answer, but they say you down in Mississippi now, where whole things is made half. Why they tell me that, I don't know. What mother wanna hear her child finna be carved up and carved out for no reason at all? I guess it don't matter. Here or there, us all gone be made to pay somehow.

Ephraim ain't said a word since they took you. Not a single word in all this time. Can you imagine? I see his lips move, but I be damned if any sound come out his throat. Sometimes, I wanna say your name, the name we gave you, not the ugly one Massa throw on you and we act like it's okay. I think saying your name maybe bring him back to me. But the way he hang his head, like a noose around his neck that I can't see, I don't have the courage. What if saying your name be the thing that take him from me altogether?

"Can I see him?" I ask the dark. "Can Ephraim? We ain't even gotta touch him. Just take a quick look to know he still ours, even if he belong to somebody else." They say all Ephraim need to do is have a peek in one of those looking glasses. "How 'bout me?" I ask. They tell me look in Ephraim's eyes. "How can I do that," I ask, "when he won't look at me no more?" All I hear is the wind blowing through the trees and the **creek-creek** of bugs in the grass.

You like your people. You is **like your people.** I hold on to that and let that fill the empty space inside me. Swirling, swirling like fireflies in the night. Holding, holding still like water in the well. I's full. I's empty. I's full, then I's empty. I's full and I's empty. This must be what dying feels like.

It ain't no use. No use in hollering at folks who won't hear you. No use in crying in front of folks who can't feel your pain. They who use your suffering as a measuring stick for how much they gone build on top of it. I ain't nothing here. And ain't never gone be.

What he trade you for? To keep this rotten land that breaks spirit and bleeds mind? I tell you what: ain't gone be too much more of this here. Nah, sir. Take me and Ephraim and us leave here. Don't have to go nowhere, but leave. It be the same like slaughtering a hog. Just a sharp blade quick and deep across the throat and it be over just like that.

And then us get to be whispering voices in the dark telling some other people how they babies is getting along out there in the wild.

Oh, my poor baby!

Can you feel me?

I's Middle Anna and that there is Ephraim. We your mam and pappy, Kayode. And us sure do miss you.

PSALMS

July had tried to kill them.

First it tried to burn them. Then it tried to suffocate them. And finally, when neither of those things was successful, it made the air thick like water, hoping they would drown. It failed. Its only triumph was in making them sticky and mean—sometimes, toward each other. The sun in Mississippi even found its way into the shade so that on some days, not even the trees were comfort.

And, too, there was no good reason to be around other people when it was hot like this, but longing for company made it in some ways bearable. Samuel and Isaiah used to like being around other people until the other people changed. In the beginning, they had thought all the curled lips, cut eyes, turned-up noses—even the shaking heads—signified a bad scent emanating from their bodies because of the toil in the barn. The odor of swill alone had often made them strip bare and spend nearly an hour in the river bathing. Daily, just before sundown, when the others were bent out of shape from fieldwork and tried to find an elusive peace in their shacks, there Samuel and Isaiah were, scrubbing themselves with mint leaves, juniper, sometimes root beer, washing away the layers of stink.

But the baths didn't change the demeanor of the sucked teeth that held The Two of Them in contempt. So they learned to keep mostly to themselves. They were never unfriendly, exactly, but the barn became a kind of safe zone and they stuck close to it.

The horn had sounded to let them know work was ending. A deceitful horn, since work never ended, but merely paused. Samuel put down a bucket of water and looked at the barn in front of him. He took a few steps back so that he could see the entire thing. It needed a new coat of paint, the red parts and the white. **Good,** he thought. **Let it be ugly so it could be truth.** He wasn't going to paint anything, provided the Halifaxes didn't force his hand.

He walked a little to the right and looked at the trees in the distance, the ones behind the barn, down by the bank of the other side of the river. The sun had dimmed and began to dip into the forests. He turned to his left and looked toward the cotton field and saw the silhouettes of people carrying sacks of cotton on their backs and on their heads, dropping them off into wagons waiting in the distance. James, chief overseer, and a dozen or so of his underlings were lined up on either side of the constant flow of people. James's rifle was slung over his shoulder; his men held theirs in both hands. They pointed their rifles at the passing people as though they wanted to fire. Samuel wondered if he could take James. Sure, the toubab had some weight to him, and the benefit of firepower, but putting all that aside, if they were to have a right tussle, fist to fist and heart to heart like it was supposed to be, Samuel thought he could eventually break him—if not like a twig, then certainly like a man near his edge.

"You gon' help me or not?" Isaiah said, startling Samuel.

Samuel turned quickly. "You know better than to creep," he said, embarrassed for having been caught off guard.

"Ain't nobody **creep.** I walked right up. You so busy minding other folks' business . . ."

"Bah," Samuel said and waved his hand as though he were shooing a mosquito.

"You help me put these horses in they pens?"

Samuel rolled his eyes. There was no need to be as obedient as Isaiah always was. Maybe it wasn't that Isaiah was obedient, but did he really have to give them so much of himself and so readily? To Samuel, that spoke of fear.

Isaiah touched Samuel on the back and smiled as he walked toward the barn.

"I reckon," Samuel whispered and followed.

They put away the horses and watered them, then fed them a shovelful of hay and swept the remainder back into a neat stack near the front left corner of the barn, near the straighter bales. Isaiah smiled at Samuel's unwillingness, his grunts and sighs and head shaking, even though he understood the danger in it. Tiny resistances were a kind of healing in a weeping place.

By the time they finished, the sky was black and littered with stars. Isaiah walked back outside, leaving Samuel to his grievances. This was how he would engage in his own bit of rebellion: he leaned against the wooden fence that surrounded the barn and stared at the heavens. **Crowded,** he thought, and wondered if, perhaps, the abundance was too much; if the weight of holding on was too heavy, and the night, being as tired as it was, might one day let go, and all the stars would come tumbling down, leaving only the darkness to stretch across everything.

Samuel tapped Isaiah on the shoulder, waking him from his reverie.

"Now who ain't minding they business?"

"Oh, now the sky got business?" Isaiah smirked. "Least my work is finished for now, though."

"You a good slave, huh?" Samuel poked Isaiah in the belly.

Isaiah chuckled, lifted himself off the fence, and began walking back toward the barn. Just before he reached the door, he stooped to pick up a few pebbles. In quick succession, he threw them at Samuel.

"Ha!" he yelled and ran into the barn.

"You missed!" Samuel yelled back and ran into the barn after him.

They ran around inside, Isaiah dipping and dodging, laughing each time Samuel reached out to grab him, but he was too quick. When Samuel finally leaped and crashed into his back, they both stumbled face forward into the freshly piled hay. Isaiah wriggled to get loose, but the laughter made him too weak to make any headway. Samuel saying, "Uh huh," over and over again, smiling into the back of Isaiah's head. The horses let out loud breaths that reverberated through their lips. A pig squealed. The cows made no sounds, but the bells around their necks clanged with their movements.

After a moment more of struggle, Isaiah surrendered and Samuel relented. They turned on their backs and saw the moon through an opening in the roof; its pale light shot down on them. Their bare chests heaved and they panted audibly. Isaiah raised a hand up toward the opening to see if he could block out the light with his palm. There was a soft glow in the spaces between his fingers.

"One of us gotta get to fixing that roof," he said.

"Don't think of work now. Let yourself be," Samuel said a little more harshly than he intended.

Isaiah looked at Samuel. He examined his profile: the way his thick lips protruded from his face, less so his broad nose. His hair twisted and turned any which way. He looked down at Samuel's sweaty chest—the moonlight turned his dark skin to glitter—and was lulled by its rhythm.

Samuel turned to look at Isaiah, met his gentle stare with his own version. Isaiah smiled. He liked the way Samuel breathed with his mouth open, lower lip twisted slightly and tongue placed just inside the cheek like the expression of someone up to mischief. He touched Samuel's arm.

"You tired?" Isaiah asked him.

"Should be. But nah."

Isaiah scooted over until their bodies touched. The spot where their shoulders met grew moist. Their feet rubbed together. Samuel didn't know why, but he began to tremble, which made him angry because it made him feel exposed. Isaiah didn't see the anger; instead he saw beckoning. He rose to move on top of Samuel, who flinched a bit before relaxing. Isaiah slid his tongue, slowly and gently, over Samuel's nipple, which came to life in his mouth. Both of them moaned.

It was different from the first kiss—how many seasons ago was that now, sixteen or more? It was easier to count those than the moons, which sometimes didn't show up because they could be temperamental like that. Isaiah remembered that it was when the apples had been fuller and redder than they had ever been before or since—where they stumbled, and shame had kept them from looking into each other's eyes. Now Isaiah moved in close and let his lips linger on Samuel's. Samuel recoiled only a little. His uncertainty had found cover beneath repetition. The struggle that had once made him want to choke Isaiah as much as his self was in remission. There were only traces of it now, insignificant battles in the far corners of his eyes, maybe a smidgen at the back of his throat. But it was overcome by other things.

They didn't even give each other the chance to fully disrobe. Isaiah's pants were down around his knees; Samuel's dangling from an ankle. Impatient, thrusting into each other in a haystack, the moonlight shining dimly on Isaiah's ass and Samuel's soles—they rocked.

By the time the one slid off the other, they were already tumbled off the haystack, deeper into the darkness, spread out on the ground. They were so spent that neither wanted to move, though both craved a thorough washing in the river. Silently, they decided to remain where they were, at least until after they had regained control of their breathing and the spasms subsided.

In the darkness, they could hear the animals shuffling, and they could also hear the muffled sounds of the people nearby in their shacks, singing or maybe crying. Both were viable possibilities. More clearly, they could hear laughter coming from the Big House.

Though there were a least two walls and not an

insignificant amount of space between him and the laughter, Samuel looked in the direction of the house and tried to focus on the voices emanating from within. He thought he could recognize a few.

"Nothing never changes. New face, but same tongue," he said.

"What?" Isaiah asked as he stopped staring at the roof and faced Samuel's direction.

"Them."

Isaiah inhaled deeply, then exhaled slowly. He nodded. "So what we do? Bash the face? Split the tongue?"

Samuel laughed. "Face been bashed. Tongue already split. You've seen a snake before. Better to get far away as we can. Let them slither here on they own."

"That's the only choice, then: run?"

"If the face don't heed, don't even know it's not heeding. If the tongue don't yield. Yes."

Samuel sighed. Maybe Isaiah was afraid of the dark, but he wasn't. It was where he found shelter, where he blended, and where he thought the key to freedom surely rested. But still, he wondered what happened to people who wandered off into a wilderness that wasn't their own. Some turned into trees, he reckoned. Some became the silt at the bottom of rivers. Some didn't win the mountain lion's race. Some just died. He lay there silently for a moment, listening to Isaiah's breathing. Then he sat up.

"You coming?"

"Where?"

"To the river."

Isaiah turned on his side but said nothing. He looked in the direction of Samuel's voice and tried to differentiate his shape from the surrounding darkness. It was all one endless mass until Samuel moved and delineated the living from the dead. But what was that sound?

A scratching noise was coming from somewhere.

"You hear that?" Isaiah asked.

"Hear what?"

Isaiah was still. The scratching had stopped. He laid his head back down on the ground. Samuel moved again, as though preparing to stand.

"Wait," Isaiah whispered.

Samuel sucked his teeth but returned to his position, lying next to Isaiah. Just as he got comfortable, the scratching noise returned. He didn't hear it but Isaiah looked in the direction it was coming from, close to the horse pens. Something took shape there. It was first a tiny point, like a star, and then it spread until it was the night he was brought to the plantation.

Twenty of them, maybe more, piled into a wagon drawn by horses. All of them chained together at the ankles and at the wrists, which made movement labored and unified. Some of them wore iron helmets that covered their entire heads, turned their voices into echoes and their breathing into rattles. The oversized contraptions rested on their collarbones, leaving behind gashes that bled down to their navels and made them woozy. Everyone was naked.

They had traveled over bumpy, dusty trails for what, to Isaiah, seemed a lifetime—the sun burning their flesh in the day and mosquitoes tearing it up at night. Still, they were thankful for the torrential showers, when those without helmets could drink at their leisure rather than at the gunmen's.

When they finally reached Empty—which was what, in the quiet places, people called the Halifax plantation, and for good reason—he couldn't make out anything except a dim light coming from the Big House. And then they were pulled one by one from the wagon, each of them stumbling because none of them could feel their legs. For some, the weight of the helmet made it impossible to stand. Others had the burden of being held down by the corpse they were chained to. Isaiah, who was just a child, didn't even know enough to consider the man who lifted him up and carried him even though his own legs were about to give.

"I got you, little one," the man said. His voice labored and dry. "Your maw made me promise. And I gotta tell you your name."

Then everything went black.

When Isaiah came to, it was morning and they were all still chained together: living and dead alike. They were lying on the ground near the cotton field. He was hungry and thirsty, and the first to sit up. That was when he saw them: a group of people holding pails marching up the path, headed right for them. Some were as young as he was. They came with water and food—well, at least as close to food as he was liable to get. Pig parts that were seasoned enough to cover up the acrid taste and alleviate gagging.

A boy with a ladle approached him. He moved the ladle toward Isaiah's face. Isaiah parted his lips and closed his eyes. He gulped as warm, sweet water leaked from the corners of his mouth. When he was done, he looked up at the boy; the sun made him squint so that at first, he could only see the boy's outline. The boy moved a little, blocking the sun. He looked down at Isaiah with big, skeptical eyes and a chin too proud for anyone to have under those conditions.

"You want some more?" the boy called Samuel asked him.

Isaiah was no longer thirsty but nodded anyway.

When the darkness returned to itself, Isaiah touched his own body to make sure he wasn't a child anymore. He was himself, he was sure, but what had just come to him, from a pinpoint in the dark, proved that time could go missing whenever and wherever it pleased, and Isaiah couldn't yet figure out a way to retrieve it.

Isaiah couldn't be certain, but the remembrance that showed itself reminded him that he and Samuel were about the same age, sixteen or seventeen now, if every four seasons were properly counted. Nearly twenty years old now and so much had remained unspoken between them. To leave it in the silence was the only way it could be and not break a spirit in half. Working, eating, sleeping, playing. Fucking on purpose. For survival, everything that was learned had to be transmitted by circling the thing rather than uncovering it. Who, after all, was foolish enough to show wounds to folks who wanted to stick their mouth-sucked fingers into them?

The quiet was mutual, not so much agreed upon as inherited; safe, but containing the ability to cause great destruction. There, lying in the dark, Isaiah, exposed too closely to a living dream, heard it speak.

"You ever wonder . . . where your mam?" Isaiah heard it say.

He then realized it was his own voice, but he didn't remember speaking. It was as though another voice, one that sounded like his, had escaped his throat. His, but not his. How? Isaiah paused. Then he moved over, closer to Samuel. He felt his way around Samuel's body and settled his hand on Samuel's belly.

"I ain't mean . . . what I mean is, I ain't say . . ."

"You spit then try to grab it after it leave your mouth?" asked Samuel.

Isaiah was confused. "I ain't wanna say that. It came up by itself."

"Yeah," Samuel said, groaning.

"I . . . You never hear a voice and think it's not yours but it is? Or it kinda is? You ever see your life outside you? I don't know. I can't explain," said Isaiah.

He thought that maybe this was the witlessness that he saw take hold of a person, because the plantation could do that—make the mind retreat so that it could protect the body from what it was forced to do, yet leave the mouth babbling. To calm himself, he rubbed Samuel's stomach. The motion lulled the both of them. Isaiah had started to blink slower and slower. He was almost asleep when his mouth woke him up.

"Maybe a piece of you, somewhere inside, maybe your blood, maybe your guts, holds to her face?" Isaiah said, surprised at his words, rushing forth as though they had been dammed up. "Maybe when you look in the river, her face is what you see?"

There was silence and then Samuel inhaled suddenly and quickly.

"Maybe. No way to ever know," Samuel finally replied.

"Maybe a way to feel, though," Isaiah blurted.

"Huh?"

"I said maybe a way . . ."

"No. Not you. Never mind," Samuel said. "Let's go to the river."

Isaiah intended to stand, but his body preferred lying there with Samuel's.

"I know my mam **and** my pappy, but all I remember is their crying faces. Someone take me from them and they stand there watching me as the whole sky open up on them. I reach my hand out, but they only get farther and farther away until all I hear is screams and then nothing. My hand still reaching out and grabbing nothing."

Both of them stunned by this, Isaiah by the recollection and Samuel by hearing it, but neither of them moved. They were quiet for a moment. Then Samuel turned to Isaiah.

"You knew your **pappy**?"

"A man carried me here," Isaiah said, as he heard his history being recounted by his voice. "Not my pappy, but somebody who said he knew my name. Never told me, though."

Just then, Isaiah saw his own hand reaching out in the darkness of the barn, small, frantic, just like that day. He thought that perhaps he was reaching not just for his mam and pappy, but also for all those faded peoples who stood behind them, whose names, too, were lost forever, and whose blood nourished the ground and haunted it. Whose screams sound like whispers now—whispers that will be the last noise the universe will ever make. Samuel grabbed Isaiah's hand and put it back on his belly.

"Something here," Samuel said.

"What?"

"Nah."

Isaiah started to rub Samuel again, which encouraged his voice.

"The last thing they said to me was 'Coyote.' I ain't figure that one out yet."

"Maybe 'beware'?" Samuel said.

"Why you say that?"

Samuel opened his mouth, but Isaiah didn't see. He stopped rubbing on Samuel and instead laid his head on Samuel's chest.

"I ain't wanna say these things," Isaiah said, his voice now a croak. His cheeks were wet as he nestled his head deeper into Samuel.

Samuel shook his head. "Yeah."

He looked around, held Isaiah tighter, then closed his eyes.

The river could wait.

DEUTERONOMY

Samuel was second to wake, his face orange from the glow of a sun slow to rise. The rooster was making its noise, but Samuel had heard it often enough that it faded into the background as though it were silence. Isaiah was up already. Samuel had told Isaiah earlier in the morning to let himself lie, let himself rest, remember the moments. It would be considered theft here, he knew, but to him, it was impossible to steal what was already yours—or should have been.

He lay there, as tranquil as the morning that had dyed his body with the coming light, adamant on not budging until he absolutely had to. He didn't see Isaiah, but he could hear him just outside the opened barn doors, heading toward the henhouse. Samuel sat up. He looked around the barn, observed the scattered hay from the night before, noticed how the dark hid those things and the day left behind trails that weren't exactly clear. One wouldn't necessarily assume that the cause of the mess came from pleasure. More likely, they would think it the result of carelessness, and therefore worthy of punishment. He exhaled and stood up. He walked over to the barn wall where the tools hung in rows. He went to the nearest corner and retrieved the broom. Reluctantly, he swept the evidence of their bliss back into a neat pile, nearer to where their misery was already neatly stacked. All of it to be sustenance for beasts anyway.

Isaiah came back into the barn holding two pails. "Morning," he said with a smile.

Samuel looked at him with a half grin but didn't return the greeting. "You up too early."

"One of us gotta be."

Samuel shook his head and Isaiah smiled at that too. Isaiah put down his pails, walked over, and touched Samuel's arm. He slid his hand down until their hands were joined. Isaiah squeezed, and eventually Samuel squeezed back. Isaiah watched as Samuel's untrusting eyes fully embraced him. He saw himself there, in the gaze of the deepest shade of brown he had seen outside of dreams, warm and enjoyed. He opened his own eyes a bit more, inviting Samuel in so that he could know that warmth was waiting for him, too.

Samuel let go. "Well, since we up, we might as

well . . ." He gestured at the plantation broadly. Isaiah took Samuel's hand again and kissed it.

"Not in the light," Samuel said with a frown.

Isaiah shook his head. "There's no bottom below bottom."

Samuel sighed, handed Isaiah the broom, and walked outside into the morning onto which a humid sky was descending.

"Don't feel like doing this."

"What?" Isaiah asked, following behind him.

"This." Samuel pointed outward at everything around them.

"We gotta do it," Isaiah replied.

Samuel shook his head. "We ain't **gotta** do shit."

"So you risk whupping, then?"

"You forget? We ain't even gotta do **this** much to risk whupping."

Isaiah folded in on himself at that. "Can't stand to see you hurt."

"Maybe you can't stand to see me free neither?"

"Sam!" Isaiah shook his head and began to walk toward the chicken coop.

"Sorry," Samuel whispered.

Isaiah didn't hear him and Samuel was glad. Samuel walked over toward the hogs. He grabbed a pail and then, still watching Isaiah, it crept up behind him. Recollections often came back in pieces like this.

That day—it was night, really, the black sky all

but stardust—they were still too young to understand their conditions. They looked up into that sky,
through the knothole in the roof wood. A blink was
all it was. And exhaustion held them down on a pallet of hay. Dizzy from work that their bodies could
barely manage. Earlier, their hands brushed at the
river and lingered longer than Samuel expected. A
confused look, but then Isaiah smiled and Samuel's
heart didn't know whether to beat or not, so he got
up and started walking back to the barn. Isaiah
followed him.

They were in the barn and it was dark. Neither felt
like lighting a torch or a lamp so they just pushed out
some hay and covered it with the piece-cloth blanket Be Auntie had made them, and then they both
lay down on their backs. Samuel exhaled and Isaiah
broke the quiet with "Yessuh." And that hit Samuel's
ear differently then. Not a caress exactly, but still
gentle. His creases were moist and he tried to hide
them even from himself. It was a reflex. Meanwhile,
Isaiah turned on his side to face Samuel and all
his soft parts were open and free, tingling without
shame. They looked at each other and then they were
each other, there, both of them, in the dark.

All it took was a moment, so both of them understood how precious time was. Imagine having
as much of it as you wanted. To sing songs. Or to
wash in a glittering river beneath a lucid sun, arms
open to hold your one, whose breath was now your

breath, inhale, exhale, same rhythm, same smile returned. Samuel didn't know he had the heat until he felt Isaiah's.

Yes, recollections came in pieces. Depending on what was trying to be recalled, they could come in shambles. Samuel had started slopping the hogs when the pin that had been stabbing at his chest all morning had finally broken through. It had only a little blood on its tip, but the blood was there all the same. Who knew blood could talk? He had heard others speak of blood memory, but that was just images, wasn't it? Nobody ever said anything about voices. But last night, Isaiah had brought so many of them with them into the barn on the end of his question, a question that had smashed all of their established rules, the ones that they had come up with between them, the ones that so many of their people understood.

Samuel tossed the hogs more food. He ignored the pin sticking out from his chest and the whispering blood, which was now coming forth as a droplet, not unlike rain, carrying within it its own multitude, its own reflections, a world—a whole world!—inside.

He began to feel hot and itchy inside.

You ever wonder where your mam?

Before then he was able to avoid the pinch of such inquiries, lose them in the abundant sorrow that permeated the landscape. No one asked each other about the scars, missing limbs, tremors, or night terrors, and so they could, therefore, be stashed in corners behind sacks, cast in waters, buried underground. But there was Isaiah digging around for shit he had no business digging around for, talking about he "ain't mean." Then why did he say? Samuel thought they had a deal: leave the bodies where they fucking lay.

They were in the dark last night, so Isaiah couldn't see, thankfully, that Samuel shifted on the ground, almost stood up, and announced that he was heading to the river, where he would submerge himself and never resurface. Instead, he sat there, muscles flexing under the strain of grasping for something not there. He blinked and blinked, but it didn't stop his eyes from burning. **What kind of question was this?**

He had let out a breath in a huff. Even in the dark, he could feel Isaiah's calm anticipation, its steady, relentless tugging, coaxing him to open himself up yet again. But had he not opened himself up wide enough? No one else had known what it was like—what it looked like, felt like, tasted like—deep inside of him but Isaiah. What more could he give that wasn't everything already? He wanted to hit something. Grab an ax and hack at a tree. Or maybe wring a chicken's neck.

The quiet between them was stinging. Samuel took a deep breath as the shadow of a woman rose in the dark just at his feet. Darker than the dark, she stood naked: breasts hanging, hips wide. She had a face that was somehow familiar, though he had never seen it before. Further, a shadow in the dark made no sense. They were daytime denizens. And yet, there she was: a black that made night jealous with eyes that were, themselves, questions. Could this be his mother, stirred up by Isaiah's broken pact? Did that mean he was a shadow, too? Suddenly, she pointed at him. Startled, he spoke suddenly.

Maybe. No way to ever know.

Maybe she made Isaiah speak, too?

As the hogs ate, Samuel tried to wipe the blood from the pin and remove it from his chest. He stopped when he heard a noise in the distance. He wasn't sure if it was the rustling of weeds or a yell. He looked toward the trees and he saw something. It looked like the shadow. It had come back in the morning light as a reminder. Conjured up by an inquiry, it would now roam everywhere he roamed because that is what he had heard mothers were supposed to do: watch every move their child made until such time that the child was no longer a child and it was then the former child's duty to create life and watch it bloom or watch it wither.

"'Zay! Come on over here and see this." Samuel pointed out toward the woods.

Isaiah ran up beside Samuel. "Ain't you gon' apologize for what you said to me?"

"I did that. You just ain't hear me. But look. There. That there. Moving."

"The trees?" Isaiah was quick with those words, distracted, wanting to discuss the other thing.

"No, no. That thing there. Don't know what . . . a shadow?"

Isaiah squinted and he saw a flutter.

"I don't . . ."

"You saw it?"

"Yeah. Don't know what it is."

"Let's go see."

"And get whupped for being near the edge?"

"Bah," Samuel said, but he also didn't budge.

As they both peered into the edge, what had at first been black became white as James the overseer emerged from the army of trees. He was followed by three of the toubab in his charge.

"You think they found somebody?" Samuel said, oddly relieved that it was James and not the shadow.

"They say you can tell by they ears," Isaiah replied, looking at James and his men. "By how the bottom part hang. But I can't see from here."

"Maybe they just patrolling. Ain't it time for the call to the field?"

"Uh huh."

Neither of them moved as they watched the men work their way across bush and weed, still walking along the perimeter toward the cotton field, which stretched to the horizon and sometimes looked as though its clouds touched the ones in the sky.

Empty began to show signs of life as other people emerged from their shacks to look the light in the face. Samuel and Isaiah waited to see who, if anyone, would acknowledge them. These days, only Maggie and a few others had kept them in their graces, for some reason.

The sound of the horn startled Isaiah. "I ain't never gon' get used to that," he said.

Samuel turned to him. "If you right-minded, you don't have to."

Isaiah sucked his teeth.

"Oh, you happy here, 'Zay?"

"Sometimes," Isaiah said, looking into Samuel's eyes. "Remember the water?"

Samuel found himself smiling even though he didn't want to.

"And one gotta think and not just do to be happy," Isaiah said, returning to the question Samuel asked.

"I reckon we should get to thinking, then."

The horn sounded again. Samuel looked toward the sound, over by the field. His eyes narrowed. Then he felt Isaiah's hand on his back. Isaiah held it there, calm and steady, the heat from it not making things worse. A moment, which would pass too quickly and yet couldn't pass quickly enough. It was almost as if Isaiah were holding him up, pushing him forward, giving him something to lean on when the legs got a little weary.

Still, Samuel said, "Not in the light."

Still, Isaiah kept his hand there for a moment more. He then started to hum. He would do that sometimes while stroking Samuel's hair as they lay together in the dead of night and that would make Samuel's sleep a bit easier.

Samuel wore an expression that said, **Enough now!** But in his head, etched across his mind, in bright shining voice, was:

Isaiah soothing. He always a soothing thing.

Maggie

She woke.

She yawned.

A burial place. This be a fucking burial place, Maggie whispered, before it was time to go to the other room, the kitchen that she was chained to even though not a single link could be seen. But yes, there it was, snapped around her ankle, clinking nevertheless.

She mumbled the curse to herself, but it was meant for other people. She learned to do that, whisper low enough in her throat that an insult could be thrown and the target would be none the wiser. It became her secret language, living just below the audible one, deeper behind her tongue.

The sky was still dark, but she lay in her hay pallet

an extra moment, knowing it could cost her. The Halifaxes each had their own way of communicating their displeasure, some less cruel than others. She could tell you stories.

She climbed out off of the pallet and rolled her eyes at the hounds that lay on the floor by her feet. Oh, she slept on the back porch with the animals. Not her choice. Though it was enclosed and provided views out onto Ruth Halifax's garden. Beyond it, a field of wildflowers bursting with every color, but the blues were the ones that were perfect enough to hurt feelings. Several rows of trees marked the end of the field and gave way to sandy ground that opened onto the bank of the Yazoo River. There, the people, when permitted, would scrub themselves down in the sometimes muddy water under the watchful gaze of the man whose name Maggie stopped saying for a reason. On the other side of the river, which seemed farther away than it was, a mess of trees stood so close together that no matter how hard she squinted, she couldn't see past the first row.

She wanted to hate the fact that she was made to sleep there on the porch, low to the ground on some makeshift bed she piled together herself from the hay she got from Samuel and Isaiah, whom she referred to as The Two of Them. But so often the smell of the field calmed her and if she had to be in the damn Big House with Paul and his family, then it was best she was in the space farthest from them.

The hounds were Paul's choice. Six of them that got to know every living soul on the plantation in case any of those souls tried to drift. She had seen it before: the beasts chased people into the sky and managed to snatch them down no matter how high they thought they could float. Them dogs: ears just a-flopping, woofing in that gloomy way they do, sad eyes and everything. You almost felt sorry for them until they got ahold of your ass and bit it all the way back to the cotton field—or the chopping block, one.

They whined and she detested the sound. Why they kept the animals enclosed was beyond her reasoning. Animals belonged outdoors. But then again, the Halifaxes were indoors so that meant all of creation had some right to be inside as well.

"Go on," she said to the hounds, unlatching the door that led out to the garden. "Go find a hare and leave me be."

All six of them ran out. She inhaled deeply, hoping she took in enough of the field to last her through the day. She kept her hand on the door so that it would close quietly. She limped over to another door on the opposite side of the porch and went into the kitchen. It could have been its own cabin given that it was twice the size of even the largest of the shacks people lived in at Empty. Still, she felt cramped in it, like something unseen was pushing her down from every direction.

"Breathe, chile," she said aloud and dragged her

hurt leg over to the counter that ran underneath a row of windows that faced east and looked out onto the barn.

She grabbed two bowls and the sack of flour stored in the cupboards beneath the counter. She removed a jug of water and a sifter from the cabinet left of the counter. Once combined, she began kneading the ingredients into dough for biscuits: a heavy thing that, with heat, time, and her bruised knuckles, became yet another meal that failed to satisfy Halifax appetites.

She moved over toward the front of the kitchen to get some logs to heat the stove. There was a pile of them under another window, one that faced east. During the day, that window allowed her to see past the willow tree in front of the house, down the long path that led to the front fence and intersected with the dusty road to Vicksburg's town square.

She had only seen the square once, when she was dragged from Georgia and hauled off to Mississippi. Her old master had loaded her up onto a wagon, chained her feet, and sat her among some other frightened people. The journey took weeks. Once they got past the lumbering trees, the road opened up upon a great number of buildings, the kind of which she had never seen. She was marched from the wagon onto some platform, where she stood before a great crowd. A toubab, filthy and smelling of ale, stood next to her and shouted numbers. The people in the audience looked at her, none raised their hands in pursuit of her—none except Paul, whom she heard tell his young charge that she would make a good kitchen wench and companion for Ruth.

She picked up two logs and headed for the stove, which sat near one of the doors. The kitchen had two doors. The one closest to the stove faced west and led to the covered porch where she slept. The other, facing south, led into the dining room, beyond which was the foyer, the living room, and the sitting room where Ruth entertained when she was up to it. One of the windows in the sitting room faced the cotton fields. Ruth often sat and stared through it for hours. On her face, a smile so delicate Maggie couldn't be sure it was a smile at all.

At the back of the house was Paul's study, which contained more books than Maggie had ever seen in one place. Glimpses of the room only intensified her desire to be able to open one of the books and recite the words, any words, as long as she could say them herself.

On the second floor, four large bedrooms anchored each corner of the house. Paul and Ruth slept in the two rooms facing east, adjoined by a balcony from which they surveyed most of the property. At the back of the house, Timothy, their only surviving child, slept in the northwestern room when he wasn't away at school in the North. Ruth insisted that his bedsheets be washed weekly and his bed be turned down every night despite his absence. The last bedroom was for guests.

Perceptive folks called the Halifax plantation by

its rightful name: Empty. And there was no escape. Surrounded by dense, teeming wilderness—swamp maple, ironwood, silverbell, and pine as far, high, and tangled as the mind could imagine—and treacherous waters where teeth, patient and eternal, waited beneath to sink themselves into the flesh, it was the perfect place to hoard captive peoples.

Mississippi only knew how to be hot and sticky. Maggie sweated so profusely that the scarf wrapped around her head was drenched by the time she began gathering the cookware. She would have to change it before the Halifaxes got up to eat. Her neat appearance was important to them, these people who didn't even wash their hands before they ate and who didn't clean themselves after leaving the outhouse.

With powdered hands, Maggie rubbed her sides, content with how her figure—not just its particular curves, but also how it never burned and became red under a beaming sun—separated her from her captors. She loved herself when she could. She regretted nothing but her limp (not the limp itself, but how it came to be). The world tried to make her feel some other way, though. It had tried to make her bitter about herself. It had tried to turn her own thinking against her. It had tried to make her gaze upon her reflection and judge what she saw as repulsive. She did none of these things. Instead, she fancied her skin in the face of these cruelties. For she was the kind of black that made toubab men drool and her own men recoil. In her knowing, she glowed in the dark.

When she felt her shape, it evoked in her another outlawed quality: confidence. None of this was visible to the naked eye. It was a silent rebellion, but it was the very privacy of it that she enjoyed most. Because there was precious little of that here—privacy, joy, take your pick. There were only the four dull corners of the kitchen, where sorrow hung like hooks and rage leaped in from any opening. It came in from the spaces between floorboards, the slits between door-jambs and doors, the line between lips.

She threw the logs into the belly of the stove, then grabbed a pan out of the cupboard above. She went back to the counter and removed the dough from the bowl. Tenderly, she molded. Properly, she spaced the shapes into the pan. Then into the oven. But that didn't mean she could rest. There was always more to do when serving people of invention. Inventors for the sake of inventing: out of boredom, solely to have something over which to marvel, even when it was undeserved.

Their creativity puzzled her. Once, Paul called her into his room. When she arrived, he was standing near the window, the sun rendering him featureless.

"Come here," he said, his calm laced with venom.

He asked her to hold his manhood while he uri-nated into a bedpan. She thought herself lucky con-sidering the other possibilities. And when he ordered her to point its slit at her chest, she left the room splashed yellow and drawing flies. She counted her blessings, but still: how confusing.

She tried to remember something Cora Ma'Dear— her grandmother from Georgia who taught Maggie who she was—said to her. She was just a girl then, and their time together had been so brief. But some things printed on the mind cannot be erased—made fuzzy maybe, but not gone. She tried to remember the old word from the other sea that Cora Ma'Dear used to describe toubab. Oyibo! That was it. There was no equivalent in English. The closest was "accident." Then it was simple: these people were an accident.

Maggie didn't much mind their brutality, though, because it was what she had come to expect from them. People rarely deviated from their nature, and although it pained her to admit, she found a tiny bit of comfort in the familiarity. Their kindness, however, sent her into a panic. For it, like any trap, was unpredictable. She rejected it and risked the consequences. Then, at least, the retaliation took on a recognizable form and she wasn't rendered a fool.

When she first arrived at Empty, years ago, she was greeted so warmly by Ruth, who looked to be about the same age as she. Both of them still girls despite the newly flowing blood.

"You can stop crying now," Ruth said to her then, eyes cheerful and thin lips pulled back into a smile, revealing crooked teeth.

She rushed her inside what was the biggest house

Maggie had ever seen. Ruth even took Maggie up-stairs to her room, where she pulled a dress out of the bureau. Maggie had the nerve to adore it. She was seduced by its pattern of orange rosebuds so tiny they could be mistaken for dots. She had never had anything so pretty. Who wouldn't quiver? Ruth was with child at the time—one of the ones who didn't survive—and used her body's new shape as justifica-tion for giving away such a fine thing.

"They say I'm due in the winter. Terrible thing to have a child in the winter. Don't you think so?"

Maggie didn't answer because any answer damned her.

"Well, we'll just have to make sure the death of pneumonia don't reach here, now won't we?" Ruth said to fill in the silence.

Now that was a safe one to answer. Maggie nodded.

"Oh, you're going to look so pretty in this dress! You so shiny. I always thought white looked better on niggers than it did on people."

Maggie was young then and couldn't know the price. How dangerous to be so accepting. The dress could have been reclaimed at any moment, accompa-nied by an accusation. And, indeed, when it was said that Maggie stole it, after Ruth had been nothing but kind to her, Maggie didn't deny it because what would be the use? She took her licking like a woman twice her age with half the witnesses.

Oh, Ruth cried her conviction, imagining that it would make her sincerity indisputable. The tears looked real. She also spoke some silliness about a sisterly bond but never once asked Maggie if it was an arrangement she desired. It was assumed that whatever Ruth wanted to piss, Maggie wanted to cup her hands under and drink. So Ruth cried and Maggie learned right then and there that a toubab woman's tears were the most potent of potions; they could wear down stone and make people of all colors clumsy, giddy, senseless, soft. What, then, was the point of asking, **So why didn't you tell the truth?**

Winter came and Ruth gave birth, a girl she named Adeline. She brought the child—pale and discontent—into the kitchen and said to Maggie, "Here. I'll help you unfasten your dress."

Maggie had seen other women submit to this and had feared this day for herself. Only with a great deal of restraint could she act as a cow for this child. It had dull eyes and eyelashes so close to the color of its own skin that it might as well not have had any at all. Maggie detested the feel of its probing lips on her breast. She forced herself to smile just to keep from smashing its frail body to the ground. What kind of people won't even feed their own babies? Deny their offspring the blessing of their very own milk? Even animals knew better.

From then on, all children disturbed Maggie, including her own. She judged harshly all people who had the audacity to give birth: men who had the nerve to leave it inside; women who didn't at least attempt, by hook or by crook, to end it. She regarded them all with great suspicion. Giving birth on Empty was a deliberate act of cruelty and she couldn't forgive herself for accomplishing it on three out of six occasions. And who knew where the first or the second were now. See? Cruelty.

Chirrun, as she called them, didn't even have the grace to know what they were, and neither did many of the adults, but that was on purpose: ignorance wasn't bliss, but degradation could be better endured if you pretended you were worthy of it. The youngins ran around the plantation, in and out of the stables, hiding in the cotton field, busy as manure flies. Their darting, knotty heads were unaware of the special hell tailored for each of them. They were foolish, helpless, and unlovable, but whatever loathing Maggie felt for them was mitigated by what she knew they would one day endure.

Toubab children, however, would be what their parents made them. She could do nothing to intervene. No matter what kindly tricks she employed, they would be the same dreary, covetous creatures they were destined to be, a blight their humorless god encouraged. For them, Maggie could only muster pity, and pity only served to magnify her disgust.

It had occurred to her early on to rub nightshade petals on her nipples just before being forced to suckle. Against her skin, purple was disguised. It worked. Adeline died for what appeared to be inexplicable reasons. She foamed at the mouth. But this created no suspicion because Ruth had miscarried once and had a stillborn child just prior.

The fourth child, Timothy, however, had a will to survive nearly as strong as Maggie's. Grown now. Handsome, for one of **them.** Kinder than she would have imagined he could be given what he was. **What is he doing now?** she wondered. Painting, probably. He had a talent for such things. Ruth had made Maggie scrub the house down in anticipation of his return, which wouldn't be for weeks still. Scrubbed or not, everything looked the same to Maggie and would probably look the same to Timothy too.

She didn't spare the adults. She knew her attempts would be puny, insignificant rootwork that was more dangerous to her than to her targets. But minuscule power was still power. Therefore, when she was able, when not under surveillance, which was rare but not unknown, after she believed she had gained a modicum of their trust, she would seek all manner of things to add to her recipes. Slowly, patiently, a few drops of snake venom in the sweet tea. A tiny bit of heel-ground glass dust in the hominy grits. Never feces or urine because that was too personal. Not even a hair from her head, which is why the head wrap was so important. She wouldn't allow them the pleasure, the privilege of having any part of her freely given. And beyond that, it was simply insulting; it would only grant them even greater mastery over her. As with any good magic, she topped it off with a gentle humming that listeners often mistook for an ode to some far-off trickster in the sky. At the very least, if she couldn't kill them, she could make them uncomfortable. Cantankerous bellies and the rare bloody stool were pleasant, reassuring results.

But she remembered that she mustn't raise suspicion. She didn't put anything in the biscuits this time. She recently received a warning in her dreams. Typically, she dreamed only of darkness. Sleep of the dead, they called it, and she suffered at Paul's hands for it more than once. So when her mother came to her whispering, dressed in white with a veil over her face, Maggie recognized all the signs for danger and knew that she would have to be particularly cautious. Just bread for now.

The dogs were back, fussing and whimpering at the back door, aroused by the scent of the pork she started frying in the pan. She stepped out onto the back porch and into the dark morning. The sky had just begun to get pallid at the edges, but the sun was nowhere to be found. She kissed the air out loud in the hopes of getting the dogs' attention, get the pack of them to hush. For a moment, they quieted. Then they started up again. She stepped down into the field and picked up a stick. She shook it at them and then threw it as far as she could into the brush. They gave chase.

"Thank goodness," she said.

She gazed into the darkness, the same direction toward which the dogs ran. Whatever was in those woods, and beyond, was sure to be better than here, she thought, certainly couldn't be no worse. When she was younger, she let herself think about what could be behind the clusters of trees. Another river, surely. Maybe a town with people who almost looked like her. Perhaps a giant hole where creatures lived. Or a mass grave where people were thrown when they were no longer useful.

Or maybe the toubab were right and there wasn't a single thing beyond the woods but the edge of the world and those who ventured there were doomed to be swallowed up by nothingness. Nothingness seemed as good a choice as any, though. She stared and stared but didn't move. She didn't admit it, not even to herself, but she was broken. Her years on Empty had succeeded in hollowing her like its name promised. From friend to rag doll to cattle to cook, and not a single one with her permission. Wouldn't that bust anyone up? So yes, she was broken. But she wasn't shattered. She could keep passing her misery back onto its source. Maybe that could be a mending.

Essie, who helped Maggie in the house sometimes, would be up by now. Surely tending to that crying burden of hers, the one that nearly killed her coming into the world.

"Mag, I don't know what I gon' do. He look at me with those glassy eyes and scare me so," Essie said to her once. Maggie looked at her: Essie's hair was disheveled, her dress crooked, her face ashy with tearstains. She had only seen Essie like this once before. Both times, it annoyed her.

"Woman, ain't nothing you can do now. What's done is done. That baby your'n. If it's the eyes that scare you so bad, close yours. Or hand him off to Be Auntie, who love that color more than her own." Maggie replied with more sharpness than she had intended. She paused and rubbed Essie's shoulder.

"Maybe," Maggie then said softly, "maybe I could come by every now and again to help." She forced a smile. "And we can get Amos to pitch in; I don't care what he say 'bout it—'specially now that y'all done took the broom leap."

Maggie didn't really care what Amos said about most things. She remembered when, some time back, he walked into the study with Paul Halifax and emerged transformed into something unrecognizable; more beautiful to some, but to Maggie, every glint in his eye and click of his tongue was deception. Yet he was so proud. People liked pride. Mistook it for purpose.

"Good morning," Amos would say with a smile too earnest to be honest. Maggie would nod in return as she walked by him and then cut her eyes the moment she was clear. She did, however, understand what Essie saw in him when Paul sent him in to her. It was nice to be asked rather than taken, to be held close rather than held down. Nevertheless, a snake was still a snake and its bite hurt whether it was poisonous or not.

Sometimes, when Maggie watched Amos closely—the gait of his walk, the upward tilt of his nose, how his habbage rode his back—she laughed. She knew what he was trying to do, whom he was attempting to imitate, and she knew why. She had no contempt for him but had no warmth either. He had a kind face, though sorrowful; the latter connected him to their people and this place. He was as black as virgin soil even if his loyalties seemed to lie elsewhere, where the potential for backfire was imminent.

Maggie shook her head and put her hands on her hips.

"Just plain foolish," she said to no one.

She turned to walk back into the kitchen and saw that the sky had begun to lighten a bit and she could make out the shape of the barn among the shadows. That was where Samuel and Isaiah spent most of their time working, tending to the animals, breathing, sleeping, and other things. Those poor boys: The Two of Them. They learned, and learned early, that a whip was only as loathsome as the person wielding it. Sometimes, they made it even harder for themselves by being so damn stubborn. But never had stubbornness been so enchanting.

She didn't take to them at first. Like all children, one was indistinguishable from the other. They blended into a mass of ignorant, pitiful bodies, and they laughed, high-pitched, without reserve, which made them too tempting to ignore. There wasn't a single blade of grass that didn't bend to the sorrow of this place, but these little ones behaved as if it could be openly defied. But by the time hair began to sprout around their sexes, The Two of Them had figured out (maybe not figured out as much as revealed) an ingenious way of separating themselves from the others: by being themselves. And the split exposed a feeling in her long hidden.

Even now, she couldn't explain it, but her breasts became tender around them, like they should have, but didn't, when she was forced to be Empty's mare. Along with the tenderness of breast came a tenderness of heart. It wasn't simply that they were helpful, that she never had to lift a bucket of water from the well or a log for the fire or a boulder to beat the wash when they were around. It wasn't just that they had never asked anything of her, not even her approval. It might have been that the feeling had nothing to do with them at all, but rather with something they helped her to remember.

She saw something once. Just as the moon had gone as high as it would go, she crept over one night to bring them the food that she had hidden earlier that morning: a strip of fried quail, half an egg, a few apple slices that she mashed into a sauce, no poisons. She moved quietly from the house to the barn. She came up from the backside of the barn and intended to enter from a side door, but it was latched. She heard noises and pressed her ear up against the wall. A moan, perhaps; a gasp; the longest sigh ever. Then she peered through a crack between the boards of the wall. She could only see them because of the moonlight that shot in through the parts of the roof where the planks needed repair. Shadowy figures. From a distance, they seemed to be tussling.

She was certain she saw Samuel bite Isaiah's shoulder in an attempt to be free from his grasp. They fumbled around the haystack, crushing misplaced saddles and frightening wayward crickets into the air. They were naked, sweaty, as twisted together as earthworms, and grunting pig songs. When they had finally come to a stop, their faces were pressed together, held there, seemingly, by their quivering tongues. Then one turned on his stomach. She hurried back to the Big House.

To ease some other pain, surely. Surely.

But what was that flitting around in her head and why had she begun to sweat so? What was she remembering?

Her journey to the barn became nighttime routine. Quietly, she peeked into it, gladly offering her soul for just a sliver of moonlight. She watched them from underneath ladders, behind stacks of hay, or through the back walls of horse pens. She had no desire to interrupt or even to discuss what she saw; simply bearing witness was treasure. For they were as frisky and playful as crows and her proximity made her feel as if she were in the dark sky, suspended upon the surface of their wings. Oh so black. Oh so high. Up there, where there was safety and glow.

But down here, they had better be careful.

She had tried to find a word for what she witnessed. There was none she could think of; at least, there was no word extraordinary enough, particularly not in the tongue she spoke now.

Why aren't they afraid? Maggie found herself asking as she stood in the kitchen, still staring at the barn from the northern windows. She rubbed her face. Out of the corner of her eye, she saw something blink into existence, shimmer, and then fade out as soon as it had arrived. It was the edge of something black. Then something swirled. With it came the stench. She could only see the outline, but it might have been someone on fire. By the time she reached for a jug of water, it was gone. A spot of dried blood on the floor right where the haint had visited was the only evidence she had that she was not imagining things.

The pounding in her chest subsided and she scratched her cheek to stop from weeping. Was it memory or prophecy? She couldn't tell. Sometimes, there was no difference. She held on to herself regardless and put past and future things as far away as they would let her—as though that mattered. Visions had the keys to the cage and would let themselves out whenever they pleased. This condition had to be lived with. There was no other way.

The cage was unlocked when thinking about The

Two of Them. And it was, then, no surprise to her that they chose each other above the other, more readily available options. It was unremarkable that they mostly didn't pay attention to a woman, not even when forced. Not even in July, when toubab women would wait for toubab men to render themselves unconscious from spirits. These women—who went on and on about what it meant to be a lady (a term Maggie thought foolish)—got down on barn floors, pulled their dresses up over their breasts, spread their legs from one corner to the other, and writhed for the men they publicly despised.

Isaiah and Samuel weren't moved in January either, when people sometimes huddled together for warmth. This close to a woman—whose skin and hair were dark with readiness, whose breath comforted and agitated, whose nether-scent threatened to make the insides of men shatter from longing—and neither of The Two of Them so much as twitched a pinky finger. No, those boys risked more than was necessary searching each other's faces, again and again, for the thing that made rivers rush toward the sea. Always one smiling and always the other with his mouth angry and ajar. Reckless.

She looked out the window again at the barn and saw the sun peek its head through the eastern trees. The pork was almost done. She took a plate and wiped it with the edge of her dress and went to the dining room table.

She had set the table with unfathomable resentment.

White table linen, sharp at the corners, napkin rings strangling, cutlery already its own kind of deadly. All living things smothered, even the picked-wildflower centerpiece. The dim candle lighting cast a brass shadow, making everything, even Maggie, appear appropriately solemn.

She had to arrange the table the same each day: Paul always at the head; Ruth always to his right; Timothy, when home, always to his left, and three extra settings for the occasional guests. She would stand around after she had set the table and listen to the family give, in unison, thanks to the long-haired man whose gaze always turned upward—probably because he couldn't bear to see the havoc wreaked in his name. Or maybe he just couldn't bother to look. Maggie only knew about this man because she let Essie talk her into going to one of Amos's sermons one Sunday.

They held court in the woods, in the circle of trees at the southeastern edge of the cotton field. The man whose name she couldn't speak for a reason was there with a few of his scraggly minions and she wanted to turn right around when she saw him. But Essie had begged her to stay. She seemed so proud—and something other than proud, but Maggie couldn't tell what.

Amos stood upon a big rock that neither time nor water had worn down. But that was exactly what the clearing smelled like to her: the moist and tired things that hid beneath rocks—or, in this case, stood

on top of them. There were about thirty people in
the crowd then, sitting on logs or on the ground.
That was before people started to believe Amos. He
opened his mouth and she sucked her teeth. He
wasn't doing anything but repeating some bits and
pieces she heard Paul discuss around the dinner
table. She knew from experience that no good could
come from folks spending so much time alone with
the toubab.

She found it rather dreary. Amos did have a way
of talking, though. More like singing than anything
else. The rock showcased him in a new light. Sunrays
came down through the leaves, giving his blackness
a kind of golden hue, showering him, too, with the
kind of jagged shadows that made men mysterious,
which was another way of saying strong. And Essie
seemed so pleased. That was what made Maggie
promise Essie that she would come back and sit with
her in the same shady spot Essie reserved just for
them. Until it could be so no longer.

Until the day Amos's words took a different turn,
spoke of things that made Essie look down and
Maggie lean back. Maggie immediately placed the
meanness in them—toward The Two of Them, of all
people!—and she gave Amos only a stern eye when
she wanted to give more.

Uh huh, she thought, **there it go!**

"It's a old thing," she told Amos. But he didn't
listen. She didn't wait around to hear another word
come out of Amos's mouth. She unlocked her arm

from Essie's, stood up, and marched her way back to the Big House, tall with lips curled, shadows falling down her back and light fluttering across her chest. She only looked back once and that was to let Essie see her face so she would know that it wasn't because of her.

She stopped setting the table for a moment and turned to look at the barn from the window.

"Mm," she said aloud.

Maggie suspected Essie knew about The Two of Them and never said a word. That was good, though, because some things should never be mentioned, didn't have to be, not even among friends. There were many ways to hide and save one's self from doom, and keeping tender secrets was one of them. It seemed to Maggie a suicidal act to make a precious thing plain. Perhaps that was because she couldn't imagine a thing—not a single thing—worth exposing herself for. Whatever she might ever have loved was taken before it even arrived. That is, until she crept up and saw those boys, who had the decency to bring with them a feeling that didn't make her want to scream.

She made her way back into the kitchen, grabbed a rag, and removed the biscuits from the oven. They had browned perfectly. She slid them into a bowl lined with a square of linen and set the bowl on the table. She held two biscuits in her hand and squeezed until the crumbs pushed through her fingers.

She looked around the room and then back at the

table again. She wondered if she had the strength to flip it over because she already knew she had the rage. She placed her hand on a corner of it and gave it a little tug.

"Heavy," she mumbled to herself.

She heard the sound of footsteps coming down the stairs. She knew it was Paul because of how deliberate each step was. He'd come in the dining room and sit at the head of the table and watch her, like her wretchedness brought him joy. He might even have the nerve to touch her or stick his tongue where it had no business being. She wished she knew a spell that could slit his throat, but alas, that would require her hands to be used and she wasn't certain that she could take him.

"Shit."

ESSIE

Though goddesses made more sense, she agreed to kneel to Amos's secondhand god—especially if it meant more rations and a wall between her and numerous sufferings.

Maybe not a wall, exactly. More like a fence, a wooden fence, not unlike the barn's, staked out in uncommon ground, jutting from the earth, meant to keep animals in and people out. A fence and not a wall because crafty as some childish anger was, it didn't have the legs to climb something so tall. But it could slip through spaces between planks. It thought itself innocent like that. And sometimes, that's what toubab reminded Essie of: children of everlasting tantrums, ripping and roaring insatiably; stomping through fields with boundless energy;

finding everything curious and funny; demanding mother's teat; falling, finally, into rest only if
gently swayed.

They were too young, then, to understand treaties,
much less honor them. Signing them must have been
penmanship practice or flourish. Still, it was the only
assurance people had. So, she knelt; with the pale
baby held snug at her waist, she knelt. Sultry in a
way that her tattered dress, dusty skin, and loosening braids should have never allowed her to be. The
strategy told to her was a lie. Toubab men were, in
fact, not discouraged by an unkempt woman. Paul
Halifax simply peeled back the layers, saw past the
pricked and bleeding fingers that gathered a respect-
able 150 pounds of cotton every day except Sunday.
For him, Essie's thick thighs and delicate wrists were
a kind of currency. She knew then that they purchased everything except mercy.

"It won't never happen again. This, I promise you,"
Amos said to her seven days after he failed her.

Later, much later, she showed her broom-husband
her commitment by muddying her knees beside his.
However, she would remain skeptical. Skepticism
was the only thing that she could truly claim as hers.
She took it with her to the barn the day Amos sent
her there with a message.

"This ain't pie; this peace," she said by way of
greeting to Isaiah as she balanced the wildberry con-
fection in one hand; the pie was covered by a piece of
cloth so white it glowed. In the other hand, she held

the pale baby she named Solomon for her own good reasons. She carried the apprehension atop her head, balancing it like they did in the old days.

Solomon was fussy. He threatened to topple everything by pulling at her dress, right where the milk had made it damp. She hated that he had that sort of power over her body, his cries like a spell making her breasts respond by leaking drops of her serum-self out for his nourishment. She nearly dropped him, but Isaiah caught him by the bottom and took him from Essie's loose grasp. Solomon looked at Isaiah with big, flat eyes, blue as birdsong, set at the edge of a face that seemed nearly skinless. And yet, in the natural curl in the baby's sun-colored tresses, Isaiah found something familiar enough.

"You hungry, huh?" Isaiah said to the quieting baby, who touched his nose as he looked at it, transfixed, before he slid his tiny hand down to Isaiah's lips and tugged on the bottom one. "We eat together then, I reckon." Isaiah looked at Essie. "How you?"

"Here in this body. You know how it be," she said, frowning first before gradually allowing the corners of her mouth to curl into a smile.

"Surely," Isaiah said, looking at her, then back at Solomon, whose nose he rubbed with his own.

"How old is he now?"

"Almost two."

"And ain't walking yet?"

She shrugged.

"You wanna come inside? Sit for a spell?"

"Kindly," Essie said as she followed him into the barn.

She was always surprised at how clean Isaiah was given how close he lay to animals. He smelled like juniper at the height of May, glistening in pitch blackness. She was there when Samuel first brought him the water. Too young herself, but still knowing a shining when she saw one; it was almost if the water had become silver, catching every light in the pouring, rainbows in drop formation, dripping from the concerns of Isaiah's mouth while he attempted to take in too much at once. Ain't that a shame—for someone to have been wasting colors like that, no matter what their age? Still, hovering over them was something unseen because it was unseeable, but its vibration could be felt. That was why her hands trembled then and why her hands trembled still whenever these two were around.

Inside, Samuel had his arms raised. His back was facing Essie, Isaiah, and Solomon as they entered. Essie couldn't tell if he was paying tribute to creation, holding court with degenerate beasts, or merely stretching out of himself. Sometimes, the space inside the body could get to be cramped and it was necessary to extend the limbs to give the spirit more room or, maybe, an opening to fly from. He wore no shirt, so every bit of sweat on his skin was visible, racing from top to bottom. His flesh evinced no **natural** blemishes, but the moisture highlighted the ones marked there by cowards. She hated to admit to herself that she found beauty in the way those scars snaked across the broadness of his back with delicate curves.

"You got room for pie?" she said to Samuel's behind, which was raised up like heaven.

He came down hard but turned slowly. He had no grin on his face, but one suddenly appeared after he looked at Isaiah and Isaiah nodded. Essie could tell then it was manufactured, but she revealed her teeth in a wide smile in return anyway, didn't even try to hide the space of the missing one.

She had known Isaiah longer than she did Samuel. She appreciated his gentle nature and how—when Paul holed them up for what seemed like days, in that rotten old shack they called The Fucking Place— Isaiah held her hand first. He tried, awkwardly, to put his limp self into her in-between that in no ways welcomed it, but they pretended that they were full-scale rocking anyway. **Hurt hard when somebody make you fuck your friend,** they both thought later.

Paul set James about the business of watching them, and sometimes, James would pull out his thing, leaving, for anyone to see, the puddle that Isaiah faked. Afterward, pulling up their clothes as though they had actually done something, she and Isaiah shared squinted eyes, quiet giggles, a song where their harmonies blended and echoed, and the first everything-hotcake she ever made, which they gobbled up together sitting side by side. But it was still doughy on the inside, so it gave them both cramps—and squatting among rocks and trees to share as well.

Amos didn't have Isaiah's decency, but that was no special mark against him because neither did most men. Most men followed their impulses without considering where they might lead, perhaps in spite of considering where they might lead. It was hard to blame a turd for smelling the way it did. Best to just make the most of it and let it fertilize the soil so something could grow. There was never any guarantee, however, that there would be anything worth harvesting.

Out of all those unprivate moments in the dank of it, under James's steady gaze, Essie and Isaiah created a friendship—that was it. Displeased, Paul lashed Isaiah three times and sent him hollering back to the barn. It wasn't even five minutes after Essie had fastened her dress to the neck that Paul had James line up a group of nine men. Essie looked at them as intently as Paul did. Did he mean to give each of them a turn in succession? Would she be left so numb that afterward, her walk back to her shack would have to be done with legs far apart and clutching the agony at the pit of her stomach?

Paul surprised her. He chose one: the one who looked at her in her face and didn't look away or dissect her by wondering the shape of her breasts or what contours might be hidden behind her clothing. It was Amos who was told to come forward and when he did, he took Essie's hand and rubbed it against his cheek.

For months, Essie was astonished by Amos. She didn't realize she could feel such tenderness toward a man. She didn't know that body union could feel like something interesting and not just labored. She thought the tingling that shocked her body was only possible through the use of her fingers. When Amos held her tightly after it all, adding his spasms to hers, she allowed herself to go limp in his arms.

But those months hadn't put her in the way Paul imagined it might. Rather than have James form another line, Paul interfered himself.

Being forced to do their own work only made toubab doubly vicious, made them feel unsteady and revealed them as . . . regular, which was another way of saying it killed them. Therefore, they wanted everything else to be dead, too.

Essie felt like that now: dead, but somehow, walking—playing, smiling, cooking, picking, clapping, shouting, singing, and, in the nighttime, lying down—just like a living person, so all were fooled. Or maybe none were because the dead recognized one another, in scent if not in sight. She wondered then what Isaiah might see, if the reason they were no longer friend-friends wasn't because Amos occupied all her time and kept her fastened to the clearing, but because the living and the dead could never mix without some grave omen coming to pass.

"I brought a peace," Essie said to Samuel, holding up the cloth-wrapped pie.

Samuel closed his eyes and smelled the air.

"Hope it ain't raw in the middle," Isaiah said with a laugh, holding Solomon close to his chest and rocking him.

Essie cut her eyes and kissed her remaining teeth before sticking her arm out and handing Samuel the pie.

Isaiah pointed. "You can sit over on that there stool if you feel like it. You want the baby back?"

Essie signaled her indifference by flipping her hand in the air. She turned knowingly to the side and plopped down on the stool. Isaiah sat on the ground in front of her.

"So what Amos want?" Samuel said while looking down at the baby in Isaiah's lap.

Essie smirked because she appreciated the way Samuel called the truth forth from its hiding places. She smoothed her dress and swiveled her behind firmly on the stool. "Peace, he say."

"And what you say?" Samuel shot back, looking her dead in the face, but with not a hint of animus.

"Well, y'all already know y'all got two different ideas of peace."

"Don't everybody?" Samuel asked, looking at Isaiah.

Isaiah continued rocking the baby.

"I reckon," Essie said. "We can talk about that there

over the pie. Ain't that what Mag always say toubab like to do—talk over they meals instead of eat?"

The vibration came from shared laughter. Even the baby cooed and giggled, which was what silenced Essie suddenly, pulled her out of herself, and caused her to seek the pretend shelter of the fence once more.

"Pie," Isaiah said aloud to himself as though thinking of how the word sounded. His rich voice brought Essie back with memory.

"What kind of pie you make?" Isaiah asked as he jiggled Solomon's arms to make him smile.

"You know that bush over by the river, the one by the hump-log, about two skips behind, where Sarah caught that black snake and scared Puah halfway out her mind?"

"Yes! I need me some blackberries," Isaiah said.

"That and some other red ones back there in them woods. Funny how they taste tart apart and sweet together." Essie looked around. "You got something to cut it with?" she asked, and Samuel walked over to the barn wall to get one of the tools hanging on it.

"I know you better take it to the well and wash it first," Isaiah said.

"I know it! What you think I am?" Samuel shot back, marching out of the barn with the heat of a lie burning over his head.

Essie and Isaiah both smiled, and then the smiles left their mouths as they both looked at the baby. The quiet lingered between them, interrupted occasionally by Solomon blowing through his lips. Isaiah bounced him on his leg.

Essie tilted her head and looked at Isaiah. How he had grown from the boy whose mouth wasn't yet big enough to hold a bounty of rainbows. She was going to ask him if he still remembered the smell. In The Fucking Place, the mildew and moss had grown thick, such that it brought with it a smell that not even rolling around in the soil as pretense could cover up. To her, she wanted to say, it smelled like eyes watching. She knew that didn't make any sense but thought that if anyone could understand, it would be Isaiah.

The smell, or the way the morning sun shot through the decaying planks of wood, lighting up dust and giving horseflies paths to freedom. The light that offered no comfort but only illuminated a damn shame and made the air too thick to breathe. The aggravation might have been tolerable, to some degree, if not for James standing right there between light and shadow with his britches open just enough to point his weapon at them. They pretended not to see.

She wanted to know: Did it all still clutter Isaiah's days like it did hers, both the kindness and the humiliation, each liable to show up in full form at any time—whether plucking in that confounding cotton field or after having found the perfect log on which to sit in the clearing? Sometimes, it got mixed in with Amos's morning messages; hovering right next to the Jesus talk was the image of James's grin.

Maggie said the way to get rid of anyone from the recesses of the mind was to never speak their name again, not even think it. Which is why James seemed to avoid Maggie wherever she showed up. But how not to think a name when the mind was already so hard to control?

Sleep was the best place to hide because dreamlessness at least provided shelter. Tucked away in the darkness, no one could see, and therefore everyone was safe. Isaiah should at least recognize that place in her because she recognized it in him. Wasn't that made clear when they squatted together, aching and sweating, in those bushes next to rock and below tree?

Was the barn a better place? How better? And if it was, indeed, love that laid itself down over everything so that there could be beauty even in torment, where possibly could Isaiah have gotten the courage to do it and only it, knowing what Paul wished to use Isaiah's body for? It was dangerous to embrace anything but the Lord like that. Everything else could only ever be fleeting. And who wants to lose a foot, or their soul, chasing behind the wagon dragging your love deeper into the wilderness?

In that place where they pretended, what had they found? That Fucking Place where they lay in the mustiness of other bodies, some who made it out and others who didn't, who could be buried right there beneath them or, instead, who could be hovering just above them, watching, too, and also giggling at their charade, understanding in their haint-state what they couldn't before: however we are is however we are.

The dancing shadows were a clue. Essie might have mentioned this to Isaiah before, but she had forgotten now that her heart was filled with the blood of Jesus, who had but intervened too late and had only half promised to do so should the menace arise again. Amos said don't worry, he would be an example. Essie wondered why since she had already been made one.

And now here Essie was, in a dusty barn, sitting right in front of decency as it held on to its enemy. Bounced it in its lap and smiled as it cooed. So she was right: she and Isaiah were no longer friend-friends. Given enough time, betrayal—no matter how tiny—makes its way up the steps and sits on the throne as though it had always belonged there. Maybe it did and it was actually **surprise** that had no place.

Samuel returned from the well, wet and laughing.

"You fall in, fool?" Isaiah asked.

"Nah. James and them was at the well so I went to the river. Puah was down there. She splash me with her silly self."

"Oh," Isaiah said. He and Samuel exchanged glances.

"Well, here," Samuel said, extending the hay knife. "Who gon' cut it?"

"You got the knife," Essie said.

The knife was damp and glistening. For a moment,

it crossed her mind that the barn had all manner of
sharp object. There were axes and pitchforks, but also
the blunt edge of a hoe or shovel that, with great force
behind it, could also be useful. She looked around the
barn, ignoring Isaiah, Samuel, Solomon, the animals,
the insects, the smell, but not the various-shaped ob-
jects that hung on the walls or leaned against them.
Why hadn't the men gathered these things, placed
them in a pile at the center of a circle, where they
could choose the tool to which they were most accustomed? But it had to be all of them. At once. Because
bullets were quick and would take some down. The
guns couldn't take out every one of them, however,
and in that was the chance.

It would **never** be everyone, though. Other than
suffering, spite was the only other thing they all
shared. She had heard the story once from Sister
Sarah when Sarah was mumbling it and thought
Essie wasn't listening because Essie made it seem, for
her own interests, like she wasn't listening. All it took
was one to run back to Massa and tell tales of the
plot to leave. It wasn't like any of them wanted to do
any harm, though they would be well within their
rights to do so if they did; sold-off loved ones alone
made that righteous. They just wanted to be somewhere free and free **of.**

Samuel cut three pieces. He handed the first piece
to Essie, who took it into her palms. He handed
another to Isaiah before he sat down holding the
last piece.

"The baby can eat this?" Isaiah asked Essie, who shrugged her shoulders, then nodded.

Isaiah broke off a small piece, mashed it between two of his fingers, and then held those fingers near Solomon's mouth. Solomon sucked the bits from Isaiah's fingers. The baby scrunched his face and chewed. Some of it spilled out of his mouth and Isaiah pushed it back in. When he was done chewing, Solomon opened his mouth again. Samuel and Isaiah laughed.

"You ever imagine that? Two mens raising they own baby?" Essie, leaning forward, whispered.

Isaiah laughed nervously. "I seen two or more womens do it plenty. Only thing stopping mens is mens."

"That the only thing stopping them?" Samuel asked Isaiah.

Isaiah didn't respond. The baby tugged at him and he broke off another small piece of pie and fed it to him. Then he took a small bite of the pie himself. Isaiah smiled at Essie and nodded his head.

Samuel looked at Isaiah but was talking to Essie. "So peace. You say Amos want peace? From what?"

Essie sighed, rubbed her face, and tucked a stray braid behind her ear. "He say the punishments been getting worser. He think it have something to do with y'all not doing what you should be."

But what should they be doing? Essie thought. The shape of them was already illuminated and cast in the sky, one a water carrier, the other the water.

And why should that ever be a source of pain? Scarce though it was, she was here out of duty, out of loyalty to a man who bargained for her but overestimated the integrity of the dealmaker.

"But he say he keep away from me?" Essie asked Amos then.

"It don't work like that, honey child," Amos said softly. "Toubab never so plain. Is ritual that protect you whether his mouth say it or not. They rituals is what they respect. We gon' do it their way. We jump. We take care of his seed. We preach his gospel. And you be safe. I swear it."

This is what Essie's silence said, but Amos failed to hear: **Oh! But didn't he break his ritual to Missy Ruth to do what he did to me? Which gospel say, "Do the most terrible thing?" And here, this Solomon, is the evidence! You a fool, Amos. But, mercy, a fool with his heart intact.**

Essie refocused her eyes on Isaiah and Samuel. Samuel looked at Isaiah.

"I told you," said Samuel.

Isaiah didn't respond. He looked down at Solomon sitting in his lap. "Not doing what you should be," he whispered. He smiled at Solomon, raised him in the air, which made the baby kick and giggle and chew on his own hand. Then he brought him back down and looked over at Samuel.

"Sorry," Isaiah said, still whispering.

Samuel shook his head and moved deeper into the barn. In front of the horse pens, he lifted himself up on his toes, calves taut, ass high, and arms out-stretched like he was reaching for something that he knew he couldn't reach.

Essie looked at Isaiah. "What he doing?" she asked quietly.

"This place too small," Isaiah said, his eyes trained on Samuel's back.

"Oh," she said, interpreting "this place" as "this life."

Essie smiled anxiously. She looked at Samuel's back. She had been sent to make an opening but had only succeeded in making the pursued retreat even farther in. She got up from the stool and stuck out her arms to take Solomon back from Isaiah.

"I hold him," Isaiah said as he stood with the baby. "I walk y'all to the door."

They moved slowly. "I almost don't wanna put him down," Isaiah said.

"I don't know that feeling," Essie replied before stretching out her arms for the baby just as they reached the frame of the door.

"Listen. Isaiah. Come on by. Make your case. He ain't finna listen. But . . ."

She looked at them, Samuel's back and Isaiah's face, tilted back as though signaling his openness to receive glory. Her lips parted, but the words remained on her tongue.

I ain't never gon' say this out loud ever, but I name him Solomon because he half mine and half ain't. Ain't that terrible?

She focused on Isaiah's mouth before looking at the baby in her arms. **He put inside me whether I want him there or not. He come out of me raising hell behind him. And I gotta be the one to nurse him. I gotta be the one to bounce him on my knee when he cries too long. While Amos just sit across from me watching that I don't do nothing of what he call "silly." But what silly about me having say over what I am?**

Essie stepped outside. She saw the pigs in their pen and it was the first time that she ever noticed that they were the same kind of pale as Solomon. She heard Amos's voice: **"But the fence, Essie. Remember the fence!"**

What for? she thought. **'Cause it lets the things through anyway. 'Cause wood rots. And fences come down. All you need is a bad storm. And ain't that where they come from to begin with? Ain't the truth right there in the way they spin and destroy everything that get any kind of close to them? Ain't they just creek waters God willing to rise?**

Essie turned away from the pens and began walking slowly toward the gate. **I came here with a pie I didn't wanna make because Amos is the best I can do. He** see **me. Don't you understand?**

She turned back to look at Isaiah and Samuel, who hadn't yet moved from their spots. **Amos make a bargain, even if in his own head, that so far hold up and I won't let that just fall apart and become**

broodmare again. Where were y'all when I needed some good, huh? In here carrying on, I reckon. Now here I am, carrying my burden in the flesh and Amos tell me I supposed to love it because that what the blood of Jesus demands. Small price to pay, he say. But who paying? He don't bring that up because he already know the answer.

Solomon looked up at Essie as the tears began to form in her eyes. She wiped them away quickly. She blinked and came back to herself.

"Y'all be good now," she yelled out as she began to step backward.

Isaiah waved. Samuel stood motionless, trans-fixed, a humming in the air that seemed to come from both him and not him, which frightened her. She turned and walked toward the gate and stood briefly at its opening. It framed her like a picture and continued to do so until she walked beyond it and headed due north.

Amos

Amos had seen strange things before: living babies retrieved from the taut-faced corpses of their mothers; beat-down men talking out loud to shadows; bodies swinging high from trees. One body in particular was that of a man named Gabriel, a friend of Amos's father. There wasn't much he remembered about Gabriel; it was, after all, so long ago. There wasn't much more Amos remembered about his father, either—except his name, Boy, and his ever-stooping silhouette in the field, sometimes against a red horizon.

But what remained clear about Gabriel was the missing thing: a bloody, discarded clump at the base of the tree. Amos cursed himself even now for mistaking it for rotten fruit, for wanting to claim it for his mother so that she could use it for jam or a pie. To this very day, the thought of what might have happened made him grab himself and wince.

He arrived at Empty full-grown with his head fastened inside something that looked almost like a rusty birdcage because a toubab woman in Virginia said something untrue, and death was too expensive. With no space to fly, the bars sliced his vision to pieces, permitted him to see only in thin slices. A smiling face here, a sobbing one there, but he couldn't put it all together for the obstacles in between. Coming down off that creaking wagon, shackled to twenty other people, holding up a boy because he made his mother a passing promise. The metal chains roared as they slid from wood to dust, heavy feet stirring up orange clouds that made them all cough as they were rushed onto a patch of land and then, in the morning, out to the cotton field. It all appeared before him in fragments: safe, manageable fragments that made him think that perhaps the birdcage wasn't so bad after all. It wasn't good to think about the past because thinking about it could conjure it up. Sometimes, the past was gracious. Loneliness had hands, but it was much more than wanting a steady piece. Piece wasn't even on his mind when he first saw Essie in the field, crouched and sweating, a scarf holding her hair up like a hill. His gut told him that they should be cleaved together, smile together, endure trials together because that is how they belonged: together. And there was nothing in The Fucking Place that could ever make that untrue. So when Paul chose him out of the nine lined up, Amos knew it was a sign.

Amos sighed. He had seen strange things, so he closed his eyes. The first time Paul demanded Essie, Amos pleaded until he was hoarse, promised unthinkable favors that only managed to make Paul angry. It was only after Paul threatened to whip him that Amos became silent. He didn't think of that as cowardice, just futility. When Paul finally took Essie and left, Amos choked on her quiet obedience, stumbled over the impasse. He imagined actions that he knew he could never indulge in without great cost, and not just to himself. Breaking Paul's bones would have been simple, but grinding them into dust for the paste that Amos would smear on his own face for the dance, shaking a staff, and calling out forgotten words to ancestors who he wasn't exactly sure could hear: that would be the hard part because there was no guarantee that he wouldn't remain alone.

He sat in that dark shack for hours. He saw the darkness turn in upon itself, churn, and spasm. He watched it reach out for him, felt it first caress, then clutch and fondle him. When Essie finally returned— eyes bruised, hair awry, limbs weary, bleeding, and missing something—he wanted to handle her like he would a newborn. Instead he whispered to her viciously against his better judgment. He couldn't help it. She had become a looking glass for his incompetence and he had no courage to place the blame where it actually belonged.

"They earlobes always tell their intentions. I don't know why, they just do," Amos said as though it mattered. Spoken like a true fool, he let the words trip out, jagged from being dragged over his teeth, thus sharp on Essie's skin.

"You coulda killed him," he added after he got no response from her. He had the nerve to say it because it was dark and he couldn't see her. Essie's quick inhalation startled him. She must have intended for him to feel the scolding in it. The words he knew she left behind her lips: **You coulda, too.**

The next morning, in the picking field, his hands had curved into the position ripe for killing (it wouldn't be murder because the laws saw no humanity in his kind). He saw how his fingertips touched and bled from the spines, but never had his hands been so strong. With a little gumption, he could strangle at least **one** of the overseers, starting with James, with little effort. It wouldn't be so different from pulling cotton: pluck the life from people just as mean, in the same hot sun, stooping, too, into the ache of bones. What would it be to watch another person drop dead for the wages of their condition? For this, he could be of great assistance.

It boiled inside of him, troubled his mind. He entertained, for a moment, suffocating James, shoving the seventy pounds of cotton he had picked thus far

right down the man's throat. Briefly, his lips crept
into a grin.

One hundred pounds, finally, when he could have
picked double that. But it was important to manage their expectations. Give them your peak and
then the moment you don't perform at that level, the
fools want to split your back open and deny healing.
Unconcerned with the blood splatter, they would
send your sick ass right back into the field and ferret
out hundreds of pounds from you at gunpoint. He
kept it easy for just that reason.

But Amos felt the managed drudgery dull his
mind, close the world in on him, collapse the sky
and the ground into one indistinguishable whole. He
longed to stretch out his arms, maybe take a deep
breath, but the squeeze, the push, the tightness roped
around him like he was swinging from a tree. Just a
little air, that's all he needed. And he wouldn't even
take it in through the mouth. Give him some, and
he'd be happy to inhale and exhale through his nose.
They wouldn't even know he took it.

But maybe rest, of a kind, was on the horizon.

Seven days later, he made a promise to Essie.

"Never again. I swear it."

Just as her morning vomiting let them know that,
flat stomach or not, she was with a child whose pappy
would be unknown until they saw the baby's skin,
Amos went about the business of securing Essie's refuge. He was loading his final sack of cotton onto the
awaiting wagon when the pink sky signaled an end

to one dreary day but never tomorrow. He removed his straw hat, which Essie had weaved for him herself, held it to his chest, and looked down at his feet. This was the only way ever to approach a toubab, but especially if you intended to ask for something. They didn't appreciate gumption; they saw it as arrogance. Amos waited until the others were on their solemn walk back to their shacks, slumped over and sweating, weary and death-glazed. He hoped that the sight of their misery would satiate at least some of the malice in Paul's heart and leave room for mercy, however minute.

Paul and James were on the other side of the wagon, talking about Isaiah and Samuel. Amos heard the word "bucks" and Paul asked if James watched them in The Fucking Place or not, and James said, "Yeah," and Paul replied, "If yes, then where are the nigglets?" James had huffed that if they were lame in some way, maybe Paul should consider "replacing them with any manner of good nigger," but Paul said, "It makes no sense to sell the best two."

Amos crept around the wagon.

"Massa," Amos said, shuffling up to them, hoping his insolence would pale in comparison to his suggestion. "I beg your pardon. I don't means to interrupt. Neither do I means to hear your'n business. But I hope you hear me as I ask: Maybe us niggers need Jesus, too?"

It was the first time Amos had ever used either word—nigger or Jesus—and he had decided that the betrayals would be worth it given that he had already given Essie his word on the seventh day. Paul removed his hat and looked to James.

James chuckled, removed his hat, fanned himself with it, and swatted away some flies.

"Cousin, you look like you could use a drink."

Amos watched their backs as they walked away from him to the barn, took hold of the horses led to them by Isaiah, and rode off together, leaving him standing in the middle of the cotton by himself. The question high above his head.

He knew better than to ask again. So he waited. His patience was true. For not two weeks later, Paul sent for him. Amos was going to go around the back of the Big House, but the messenger, Maggie, led him to the main stairs. Typically, people weren't permitted to step foot in the Big House at all, much less enter where toubab usually entered. Other than Maggie, Essie, and a few others, people knew to respect the boundary represented by the stairs that led to the massive front doors. Because of that border, there was room to imagine what was inside. Some people thought it might be a cave or a canyon. Others thought it might be the end. Amos said, "Naw. Just greed, I reckon." He was right. But it wasn't that he had some second sight, not yet anyway. It was because he had been such a good witness for Essie.

During the months prior to their bliss being torn up, Essie told Amos that the Big House was too much for three people and that they hung animal heads on the wall like art. "Right next to their own faces and you can't tell the difference," she said with a sweet chuckle.

She said that she didn't realize three people could make so much **mess** that it took days to make right. Over and over, they demanded order only to wreak havoc and then demand order anew. She said people as cutthroat as they didn't deserve beds so soft, though she allowed Timothy to be an exception because he evinced a gentle nature.

Essie never saw so many candles lit at once, she said, the soft light coming from so many points, casting the most joyful shadows on every wall, growing and growing until, oddly, they became menacing. At which point, what flooded her mind, and Maggie's too, she reckoned, was that all it would take was a delicate tap to tip one of the candles over, and maybe the resulting blaze would, likewise, begin as splendor before it became tragedy.

Paul stood outside at the bottom of the stairs. He ascended them slowly, occasionally glancing back to see a stunned Amos, lost in the thoughts put into his mind by Essie. This was the closest he had ever been to the Big House. The four white columns at the front of it never seemed this huge before. He was afraid to take a step forward. He had the distinct feeling at the nape of his neck that once he passed through them, he might not make it back out.

In a sense, he was correct. He stood there at the bottom of the steps, between the two stone pots of

red roses that anchored them, and wondered if he
had made a terrible mistake. The sun was setting behind him. He couldn't see the blood orange his back
had become under its shrinking light. It had been
other colors before: black, purple, red, blue, but this
time honeyed enough to seem without pain.

"AMOS!"

Paul's sharp tone shocked Amos back to life and
he took to the steps two at a time, careful to remain
bowed and behind.

"I beg your pardon, suh."

He wondered if he should add a compliment, tell
Paul that he had been taken by the house's beauty.
The white wasn't pristine; Amos noticed some of the
paint chipping, and a bit of mildew grew at the bases
where wall met ground. And just now, a couple of
leaves descended and scraped themselves against the
floor of the front porch before coming to a complete
stop in the company of a pair of oak rocking chairs.
But the windows were gleaming, and the shutters
that framed them were delicate enough to make him
question whether anything horrible could possibly
occur behind them. Would ivy cling so closely to a
lover who failed it?

Once Paul crossed the threshold, Amos knew that
he would have no choice but to cross it, too. There
was still time to turn back. It would cost him skin,
but it would heal. Maybe that was why toubab per-
petuated the cruelties that they did: people seemed
to be able to take it, endure it, experience and witness

all manner of atrocity and appear unscathed. Well, except for the scars. The scars lined them the same way bark lined trees. But those weren't the worst ones. The ones you couldn't see: those were the ones that streaked the mind, squeezed the spirit, and left you standing outside in the rain, naked as birth, demanding that the drops stop touching you.

With all the reverence he could muster, he moved his legs past the doorway and suddenly felt small and unclean. Forgetting himself, he looked up. Even if he were to stand on his toes, he wouldn't be able to reach the ceiling. And no matter how hard he tried, and he tried hard, he couldn't spot a speck of dirt anywhere.

"Move faster," Paul said, interrupting his thoughts. "Why are you all so slow?"

But any faster and Amos would have surely crashed into Paul, or worse, wound up beside him, which was also a crime. So Amos shuffled a bit, turning his one step into two quicker but smaller ones. That seemed to please Paul.

In the periphery, Amos saw Maggie dusting a piece of furniture, a chair with a cushion that had a scene embroidered into it. From his distance, it looked to Amos as though it might be a depiction of the Halifax cotton field itself, at high noon, when the sun is at its peak and the pickers are under the strictest surveillance, when the throat threatens to collapse and crumble from lack of water, and yet the overseers look at you as though taking a natural human pause is unthinkable, reminding you that it could be worse: you could be chopping cane at an increased risk of severed limb; you could be at the docks with men who hadn't seen civilization in quite some time and wouldn't discriminate one hole from the next; you could be pulling indigo, which meant your work would forever mark your hands as tools. Or you could be the property of doctors who needed cadavers more than they needed anything else. All of that to say: Be thankful that you're a cotton picker and an occasional bed warmer. It could be worse.

Amos wondered if it was him Maggie was cutting her eyes at. Their interactions hadn't been enough that he would deserve such regard. He knew she was a good friend to Essie, so she had to know that all of this was for her.

Did Maggie not understand his humiliation now would be his dignity later? She would regret the looks she was giving him as he trailed Paul on his way into the room where the door was now closed. She would marvel at his plan once he made it clear. Yes, it would be a tacit agreement if not an explicit one: in exchange for being learnèd in the ways of Christ, which meant being learnèd in ways forbidden by law, Amos would ensure docility was treasured over rebellion; earthly rewards, if there truly were any, were no match for heavenly ones. No blade should ever be raised against either master or mistress anywhere within the confines of Empty.

And further, disobedience would be likewise cast out. And wasn't that, after all, exactly what Isaiah

and Samuel's obstinance amounted to? There was
nothing wrong with the wenches given to them; Paul
had already proven that. It was impossible that they
were **both** infertile. So it had to be willful, some intentional measure to thwart Paul's plan to multiply
them as he saw fit. It was as though they believed
that the line should stop with them and they would
thus be able to spare the blood of their blood whatever it was they believed they, themselves, suffered.

Ha! Glory! What the whip couldn't remedy, Jesus
could. And that was a good thing!

But that wasn't all. In the blank spaces between
the letter was the spirit. And that held weight. Amos
knew that success would also garner him sway. Not
too much; a person should never think a toubab
could be so brazenly molded, especially not by a darkie. All influence had to have the appearance of confirmation. And what he would eventually be able to
have confirmed was that Paul had no further use for
Essie. Hallelujah.

To give Paul the benediction he sought, a newly
christened Amos would take Essie's hand in marriage. A simple broom jump, as Amos had seen
performed in kinship circles as a child. He had
to, of course, first ask for Paul's permission. These
were traditions that followed strict rules and could
only be ordained if the master of the manor gave
his blessing. And while their ceremony could never
be as astounding as a toubab's—there would be no
horses or trumpets, no impeccably tailored clothing,

no one coming from far to join in the merriment, and Essie's parents wouldn't be on hand to give her away because, as it turns out, they were given away themselves—there was no better view than the waters of the Yazoo, rushing not at all haphazardly to meet the grand Mississippi before, finally, joining in their long journey to the Gulf of Mexico.

It was that last thought, not the door opening onto Paul's private study—a room lined, on two sides, floor to ceiling, with volumes and volumes of books—that made Amos gasp. Though Paul smiled and Amos took that to mean that he thought the inhalation was a tribute to the grandeur they both stepped into. With a flourish, Paul stepped behind a dark maple desk, on top of which there were neat stacks of papers and, to the right, a closed jar of ink with a pen laid neatly on top of it. Paul sat and gestured for Amos to step forward. Crushing his poor hat between both hands, crumbling it as though he was about to discard it, Amos took timid steps and kept his eyes to the ground as Paul lit a candle in a brass holder.

"Tell me what you know about the Christ," Paul said, louder than necessary.

Amos knew that Paul liked to hear himself speak, was dazzled by the display and encouraged, by the embellishments biblical references allowed him, to opine without regard to the desires of his audience. Essie talked about how Paul hogged the ears of his guests at the parties he and Ruth would sometimes host. That was when he would have the most people in the Big House, and give them the best dresses to wear so as to impress his guests, who saw beauty in white cloth against black flesh. Wide-eyed and gaping, the contrast seemed to bring them a kind of comfort that Essie could only guess at.

They all saw it, though, Essie said. How Paul's guests would yawn and roll their eyes and pull their watches from their pockets, pretend to be called elsewhere, give every indication that they had heard enough. But none of that stopped Paul. If they were in his house, they were honor bound to be taken by the words God Himself put in his mouth.

Amos observed something more: how Paul was delighted by his ability to connect these words of accumulation, dominance, and piety in the language of his birth. And not for the first time, Amos envied him. What must it have been like to wake up each day and greet the morning with the tongue of your mother's mother's mother? Hell, to even know who your mother's mother's mother was!

"What I'm telling you, nigger, is that this journey you are set to embark on is not a fool's errand. If you are called, your allegiance is to the Almighty and your loyalty is mine for all eternity, for it is I who permitted it."

Amos bowed his head deeper into his chest and mumbled, "Yes, Massa."

"What you say?"

"Yessuh, Massa," Amos said louder, his hands now fidgeting at his sides.

It wasn't the first time he felt a twinge in the pit of his stomach that he had tried to avoid interpreting as defeat. To stand there, head necessarily bowed before the man who spoiled his soon-to-be broom-wife—no, spoiled **himself**! What Paul committed was an act against his own humanity, and no manner of expertly tailored clothing or well-enunciated diction would change that. Nor would any perfectly framed renderings of him and his family—all of them looking at the viewer, hiding smiles, with the "lady," as they called her, seated, as was her right to be, and her husband and son flanking her as though their role was to guard her against anyone looking at them. This painting, taunting anybody who gazed upon it, hung above a fireplace that had the audacity to be roaring in August.

Nah. None of that shit would spare him. Neither would the stacks of coin, nor the promissory notes, nor the wagons full of people, nor the acres and acres of land that held the dead and dying but remained a fetching green nevertheless. None of this gave Paul immunity from what would be an honest comeuppance if only Amos fell full into his part; fell so hard, in fact, that he would lose himself to the descent, **become** it even, wingless to the very bottom of it, if that was what was required to keep Essie from the heart of the bull's-eye. So head bowed, yes, head bowed. Let Paul's fury see where the crown should go.

For months, Amos learned from Paul, word for word, what Paul called "the book of creation and the source of names." At night, Amos had shared some of what he learned with Essie, spoke, also, to her belly so that their child would know. She was fascinated by it all because she hadn't heard the stories quite in this way before. Amos realized that he gave the words a rhythm that Paul couldn't. This pleased Amos. And that was when he began to feel it: lifted.

He had almost reached the summit when Essie gave birth to a disappointment. Amos looked at the baby's skin and knew its origin immediately. The midwife wept; the child screamed; and Essie yelled, "Solomon!" Amos stepped back, inhaled deeply, and then let it out quickly.

He knelt down next to Essie. He understood what she was suggesting because he knew the story all too well. **Split a baby in half?** "No ma'am. So sorry. We can't. Can't do that and keep you safe, too. Trust me. I know it."

Nearly at the top, but the double screaming, day and night, had yanked Amos right back down. When the dreams began, Amos could make neither heads nor tails of them. The lightning, the howling wind, the thunder, the singing magnified, the colors, the blurred figures, the spinning, the music—all of it swirling together. It only confused him. The falling he recognized because that was what he told himself

he would do. But he imagined that he would be falling forward, as one might after a long day, a pallet
just within reach, so that the arms could extend and
protect oneself from damage. But the backwardness
of this new tumbling was unexpected. Outstretched
arms provided no buffer. And there he was, kicking and screaming in the blinding expanse of white
where not even his voice was echoed back to him.

There **was** someone living in the clouds, someone
who had turned the world now into the same blanket
of fog that Amos found himself spinning in. And
it wasn't that this someone was invisible but that,
instead, it had given the world its own color so that
it was merely camouflaged. Amos knew that all he
had to do was wait. If he was resolute in his patience,
the somebody would blink, revealing ever so briefly
the precise location of its presence into which Amos
could find a fool's refuge, soft as cotton. And then,
in chorus, it could say his name.

But there was no chorus to be found. He heard
only a singular voice, hard, like it had been scraped
across gravel or frozen. When it said his name, Amos
felt his blood chill.

He woke up: sticky, wet, and dizzy; short of breath;
parched and starving; his voice, also, a croak; too
tired to move. But he had been touched. In his face,
there was a knowledge that he didn't have before, a
certainty and a seeing that came upon him through
the communion with the baffling every-which-way he
encountered while unconscious. Its meaning couldn't

be interpreted, but he somehow knew he could be a conduit through which understanding could be conveyed to others. When the time came, whatever forces communicated with him would communicate through him. This was the mark of tongues. The wretched, despite all other things, anointed. Amos knew Paul evinced no similar experience. This thing was Amos's and Amos's alone.

As Essie lay next to him, he looked upon her with his newest eyes, tracing every kink and curl on her head, jet-black tresses that blanketed her neck until they gave way to the curve of her back. He could see the bumps of her spine leading down to the splendor that was her own and that was the gift he had hoped his transformation would be able to provide: that she would be able to reclaim what was rightfully hers and give herself back to herself while he witnessed and recited a psalm.

At the first sermon, Amos spoke to the four people who had it in them to get up on their day of rest. Amos asked Paul's permission to use the spot just beyond the cotton field, but still on Halifax land. Paul told James to watch over.

Amos climbed upon the rock, like a mount. The light and shadow both hit him at once. From that moment, the people could look nowhere else.

"What God wouldn't give for a jug of lemonade," he said to them as he dabbed his head with a torn piece of cloth, folded to absorb the sweat beading at his hairline.

"Or potlikker," A Man Called Coot shot back, and they all laughed.

"You are not your body," Amos said softly to the people, as James stood armed in the canopy of trees.

"What you mean?" a woman named Naomi asked. "I sure is my body. Got the scars and tired hands to prove it."

Amos smiled and went closer to her. He touched her on the arm, which she eyed suspiciously. Then laid his other hand right on the woman's chest, felt the pulse of her heart beneath his palm, and shook his head. Amos shot up suddenly and clapped his hands together. He looked up, past the trees to the sky above, then closed his eyes to listen to the inside voice that was only a whisper, an incessant whisper that was too low to disturb the quiet, and quiet was what he needed in order to hear it properly. He needed to still everything, even the drag of his breath, to absorb the murmuring words that he was certain came from the center of everything, where the fog had only to blink to let him know where the hiding place was.

He opened his eyes and looked down at Naomi, seated before him.

"Ma'am, I got some good news for you."

Naomi, as though she had heard the same whispering voice, placed her hand on her cheek.

From the edge, James removed his hat. He put his rifle down and leaned on it like a cane. Loud enough for Amos to hear, he said:

"Well, I'll be damned."

———

"DID YOU LIKE THE PIE?"

Amos's question swept up like dust and lingered in the air momentarily before being caught by a breeze and blown over Isaiah's shoulder. Isaiah and Samuel stood, arm to arm, at the entrance of Amos and Essie's shack. Their stance struck Amos as war, but he wasn't afraid. Behind them, a blue cloth draped the doorway, keeping the sun at bay. But it also made it so that their faces were cast in shadow and Amos could only make out vague details: lips, bright eyes, and not much else, which didn't matter because their blackness, which the interior of the shack merely magnified, was comforting enough.

"Essie cook good, don't she?"

"What you want from us?" Samuel asked in a hushed but deep tone.

Amos, seated, folded his hands, pressed his lips together, and closed his eyes.

"Speak plain, Amos," Samuel said.

Amos opened his eyes and looked at Samuel. "It don't get no plainer than this: you gotta give Massa babies."

Samuel leaned forward, bringing his face closer to Amos's. He seemed to inspect it, search it for something. When he found it, he raised an eyebrow.

"What he promise you? Extra vittles? A pass to town? Freedom papers? Show me when a toubab ever keep they word."

Amos smiled. He leaned back and nodded his head.

"Be Auntie's daughter Puah is just at that age, you know," he said. "You could give Massa some sturdy children with her."

Isaiah looked at Samuel, whose darting eyes seemed to be communicating without words. Amos looked at them directly.

"What you say?" he asked. Neither Samuel nor Isaiah answered.

"I don't understand why y'all make this so hard," Amos said casually. "Y'all ain't being asked to do what no man ain't never been asked to do before. What make y'all so different?"

Silence.

Isaiah looked at Samuel. Samuel grumbled.

"Why you putting this on us, Amos?"

Amos saw Samuel standing steady for a moment, then watched as he stormed outside, stooped, and picked up the nearest rock he could find. It was of moderate size, smaller than the palm of his hand, and fit snugly inside it. He came back into the cabin. He raised his arm and threw the stone at Amos, just missing his head. Purposely missed, because at that close range, it was a sure shot. Nevertheless, Amos fell backward, then stood up quickly. He made no move toward Samuel. Isaiah touched Samuel's tensing arm and Samuel snatched it away before running back out of the shack, leaving Isaiah alone with Amos.

Amos dusted off his pants. He chuckled a bit before walking toward Isaiah.

"That one got some temper, huh? You gotta show him how to keep that in check. If you won't, the lash will."

Isaiah said nothing. Amos put his hand on Isaiah's shoulder. Isaiah looked at it. He removed Amos's hand, but gently, without malice. He didn't look at Amos when he did it. He was watching the spot where there should have been a door, but there was only a blue cloth. Amos moved into his line of sight. He tilted his head slightly and looked into Isaiah's eyes.

"You remember, right? The wagon. You remember?" Amos was bent. He held out his arms, like he was carrying, no, cradling a child in them. Nothing was there, but something was there.

Isaiah's eyes widened; his mouth opened and, at first, made no sound. Then:

"That was you?" he said, his voice quivering when it finally formed words. "I don't understand. Why you never tell me? Why you wait so long?"

Isaiah moved closer to Amos. Amos stood his ground.

"I . . ."

"You told me you tell me my name. You said a promise. You said."

"I was waiting 'til you reach the age of manhood. I ain't wanna waste something like this on a boy. It be too big for him to carry."

"You knew it was me and you ain't say nothing?" asked Isaiah, voice trembling.

Amos placed his hand back on Isaiah's shoulder. "I knew it was you and was fixin' to tell you when the time was right."

"Time right now, ain't it? So tell me."

"When you earn it, I tell you."

"Which is it? Manhood time or when I earn it? You talk slippery."

"Come to the woods on Sunday," Amos said finally, resting his arms at his sides. "Son."

"My. Name!" Isaiah shouted.

The tears had made their way out. There were streaks down his face now. Though they brought Amos no joy, he smiled again. **Isaiah could be reached,** he thought.

Isaiah was quiet. His gaze returned to the cloth, which had begun to move a little in the breeze.

"I know more than your name," Amos said. "Talk to Samuel about Puah. And we find you somebody. But not Essie. Not Essie, no more."

Isaiah looked at Amos as though he couldn't speak an answer. Isaiah closed his eyes. Amos watched as he muffled a covenant with despair. But the sound, not as mellow as birdsong, nor as thunderous as a midday storm, could be heard, resting somewhere between the two, and made Amos long for the old place—Virginia. The longing was misplaced. That wasn't home and neither was this: not these shores, certainly, but which ones, exactly, he knew he would never know, and that was where the pain was.

Isaiah opened his eyes.

Amos's mouth opened slightly, as though to whisper or to kiss, his tongue not restful behind his teeth. Then he closed it quickly. What he wouldn't give to have his pain eased, too. He shook his head and let out a frustrated breath.

"Puah. And we find somebody for you. But not Essie."

Isaiah walked outside. He looked down briefly. Amos could see in the slump of his shoulders that the boy whom he had once lifted up was now pressed under the weight of Amos pushing him down. And no matter how necessary, Amos felt a little broken himself for this. Suddenly, Isaiah took off, ran in the direction of the barn, disappearing behind the clouds of dust his feet stirred up. Now it was Amos's turn to stare at the blue cloth, moving slightly in a too-gentle wind.

A FEW DAYS after Samuel almost smashed a rock into his head, Amos walked, with only minor trepidation, to the barn. He was praying the entire time so he ignored the children playing in the weeds and the folks who waved to him as he passed their shacks. They would have to forgive his rudeness. When he reached the fence of the barn, he saw Samuel and Isaiah kneeling near the barn door, a slop pail between them. He refused to be seduced by their glowing.

"You come to service?" Amos shouted to them, smiling as he scooted between the slats of the fence and walked toward them. His eyes darted from one boy to the other as they stopped what they were doing and turned to him. His eyes landed on Isaiah.

Samuel let air whistle out from between his teeth and then returned his attention to the pail.

"'Zay told me what you said to him, what you won't tell him. I like to knock you down where you stand." Samuel squinted, looked at Amos, stood up, and balled his fists. "Get on out of here."

Amos took a few steps back. "Y'all young," he said. "I ain't just trying to find **y'all** favor, but **everybody.**" His hands were pleading; they were **pleading.** "Just once. Both of y'all. Just one time."

"When it ever been just one time?" Isaiah replied. "Ask Essie."

Amos felt that in his gut. He closed his eyes. He retreated within with the hopes of coming back out with something that might be more healing.

"Y'all mean to tell me you would have us all beat, leaned on, sold, maybe even put in the ground because y'all won't bend a little?" Then he said, but not with his mouth: **Don't you know us all gotta bend, got to, if we want a little bit of anything that might be shaped like serenity? Nobody don't like to give Massa want he want, but we like even less to give him a reason. And here y'all are giving him all the reason in the world. Before I found**

Jesus, I understood you. I felt the praise of y'all's together time and rejoiced. But now, mine eyes have been opened and I see, I see. I tumbled for this. I tumbled and I made a deal to keep a small hush for Essie and for me and for y'all. Take it. Why won't y'all take it?

Yes, even now he noticed the reality flickering between them. It was like the finest of spiderwebs with a tenuous amount of dew trembling on the strands of it, suddenly snatched away and then reconstructed within the blink of an eye, delicate tendrils that were somehow stronger than they appeared, holding the weight of a rainstorm before finally giving way and allowing an unobstructed view. But that was no reason to be sad because the morning, after rain, offered up beauty of which the smell of hawkweed was just the beginning.

Neither Isaiah nor Samuel could answer a silent question, though it seemed like Samuel was about to kneel. But no, nothing. Samuel simply returned to his pail. Isaiah got up then and moved closer to Amos.

"My name. Please," said Isaiah, the last word stretched, making his bottom lip quiver.

Samuel reached over and nudged Isaiah's hand, then shook his head. "Don't beg like that."

"Son, we gotta wash each **other's** hands. Can't be just one of us," Amos said, looking directly at Isaiah.

Isaiah bit his bottom lip and walked into the barn.

Samuel puffed his chest and Amos thought this might be the tussle he was ready for this time, but no. Samuel just followed Isaiah into the barn, leaving the pail as Amos's only company.

Isaiah and Samuel were gone, disappeared into the barn. But the spot outside, where they were just on their knees, was still covered by their shadows.

HE KNEW IT WAS WRONG, because what happened in The Fucking Place should be locked up there and burned, but he had asked Essie about Isaiah anyway and, as always, her response was no response. She just looked at Amos with those big, probing eyes, big because she kept things secreted within them, and despite that, all Amos wanted to do was protect her, let her be her.

She rested soundly beside him now, worn out from fieldwork. He looked at her glistening face. Beautiful as she was, it made no sense to him why she and Isaiah had a camaraderie that produced nothing but whispers and laughter. Amos could understand himself taking a while to do what he had to do. He was older. Gray hairs had come to outline the edges of his scalp. Older men were sometimes not as virile as they were when they were younger. Had Paul given him just a little more time, he and Essie would have given him enough children to meet his fancy. Paul's time—time for any toubab—moved differently, though; it was quick and unpredictable.

Essie couldn't bring the good tidings and Amos understood. Bury it, then, in the wild ground of The

Fucking Place. He didn't know if he would find it, even with a shovel in the middle of the night, but he had to try for her sake. He had to.

The barn was dark. Inside, there were nothing but the horses and two twisted shadows on the ground. Two shadows! Twisted together on the ground. Yes, Amos had seen strange things. But this—this beat all!

He was astonished by how obvious it was, by how easily it could be missed by those who weren't curious enough to seek the answer right in front of them because the answer, even when revealed, remained unbelievable.

He had thought their kinship merely hazardous at first, never thinking it wise for any two people to be so close, not here anyway. Even with Essie, his embrace was one arm **only.** The other arm had to be free to cry into the crook of when the warmth of other bodies turned cold. It hadn't occurred to him until the veil was lifted, and the world was clearer to him, what Samuel and Isaiah's peculiar closeness meant.

In the absence of women, he understood the necessity of turning to a hand or a hog, or, in a last-ditch effort, begrudgingly and with falsehoods intact, the uncleanliness of other men. Hot was hot and release, for a man, was always imminent excepting into death. But to not have a desire for women to begin with, to produce no physical response to them whatsoever, above all, to willingly choose a male to cradle you gently into sleep, even when women were as soft and abundant as cotton . . .

Amos shook his head to clear the image from his mind. Man on top of woman: that wasn't just Christlike, it was sensible, right? He asked the question, but rhetorically, because he was apprehensive and uncertain about an answer. There was no suitable name for whatever it was that Samuel and Isaiah were doing, at least, none that he could remember. That he couldn't remember bothered him as much as the act itself. They weren't women. Women were weak, and by God's design. Nevertheless, by carrying on as though at least one of them was female, they threatened to only further diminish what Amos imagined was already diminished to death. For Samuel and Isaiah to wear their sex this way—dewy, firm, trembling, free—even under the cloak of night, was folly. If they had cared at all for any of the others, they would have, at the very least, masked their strangeness. Hushed it better, goddamnit, so that toubab wouldn't discover it. Didn't they understand that here, under Paul's word, they were nobodies?

Hold on.

There **were** bodies. They were **in** bodies. They just had no authority over theirs.

Amos could look at the embracing shadows no more. Especially the one he carried from the wagon all those years ago. Can you even imagine that? Someone throwing a child into a wagon as simply as you would a sack of cotton. A child screaming and his parents being beat into the ground for daring to protest. He was impressed, though, that the boy survived the trip. A little woozy at the end of it, of course, what with the way food and water were rationed, and how the insects bit. But Amos ignored his heavy shackles to catch the boy before he passed out in the dirt. Holding him, he wondered what it might be like to have his own child, to hold him close to his chest that the baby might be tickled by the coils of his father's hair. And looking down at son, son would look up at father, smile, and tug at the strands of his beard so that they both would be glad.

He began walking back to his cabin, avoiding the lantern light of the patrollers in the distance. He traced his steps, recalling that he had seen Samuel and Isaiah often since they were boys, mostly near the barn and, therefore, mostly segregated from the others. One black, the other purple; one smiling, the other brooding. Maybe if someone had carried him, weak-kneed, off a wagon, Samuel might be a son, too.

"You knew?" Amos asked folk.

He paid close attention to their whispers. The women were thankful for the reprieve, the others grateful for their courage. Maggie said it was something old, from the other time, before the ships and guns came. Amos knew of no such thing. He didn't even have to ask Essie because her and Isaiah's shared laughter now made sense. But there wasn't anything funny. He didn't understand how she didn't connect Isaiah's failure to Paul's.

Paul. Amos knew that once Paul discovered that
the nature of Isaiah and Samuel's stubbornness was
something other than bad aim, they would inspire
a passion in him that would become uncontainable.
At some point, Paul's restless mind wouldn't be content with just The Two of Them; he would seek to
inspect the others, to find increasingly creative and
heartbreaking methods of preventing Samuel and
Isaiah's unholiness from spreading. Because of those
two, suffering would prosper.

Amos felt spite growing in the midpoint of his
ribs, even though it was well known that Samuel
and Isaiah inspired everything around them to
dance: some old folk, the children, flies, the tips of
tall grass. Everything except the black-eyed Susans,
which turned their heads up at whomever. Skeptical
by nature, they swayed a little when the boys walked
past, but never any more than that. They were secure
enough in the golden of their petals that they didn't
have to worship anything else, except, maybe, the
rain. Shout when she came down. Amos wished his
people could be more like that.

When he himself saw them together—now that he
saw them saw them—frolicking in the marsh, heft-
ing bales of hay, and tending to the animals, or just
sitting silently side by side with their backs against
the barn feeding each other with bare hands, feet
too close together, he nearly glorified their names.
He covered his eyes because Isaiah and Samuel were

bright and coated in a shining the likes of which he had never seen. A shame that he would have to be the one to smash it.

It was necessary, then, that the nature of his sermons change. If the entire plantation could unite in this purpose, not just him, maybe . . . With a chest full of regret, and with his softest voice, away from the circle of trees so that no toubab might hear and unleash chaos before it had the chance to be thwarted, sometimes in the confines of his shack, he chastised any person who accepted, condoned, or ignored Samuel and Isaiah's behavior. Most people were frightened by this sudden shift because they weren't accustomed to his river-water voice sounding so drought.

"You think God don't see?" he would say quietly as he pointed in the direction of the barn, his dark fingers hanging in the air, quivering like tree branches shed of leaves, hoping uncertainty wasn't wearing him like Sunday clothing. For it had been he who Paul trusted with the words of the book and in there it had said **multiply and give God His glory-glory.** This is what he tried to explain above the tumult of whys that had bombarded him from the lips of almost everyone he whispered to.

He had anticipated difficulty, resistance, since his own legs were unsure. Samuel and Isaiah were, after all, boys, oftentimes helpful ones who were one bluster and the other tranquil, but never callous or aloof. He knew some of the people had thought of

them as their own children since the two were orphans. People took a special interest in orphans, secretly gave a little extra in terms of affection, though
they had none to spare. The women, especially, cared
for Samuel and Isaiah more than they should have,
Maggie being the worst one and the one who should
have known better.

"Shiiiiit," A Man Called Coot whispered back to
Amos. "Excuse my tongue, but a tiny bit of nice-nice
between us ain't killed nobody yet."

"They don't bother nobody 'round here," Naomi
said quietly. "Some of us ain't got a lot of time no
way. Might as well steal some kind of easy before the
hard have its way with you."

But the majority of those whom Amos invited in
remained silent, turned to one another with a look
that Amos had seen only on the faces of toubab.
It jumped from one face to the next, like lanterns
being lit in quick succession. Instead of too much
resistance, Amos found a frightening commonal-
ity between toubab and his own people that could
be exploited quite easily. The idea that they could
be better—more entitled to favor than others, have
a kind of belly breeze of their own—hadn't really
occurred to them. Occasionally, Paul would show
more approval toward some of them based on the
speed and dexterity with which they pulled cotton,
but the reward for that was more work and greater
expectation, not less. Sometimes, he was a bit more
lenient with the people whose color was diminished

by Paul's interference, but the cost of that was evident. Now, because of Amos, they had this new concept to reckon with: they could have access to some kind of **sometime** just by virtue of not being one of the excluded.

They had come to Amos two by two, but they were seduced one by one. People began avoiding Samuel and Isaiah. They would deliberately walk the long way, past the overseers and through the weeds, to dodge them on the common path to and from the field. They left tools on the ground outside the barn instead of handing them over directly to them. They bathed farther up the shore away from them. They left no room for them at fire circles. They cut their eyes and screwed their faces each time Isaiah and Samuel dared displays that remotely resembled affection.

Amos was there, down by the river, when Big Hosea attacked Samuel. Hosea had said that Samuel looked at him funny. Hosea was one of the few on the plantation who was sure he could take Samuel on. He always sought Samuel out to play-wrestle in the high weeds as a means to test his own strength. So it took nothing for him to punch Samuel square in the jaw right there at the river in front of everyone. For his trouble, Samuel nearly split Big Hosea's head open against protruding rocks. Amos and others helped Hosea up as Isaiah held Samuel back. Hosea said Samuel looked at him in a way that made him feel defenseless, naked. Never mind that they were all naked from bathing. That look, he said, made him lunge for Samuel. Hosea's chest was heaving. Amos told him to calm down, told him that no one blamed him for doing what came natural for men to do. No one mentioned, either, that between Big Hosea's legs, his flesh was stiff and throbbing.

Now it was Sunday. Amos was alone as he walked through the weeds, along the cotton field, and into the clearing beyond it. Just before he entered, he could see how the light fell down in that space and made things a pale gold, but the silence, too, gave things a color. He didn't have the language to describe it. It wasn't like it was blue, though that is what he would have said were he less observant. He would have to be content with not having an answer for everything. "Humble yourself, Amos. Be humble."

Once in the embrace of the clearing, he sat on the rock, crossed his legs at the ankles, brought his hands together, and started to pray. When he was done, he opened his eyes wide, for he had heard the whisper. He brought his hand to his mouth. There was a faint frown on his lips. **No,** he thought, but the whispering voice was quietly **Yes.**

The first of his congregation broke through the trees and into the clearing. Amos straightened up. It was Be Auntie, and she was holding Solomon, who was whining just a little.

"Good morning, ma'am. Good morning," he said.

Amos looked down at Solomon. His mouth tried to smile, but his eyes didn't.

Hush.

GENESIS

Here is not where we begin, but it is where we **shall** begin. For you to know us. For us to know you. But mainly, for you to know yourself.

We have names, but they are names you can no longer pronounce without sounding as foreign as your captors. That is not to condemn you. Believe us: we know the part we played in it, even if just through our ignorance and fascination with previously unknown things. Forgive us. The only way we can repay that debt is by telling you the story that we give to you through our blood.

All memory is kept there. But memory is not enough.

You are the vessel, you see, so that is why you must

not give in to the temptation of the long sleep. Who will tell it if not you?

You can never be an orphan. Do you understand? The night sky itself gave birth to you and covers you and names you as her children above all others. First born. Best adorned. Highest thought. Most loved.

And despise not the dark of your skin, for within it is the prime sorcery that moved us from belly-crawl to tall-walk. From the screaming, we brought forth words and mathematics and the dexterity of knowledge that coaxed the ground to offer up itself as sustenance. But do not let this make you arrogant.

Arrogance brings you lower, down from the moun-taintops where you were breastfed. Like where you are now, down in the bottomless. Where separation is normal and joy is found in indecent places.

To fold yourself in on yourself is where you will find power. Risen out of circles at the bottoms of oceans. By hands that stitched the cosmos so that it might be primed at the beginning of everything. A little pageantry never hurt anyone. It is all right for you to find humor in that. We like to hear your laughter.

You must know that you come from the place where fathers held you and mothers hunted for your pleasure. Holding great spears and dancing, carrying you shoulder-high and celebrating victory. You still do the dance. We see you. You still do the dance. It is part of what you are.

A hand is unfurling. In its own time, which seems

too long to you, we know. But you must be patient. We will not judge you harshly if you succumb to the pain. It is a lot to ask of everyone, especially you, so cut off from where you are supposed to be. Return to memory when you are filled with doubt (though memory is not enough). There are no lines. For everything is a circle, turning back on itself endlessly. This is not to make you dizzy, but to give you the chance to get it right the next time.

We know that you have questions. Who are we? Why do we only whisper to you? Why do we only come to you in dreams? Why do we dwell only in the dark? Answers soon come. We, the seven, promise.

Fold in, children. Fold in.

I Kings

The day the devils walked out of the bush, King Akusa was in her royal hut in the heart of Kosongo territory, in good spirits. Two of her six wives, Ketwa and Nbinga, had brought in her dinner: bowls of yam, fish stew, and enough palm wine to make her feel mellow.

Her second wife, Ketwa, whom she favored, was much more adept at cooking than any of her other wives.

"Did Ketwa prepare the meal?" the king asked. She knew that he did but liked the way a smile appeared on his face, tender and gently curled, whenever she asked.

"Yes, my king. As always," Nbinga replied.

"Well, not always," Ketwa corrected. "When we

smell that burning scent, when the fish is too soggy, we know that I am not the cook."

The king laughed as she washed her hands in a bowl filled with water and sage.

"And you will help prepare the feast for the ceremony? It is only a week away, you know," she said with a wry smile.

"Of course," Ketwa said. "Kosii is my favorite nephew. But his mother is an even better cook than I. She is the one who taught me."

"I am sure she would appreciate the help in any event," the king said.

She reclined onto the smooth bundles of red, orange, green, and yellow blankets at her back. She looked up at Ketwa.

"Are you not going to join me for some palm wine?"

Ketwa looked at her. He felt drawn to her nighttime skin; her clear, bright eyes; and the silkiness of her breasts as they lay beneath her beaded necklace. He noticed her head as she tilted forward to reach for a cup: bald as her behind, clever in its shape, adorned with blue paint and red gems. She had a king's head and a warrior's mind inside of it.

"Will the others be jealous?" Ketwa asked as he poured the wine.

"Why? They will be joining us too," said the king, and she smiled.

"And who will tend to our children if I am here?" he retorted.

"You are one of many."

She brought the cup to her lips just as young Reshkwe ran into the hut. He was panting heavily and fell to his knees at the edge of the bowls of food laid out before the king.

"You dare enter without announcement?" Ketwa rebuked.

Reshkwe's forehead touched the ground.

"Forgiveness," he shouted between pants. "Forgiveness, King Akusa. But you must come! It is a nightmare. A nightmare has come to us!"

What could have reached the village so far from the sea as it was: days and days of trekking through the savanna where lion and hyena lurk, not to mention across a river teeming with hippo and crocodile? The nearest neighbors, the Gussu, were days away and were respectful enough to come always bearing gifts, nothing nightmarish as the boy described. King Akusa wondered about the possibilities of a curse, but reminded herself of the wards: the village was large; the drumming was regular, sometimes loud enough to frighten birds from trees; and the ancestors were relentlessly respected with offerings of only the most magnificent bananas from the harvest. There was no reason to believe that they were angry and had sent some form of plague. If anything, they would be pleased by how the village thrived, populated with five generations of people upon whose faces the ancestors lived. And soon, they would have gate guardians for the first time since the war.

The king reached behind her blankets for her

spear and shield. Upon the latter was a carving of her family's avatar: a jagged little warrior, shaped like a lightning flash, with their weapons raised high in triumph.

"Shall I summon the guard, my king?" Nbinga asked.

"Have them meet me on the way to the gate."

King Akusa darted out of the dwelling with incredible speed. She rushed past dozens and dozens of huts, a trail of red dust flowing behind her. The ground was dry because there were still at least two months before the rainy season. The sun was just beginning to descend behind the trees. She looked down to see her shadow, quick and long, beneath her. Soon, she heard the pounding of her guards coming up from behind. They moved in like a coming storm and eventually caught up to her. Together, they reached the village square. And together, they came to a screeching halt.

One man gagged. Another vomited. Three women recoiled. Four men nearly retreated. King Akusa the Brave merely narrowed her eyes and tightened her grip on her spear. The boy was right. Demons had somehow made it to their home.

Not somehow. Next to these strangely dressed things, whose skin was like having no skin at all, was a Gussu. He stepped forward and knelt before the king. He had the apologetic eyes of a friend, but she did not trust him.

She turned to see the guards in various states of

disarray. She banged the dull end of her spear against the ground and suddenly, they all came to attention. She cautioned the guards not to go near the strangers and to avoid touching them. Grateful for her wisdom, they surrounded her in a protective half circle and pointed their spears at the intruders.

"Are they dead?" Muzani, the tallest, asked.

"Move away," the king ordered, not at all masking her irritation at their forgetting she was the greatest warrior among them and could readily protect herself, even against the unliving. She looked down at the Gussu who knelt before her.

"I'm confused," she said as she dug her spear into the ground. "Your position indicates respect, but you brought pestilence to my village. Explain yourself immediately or you and these demons shall suffer together."

She would have expected such things of the mountain people with no name, who had once come down from their perches in the clouds and attacked her village unprovoked. She was a girl then but remembered them clearly because of their sharpened teeth and the white paint that garishly adorned their faces. The no-name mountain people more than liked war; it seemed for them a kind of religion, the thing that defined them. To remove war from their hearts would be akin to removing the ancestral bonds from her own people. They would merely dissolve and all that would be left would be smoky wisps and a foul odor. But none of that meant that the Kosongo wouldn't fight back. On the contrary, the king's mother led the charge against them, her spear held high as though she had grabbed lightning from above.

"Not demons," the frightened man said in service-able Kosongo tongue. "Friends."

He signaled for the demons to bow and they did. They were less ugly in that position. The king ordered the guards to lower their weapons but to also exercise caution. With an easily understandable hand gesture, she instructed the intruders to stand. She couldn't stop staring at them. They had hair the color of sand. She looked each one in the eye. One wore a curious object over the eyes that made them look small and beady. And her initial assessment was correct: all three demons were missing skin. One of them opened its mouth to speak. Broken as it was, she recognized it and suspected bad magic.

"Greetings," it said. "I am Brother Gabriel. And I am here to bring you the good news."

BEULAH

Wide as two women, Beulah—now Be Auntie—
had the space to dream when everyone else on
Empty knew better. The smile on her face wasn't
permanent and it wasn't an indication that she was
witless. Rather, it was a kind of armament against
the sorrow that bending over in the cotton field,
and in other places, rubbed into the skin. It wasn't a
perfume, and yet it had its own scent. Smelled like
something buried for a long time and then dug up.
Now exposed to the sun, the thing didn't begin to
resurrect itself, but it did unfurl its stench—old, rotting, sharp—inspiring gagging and heaving, but
also telling you something about itself, about whoever put it there, and about who uncovered it.

She felt like she was that buried thing. Covered up

against her will. For so long forgotten. Left to decay. Discovered too late, but still useful to thieves who fancied themselves explorers. All of this left her in a very delicate condition. The forbidden dreams that had once been the source for the jubilation of she didn't know how many people, singing in a key that made her feel fine, had begun to fracture such that they sat side by side with some other discordant thing that likewise doubled her. Not just her body, though, but also her mind, heart, and, she would like to believe, soul (she had one—two!—despite toubab telling her she had none). What choice did she have but to burn every slight until it shined like a comfort?

She didn't mean to give herself to Amos, not at first. Essie was with child and they still had her out in the field. Essie couldn't sing to keep everyone on rhythm; it was just too much. Be Auntie told a rhyming story to make up for it. Something about a town down in a valley and how the people were going to prepare a banquet even when they knew a storm was a-coming. Not only that, but Be Auntie (or maybe it was Beulah) picked her share of cotton and half of Essie's too so that Essie would avoid the lash. Yes, ma'am, they would even whup a girl plump with child, which made no practical sense. If the goal was to magnify your glory, why would you take your blessings out two at a time?

"You still trying to climb on top of her, after what she been through?" she was bold enough to ask Amos after the horn sounded and the sun mellowed.

"She my woman. I do anything for her. Trying to make her forget. Trying to make her know tain't a ounce missing of her beauty."

"And you doing that by going to her instead of letting her come to you?"

Be Auntie knew it was futile by the confusion on Amos's face. She knew men, ones in heat or ones who had something to prove, were senseless. They would rearrange land and sea to get them both to lead to satisfaction when one was enough already. Afterward, when their minds returned to them, the kind ones experienced regret, the cruel ones sought more cruelty, and the two were indistinguishable to her. It didn't have to be some grand act. All they had to do was look at her like they were disgusted by **her** for the act **they** just committed. They get on up from the pallet and walk out of the shack without so much as a "thank you" or "evening," not even a "beg your pardon." She thought they could at least act like they were forced to sometimes and give her the redress she was rightly due. Instead, they left her to lie there in her own stink **and** theirs like doing so was the gift she was waiting on. And so often, she was just there crying on the outside and hoping that what they left inside her didn't catch, and if the blood came, then mercy somewhere had heard her.

What was most insidious about it all was what the repetition did to her. At some point, in spite of herself, she started to enjoy the rhythm. The sly smile. The cool words. The giddy sway. The pressing down.

The steady pump. The last thrust. The slap. The kick. The punch. The forgotten gratitude. The lost good night. She found herself molded into the shape that best fit what they carved her into. Water done wore away at her stone, and the next thing she knew, she was a damn river when she could have sworn she was a mountain.

Mountain to river was a place. More than a place, it was a person. Beulah was a mountain. Be Auntie was a river. In between, fertile or arid land, depending on the location. The others judged her harshly, she knew, for being the first of them to go from up high to down low. But she was just the first, and her sacrifice, one of them anyway, was this: she made it so that there would be more grace waiting for them when they, too, made the descent.

And it wasn't like she climbed down all of her own volition, carefully navigating the peaks and slopes, securing her footing so that she didn't slip on any smooth and icy crevices. Nah. She was pushed. It mattered not whether she smiled or screamed as she plummeted. Some tumbles were worthy of pity regardless.

Because look what had become of her in the bottom-bottom: she was men's rest stop and peace of mind; she was their cookhouse, flophouse, and out-house; she bore them children for whom they could bear no attachment and collected the children not of her blood to replace the ones snatched away on a whim or a bill come due.

She knew she could spare Essie (not stop, but slow her fall) because **womens had to look after womens**—particularly when refusal meant death. Yes, she opened her arms wide to Amos, legs too; let him not only laugh, talk, rock, bump, grind, hit, and fail to say sweet dreams or farewell, but she also let him do it over and over and over again until it felt like something divine—if just for the ritual of it.

Another thing defined her worship. **See, Maggie was wrong: if you get them early enough, they won't be corrupted. You might just could turn boys' natures such that when they see a woman, their first instinct ain't to tame her, but to leave her be. You could coat them in enough salve that when they started preferring the outdoors, to be around the older men—who didn't have the benefit of what they call "womanly things" precisely because they wanted the right to be reckless and pilfering; if they had embraced their whole mind instead of half of it—the error of their ways would be revealed to them, and they knew they couldn't see that and survive intact.**

Be Auntie (not Beulah) doted over every boy-child—especially the ones whose color had been meddled with. Every girl-child, particularly the ones whose skin was raven, she lorded over or left to fend for herself (as Beulah wept). **Womens had to look after womens,** yes. But first there had to be trial and she refused to interfere with that sacred passage for any woman, young or old.

She got Puah after the mother and father were both sold off. Puah wasn't even walking yet and still in need of milk, which Be Auntie gave to her only sparingly, supplementing it with pieces of bread and hog parts she knew the baby to be too young to be eating. When Puah's stomach pained her all night and her cries wouldn't cease, Be Auntie blamed the child for her own condition and just let her scream until her throat was raw, after which she would just whine gently. It's a wonder the child had any voice at all.

The baby was too young for grown-up food and also too young to have sown such resentment in Be Auntie, but there both of those things were, sitting uncomfortably in one tiny little body, futile but resolute.

What Be Auntie did know was that one day, Puah would be of use. It would either be as a sword or it would be as a shield, possibly both, but whatever the form, it was inevitable. Maggie wasn't the only one who knew of the deep and hidden things.

One sticky night, Be Auntie was lying with Amos. He had come into her shack in a huff, complaining about how he tried to be reasonable with Isaiah and Samuel, but they just wouldn't submit.

"Submit to what?" Be Auntie asked rather innocently.

Amos looked at her as though she had cursed. "A nature grander than they own! You ain't been listening to what I been trying to tell you?" he said loudly before lowering his head to allow his voice to reach that level. He sighed. "Some folk will never understand that the part ain't more important than the whole," he said to her darkly. "But you hear me, Be. Huh?"

Amos's eyes were kind. He had an open face. His tones were not unlike a story being told around a fire at night. You had to lean in, and not even biting mosquitoes could distract you once you were there. She had that, too, the voice for story, but people only wanted to hear hers as comfort, not as inspiration. But Amos also had a breezy touch. He brought himself down with her, down the mountain and into the stream. He touched the water. He slid his hand right between her thighs and she didn't flinch at all. She knew he cared about her pleasure, but that her pleasure wasn't the point. Still, she squirmed a little at what he had tickled. They were close together, him smiling, her with drowsy eyes.

"You need me to do what?" she whispered.

Amos sat up and looked over to the side of the shack where the children lay, piled together like refuse somebody had swept up (and perhaps someone did), and he looked at a trying-to-sleep Puah.

"How old Puah is now?" Amos scratched his chin. "Fifteen? Sixteen?"

"Just about."

"And you manage to keep her still locked up in here with you? Massa or nobody don't come 'round to mess with her?"

Be Auntie looked at Puah with an envious eye. What guts this girl had to first survive whatever Be Auntie put in her belly and then to live on Empty still full. Nah, maybe that wasn't as much guts as luck. Luck that had escaped everyone else on the plantation except Puah, it seemed. Lucky people were of no use to anyone but themselves. (Sarah was another story, but Be Auntie didn't have that much fight, or yearning turned 'round to face itself, in her to do it Sarah's way.)

"Hm," Be Auntie said. "What you asking about her for?"

"I need her. For them."

The twinge of pain she felt in her temples was for her, not Puah, she told herself.

"What for?"

"You know what for."

Be Auntie knew Samuel and Isaiah as not-hers. They were two children who she was never able to incorporate into her tribe—one, in particular, for good reason. They weren't raised by anyone but looked after by everyone, vagabonds of a sort, but beloved ones. They were the ones who were in the barn and had to have had good natures because they took care of the animals, of life, didn't just plant it, pick it, and put it in a sack. But one of them was also the one with the ax. Sometimes, she heard a pig squealing. Pigs somehow always knew what was coming. They fidgeted on the day of. They would try to run, but Samuel's hands were firm. There was no expression on his face before or during. But after, when he was down at the river, washing the blood from his hands, his bottom lip would droop, and his drool splashed into the water's rush. **Boy not boy,** she thought. **Boy now man.**

Amos kissed Be Auntie deeply. He brought his lips down to her neck. He looked at her and rubbed his nose against her.

"Let me see what I can put in her head," she said. "I gotta be careful about it. That girl always do the opposite of what I tell her."

It pierced Be Auntie's heart that despite her disobedience, Puah walked through Empty relatively unscathed, as though she had taken all of the advice and cues Be Auntie offered, rather than tossing them to the ground and kicking them away. It meant that perhaps Be Auntie had erred and that Puah's scorn and her hope, rather than the advised split then submission, could be a way, too. Oh, well. It didn't make much difference anymore. Here it was, and Be Auntie knew it would come sooner or later: the time for Puah to know the grace that none of the others had the foresight to show Beulah, which was Be Auntie's dawn. **Don't matter who do or don't like it. At least I got to choose my own name.**

"I think she sweet on that there Samuel. That's the bigger one name, ain't it? The purple one, not the black one?"

"The one that keep his mouth open, yeah."

"Hm. All right then."

Be Auntie pulled on Amos. Puah and the other children all huddled even though it was too hot to do that, but they seemed as though they didn't want to take up too much space, which was wise because shrinking down kept you out of the minds of toubab, and if you weren't sturdy enough to withstand what their minds could do (who was?), then it was best that you just be smaller than you had ever been before.

She looked at Amos. "Come on."

He had interrupted the beat of their song. They couldn't do their dance if the music stopped.

"Let me."

She wrapped her arms around him and pressed her plush into his.

"Can I tell you 'bout the thunder?"

She wasn't the singer Essie was, but she could tell one hell of a story to keep time.

PUAH

Puah hated the way the cotton got stuck beneath her fingernails. She hated even more what the picking did to her fingers: made them raw and heavy, made her feel like she had something in her hands even when she didn't. She was thick with grievance, which she had to continuously tuck back into her crevices, inhale to give it more room and hold it in place.

She held on to her sack with a grudge, snatched it from spot to spot as she robbed one plant after the next, thievery on behalf of a man who, if she could, she would pluck the hairs from, one by one, even the eyelashes, in the same way. In the corners of her eyes, the only thing that threatened to form, ever, was anger. But in the shape of her body, which marked her as vulnerable from every direction, with danger lurking in the company of anybody, she kept her vengeance pillowed and well blanketed in the nest of her soul.

At the end of the day she threw her pickings in the wagon, watched by James, whom she never looked in the eye, for Maggie, yes, but also because she wanted to deny him the courtesy of her gaze. Her wide eyes, bushy eyebrows, and long lashes would be for her own offering and hers alone. And the only people to stand at her altar would be those of her choosing. These were the things she told herself in places where she could afford to be resolute.

She lifted her dress by its hem, exposing the obsidian of her calves, and started back toward the shacks. She wanted to bathe in the river, but the men were there. She would find a bucket and fill it with river water and wash herself in the night, behind Be Auntie's shack, instead.

She pulled on her hair, touched the roots of it, noticing the new growth that had made her braids puffy and fuzzy. It needed a good washing and greasing before being tied up before bed to keep it pressed against her mind. As she brought her hand back down to her side, she noticed movement in the distance. She walked over toward it, toward the barn. She stopped at the wooden fence circling it and saw Samuel leading a horse toward the pens and wanted to catch him before he went inside.

"Samuel," she shouted, impressed by how far her voice carried.

He turned and smiled. He walked over to where she was standing on the bottom rung of the fence. He pulled the horse along with him.

"Oh, y'all done in the field?" he asked.

"Well, you see me right here in front this barn," she said, putting her hand on her hip.

"All right then," Samuel said with a laugh.

She swung her leg over the fence, then the other, and sat on the top rail.

"What you got planned for your rest day?" she asked, looking beyond him and into the barn. She saw a figure moving around inside and knew it had to be Isaiah even if she couldn't see him clearly. She returned her focus to Samuel and grinned at the way the tender sun and dawning starlight had lit his skin so that the pitch of it was obvious.

"Ain't nothing. Gon' be right here with 'Zay."

There was a moment of silence between them that gave her the chance to notice the moist of his lips. She forgave him for not asking her about what she would be doing with her Sunday.

"Probably going over by Sarah to have her plait my hair. She do plaits so nice." She touched her hair and pulled a braid down over her forehead and held it by its tip.

"Where Dug?" Samuel asked after her pretend baby brother.

Puah sucked her teeth. "Somewhere up underneath Be Auntie, I guess. Boys shouldn't follow behind they mamas like that."

Samuel looked at the ground and gripped the reins of the horse a little bit tighter.

"Oh, I didn't mean—"

"I know," Samuel interrupted. He kicked at the weeds and bent down to pick up a pebble. He threw it over the fence. Puah watched it travel and land in the distance.

"You throw far." Her lips parted for a smile, which Samuel returned.

"You should come with me to Sarah tomorrow," she said.

Samuel twisted his lips at the idea.

"What? You don't like Sarah?"

Samuel laughed. "I like Sarah just fine. But what I supposed to do, just sit there and watch her plait your hair?"

Puah jumped down off the fence.

"Yeah," she said and moved closer to Samuel. She reached up and touched his hair; it was beady and dusty.

"And maybe she plait your'n."

They stood there just breathing and not saying anything. Samuel couldn't look her in the eye, and Puah couldn't look anywhere else but in his. Samuel had the kind of eyes that invited people over, greeted them, and then quietly shut the door in their faces. And for some reason, standing out there on the

wrong side of it, people felt compelled to keep banging on that door until, by some mercy, he opened it.
His hair coiled in her fingers and Samuel closed his
eyes just as Puah's mouth parted.

Over his shoulder, she saw Isaiah leaning against
the barn door. His arms were folded and one of his
legs was raised so that his foot was flat against the
door. He didn't have a frown on his face, nor did he
have a grin. He seemed to be lingering in the middle
of both, looking outward, but seeing inward. Now
and again, he shooed away flies, but other than that,
he didn't move. She stopped playing in Samuel's head
and waved at Isaiah, but he didn't seem to notice. So
she called him. He uncrossed his arms and moved
away from the barn. He seemed hesitant to come over
to them. He looked at Samuel and Samuel turned to
look at him. If they said anything to each other, she
didn't hear it. But it certainly seemed like there was
some sort of exchange. Isaiah walked toward them
slowly. He came up from behind Samuel, touched
his back as he moved beside him. The horse took two
steps and then was still again.

"Hey, Puah," Isaiah said in such a reassuring voice
that she nearly felt welcomed in a space that usually felt shut off from everything else. Under that,
though, she detected something in the calmness of
his tone, a prickly thing that made her scalp itch.
She looked at him and saw something quickly flash
across his face.

"I was just telling Samuel he should come with me

to Sarah tomorrow and get his hair plait. Won't he look good?"

She didn't say that to hurt Isaiah's feelings. She meant it genuinely. Isaiah looked at Samuel from head to toe.

"I reckon he look good either way. Up to him how he wanna show that good," Isaiah said, grinning. He put his hand on Samuel's shoulder. "I gotta finish up, Sam. Let me take this here horse back in the pen. Come on, boy. Good evening to you, Miss Puah."

"Just Puah," she said. Isaiah nodded his apology and strolled off with the reins of the horse in his hand, pulling the buck along. Puah watched them walk into the barn and then returned her attention to Samuel.

"He right. You look good either way. Still, I hope you choose plaits." She smiled and turned to climb back over the fence.

"Night, Sam-u-well." She winked. Then she jumped down and headed to her shack.

Puah was one of two of Be Auntie's girls; the other, still a toddler, named Delia, a child that Puah swore Be Auntie named with spite in her heart because the baby and Puah shared the same midnight color.

They all slept on one pallet. Puah didn't like lying down next to her imitation brothers. For some of them (irrespective of their age, and that surprised her), the mere acts of closed eyes and the rumble of snoring were calls to actions she never authorized. Most nights, she slept curled in a corner, the edge of her dress tucked under her soles, creating a kind of tent in which she could hide her body from those who would dare pry.

Be Auntie told her to forgive them, that beat-down people did beat-down things. Toil made them hot and cruel, but mostly hot, and sometimes the best a woman could do was be a sip of water. That was how Puah knew that Be Auntie could never be her real mother, no matter how many lullabies sung or pains rocked. Her real mother would never ask her to be a sacrifice to ungrateful, nonreciprocal fools. Her real mother wouldn't baby every boy no matter how grown and chastise every girl no matter how sweet.

"Shameless," Be Auntie mumbled at any girl within earshot, and Puah didn't like the way it was hissed at her. It was like no matter what she did or didn't do, any evil would be laid at her feet and regarded as the product of her own belly. "Grown," she heard Be Auntie say when any kind observer would have said "growing."

There was no one else in the world, she thought, cursed to carry such a burden. Everywhere a girl existed, there was someone telling her that she was her own fault and leading a ritual to punish her for something she never did. It hadn't always been this way. Blood memory confirmed this and women were the bearers of the blood.

It was worse when the cruelty came from other women. It shouldn't have been; after all, women were people, too. But it was. When women did it, it was like being stabbed with two knives instead of one. Two knives, one in the back and the other in a place that couldn't be seen, only felt.

Maybe Be Auntie had no choice. Maybe after so many times of being beaten in the fields by Massa only to return, scarred, to the shack to be beaten by her lover's hand, she had finally decided to yield. Maybe she thought she could influence manhood in another way, shower them with a tenderness they could carry with them and share with other women they encountered, if they remembered. That was the problem. The desire for power erased memory and replaced it with violence. And Be Auntie had the bruises to prove it. Nearly every woman did.

That was why Puah despised Dug so. She knew all the attention, all the energy, all the titty milk Be Auntie was giving him was a complete waste of time. No matter what she did—no matter how blessed the kisses to the cheek or how mellow the song sung, even deep into the night—his hands would still grow to a size that could snugly grip the throat and easily crimp into a fist tight enough to smash teeth.

Men and toubab shared far more than either would ever admit. Just ask anyone who had ever been at their mercy. They both took what they wanted; asking was never a courtesy. Both smiled first, but pain always followed. And, too, both claimed they had good reason for this absurd behavior: whatever forces in the sky had declared that this act had to take place, that what could have been pleasure if both parties were willing had crumbled into a gagged and lying thing, it was as much beyond their control as sunshine; it simply wasn't and couldn't ever be their fault. Nature was stubborn.

Whatever. Puah had a plan to escape Be Auntie's fate, the whims of false brothers, and toubab. She had a place to retreat to.

In the imaginary—where the Other Puah lived, which wasn't too far, which sat right up against where This Puah lived, parallel, but crisper in color, more textured in sound, only seen by This Puah when she tilted her head in just the right position and paid close attention to the rhythm of her heart—there was enough to eat.

The Other Puah feasted lazily on strawberries and other sweet-smelling fruit, licked honey from her palms, and used a knife and fork to eat roasted chicken, which fell delightfully from the bone. There, her laughter was a mask for nothing and the tingling at the tips of her fingers came from how willingly they were kissed. She frolicked, the Other Puah, because there was no one lying in wait, anxious to take advantage of her kindness, misuse it, and leave it squirted on top of her like a shooting-star-shaped stain, drying and, in time, flaking, to be lifted off by breeze or troubled water.

Her suitors walked on black-sand beaches, skin like they had been made from the substance upon which they stood, each more loving than the next. They each sang songs about her, using words that she didn't recognize but knew to be charming because of how smoothly they left their lips. And in the imaginary, just like in the Empty place, she chose one above all others, the one who had eyes like gently closed doors and made everyone who looked into them conjure up a masterpiece to knock. But like all dreams, these too were interrupted by the sharp point of toil.

Dug's crying brought her back. He fussed like he knew it would snatch her into the now, dissolve the imaginary in the palm of her hands. She cut her eyes at him.

"What you want, Dug?"

He just smiled.

It starts young, Puah thought before she retreated to the corner.

SARAH'S SHACK ALWAYS SMELLED like outdoors. She kept dandelions tucked in corners and stuffed some inside her pallet. As big and sturdy a woman as she was, with skin that Puah thought could be shadow's substitute, she did little dainty things like that; that, and she would also adorn her head with baby's breath. She said she did it to trick herself into thinking she wasn't trapped, that when she closed her eyes, she could think of herself gallivanting with nowhere in particular to go, wide as a meadow and unchained, and not a single toubab face for a thousand miles.

Puah walked through the cloth that hung, dirty, in Sarah's doorway.

"Can you do it up?" Puah asked her. "So it ain't touching my neck. Cooler for when I in the field."

Sarah sucked her teeth. "Hello to you, too."

Puah smiled. Sarah looked at her head.

"Gal, you wouldn't be asking me that if you just wrapped it when you was out there like everybody else do."

"Chile, I can't be bothered with all that. Besides, wrapping makes it even more hot."

Sarah shook her head. "This why your braids never stay long. You wild with your head."

Puah put both hands on her head, shook her hips, and walked around the shack on her tippy-toes.

"What you call yourself doing?"

"Missy Ruth. Don't you see how dainty and delicate I is?" Puah batted her eyes. Sarah rolled hers but couldn't help but laugh.

"Gal, you is a fool," Sarah said, and she pulled a stool from under the table. She flopped down on top of it. "So, you wanna be her?"

Puah came down onto her heels. "No'm!"

"Stop conjuring that up, then." Sarah rubbed her temples. "Quit all that foolery and let me fix your head."

Puah sat down on the floor between Sarah's legs.

She drew her knees up to her chest and hugged them, the hem of her dress safely underfoot. Sarah began to undo her braids starting from the back.

"Your hair growing," Sarah said during the unfastening.

"I feels like shaving it all off is what I feels like."

"You must be remembering an old thing," Sarah whispered, staring at the back of Puah's head. "Like I can remember old things."

Puah yawned and scratched a spot behind her ear.

"Stop moving!" Sarah scolded.

After a moment of silence Puah spoke.

"I had asked Samuel to come on over to get his hair plait, too."

Sarah stopped undoing. "And what he say?"

"He ain't say no."

"But did he say yes?"

"No."

"Mm hm!"

Puah shifted. It was the first time that she had considered that he might not come, might not want to come, might be prevented from coming because . . . It wasn't like Samuel to be rude, to say he'd be somewhere and then not show up. Then again, he never said he would show up.

He was the only man on the entire plantation who ever cared about what she thought, who really, genuinely gave a damn and didn't feign interest as an oh-so-transparent ruse to get in under her dress. He was the first man who wanted nothing but her company and conversation, who cheered her up when she was down by sticking daisies in his hair and walking around like a chicken. Big as he was, he never once shifted his weight in her direction or tried to block out her light with his shadow. Where she felt like Isaiah ignored or only tolerated her, she knew Samuel truly saw her and didn't recoil at the notion of her grace.

"I hope you ain't letting Amos fill your head with no foolishness," Sarah said.

"No."

"Hmph. Just like Amos to send you out to that barn to cause havoc."

"I ain't causing no havoc, Sarah. And Amos ain't send me."

"Who send you, then?"

Puah rolled her eyes.

"You need to go on ahead and leave them boys be."

"Samuel is my friend," Puah said, her eyebrows bending into her frustration.

"How many of your 'friends' make your neck-back goosebump like it is now?"

"Those heat bumps."

"Gal, go on with that mess."

Sometimes it was hard to endure Sarah's truths, as unsweetened and thorny as they were. They had no roundness, no smooth edges, and every point was pin sharp. Still, from every pin-sized wound, only a little blood was let. In the small, manageable droplets, Puah could see the answers that even Sarah never intended to confront. That was a blessing that most people turned away from. Not Puah, though. Puah knew that the secret of strength was in how much truth could be endured. And on a plantation full of people asleep in lies, she intended to stay awake, no matter how much it stung.

"Well."

"Well nothing. Leave him be." Sarah sighed.

Heat came off Puah. She had hoped that Sarah felt it, that it soothed her enough to know that she had said enough and that Puah had heard enough. Tiny wounds, that's all. Better hurt now in the company of sisters, than hurt later wearing the chuckles of men down her back. A moment passed before Sarah spoke again.

"I don't wanna be up in here talking 'bout no mens, no way. They take up too much space in us as it is. Leave no room for ourselfs to stretch a bit or lay down without being bothered."

"You right," Puah conceded, if only with her words.

"So you want your hair up you said?"

"Yes ma'am."

Sarah gently pushed Puah's head forward, exposing the nape of her neck. Puah leaned into it, her chin touching her chest.

"My Mary used to be so tender-headed. I had to do her hair in big box braids. Two or three was all she could take." Sarah laughed. "You ain't tender-headed a bit. I can do nicer plaits, smaller. And take my sweet ol' time."

Puah closed her eyes and took in as much as she could.

Time, that is.

THE SUN WAS CREAMY at the horizon when she decided to go see Samuel. Some of the other people sat outside their shacks trying to relish as much as they could of the day as it was being pulled out of their grasps. Even the children who, earlier, had an energy that couldn't be sapped had slowed, sat down to mourn its passing.

Puah walked off the path, onto the weeds that grew on either side of it. They cushioned her step and were cool against her feet. She was in the mood to pamper herself.

By the time she reached the barn, the sky had moved from rose to indigo and her skin had a sweat glow that only magnified her beauty. She couldn't wait to show Samuel what Sarah did with her hair.

The barn doors were open and there was a faint light emanating from within. She didn't want to enter unannounced, so she called for Samuel and she broke his name up into threes like only she could and only when speaking to him.

"Over here," Samuel responded.

She spun around and she saw them. Her lips parted, ever so slightly, just enough to let her tongue slip out to wet her lips. But no matter how many times she moistened them, they would dry again.

There was Sam-u-well sitting on the ground, his legs crossed flat in front of him. Behind him, Isaiah sat on a bale of hay. He was braiding Samuel's hair.

"Oh hey, Puah." Samuel smiled. "I take your advice. Look at me. Me! Getting my hair plait. Don't that just beat all? Ouch, 'Zay. That too tight!"

"Hey, Puah," Isaiah said.

Puah walked over to the pail on the ground next to them. She dipped the ladle in it and took two big gulps of water. She sat down on the ground.

"Your hair looks nice," Samuel said to her. Isaiah nodded in agreement.

She sat there watching them, a dazed look on her face.

"You all right?" Samuel asked her.

She didn't answer. She was too busy cocking her head to the left, trying to bring the imaginary into focus. It shimmered upon fading into view. It was night there, too, and fireflies blinked a serenade. Beyond them, she saw two figures. They leaned into each other as they sat at the shore of a shiny river where fish that could fly took turns leaping into the air and then diving back down into the water. Then the two figures stood and walked toward the flurry of lightning bugs. The male figure, brawny and tall, took the curvaceous female figure into his arms and they twirled round and round to a music that Puah only scarcely heard. It was a cradlesong. Then all the flies lit up at once and illuminated the couple. It was the Other Puah and Her Samuel. She was smiling and looking into his eyes, deeper and deeper, and, to her surprise, there it was. Unmistakably. The door that had always been sealed was cracked open. There was a light coming from the opening, faint like from a candle, but light nonetheless. And the light spoke. It said, "Been waiting on you."

Puah reached out her hand at the scene, tried to grab and hold on to it as it began to recede. No matter which way she cocked her head, it wouldn't return.

"Puah?" Isaiah said.

A tear rolled down her cheek.

"Puah?" Samuel said.

And she folded in on herself, taking comfort in her own arms. The hem of her dress tucked safely beneath her feet.

LEVITICUS

Y ou too much like a woman," Samuel said as
he pitchforked hay into a pile near the horse
stables. Sweat dripped from his temples to his jaw
before collecting, quietly, in the dimple just above
his collarbone.

Isaiah had pails in his hands. He was preparing to
go milk the cows but stopped suddenly with Samuel's
observation. He was particularly struck by Samuel's
tone: not exactly coarse, but definitely the sound of a
man who had been thinking about it, had allowed it
to roll around his head, and in his mouth, had grown
tired of keeping it locked away in his chest, and could
only find reprieve in its release. Isaiah turned to look
at Samuel and smiled anyway.

"I thank you," he said and winked his playfulness.

"I ain't trying to flatter you," Samuel responded as he continued to pile the hay, which was now waist high.

Isaiah chuckled. "Look at that. Sweet-talking me and ain't even trying."

Samuel sucked his teeth. Isaiah walked over to him with pails in hand. The pail handles squeaked with each step. The sound irritated Samuel and made him bristle.

"Now I bother you?" Isaiah asked.

Samuel stopped shoveling. He stuck the pitchfork into the ground with enough force that it stood on its own. He looked down at it, then faced Isaiah.

"I can't have no weaklings by my side."

"You know me to be weak?"

"You know what I mean."

"Nah, suh, I don't," Isaiah said. He put the pails on the ground next to the pitchfork. "But it sound like you calling me weak because I remind you of a woman."

Samuel just stared at him.

"But none of the womens you know is weak."

"But toubab think they weak."

"Toubab think all of us weak." Isaiah shook his head. "You worried too much 'bout what toubab think."

"I better be worried. And you, too!" Samuel's chest puffed like it was preparing to release yet again.

"Why?"

"Everybody can't be against us, 'Zay!" Samuel yelled.

Samuel had never spoken to Isaiah in that tone before and Isaiah could see the sweat on Samuel's brow and the pained expression on his face that announced regret etching its way in. Isaiah took a deep breath, looked down at the ground, refusing to return the volume that had just assaulted him. Instead, he spoke quietly.

"And everybody can't want us to be what they want us to be neither."

Samuel rested his arm on the handle of the pitchfork. He wiped his forehead with the back of his hand. He regretted letting himself open this way. A man, he thought, should have better control over his doors and locks. Still, some doors couldn't be locked once opened. He looked at Isaiah. He stared into his eyes and was almost convinced, by their tender shape, by how they were crowned by thick, silky eyebrows, to let it go. Almost.

"How 'bout your name?"

Isaiah frowned. "My name," he whispered. "How you could even . . ."

Samuel wiped his brow with both hands but didn't know what to do with them afterward, so he balled them into fists. He looked intently at Isaiah.

"When you know Big Hosea to have a problem with anybody, huh?"

Isaiah's lips parted, but only silence filled the space.

"I been knowing him since we both little. You see how he come after me? For what?" Samuel grunted.

"I know, and . . ."

"And what you do? Stand there instead of helping."

"It was me the one who pull you off him!"

"When you shoulda been the one helping me whup him!"

Isaiah nearly buckled under the weight of that. He leaned forward. He put his hands on his legs, just above his knees, to brace himself. He exhaled. He kept looking at the ground.

Samuel eyed him from toe to head. "Yeah."

Isaiah wouldn't allow himself to be crushed by the heaviness or by Samuel's attempt to stack more on top of it. He stood erect. He took two steps toward Samuel. He looked him in the eyes and then looked away to gather his thoughts. Samuel, meanwhile, had planted his feet and cracked his knuckles.

"You right. Sorry," Isaiah said as he returned to gaze into Samuel's squinting eyes. "I shoulda done more, but I ain't wanna do nothing to make Amos think he got the upper hand—or make the people think we was what he said we was."

Samuel's lips were dry and ashy, so he licked them. His tongue darted out, drenching first the bottom then the top. He tasted salt. He put his hand on the handle of the pitchfork.

"Folks listen to Amos. Maybe we should," he said. His grip on the pitchfork was loose and unsure.

"No," Isaiah said quickly. "I young. Young as you. But this I know 'cause it don't take long to learn it: anybody with a whip gone use it. And people without one gone feel it."

Samuel snatched up the pitchfork.

"Amos ain't got no whip!" he said as he began, furiously, to fork hay.

"But folks finna obey him just the same," Isaiah countered.

Samuel stopped and let the pitchfork fall. It hit the ground with a thud. The two of them just stood there, silent, not looking at each other, but both breathing heavily, audibly. Finally, Samuel cracked the silence in half.

"I can't stay here."

"Who can't?" asked Isaiah.

Samuel paused. He had no answer that would satisfy. The realization made his chest burn and his face itch. He clapped his sweaty palms. The sudden, sharp sound stirred a horse or two before it dissipated. It didn't distract Isaiah, however. He kept his gaze steady, his face still prepared to receive an answer to his question.

"You ain't never talk like this before," Isaiah said gently.

"Maybe not talk," Samuel replied.

"But think? Can't be. Even in the midnight hour?"

In Isaiah's eyes was a mist, nighttime, and two sets of calloused feet creeping alongside a riverbank. Owls hooted and the snap of fallen branches being cracked in half by heavy footsteps echoed in the distance. Far behind, a point of light and the voices of wild men laughing. A glint of metal seen by the shine of the moon and the two sets of feet speed up, into the wet of the river. Muddy and tired. Then two whole bodies submerge and, though frantic, refuse to make a splash for fear of attracting the attention of jackals disguised as men.

But the silence provides no shelter and the wildness catches up to them and drags them, by their feet, out of the water, over jagged rocks, through the broken woods until they come upon a row of bitter, eager trees willing to perform acts of vengeance in the name of stolen fruit. The men have ropes, laughter, and fingers hooked into triggers. The men bind their prey. Nooses burn necks. Tightened, they block air. Then the eyes constrict and throats mourn the denial of screaming. Pull. Pull. And up in the air the bodies go. Kicking the nothing around them. Flying nowhere.

After a while, tuckered out down to the soul, they go limp, an offense to the gods of wicked laughter. So they unload their weapons into the dead-already. Then they douse the bodies with oil and set them aflame. They think it's a campfire, so they sing songs. **Look at the monkeys. Look at the monkeys. Swinging. Swinging from the trees.** The flames eventually die and the bodies eventually drop. The wild men fight over the best pieces to take home.

When Isaiah snapped back to the barn, it dawned on him that he had been standing there the entire time and neither he nor Samuel had even attempted to touch the other. He moved a step closer and stroked Samuel's cheek with the back of his hand, his rough knuckles finding comfort against Samuel's smooth skin. Samuel closed his eyes, leaned into the rhythm of Isaiah's motion before finally grabbing Isaiah's hand and holding it in place against his face. Samuel kissed Isaiah's hand.

"There's danger in the wilderness," Isaiah unloaded. He figured that it was only fair that the both of them share the weight of it. Samuel lifted it, inspected it, and noticed a crack in it. Those monkey-swinging bodies: they dared go down without a fight?

"There's danger **here**," Samuel replied. He cut his eyes, almost with cruelty, at Isaiah and picked up the pitchfork again. Isaiah grabbed him by the wrist. He stared into Samuel's face, searching for an opening, however small.

"Don't break us, man."

"Ain't I here?" Samuel asked, not exactly returning Isaiah's gaze. "You see me or nah?"

He pulled himself from Isaiah's grasp and returned to the pitchfork and his drudgery. For a moment, Isaiah didn't move. He was oddly calmed by the repetitious sound of Samuel's forking, the consistency of his one-two motion.

"I could do it, you know," Samuel said at last. "Make it with all those womens. But I just don't wanna."

Isaiah stepped back, turned his mouth to one side.

"You ain't never think that?" Samuel asked him.

"So you wanna hurt two people, not just one?" Isaiah looked around the barn—at the horses in the stables, at the haystacks, at the tools that hung on rusty nails hammered haphazardly into the barn walls, at the roof and its intersections of wooden beams. He looked and looked as though it were his mind and he was searching for the answer to Samuel's question, but all he could find were cracks.

"Sometimes I don't even know you," Isaiah said out loud, still looking at the barn walls.

"You know me. I be the you you don't let free."

Isaiah was going to say, **You mean the me I been freed,** but didn't see the point. "Sure they thank you for it," he replied instead. "The womens, I mean. For being able to. Puah especially."

Samuel scowled. "You jealous."

"Maybe. But not why you think."

"Just saying. If you feel to stay here, be easier if—"

Isaiah cut him off. "Whatever you decide is blessèd."

With force, Samuel let out some air through his nose and raised it. "You different." He didn't mean to say it out loud, but it was too late. It had already middle-finger plucked Isaiah on the forehead, pinched his arm as a cross mother would. All Isaiah could do was rub the places that stung and give Samuel the eyes that conveyed his surrender.

Samuel stood there and, for the first time, was disturbed by the stench of the barn and the way it stuck to his skin. He noticed that underneath the saltiness was something sour, like food left to rot. He held his nose for a moment and suppressed an urge to heave. Finally, he walked over to the pails that Isaiah had put down.

"Let me do this. You pitch the hay," he said as he picked up the pails and headed outside. He felt Isaiah's eyes on his back, yes, but also his caress. But he didn't stop.

He went to the cows. They greeted him tumultuously, mooing their anxiety.

"You looking for 'Zay, huh?" he said to them.

He sat down on the tiny wooden stool and waved away the flies that circled his head.

"I beg your pardon," he said to the nearest cow.

Then he grabbed her teats and started to pull.

O, SARAH!

The yovo who licked Sarah's cheek said that he knew she was sturdy because she still tasted like salt water. Yovo was an old thing that Maggie told her no one else would understand, so she might as well call them toubab like everyone else did. A shared language was how they could form a bond despite subsisting on the most foreign of soils. They brought with them hundreds of languages, divine practices, and ancestors. Those who had not had them ripped from even their dreams knew better than to speak them in earshot because betrayal was also a commodity.

"Keep it behind the bosom," Maggie had told her. "Maybe inside a cheek. Close, but hidden. It'll be easy to reach when you need it. Trust that."

Despite sharing a unifying language, nobody wanted to hear Sarah's ship story. Wagon tales were hard enough. But to sit still as Sarah revealed how, when left no other choice, when closed in tight and surrounded by the heat, dank, and hands of a way-ward vessel, vomit could become a meal—that was simply too much. Most of the people she came to live with on Empty knew nothing of ships. They had been born in the stolen land, under the watch-ful gazes of a people with eyes—mercy!—eyes that seemed to glow in the dark like any pouncing beast. See, the first hands to touch **them** were without skin so she couldn't expect from them a willing audience. She wasn't insulted, then, by their choice to leave her without witnesses. That would perhaps mean that her name would eventually be lost to time, and the girls who came up behind her wouldn't have her to show them exactly who came before. That was where the real shame found roots. She kept it, then, all of it, locked up in her head with the other things that squeezed themselves into that space without even the courtesy of a "How you?"

He licked Sarah's cheek in the town square of some place called Charleston, South Carolina—where the bodies from ships washed up with the tide and clut-tered the shore—and said that she still had salt in her and that her arms were just right for chopping cane. They dragged her there from the place they called the Isles of Virgins, a name that made no sense to her given the violations that sometimes didn't even wait for moonglow. She had been seasoned there. They tried to break her in half. She was young enough so that they had nearly succeeded. But trapped within her mind were remembrances.

The first place she lived wasn't by a sea. It was deep in the bush, which had protected them, and the ground, from sun, and made their eyes suitable for night. Flowers burst all around her in colors that she hadn't seen anywhere in Miraguana, St. Thomas, Charleston, or Vicksburg. Fruit was abundant, and the plums were thick with the juice that ran from the corners of her mouth and trembled at the edge of her chin as surely as any dew.

She had not yet arrived at her name, which is to say that she had not grown enough to be given a name since names came from how your soul manifested, and that couldn't be known until it was time to transition from girl to whatever it was you chose to be after. But everyone had to begin there: girl. Girl was the alpha. Even in the womb, the healers had said, the start was there before anything might change. Circles came before lines; that was what had to be honored. When the babies arrived, they were girls irrespective of whatever peace blossomed between the legs. Girls until after the ceremony where you could then choose: woman, man, free, or all.

A girl with so many mothers, aunts, and sisters, draped in the softest fabrics, no unkind eyes or untoward glances. Sarah remembered the laughter most, but also a wagging finger when she had once tried to slip from under the bush's protection.

"You want to get gobbled up by a lion, yes?"

"No."

"Then you come over here right now, child!"

She walked sullenly back to the arms of the many mothers, but she would get gobbled up by a lion anyway. And no one would hear her testimony of the ship. Nothing about its sickening rock or the marks left on wrists and ankles from heavy shackles. Not a word to be heard about the thing in the corner that moved, and she was sure it wasn't a shadow because there was too little light to cast one. Instead, silence. **Nobody wants to hear that old Africa shit. We here now, ain't we? What difference do it make 'bout before the ship? That was the danger. The danger was alive, you hear? It was living. Nothing there can save us now.**

They silenced her, all of them but Maggie, who had a lot of an old thing in her.

Easy, Sarah, O Sarah. Breathe. Rejoice. The memories are still yours to keep.

If they were open to bearing what she carried, she could tell them about how she learned of freedom's possibility. There were words being carried across waters after she was sold from St. Dominique, that the people had had enough. The same blades they had chopped the cane with were held high, in unison and in charge, and blood spilled such that the ground itself was black and soft no more. Sarah wondered if the soil in Charleston could likewise be transformed. They all had blades. Yovo (now toubab) damn sure put the blade in her hand and expected her to chop the cane as if that was all the blade could be used for. But to raise the blade was to accept the risk that the danger was living. And how could she ever permit that slithering thing the chance to crawl toward her Mary?

Their first kiss was under the arc of sweetgum trees. No moisture in the air, but between them, yes. It was spring and their calm had come from each other's embrace. Breath. Slow. Blinking. One chin lifted and the other bowed. A stray hair that Sarah tucked behind Mary's ear.

"Plait it for you later, all right?"

"All right then."

Maybe it wasn't just danger; maybe all skin was living, too. Maybe all bodies understood gentle touch. Could bosom and bottom alike be curved precisely for a loosening hand, a knowing lip? All Sarah knew for sure was that when she and Mary were between, they were **between:** legs entangled, and the dual bushes that each held their own shining stars had joined. Bellies rose and fell and never—never once— did they fail to look into each other's faces and see what was actually there no matter how many times Charleston had said it wasn't.

Sarah saw that same look between Isaiah and Samuel, sometimes. Only sometimes because the mean one, Samuel—who seemed to be choosing **man** because he didn't understand how that made the other possibilities remote—was fighting against himself because his desire didn't look like anything he had ever seen before. The other one, Isaiah, had better imagination. She wasn't sure if he had chosen **woman** or **free,** but it was clear he had chosen one or the other because violence wasn't his primary motion.

Given the numerous times Sarah stepped onto a greedy but unwelcoming shore, it was in her to know. Against dipping suns, and airs dripping wet and smelling of honeysuckle, she saw how Samuel turned his body away when Isaiah turned his body toward. She saw the ax in Samuel's hands and the pail in Isaiah's. For Isaiah would milk the cows and Samuel would slaughter the hogs. Isaiah's hard-earned smile and Samuel's understandable fists: she could precisely attribute glee to one and despair to the other because one's spirit had clearly sprouted wings while the other took refuge in the echo of caves. Both, she knew, had a purpose, however imperfect. Life was being clung to, whether with balm or sword.

No one looking could see what she saw because no one looking knew what she knew. To everyone else, Samuel and Isaiah had blended into one blue-black mass, defined by the mistaken belief that it was a broken manhood coating their skin and not, what—courage? Though it could have been fool-hardiness, too.

Girl is the beginning, damn it. Everything after is determined by soul.

There were no sweetgum trees on Empty, so Isaiah especially, but Samuel, too, must have had no choice but to settle for the cover of a ratty barn roof that even the pallid moon could penetrate if it wanted to. Their safety was therefore less and she felt for them, but only to the degree that it was rooted in her own memory of what was lost.

Wait.

Not lost, though. This wasn't something she had incidentally misplaced on a ramble. Someone had devised a separation to be felt acutely between the two wings of her ribs. That was an unprotected space— **the** unprotected space.

Every time she saw Isaiah and Samuel, it made her curse the distance between her and Mary, and the people who placed it there. And what was in that distance but thorns, green and steely, eager to pierce not just the beating feet racing back to embrace the departed, but the chest for that was where the treasure was. When she saw Isaiah and Samuel, the distance stretched and grew more and more entangled. But seeing them also softened her because she had remembered, too, how it would end.

Was Mary still in Charleston? Probably. There was no need to have sold her, too. The cane was punishment enough. But they would teach her, for the rest of her days, the meaning of **sugar** anyway. Some days, it was safer to imagine her dead: a plump corpse condemned to the ground, under layers and layers of earth, to become nourishment of another kind. Other days, Sarah couldn't help but imagine Mary with a blade strapped to her thrashing arm covered not in her own blood. But neither of those was what unfolded. Truly, they had to pry the blade out of Sarah's hands, not Mary's. What had they even given it to her for in the first place? If it could chop cane, it could chop man. Her refusals, which they wouldn't heed, meant she could test the theory. She was too much her people and that was the way it would be.

"We was always doomed, won't we?"

That was the last thing she said to Mary as they tied Sarah down and carted her off to Mississippi. There was no point in saying the things truly felt because they were already known. Instead, Sarah figured that the time should be spent looking at the face of her One, to study it so that in the deep, deep of night, which was the only time solace could be real, when her hands were tucked between her own legs—that was the **only** face she saw. Then, and only then, could she fling her juices upward, hoping they, too, could be etched there like the sky that her Only One, wherever she was, could also see, and when the rain came down, also drink from.

O, Sarah! Empty was another thing. It was the deepest. It was the lowest. It was the down and below. It was the bluest depth. It was the grave **and** the tomb. But briefly, ever so briefly, you could still

come up for air. Despite the blood and the screams
and the smothering hot, here, too, was where Essie
sometimes sang in the field and made the picking less
monstrous, if not less grueling. Oh, she would open
her mouth and hit a pitch that made bellies rumble
because it was the same vibration as living itself. The
butterflies must have known too; Sarah could tell by
how they flirted with circling Essie's head.

And in Sarah's liminal way, she, like Essie's butterflies, skirted around the edges of Isaiah and Samuel,
giving her the room to not give **too** much of herself
because almost everything on Empty took and took
and took, and replenishing was as foreign as kindness. But the one who was the better chooser because
he had clearly chosen **woman** or **free** had loosened
her a bit—a **little** bit—against her better sense.

Isaiah was down by the river one sunset. Sarah
had hated the way the sky could do that—spread its
colors clean across creation in violet hues with hints
of orange, a moment designed strictly for joining.
Yet the rest of nature took cruel turns at denying her
breasts the warmth of her lover's touch. But Isaiah
stooped against that backdrop anyway, looking confused. He was without Samuel and Sarah reckoned
that Samuel couldn't stand to be anywhere, joined,
where there was no barn cover. She walked closer.
Her head was still wrapped from the long day and
her dress was wet from labor. She was shining with
the combining colors. Isaiah was looking at the blue
vervain that dotted the edge of the land but knew

better than to get any closer to the river's lip. He smiled at her approach and pointed to the flowers.

"Blue can hurt, you know," he said as she stood next to him. She eyed him.

"You don't know from blue," she said, waiting to see how he might protest.

He looked at the flowers again. "You right." He put his head down.

She didn't expect that. She inhaled deeply before letting her breath out slowly. She closed her eyes for a moment and then took another deep breath, which brought the mixture of wildflowers and river water closer to her tongue. When she opened her eyes, she was looking across to the bank on the other side. She held her gaze.

"Your'n thing an old thing," she said softly.

Isaiah looked at her. "You mean from before? From where you from?"

"Nobody never listened, but yeah."

"I wish you tell me," Isaiah said.

Sarah smiled. **A tiny thing, but so kind,** she thought. She held her hand to her chest.

"What I can tell you is hold on as long as you can. Nothing but pain is guaranteed. But hold." She pointed east. "I shoulda."

He again looked confused but nodded his head. The only reason she told him even that much was because she thought he picked **woman** or **free.** So there was a greater chance for a balanced response to her knowing rather than a discarded one. Isaiah stuck his foot in the water and swirled it.

"Keep on," she said, surprised at how that was even in him to do. "Now stop."

Isaiah looked at her.

"What you see?" she asked, pointing down to the water.

"Something," he responded, squinting into the murkiness. "A face? A woman's face?" Isaiah leaned in a bit closer. "She's looking . . . at you!"

Sarah's smile had caught him by surprise. She chuckled. She had wondered why Mary had sent the message through him and not her, but she was glad of it.

"Thank you," she said to Isaiah, looking at him and just briefly catching his eyes.

"For what?" he asked.

"It don't make no nevermind," Sarah said. "You helped me. And you has my sympathy."

Isaiah just looked at her.

"Can't be easy having all the peoples with they backs to you."

"Not all," Isaiah said.

"Mm," she said. Then she looked away.

Isaiah looked back down at the waters. "Oh! The face gone."

Sarah wiped her forehead and touched her head wrap as though she was checking to see if it was still in place. "It'll be back. Someday."

Isaiah nodded and was about to swirl his foot again when James approached them. He walked right up behind them without so much as shifting a dry leaf or crunching a stray pebble. He could do that: be as quiet as a trap. His hat was pulled low. His rifle was tight in his grip.

"Time to get on back to your shacks. Don't you see where the sun is? Quit this dragging. No time for mellow. Get."

There was no scorn on his face; his lips, however, were bent in sorrow. But even when toubab smiled, they had a streak of despair at the edge of whatever joy they thought they had found. Not regret, no, not that. More like they were waiting for something that they knew was coming but wished it wasn't—even if they called it down themselves. Sarah didn't look at James, but she did make a face that arched her eyebrows and shifted her lips to the side. Curious things, these yovo. She meant toubab.

She glanced at Isaiah and started on her way.

"Night, Miss Sarah," he whispered.

James shot him a look at the word "Miss." Sarah turned to see Isaiah backing away from James and then jogging toward the barn. She turned back around and stepped on over patches of weeds and sauntered her way back to the dirt path, not quite with Puah's humor or grace, but close.

See? Isaiah call me "Miss" right in front of that one whose name I won't say for Maggie's sake and

**for mine. Courage or foolishness, it don't matter.
I got another witness. Àṣẹ.**

She grabbed a handful of larkspur, and then another. She came quickly upon her shack. Alternately
moving and stooping as though in prayer, she placed
a portion of the flowers in each of the four corners
of the room.

"To keep true close and lie away," she said before
she sat down on a stool with a thud.

Legs spread out, she raised her dress and longed
for cool. When none came, she patted her wrapped
head, which had started to itch. Memories could do
that: come up prickly to poke at the scalp and peck
at the mind.

Finally, she unfurled the wrap and let it hang to
the ground. It blocked one of her eyes but she could
see with the other. She looked at the flowers she put
down, cornered.

Not hardly sweetgum. But it'll do.

RUTH

The moon went elsewhere and Ruth rose from her bed. She walked gingerly across the rug but didn't retrieve her slippers, nor did she think to cover herself in a housecoat. Her nightgown was enough. She didn't bother to light a candle or a lantern. **No light. No light.** She decided to take her chances in the dark. If she should stumble, knock her knee against some forgotten piece of furniture, tumble down the stairs after misjudging one, it would make no difference to her. It would just mean that the broken-outside would finally match the broken-inside and the chips and cracks that were known only to her would no longer be secreted away and wept over in solitude. Then everyone could see and they too would weep because they would finally know that she was innocent. Her tears. Oh! Her tears!

She walked out onto the porch and stopped right between the two main columns. She stretched out her arms for no reason, or maybe to catch the wind, which was rare enough in Mississippi. To feel it now was to welcome it. It dried the moisture on her pale but freckled skin, and she felt smooth to her herself. She closed her eyes and took it in. She swayed a little, almost as if this was a kind of worship like the kind she had claimed or, rather, was given and told it was where she belonged—there, in the secondary space where she, due to the curves of her sex, could only ever be partial and two steps behind. Head down. Not a whole body; merely a rib.

Though she was awake, she still felt the weariness of the day inside her head and moved over to one of the rockers to sit down. She sat heavily and the chair jerked backward before springing forward again. She let her head roll down so that her chin hit her chest, her bright red hair came forward to her face and hung down in front of her shoulders. Then she lifted her head and inhaled deeply. The day and the night smelled different from each other. The day was musky, the funk of animals, including niggers, spoiled what was supposed to be ruled by the heal-all she instructed Essie and Maggie to plant carefully along the edges of the first garden that belonged to her and her alone. She loved the heal-all most because of how full the purple was, given wondrous shape by how each bloom sat above the other. The flowers opened up like tiny stars and she liked the idea that there was something on the ground that could match the splendor of the night sky.

That was moot. There was too much interference in the day and very little she could do about it that wouldn't make the stench worse. It was only in the deep night that her plan worked and even the closed blooms gave her a gift to smell. The only shame was in the competing beauty that divided her attentions between where she sat and where she looked up to.

The night, too, was a place to wander. Within certain confines, of course, but it still provided a chance to explore. From one horizon to the other, this land belonged to Paul, which meant that her safety wasn't only paramount, but guaranteed. She had made all the appropriate sacrifices to solidify the contract. You couldn't see it, but there was a trail of blood that led from her womb to the woods and followed her wherever she went. Whether it was in downtown Vicksburg to visit the dressmaker, in the front row of the pew at church as the reverend looked at her with eyes that lingered a tad too long, in her needle-point circle with the women who envied her only because they imagined her in possession of a life that they wanted—and she knew none of them would want her life if they knew about the wandering that Paul's absence made absolutely necessary, or maybe they **would;** who's to say?—the trail moved when she did, always led to her no matter where she stood, and connected her, forever, to the thick and thin separating man from beast. That was why she wandered the wilderness most of all. She was tethered to it for reasons she couldn't yet understand but also felt on the cusp of the wisdom that she knew would soon come. What she knew for certain was that being in open nature was where she felt most like she was a whole body and not just a stolen piece.

The breeze felt good and she opened her legs a little wider. Maybe if she did that, other people could see the cord—she would rather think it that than a trail—and know that she was actually alive and not just some haint half existing in a spot she was chained to against her will, not being able to move on because unfinished business would never have even the slightest hope of resolution. She was here by mercy and maybe even by choice because the mercy was so reviving that she felt she owed so much to it. On her knees, then. On her knees, but only for a moment.

Still bent, she looked up to the North Star and thought maybe Timothy was looking at that same one. He was very much like his father, but he was also his mother's sole prize. She kept all of his letters in the top drawer of a small chest beside her bed. He wrote to her often to tell her that while he still thought Thomas Jefferson had a point, maybe there was another way to think of niggers, whom he called "Negroes"; that walking on two feet meant that they weren't the animals Ruth was certain they were, or maybe not as certain as she believed.

"My son. My special child," she wrote to him by lamplight, straining her eyes. "You are silly. All that book learning and you kept your childlike nature after all."

She knew that Northern ways were slippery and could slither their way through any boundary given enough will. If the North had anything, it was that: will. Loud was what Northerners were, and hypocrites. The South was a constant reminder of their roots, these U-nited States that were neither united nor stately, but were some loose configuration of tepid and petrified men trying to remake the world in their own faded image. This wasn't a framework for liberty; this was the same tyranny of Europe, only naked and devoid of baubles.

What Northerners lacked in charm, they more than made up for in speeches: heartbreaking and endless speeches that made men raise their pitchforks and torches and march to the edge of nothing-**yet** with yelling mouths and tearstained faces to declare, before all of creation, that they were ready to die so that a dream they would never be a part of should live.

That was why she told Paul that Timothy should remain in Mississippi, that any education he needed could be done here because they had enough wealth to bring to bear whatever was missing from the place where the waters gather. That's what the Natives called out, she was told, as they were mowed down and moved farther into the wild. They called on gods that held the waters together to unbind them and let them drown everything that crawled uninvited onto these lands.

And it rained. Heavy. Hard. For so many weeks that the story doesn't even mention when it ended, so Ruth had to assume it was on the day that she first remembered seeing sun. But all that did was make the soil rich and earthworms wiggle to the surface, only to be consumed by birds, which made them fat, lazy, and easy to catch—which, in turn, made nourishment abundant for the soldiers who drove the rainmakers and their gods west. They must not have known that one of God's most elegant acts was giving His people the strength to part waters and hurry through.

But Paul convinced her to send her only begotten son to the ravages of the winter lands and she knew he could only come back but changed. The baby who made it. The child who survived. The young man of many talents who was enough his mother to have the wisdom his father lacked, but was enough his father to understand his duty. Timothy assured her that all that he would bring back with him was knowledge and, maybe, a good wife, God willing. And she wanted so badly to believe him, but there was a quiver in his lip and he patted his forehead too much with the kerchief on a day that wasn't that hot. Not enough of his mother in him; too much of his father.

Ruth got up from her prayerful position, descended the stairs, and walked out onto the land. The weeds beneath her feet felt cool and the dew made the ground a bit slippery, but she didn't lose her step. She stood there in the middle and let the stars look at **her** for once, take **her** in, be in awe of **her,** whether she deserved it or not, before using her own hidden power to join them. The wind pushed against her nightgown and that was the only sound, though the night made its own noise: the insects, the animals, and sometimes, the hushed moans that the niggers thought might have been the makings of love, but she knew her husband to be the architect, so it was merely business. These sounds converged and, yes, perhaps even scratched out a melody. But it was all too plain to her ear to be a symphony, even with the thunder of her heartbeat added to the mix.

Her green-green eyes were glazed over with memory so she wasn't sure if what she saw before her was now or then, but there was a light in the distance, shining downward, from where she couldn't discern. In the light, there was the silhouette of a man, tall and straight, perhaps with a rifle cast over his shoulder, but unlikely a soldier. There was little need for soldiers now that the land had been captured and the savages that resided in this space before were tamed and would soon be erased by means she was unafraid to articulate. For the rules were different under acts of war. Though women were not permitted to fight in the official declarations of such, **official** was key for two reasons. First, some women disguised themselves as men, took on the exact visage and manner of men, from the short hair to the aggressive gait, to do what they believed was the patriotic thing. She knew of one such woman who was hanged when discovered, not for the fighting—for she heard that she had fought even better than the men—but for the deception, which they claimed was in more than just her disguise; it was in the way she lived even in times of peace, rejecting "she" for "he," an affront to Christ.

Second, women endured a more lasting, thus a more brutal combat in merely trying to survive men. Whether men had seen battle or not, each of them, to one degree or another, came home from wherever it is men go to be with themselves or to do the things they would never admit to out loud, with the same intent to inflict whatever harms they endured from the world onto the women and children closest to them. Relation didn't matter. Mother, wife, sister, and daughter were all equally targeted for the same rage. Father, husband, brother, and son all had the same blank disregard in their eyes—there, behind the glistening fury, was the thing that shook them so thoroughly that they felt the need to destroy anything and anyone who they believed could see it: nothing.

Whenever and wherever **nothing** encounters **something,** conflict is inevitable. She wondered if the figure in the light carrying the rifle was, then, coming to start a war with her. She took a step back. She blinked and the figure and the light were gone. Only unyielding blackness was there now and, strangely, it comforted her.

She took slow steps around the perimeter of the Big House until she reached the back and stood in front of her garden. The smells overwhelmed her. Not just heal-all, but also coneflowers and gardenias. She bent down to inhale. She closed her eyes and asked herself why not a bedroom right here, in the middle of the garden, under a tent, of course, but yes, in the springtime this was the place she should lay her head every night. Summer might be too grueling, but spring.

She thought maybe wake Maggie and Essie. She wanted them to smell the garden as it was supposed to be smelled, too. And wouldn't they want to be awakened? Surely after backbreaking work in the cotton field and in the kitchen, they would appreciate being in the presence of glory, even if for a short time. Ruth touched her throat. Her head rolled back. She leaned against the fence surrounding her garden. She felt faint—or, at least, she wanted to feel faint because that's what sometimes made her feel like a special woman and separated her from a Maggie or an Essie. A tear dripped from the edge of her eye. She had never before felt so generous. Never before felt it in a way so sustaining. To have wanted to invite Maggie and Essie meant her heart was big no matter what else it was also capable of. How odd to have finally come to that realization now. It must have been the flowers.

She crept through the garden. Her bare feet cracked twigs and frightened crickets into the air. She wondered how she looked there, in the dark. With no light anywhere, could she yet be seen? Did her nightgown, silky white, take on some of the ebon of the night to make it seem to glow in some violet fashion? She looked at her hands and remembered that there was a time when the beginnings of calluses were just about to come into bloom on a surface that should only ever be delicate. But then the man with the rifle flung over his shoulder came walking, even paced, right up out of the horizon to take her away from toil. He had come all the way to South Carolina to get her on the word that was whispered on the wind and carried across on wagons states away. And all he had were the whispers without a guarantee to be found anyplace. But the message itself was too compelling to ignore: a man was offering up his only daughter, fire-headed and alabaster, at the first edge of womanhood, unspoiled. That last one she had to wonder about. How was that word defined? Did untoward paternal hands count even if they were fought against as regularly as evening prayer? And what of a mother's silence? If the hands bruised one thigh, surely hush bruised the other. Children who had to contemplate such things were already denied what was theirs by right.

But there was Paul, rifle on his back pointing toward the sky. Younger then, but still much older than she was. He was possessed of a strong jaw and piercing eyes. She would gladly take her chances for whatever it was her father was willing to receive as payment.

The soil was moist and she took a bit of it and placed it on her tongue, a note of sweetness in her mouth before she chewed and swallowed. This was a part of her. She was a part of this. She lay down on the ground and let herself be hidden between flower stalks. This was, to her, a gentle act and she wondered if she should allow herself to fall asleep right there, where she felt she belonged more than anywhere else.

That was when it caught her by surprise. Out of the corner of her eye, there was a warm light that seemed to blush its way into existence. Quietly, as though not wanting to disturb or take up too much space, but simply to exist without fear of being extinguished, to share its glow with other things to bring out the golden in them, to make eyes drowsy, hearts soft, and private areas wet with the need to be intimate without malice or retaliation. This light—and perhaps it was unfair to call it that because it didn't cause her to wince—emanated from that space beyond the fence, through the weeds, over another fence, in the breach that was the barn.

She pointed at it, called attention to it with her

finger, like she was showing someone, though no one except whoever it was that hid in the heavens could see her. She wanted to call out to it, beckon it to come closer, but her throat closed, which let the light's beauty remain undisturbed. She raised herself up, her back stained with the fertile soil so that from the rear, she looked like she might emerge as her own kind of flower. She let herself out of the gate, not wanting to say goodbye to the carnations because she knew, innately, that they adored her company. She promised herself that she would give them the gift of water at the first sign of sun, and she would do it herself, with her own hands, even when she didn't have to, which would be a signpost for her sincerity, an offering of sorts.

It wasn't far, the barn from the Big House, but she felt it, still, a journey. More of a descent, actually, like when one travels from a mountaintop down to the deepest cavern, going from closer to the sun to a place where the sun can't even be discerned. It was a sojourn that made Ruth feel heavier, that if she remained there where people were bent and racked with pain some of which wasn't even visible, she somehow took on the burden, too, simply by spending a long enough time in proximity to them. This raised a terror in her heart, but it didn't dissuade her from embarking.

There was something a tad sweet in the aching and Ruth felt it in her feet. They went from moist soil, to dry, hard ground, and just as she reached the edge of the barn's gate, she stopped. The weeds at the border tickled her ankles and she stooped to pluck a dandelion that had gone to seed. She blew on it and it scattered in a dozen different directions, gently, first up, and then a slow decline until, like sleepy bugs, they met the ground and snuggled in. It was thicker there, by the barn, everything was: the air, the ground, even the darkness—except for that one point of warm glow tucked safely inside, hoarded, held.

Ruth gathered herself up and under the wooden fence, not quite on all fours, not that she would have objected, but she ducked beneath and felt a shiver as she made it to the other side of the fence in the upright position. It wasn't exactly as if she had traversed worlds, but the quality of the existence in this nocturnal place shifted. In addition to the soundlessness, the night moved. However briefly, it seemed to flutter, to ripple as a stone thrown upon pond would do to water—a quick circular pulse that she had to blink to believe. Just as fast, it was gone, leaving her to doubt her own perception.

I am here were the first words that came to Ruth's mind, but where **here** was, was still a mystery. It was the barn, obviously, but standing there looking at it, it somehow seemed like more. She felt small next to it, as if it could open up its doors and swallow her whole and she would be nothing more to it than a tender morsel. She wondered if that was what happened here at night: that some nigger magic made it so that all things came to life, that everything was given a fist to shake, a heart to beat, and a mouth to speak—and, in the dark, they could play out the forbidden things that light couldn't bear. Niggers could see in the dark, you know. They, who sprouted out of it, direct offspring, wearing it on their faces without shame. How could they not be ashamed, not even in daylight? This was the reason they had to be whipped sometimes. Not out of malice or sadism, though both of those had their piece. But to remind them of the disgrace they wore like garments and how no pride should come from it.

The ground was softer here. She realized too late why. The horse shit caked her heel and she hopped on one leg until she reached a patch of dewy grass and rubbed her foot on it until the smear was gone. It, too, was living and seemed to laugh as she scraped it from her, danced on the pointy edges of grass before sliding down, playful as a child, into the soil, and gallivanting off to some place too dark to see.

Ruth then came upon the barn doors—the lips— which were ajar like an impatient lover or a distasteful hunger, and the glowing was in there. All she saw was the small radiance that had contained itself and also become part of the inner landscape. As she inched closer, she saw that dim shadows had also made themselves a part of the quiet festival hidden in plain sight. She touched the door, expecting it to have the moisture of bated breath upon it, but while it was warm, it was also dry.

She cracked it a bit more and was disappointed. The light wasn't some otherworldly splendor waiting to bestow its grace upon her. No. The light emanated from a simple lamp, which was set between the two barn niggers whom Paul had been hoping to stud with no results; she couldn't remember their names.

They seemed to be arguing about something, but they spoke in such low tones that it sounded to her like chanting. It was only the animated way in which the eyes widened and then narrowed, how their hands clung to part of their chest and then shot outward to accuse that she was able to discern the disagreement.

She almost felt herself an intruder in a space that could only ever be hers to begin with. That was offensive to her, but with consideration, she pushed open one of the doors. The creak startled all three of them and the light somehow lost its golden arc. She stepped into the hay and ignored the prickling against her soles.

"What **is** this?" Ruth whispered. She was talking about the place. She looked around at the jumping shadows and thought she might have heard a drumbeat coming from inside the space, in the general direction of where the two niggers had just sat up, turned toward her direction, but refused to look her in the face.

"Evening, Missy Ruth," one of them said, hands folded in front of him, head bowed. "You all right, ma'am? You need us to fetch something for you?"

They misunderstood her. She saw their chests,

streaked with fear, heaving in unison. But they also glistened, which she understood as a beckoning. Men rarely spoke the truth, so it was crucial to read their signs. Since these niggers knew better than to let her see their eyes—downward gaze, downward!—she had the good sense to discern intention from their bodies. Never mind that her own eyes had already grazed them, held them down, dissected them, and consumed them. She had her own imagination, which she didn't consider because she had for so long always been at the whims of someone else's. She gave in to their misunderstanding.

"This is a barn, or something else?" she asked them, this time a bit louder.

Their silence was, to her, a delight. She wondered how she looked to them standing there, her dirty nightgown and copper hair, her skin able to shift so much more with the light than theirs and so she could take on the characteristics of every time of day or night—crystal in the day, pale blue at night. And in the in-between—at sunset, at dawn, in the twilight hour—that was the beauty she loved most of all. She moved in closer, almost like a dance, adding her shadow to the shifting ones. The light, too, seemed to fear her, flickered, dimmed.

"You. What is your name?" she asked, looking down at them.

"Isaiah, ma'am," he said. "And this here is Samuel."

"I don't remember asking you for his name." She pointed at Samuel but looked at Isaiah. "And I take it that he can speak for himself. Can he? Can he speak for himself? You do his speaking, too?"

"No'm."

There. There it was: the requisite undressing. Her words had made them disrobe. They had taken off their arrogance and let it fall to the ground before them. She had done it without the use of the whip, which illustrated, for her, the difference between women and men. Men were bluster, endless, preening bluster that needed, more than anything in the world, encouragement through audience. For men, privacy was the most frightening thing in the world because what was the point of doing anything that couldn't be revered? What difference did it make to stand on a pedestal when there was no one there to look up?

Women, most women, did it differently. Privacy allowed them the power to be cruel but regarded as kind, to be strong and be thought delicate. It was crucial, though, that she be alone in this, for men were liable, even in these spaces, to snatch from her these tiny moments of a more balanced nature in bloom. Men, it seemed, were built for the sake of catastrophe and were determined to be who they were built to be.

But Isaiah and Samuel, they were an anomaly. In this place—she had still not received an adequate answer to explain why it felt like that to be there—they had understood the necessity for privacy and the dangers of audience. Though maybe they didn't understand enough, judging from their shared welts. Perhaps they wore those outside to alleviate the ones inside. Finally, a subject she understood in the reality of this other place. She walked in the space between them and stood there facing the light so that her gown obscured their view of each other. All they could possibly see was the suggestion of each other, the roundness of head and perhaps the broadness of shoulder, through the filter that draped her body.

"This is another place, ain't it? Here is somewhere different. I can't be the only one who knows it, am I?"

"Missy?" Isaiah asked.

"I don't want to hear you talk no more. I want to hear this one speak," she said, looking directly at Samuel, whose neck was bent forward and head bent down, mouth ajar.

Ruth followed the outline of his curves: over his head, around his shoulders, along his arms, to the bend of his legs and the bottom of his rough-hewn feet. He was blessèd. The night wore him well, so well that she would have no need for the other one, the one with the more cheerful eyes, even under these circumstances, that she could feel even though they never looked at her directly. It was easy for her to picture herself wearing Samuel closely, like a shawl or beaded necklace, something simple to drape for a cold occasion or a festive one, only to remove when the sun returned to the sky or it was time to rest.

She touched Samuel and he stiffened, nearly re-coiled, but that didn't stop her from running her fingers down his back, following the path of welts, thick and thin. In her mind, she played images of what this must be like for Paul. Did he, too, touch the niggers he took before he took them? Were his eyes open? Did he hold his breath? There were enough of them now—bright-faced niggers marked in Halifax tones—for her to raise up from her deep denial about how her savior could allow himself to stoop so low. The only reprieve was in knowing that these sins were merely transactional and so weren't sins after all. If God could forgive, then she must also.

She looked down at the crown of Samuel's head. "Lie back," she whispered, and yet he didn't weep.

Pitiful. Just pitiful, which is how she preferred it. That way, she maintained her sense of control. This one was big, but he was prostrate, as he belonged. As rough as it was, the kink and coil of his hair posed no threat in this state of supplication. She wound herself around him because time was the one thing that wasn't on her side. Timothy would be home soon, stalking the grounds for a subject to paint. James might be patrolling with a few of his men, who she reckoned were only a step above nigger status themselves. Paul could be anywhere. She couldn't be seen this way, as she was, unencumbered by corset or hand in marriage, keen to let her breasts sag and not be pushed up until they threatened to constrict her lungs. No, all that did was heighten her anger and everything—every single thing—that had a source eventually returned to it. But in the meantime, in between time, it had to be let loose.

She lifted her gown to her knees, pulled it out from her legs to act as a shield between her and the why-isn't-he-weeping? nigger supine at her feet. The other one dared to raise his head even if he didn't look directly at her. She couldn't tell the difference between envy and pity, so she didn't know what to make of the look on his face.

"Look away," she commanded.

Slowly, Isaiah turned his head to the horse pens. She looked that way too. Two horses, one brown, one white with brown splotches, poked their heads forward as if they were curious, wanted to see—as if they hadn't seen enough already. But what would they hold on to? Would they remember this and, in a fit of solidarity, as beasts of burden are known for sometimes sticking together, pull her carriage off the road into some ravine, watching her tumble and break bones, and for what—a memory no creature had a right to let linger?

To hell with it all; she looked away. She fumbled first, reaching her hand down to undo Samuel's pants and then squatted down onto the lap of the thing beneath her. She threw her head back for no reason. There was no joy. There was no exaltation. Underneath her, there was no mountainous terrain, only plateaus, which would have been offensive to anyone who expected at **least** hands raised in worship.

"Are you broken?"

She didn't even look at him when she asked because no answer could smooth the offense. She cussed herself just a bit for thinking she could succeed where only failure had been spoken. Above her head, she thought she heard the roof creak, as though the weight of this place was finally too much. Should the whole thing cave in, pulling in the barn, the animals, the trees, the ground, and the sky itself, how uncomely it would be for them to find her remains sharing the same space as these unbaptized barn hands. **What was she doing there?** they would ask, knowing full well what she was doing, but because speaking ill of the dead is an affront to Christ, who rose Himself up just to make that message clear, and who will, at some unknown point, return just to confirm it, they would cry and bless her name, and the truth would be buried with her.

Ruth became aware of her weight on top of Samuel. And the weight of Isaiah's eyes. And the weight of all the children who never had the chance to be. And across her back, she felt the measure of Paul's palm, how he steadied her when she shook, and how that must have been the influence of his mother, Elizabeth, whose name was given to the land, and she felt grateful for what he could remember of his mother that helped him retain a piece of kindness reserved especially for Ruth.

She covered her head, but the roof didn't fall in on her. The creak she thought she heard was nothing more than the whimper of the nigger who was looking away at her command. There she was in the middle of a mess and couldn't remember how it had come to be. She recalled the glow and before that, the flowers and the soil. She concluded that this was a place that played tricks on the mind. Oh, and the weight. Clearly, the pressure had become just too much, and it made her dizzy. The only cure was to return to where the air made sense.

"Get off me!" she shouted before she stood up, suddenly, letting her gown's edge drop back down to her ankles. She was standing, but she didn't move any farther. She once again became transfixed by the lamplight, which flickered but wouldn't extinguish. The light itself, she noticed, had a dark spot at its core. "That," she said to herself, "that is where we are!" But how, she wondered. How could just moving from one side of the fence to the other transport her from light to no-light? She stumbled over to the lamp and kicked it over. It didn't ignite the hay and threaten to engulf the entire barn in flames. It simply went out.

Now in a dark room, with only the occasional grunts of animals, the labored breathing of the whining nigger, and the pointy silence of the forced-quiet one to remind her that she was still where she was, she looked up. She hadn't noticed it before when she thought the roof was collapsing onto her head. There was a rectangular opening that let the sky in and she saw, in that little opening, the sky that had become so familiar to her. It was peppered with tiny white stars, the only audience she felt it harmless to stand before, shining down on her at a safe distance, giving her the direction she had been asking for the entire time, but that no one was able to give her.

She walked in a circle. She raised her hands. She laughed. That last piece was a knowing. She knew she had access to things no one else had ever seen before. They would think her mad, but she knew better. She knew that there was a long line of women, from every side of the sea, who survived long enough so she could be here in this moment. And more than survived; they wanted to see to it that she wouldn't be condemned to the lives they had little choice but to lead. Each of them, now dots in an inky sky, guiding her away from witch hunts and burnings, from rapes and conjugal beds, the chastity and modesty designed by men to be foisted upon the backs and fronts of women, but only for the leisure, pleasure, and whims of men. Hosanna!

That was why she lost the children! It came to her in just that very moment. Not as punishment, but as liberation. What this meant was that Timothy, her Timothy, whom she had thanked God for, was either a help, and so was allowed to pass through, or a harm, and her misguided but well-intentioned prayers had undone centuries of careful planning because she failed to recognize a blessing when it was trying to be bestowed upon her. So then maybe his journey to the North was for good. Maybe it was to set right a grievous wrong, a spell to undo the folly of putting a throned man above a cascade of women who went down screaming so she wouldn't have to.

Now that there was no further need for the circle, she stopped. She felt dizzy. She moved away from whiny-whiny and stepped over the sharp silence. On her way back to the entrance, the life she left behind was in view, just a sliver between the crack of doors, but it was where she knew she had a better chance of belonging and she rushed toward it. She pulled open the doors and the heaviness was there. She sprinted quickly, her gown in her way, but it didn't slow her down. She climbed the gate this time, wanting to go over something rather than under it, but it never occurred to her to use the entrance because that was unnecessary if there was no one there to open it for her and close it behind her.

The garden had called her name, but she didn't have the time now. She would see it again in the daylight. She, Maggie, and Essie would come with the gift of water, the sweet kind from the well. No, it wasn't a waste to use that in the garden. Water was abundant and always would be. Besides, it welcomed the congress, for look what it produced.

She dashed into the Big House, up the stairs, and

burst into her room. It was hot and it smelled like her, which is to say that it smelled like lavender and dirt and the two together she didn't mind. She took off her nightgown and let it fall to the floor. Watching it crumpled there reminded her that she had just been rejected. How did that escape her before? The silence and the weeping, and also the heaviness and the glowing, had managed to distract her and given her too much to contemplate to even consider taking what had always been hers to begin with. Still, there was something she could extract from this to fill her belly. All she had to say was a word.

She looked down at her feet. They weren't dirty— not on the tops and not on the soles. That was impossible because she had gone from garden, to weeds, to horse shit, to dust and hay, and back again. Yet, her feet were as clean as if she had just soaked and bathed. Perhaps it was true then: she **could** float. Like some pure angel, a kind of feather, or her starry sisters, she could free herself from the confines of the ground itself, call out her own name, and be lifted, just a little, up to a more suitable air.

She went over to her dresser and took another gown from it. She put it on and it was weightless. She smiled uncontrollably. When she finally lay down to return to rest, it felt different. It felt like lying down in sky.

It felt like flying.

BABEL

At dawn, the trees of Empty were as ferocious as they were during the shade of night. Looming and towering, stationed at the borders, beckoning high above the fog, but only in the interest of luring close enough to kill. Kill whom? It depends. But lately one kind in particular. These trees are no home, not to the sparrow or the blue jay, nor to the ant or caterpillar. These trees, some upright, some gnarled, some felled, all sentinels, tasked with one bit of labor: to witness. And maybe they do, but what use is a witness who would never offer up testimony?

But, oh yes. The testimony is there, to be pried from them only. The streaks on their bodies, the gashes revealing the white meat beneath, the cracked branches snapped holding the weight. There are reasons for every split, but they never tell, not even when asked. You must know, therefore, how to prod, where to seek. Peering into the cuts that lead to the roots: roots that lead to soil: soil that doesn't lie, but curls beneath the toes of those whose blood nourishes it, who in other lands was skin-family, just like the cosmos above. One day someone will tell the story, but never today.

These trees, they guarded the edges. The most crucifying places were at the edges, there where the plantation met the land that had no owners (so said the people who were killed for challenging the idea that the dirt could have an owner). These were the roads, hot from the Mississippi sun, but not dry because the air was too thick, where even horses walked more freely than the people, insects hovering in the sovereignty they took wholly for granted, and the outer woods, the rivers rushing forward to who knows where, the arc of skies, low but forever out of reach. All these things never to be touched by any of them without great cost: a loss of limbs or a separation of spirit from body, the latter being the most preferable, but cowards would never understand that because liberty is more bitter than sweet.

And what of the homeless birds? They fly over in judgment. Almost all of them: the sparrow and the blue jay, and also the dove and the robin, but the raven is nowhere to be found. And the crashing of their voices would singe if the ones at whom they were cackling weren't already burned by summer.

So for the incinerated, the robin in particular was only music.

And there was, too, another rhythm beneath, a quiet pulse, one that had started even before the march out to the ends of Empty. Isaiah and Samuel thought they were the only ones who could hear it. Blithely, it whistled not so much in the wind as in the swaying of hands and hips, like in the midday praise in the clearing where they weren't welcome unless . . . But the sound traveled and reached some ears whether they wanted to hear or not. It wasn't, in fact, the people singing as they had first thought. It was someone else, or more than someone, judging from the harmonies. It sounded like something old and comforting, which made Samuel feel silly and Isaiah act it.

Ruth had to say but one word, and James, who had to act even if he didn't believe, rounded up his barely-men to shake Isaiah and Samuel out of slumber—even before The Two of Them had a chance to rise and shine into each other's faces, sweep up the hay they had fashioned into a bed, and greet morning with the same trepidation they would for the rest of their lives. How quickly and forcefully they snatched Samuel and Isaiah up and ordered them to stand. And the gleeful yet rough-hewn manner with which they fastened the shackles to their wrists and ankles. And then the spikes.

By the time they had been pushed out of the barn, the animals more surprised than they were, horses flexing their front legs and pigs' squeals drawn out, Isaiah and Samuel had seen what the fog couldn't hide. They expected the crowd that had already gathered, golden in the torchlight of the dawn. Some were tired. Some were smiling. The latter stunned Isaiah, but not Samuel. These were people after all. There was, therefore, some kind of happiness to be found in someone else being humiliated for once. Failure of memory prevented the empathy that should have been natural. Samuel knew, though, that it was selective memory, the kind that was cultivated here among the forget-me-nots.

The morning mist would soon give way. It would no longer crown their heads and obstruct beauty from view. Soon, it would descend and bless their knees and then their ankles before disappearing into the ground itself, revealing, then, how even a horrible place like this could be winsome. Ask the dragonflies.

How many people had already died on this land and who were they? First the Yazoo, who fought valiantly, surely, but who could never have been prepared for guns, or disease molded into the shape of one. Surely, the Choctaw were next.

And then the kidnapped people, the ones who dropped dead from toil, yes, but especially the ones who refused to mule, whose very skin was defiance. They were the ones who looked on from the darkness and occasionally whispered to their children, **How could you?** Samuel thought they meant: How could you **let them**? Isaiah thought, How could you

stay? Answers weren't forthcoming and righteousness filled the voids.

Samuel raised his head first. He figured that if
pain was going to be this day, it might as well be
earned. One of the barely-men snatched the chain
attached to the shackle around his neck, pulling
him backward. But he didn't fall. The three of them
moved directly behind him, attaching his chains, and
therefore Isaiah's chains, to the wagon that James
had already climbed into. An old rickety thing—
the wagon yes, but James too—in desperate need
of repair: wobbly and dented wheels that made the
ride bumpy and unsure, but purposely made pulling
it more of a chore; a bed so eaten through by who
knew what that the ground beneath could be seen
through it, making it a dangerous ride for passengers
as well. But it had long stopped serving the purpose
of lessening burdens.

James raised his right hand and one by one some
of the people moved from one misty spot to the
other. Isaiah had stopped counting the number of
them told to cram themselves onto the flat and focused instead on the distance between him, Samuel,
and them. Some of them rushed onto it, but Isaiah
couldn't exactly tell whose speed was cursed by excitement and whose was blessed by fear. As they
stood in the vehicle that threatened to collapse under
their weight, none of that mattered. What mattered
was the elevation. Holding on to knowledge that the
toubab didn't have yet, they could now look down,

and that, too, was irresistible. Even that tiny bit of height brought about a new perspective that straightened backs and raised chins, while arms met hips akimbo. Isaiah accepted this foolishness, for he knew the source was false. But it stuck in Samuel's throat like a bluegill bone and wouldn't dislodge.

Chained to the wagon like the animals they knew they weren't, James sitting inside with whip in hand, and a load of people cramped behind him, Samuel and Isaiah were forced to pull. And they would have to drag the wagon around the entire perimeter of Empty. And on a Sunday, too. They wondered if this whole show irritated or pleased Amos. They glanced in the direction of the people still standing among the grass and fog and spotted Amos there, a book held under his arm. They took in small pieces of his face and reassembled it inside their heads. Samuel chose irritated, Isaiah pleased. They would never agree, so they took up another project. They eyed Empty. This was how they got to know it. Every nook. Every crevice. Every blasted blade of grass. While Samuel plotted, Isaiah focused on the details.

"Hee-ya!"

James spoke to them in animal language and to move accordingly would make a lie true. So neither of them budged. The first lash sent a shock through Isaiah and his vision blurred for a moment before returning with even more clarity. That's when he noticed that they were almost pristine. The lines of Empty. How at each point, they were marked by something glorious: a flower, a rock, a tree. It might have been tolerable if uninhabited, if simply galloped through rather than owned. With no one around to mind someone stopping to speak to the bee that found its way to the heart of nectar and wish it good passage, then look up to the clouds and yell, "Me!" Nothing this calm should have such capacity for terror.

Isaiah looked down as the tears said, **I'ma coming.** He saw his feet as they dug into the squishy, slippery ground that gave no traction. The second crack struck Samuel and Isaiah trembled for him. With everything dead set on betrayal, the young men's hearts pounded a rhythm of distrust, Samuel's more than Isaiah's. It was the strain that had divided them and made them prickly.

Samuel glanced at Isaiah and resented him. It swirled in his chest for a moment before being pushed back down into his stomach with deep inhalation. It would only take both of them to wait until the chains were loosed to snake them around the necks of the barely-men and strangle them before succumbing to the gun wounds that would inevitably follow. But he knew Isaiah didn't have that in him to do. Samuel had known Isaiah for all these years and still hadn't gotten to the heart of what made Isaiah not even want to squeeze a fist tightly. What a danger to be so callow.

Meanwhile, Isaiah avoided Samuel's glances because they hid nothing and what use was it to explain to him that a last resort should be last, not first? But still, Isaiah's chest swelled with the strain of understanding that they were bound together by something much stronger than the rusty chains that held them. Tempting, though, was the thought of how much peace, however fleeting, there could be if one boy dared to be remiss in his duty and failed to bring the other boy water.

They were not oxen, but they moved and the people watched.

Isaiah would remember to tell Samuel later that he never understood the fascination with blue. Sure, it spotted the land in remarkable ways, broke up monotony, and offered a reprieve from the blinding shock of cotton, but it wasn't special. It was a distraction like everything else and he was tired of not paying attention. Still, looking upon it in the distance, peeking out of the fog, it seemed as though maybe pieces of sky had broken and fallen to the ground and perhaps it was right to give that a name. He closed his eyes and made the mistake of getting lost.

It was the first time that Isaiah thought about who came before him. Who was Paul's first victim? Was it a girl? A girl was an investment for toubab men because they could be raped into multiplying, but the rewards of such could take decades to bear fruit. A boy, then, with big arms, wide shoulders, a black and heaving chest, and iron legs, who could drag a hoe through land, digging the lines of demarcation needed to plant whatever seed the land would take.

Did Paul's father give the boy to him as a gift? First a toy and then a tool? Or was he Paul's first purchase, selected from the auction block after being picked over, prodded, inspected, and finally approved for a life of drudgery? It matters to know who was first because it should be noted who didn't prevent a second. Not that he could be blamed. That was too large for any one person to manage on his own. And death was only heroic after it was done.

But fuck the first. Samuel wondered if any of them would be the last—or, at least, the one who would leave blight in his wake so that no toubab would ever think to take up the dreadful enterprise again. A well-placed ax or stolen guns, the only difference between them being volume. One had only to decide which they preferred: submersion or thunderclap. Right now, Samuel felt like making noise. He wanted to feel the warm metal in his hands, to raise it to one eye and close the other, to wrap his finger around the trigger and pull, to watch his target riddled and bleeding. Let someone else's blood and body nurture the soil for once. How many people had he already seen destroyed? And no one with the decency to cover a child's eyes.

As they were both inside of themselves encountering forlorn moments of disgrace, Isaiah and Samuel rounded a bend, which made the wagon clearer in the periphery. The people still stood in it, straight and tall, like pillars of salt that Isaiah didn't want to look back on for fear of becoming one, too. Samuel, as always, merely kept his eyes forward because there was no reason to look back—or above. There was nobody up there who could help. The past had no use other than to dredge up pain and mystery and, thus, to confound. And there were already too many things in the present that made no damn sense. So the future was the only possible place where he might find resolution.

Isaiah, on the other hand, wondered the shape of the plantation. Was it square or rectangular? He could count the steps, but he wasn't supposed to know how to count that high. It wouldn't be a circle because toubab seemed to despise those, relentlessly worshiped right angles as though they provided order in and of themselves. It could be a triangle, but that too was unlikely because the angles could never be right. He realized then how much of this he wasn't supposed to know: shapes, angles, and the differences between them. Mathematics was forbidden because, he convinced himself, there was an equation that would reveal things that neither the Pauls nor the Amoses in the world wanted the Isaiahs to know. They spoke of trees, fruits, and snakes, but that was only a diversion meant to dissuade you from measuring the distance between here and life. But Isaiah went along. Feigning ignorance hurt as much as the lash. It was the pretending that all he was good at was toil, and not the chains, that threatened to break him. The jangling of the metal loops that connected his and Samuel's hands and their feet like the letter

I; a spike holding each shackle in place, making the walk more difficult because the legs had to be spread to avoid piercing one's own ankle with the other.

The toubab somehow imagined nudity to be degrading, so the walkers were always stripped down before they were forced to drag. Attached like a hind end of a horse so that degradation became the defining characteristic. But to be in one's natural state, save the mosquitoes, wasn't the kind of humiliation toubab imagined it should be. The skin caught every breeze along with every light. Privates were free. And the fog kissed you, left a moisture for your skin to drink, every bit as holy as any baptism, perhaps purer because it was voluntary and never purported to be salvation.

Walking on nettles was meaningless as feet had become immune because of the calluses. Isaiah, unlike Samuel, had learned to find any tiny pleasure wherever it could be found. So when James purposely steered them over a bush whose thorns were obvious, it had disparate effects. Isaiah smiled when he shouldn't have; Samuel refused to wince when he had to.

What pleasure? Samuel, in so many ways, was suspicious of it because he knew how easily it could be taken away. So if he refused to adore it, he wouldn't miss it when it was snatched from him.

Hold on.

No.

That was a lie.

There was one pleasure that he enjoyed beyond his ability to control, and were it to be removed from his grasp, he would become as empty as his pried-open hands, scraped out down to the shell of himself, a walking nothing, which wouldn't only be regretful for him. The pitchfork they used to gut him would inevitably leave impressions. Those marks would have to show something. And what was shown inevitably becomes what was done. Samuel wouldn't look up. Not now. Not never. He would look dead ahead. He could already see the blood coming. And from there, he could see the bend of the world, not that it mattered. All he could do was see it, never was he going to ride it. It might ride him, though: strap its ends onto him and kick and kick before it placed him over the stretch of its arc and rolled over him.

Here, trudging through this land that surrendered too quickly, Samuel found what most others didn't know: there is a spark at the end of a lash. A tiny speck of light, absent of any color. It's hidden behind the momentary sound of leather meeting flesh. If you blink, if you blink at all, it will be missed or discarded as a trick of the eye. But it's there, certainly. Untainted by the blood that has now darkened the whip's tongue. Unmoved by the cries of the righteous and the wicked alike. Making no distinction between the two, it floats above, almost to observe, but, like the trees, never to witness, and speeds down, not like lightning, but like thunder, and everything shakes. Everything. The past and the future together. And with the present left in such a state of quivering, the mind has no choice but to travel and join.

Isaiah looked at Samuel and the direction of Samuel's eyes led him to the spark, too. Even with the tears stinging his eyes, he saw it. Most clearly just before the sting that followed. A North Star that led no one nowhere.

Wait.

Wrong.

It led people here. To Empty. Where they, too, would become so. Capable, perhaps newly, perhaps always, of interrupting true affection and replacing it with something less, for reasons that were perfunctory and only sometimes bitter. The bombast, all that frantic posing, was designed as a cover for something even more indecent: nature.

And the spark mocked them. Flaunted how easily it could pierce reality and then retreat as though it had never been there in the first place. Failed to leave behind a path from which it could be followed into that other realm. Though there was no guarantee that anything over there would be better. It could be the same or worse, and that could be what the colorlessness signaled. Besides, a beckoning was rarely a reason to rejoice. Still, the mind, in callous circumstances, insisted upon longing for every meager delight.

Language undone by the threat of violence, they could only signal and suggest, hoping gesture could be translated and Samuel didn't mistake tucked lips for "fight," or Isaiah think a balled fist could possibly mean "patience." But they had known each other long enough not to fall victim to such easy deceptions. They placed desire above the indisputable for the sake of not wanting to think, which is another way of saying surrender. And they couldn't surrender now, not after all of this, not after they had stunned even themselves at how expert they were in uniting the entire plantation against them, toubab and person alike.

Shit. Look at how even the flowers looked at them: dandelions swaying not in the breeze, because there was no breeze except in the motion of Samuel and Isaiah passing them by. The milkweed turned away, but the obedients seemed curious, dozens of smiles laced on top of one another like treachery. That was what Isaiah smelled as they passed the huddled bushes. Everyone else might have enjoyed the fragrances, but Isaiah knew what it really was. So did Samuel.

Isaiah was tempted then to scream, to allow his legs to buckle instead of needlessly resisting. It had become clear that it was the resisting that was most despised. But acquiescence would mean nothing but more drudgery, and more abuse for error. To give up now would mean that exhausted knees could crash against pillowy weeds and the chest could collapse in on itself before it hit the ground. Lying there, ass out to all eternity, but able to catch his breath and close his eyes, if just briefly, he would raise a weak smile, but still a smile. This was tiny, but still joy. He hated himself for how much he wanted it, but hated even more the circumstances that made him want it.

Samuel wouldn't dare admit he wanted the same thing so his hate could never be turned inward. If he closed his eyes, it was only to imagine the creative ways in which that hatred could be acted out. So when his hands and teeth clenched, it wasn't only because of the lash. And just because he was bent didn't mean he couldn't see their faces. He signaled as much when he raised his chin and used his lips to point Isaiah's weary stare in the direction of the crowds of people watching them as they drudged around Empty like two white horses pulling a carriage of royalty. This was not a race, but there they were, huddled together, only some against their will, waiting at the finish line. This was not a race, but it was a race.

Why did they have to stand so close? Because most of them wanted to see. They needed to see so that they could be thankful that it wasn't them being broken right before their eyes. At the same time, both Samuel and Isaiah noticed the smiles on the faces of some of them. Maybe not smiles, exactly, but if approval could fix the lips to curl a certain way, then this was it. Isaiah noticed something more: a heaviness in their eyelids that spoke nothing of weariness. Their heads were tilted too far back. No. The downcast gazes shouted one word: **Yes!**

That was the weight that finally made Isaiah collapse at the ankles. He stumbled forward, landing square in a patch of star creeper. Stretched out like one himself, he cried into them, and Maggie was the first among the crowd to make a move: her hands trembled and her eyes were alert, but she knew better than to extend a hand. Samuel just panted, and maybe his eyelids got heavy, too.

Isaiah didn't have to say he surrendered because lying facedown stretched out like a star-fool already said it plainly. It made Samuel angry enough to pick up his disparate pieces and put them back together in glorious order. One final lash for daring and then Samuel put Isaiah's arm around his neck and together they walked, with labored and wobbly step, chains just a-jangling, back toward the barn, bow-legged because of the spikes, but not waiting to be unchained just yet. Twin backs juicy with the marks left by whips and disapproving gazes.

By the time they collapsed into each other just past the barn entrance, dust scattering as they fell, to the dreary people watching they looked like two ravens who had the nerve to become one.

Balm in Gilead

Maggie held a pail of river water. She knew the well water would be too sweet. The river would have a bit of salt in it, and any healing comes first through hurt before it makes it to peace. That was a terrible thing, she knew. Yet there was nothing truer. She knew it was why so many people saw no point, didn't have the resolve to make it through, and got stuck. A sucking mud. The sinking kind. There were a lot of people there. Knee-deep. Some submerged. Some clawing their way to solid ground. How few would make it.

The water would sting when they, she and the women, washed Isaiah and Samuel. But there was no way around it. Opened up as they were, anything even delicate would feel raw. And what wasn't bleeding was blistered, mercy, which meant that every touch would be a trial. She was impressed that they had made it back to the barn on their own, smashed into each other like warm hands, gentle but firm, quiet as a prayer, and just as plodding.

Maggie called for them: Essie, Sarah, Puah, and Be Auntie. There were supposed to be seven, but five was the next best thing. North, South, East, West, and Center, all represented, but there would be no one to balance the over and the under, to safeguard the light and the dark, to beat the drums for the call to the beyond as they did their work. Maggie couldn't risk calling anyone else in; they would be a hindrance. Maybe not maliciously, but because of their ignorance, which she didn't have the time or will to correct. Inviting Be Auntie was already pushing it. Be had already planted a willful betrayal and seemed to take pleasure in knowing where it was buried. But she also knew things happening in Empty that not even Maggie knew. Knowledge was a strength even when it hurt. So Be Auntie's talents were necessary.

Maggie waited at the entrance of the barn as her word traveled around Empty via a beautiful little girl she wished wasn't so beautiful. Hair too aglow. Eyes too bright. Skin too shimmery. Laugh too dainty. Teeth too pearly. It was only a matter of time. See? That was why she didn't like children. Their very existence foretold. They were walking warnings of the impending devastation. They were the you before you knew misery would be your portion. She was dreading having to be a witness yet again, a healer yet again. Damn it all!

She turned and looked inside the barn. Her eyes followed the trail of red droplets right to the soles of Samuel and Isaiah's feet. She shook her head. She didn't climb on that wagon, but she was among the crowd. Her pitiful gaze doing nothing except making them feel more ashamed probably. But it was all she could offer at the time. Now she would make another offering to compensate for the disgrace.

Be Auntie came first. Maggie could tell by her step that she came more out of curiosity, just plain nosiness, that seeing The Two of Them like this would give her a tale to carry back to Amos. She walked with a quick step, hands tense, back hunched, body leaning to the left, neck craning, face protruding, mouth slightly parted, eyes wide like she wanted to see.

"You call me, Maggie?"

"Yes'm. Gon' need you."

"Them two?" Be Auntie said, pointing inside the barn.

"Don't point. But mm hm. Yes'm."

"I don't know if Amos . . ."

"Fuck Amos!" Maggie said slightly louder than she intended. She raised her face a bit and looked Be Auntie in the eye. "Ain't that what you doing." She inhaled. "Smells like it and smells don't lie. So please don't come to me with his consideration when you giving him enough of your'n. He part to blame for this. And if you love him like your blushing tell me, if making a plum fool of Essie ain't enough to bring you to your senses, you could at **least** do something to clean the mess you contributing to with your severed tongue and bended knees."

Be Auntie bowed her head and nodded.

Essie arrived next, moving a bit quickly in her approach. Puah soon followed. Sarah took her time, hesitated before she got to the gate. And once she seemed to talk her herself into moving past it, she walked slowly, like she held a grudge against her own feet and everything they touched.

Maggie greeted each of them at the barn door. She raised a hand, palm forward, and looked at each woman, individually, acknowledged them with a nod and a smile. She folded her hands behind her back.

"I thank you womens for making your way here to this place where we are called to remember and bring forth something out of the dark." She took a breath. "We all suffer; ain't no doubting that. But surely we can have some say over how long and what shape it take. Am I lying?"

All of the women shook their heads.

"Now, I know usually this is for us. This ain't for nobody else's eyes but ours. No ears are supposed to hear this and goodness knows that what leaves our mouths is for the benefit of the circle only."

"How it's supposed to be," Sarah said.

"Yes'm." Be Auntie nodded.

Essie didn't know what to do with her hands. Puah stretched her neck to peer inside the barn.

"I tell y'all this because it the way we have to begin. Don't matter if you know it already. A long line of womens before us did this work. Used to be men too, until they forgot who they was. Something about men make them turn they back. Don't ask me what. Wanting nature to bend to they will, I reckon. And there was others, too, but they been split from us. Cast out and forced to be the body and not the spirit. I know because Cora Ma'Dear told me and she never did lie, not even when truth was the death of her." She paused and looked at the ground before looking out to the field and seeing her grandmother standing there with a light in her mouth. She waved. "But I think we can all come to agreeance that The Two of Them might rightly fit for our blessing."

"Yes ma'am!" Puah said so fast that it spilled from her lips like water.

"Well," Be Auntie said, looking sorrowfully at Puah, her top lip pursed in judgment. "You're young yet and don't know all of how this works. None of the cost. Don't be so quick to nod for what might come back on you."

"I deal with that when I have to deal with it." Puah forgot herself when she said this. She nearly shouted at Be Auntie, curbed, in the nick of time, only by the knowledge that she would have to return to the shack they shared that evening, and that Auntie's militia of boys, who maybe didn't even know they were her militia, might be extra unleashed on her this time. She squeezed the venom out of her tone and returned to delicate voice. "But right now—Miss Maggie, can we help him?"

Maggie looked at her with a raised eyebrow, which was then joined by a tiny smile, nearly completing the circle of her face. "We can help **them.**"

Then she put her head down. She held her arms out. "Let me be true this day," she whispered. "Let the blood guide me." She raised her face and her eyes rolled back in her head. She stumbled a bit, which caused all the women to instantly reach out for her.

"No!" she said to them, shooing away their assistance as she regained her footing. "Ground liable to be shaky on all journeys." Then, "We ready now. Come."

The women walked into the barn, moving from fierce sun into tepid shade. Their shadows moved ahead of them before fading, revealing the two groaning bodies on the ground before them. Oh, how fine! How proud even their broken bodies were slumped and no longer clutching each other in the dirt. Puah was breathless. Essie looked away. Be Auntie sighed. Sarah stepped backward, away from the circle and leaned on the barn door frame. Maggie stepped forward and leaned in to get a better look. **Two wings of a blackbird,** just like she thought. Closer: Isaiah had allowed the tears to come. They rolled out of his eyes fresh and found a place in the ground beneath

his face. Oh, yes. The Two of Them fell flat on their
faces once they knew that they were out of the sight
of judging eyes, and Maggie was certain that was
because Samuel would have it no other way. It was
also Samuel's way not to cry. He held it up inside
that massive chest of his, which was probably its own
underground pond by now.

"Essie, I need you to rip this here to pieces."
Maggie unwrapped an old white dress from around
her waist. "It ain't gotta be even, just so's I can use it
for bandages."

Essie took the dress. "Mag, this gotta be your
finest . . ."

"Go on."

Essie got down on her knees and began to tear it
into strips. She tried to look at Isaiah. She wanted to
make sure her friend, no longer friend-friend, was
still breathing.

"I can't even look at them. If I look, it feels like it
done to me," she said.

"That's blood memory. You ain't lost yet, thank
you," Maggie said to her. "Don't let the dress touch
the ground. Gotta keep it clean. Don't wanna cause
infection. Puah, I need you to go into the bush and
get me four things. We need five, but four you have
to do on your own. I help you with the last."

Puah was crouched over Samuel, who didn't wish
to be seen. Yes, he tried to flatten himself, but to
no avail because Puah's wide eyes saw all, even the
things he wanted to hide. The soft things that resided

under the layers of rock that were once flesh, but he had to make it something harder in order to exist. She reached her hand. She wanted to bring him the one thing she had to bring: a small bit of comfort, to repay him for his gentle smile, and for being able to see her in a land of creatures that turned their heads, yes, but only to look the other way.

"The marks they put on him," Puah whispered, nearly touching Samuel's back, which was laced with new lacerations, or perhaps old ones that had been reopened. "How we gon' heal this?"

"First," Maggie said sternly, turning quickly toward Puah, "we don't speak ill over what we trying to fix! That's number one. Hush, chile, and listen: Go get me these four things."

"Why me? I gotta see to Samuel . . ."

"Gal! What I tell you? Hear me now!" Holding up one finger, Maggie spoke: "Listen closely to me. And it gotta be done in this peculiar way. Go behind the Big House to Missy Ruth's garden. Get to the north side of it, closest to the barn. Pull seven stalks of lavender. You also gon' find some strands of red hair there. Bring those, too."

Maggie straightened her back. "Then you gon' walk east—walk, don't run. That's very important. You know that big willow tree in front? Take a hand-ful of weeping leaves from it."

"You ain't gon' need no handful," Be Auntie interrupted.

"Better too much than too little," Maggie shot back. She turned back to Puah. "West. Not too far from the river edge, I need as many huckleberries as you can carry. From the plant twined near the dead tree. Know the one?"

"Yes'm."

"South will be trouble. You gon' have to go to that other edge of the field, where the overseers and catchers rest. But I need that comfrey right at the edge of they shacks. Make sure your dress don't touch the ground, you hear me? Long as it don't, they won't touch you. Hold it up to your knees. Don't let it touch the ground."

"You can't hesitate, neither," Sarah added. "Snatch it up and go."

"When you get back, I lead you to the yarrow. Then we begin."

"Maybe they need a little something extra, for protection?" Puah asked Maggie.

"What you think the yarrow's for? When you get back."

Puah nodded. She got up. She felt like she should bow, so she did. Then she turned and left.

Maggie giggled. "So nervous when they new."

"She knew to bow, though. And ain't nobody told her to do that. Which means her insides are working. You was right for choosing her," Essie said.

"She choose me. Glowing the way she do, I'd be faulty to walk past her and not notice."

Maggie walked over to the boys. She got down on the ground and folded her legs in the way she was told the first women did it. She ignored the pain in her hip in favor of theirs. That couldn't become habit. **Too many women lost that way,** she thought. But this one last time was okay.

She looked around the barn. They had kept it so neat for what it was. There was no dung, even now, littering the place. Flies crowded around, yes, but there wasn't anyplace on Empty where that wasn't true. The horses were clean. The ground was swept and the hay was stacked in rectangles, except for the pile they must have been ready to work on before they were snatched up. And the smell wasn't so bad once you got used to it.

"I heard it was Ruth what got them beat. Said they looked at her with not a bit of shame. And you know that ain't nothing but a lie," Essie said.

"Devil's tongue," Sarah said.

"I ain't think you believe in their words, Sarah. You got a heart change?" Be Auntie asked.

"I don't believe they words, but it don't mean they words don't tell you something 'bout them."

"I don't see why Missy Ruth would cause trouble here. What for? She too busy chasing the tongue-face ones."

"Tongue-face?" Sarah asked.

"Ones that can't keep they tongue in they mouth when she walk past. Act like they don't even care that it could get cut off if they caught. Seem like the danger make them wanna do it more!"

"Mm!" Maggie jerked her head.

Wouldn't that be nice, though? Be Auntie thought. To have hair as straight and red as Ruth's, or blond, or any color other than deep black. To be her kind of skinny: flat on both sides. To wear pretty gowns and frilly bonnets, and bat not-brown eyes at all kinds of men who would gladly fall all over themselves to see what that put-on blinking might mean. Toubab women moved through the world gracefully. They pointed with soft hands that never knew any kind of labor that they couldn't somehow escape because every man fancied them dainty and delicate.

No. There wouldn't be any way Be Auntie could ever be that, no matter how much flour she threw at her own face, looking a plum fool or a haint, one. But she had decided on other means. She would do everything that was inside of her will to do to convince men that she was special, too. The only way to persuade any man of something like that was to agree to be the rug he wiped his shitty feet on. The key to every man's lock was going along with the untrue assessment of himself as worthy.

"What Missy Ruth want with sodomites?" Be Auntie asked.

"Don't use they words on them boys. You want the ancestors to heed or not?" Maggie scolded.

"I don't think she do," Essie said.

"How you know what I want?" Be Auntie asked.

"'Cause it's plain, Be Auntie. All your wants plain. To everybody. To me."

Sarah laughed. "See how quickly mens' needs have us at each other? Hold, I say."

"We talking 'bout a woman right now, though," Essie held.

"And what she did to mens, ain't it? How 'bout what she do to us?" Sarah looked at Essie finally.

"You know what I mean," Essie replied.

"Quit that noise! We can talk those big things later. Now we gotta be together. One hand," Maggie demanded.

There was silence except for the breathing of The Two of Them and the small weeping of Isaiah.

"What you want me to do with these strips, Mag?" Essie asked.

"Hold them 'til Puah get back. Sarah—come and sit by me. I need your steadiness."

Sarah shirked. She scratched her scalp. She twirled the end of a cornrow. She looked out on the plantation and turned up her lips. "Gon' stand right chere 'til Puah get back. Right. Chere."

PUAH WEAVED A MESS of big, green elephant-ear leaves into a pouch. She wondered how Maggie knew that strands of red hair would drape the lavender like a spider's web, marking the precise stalks that had to be pulled. She knew whose hair it was, but why was it there? She didn't have the sense to burn it so that birds wouldn't get at it? Fool.

She didn't like being so close to the Big House. Being that close meant that she was in its clutches in a way that was more tangible than pulling cotton in the adjacent field. Here, toubab were at their most merciless. Home did that to them: made them defensive, hostile, and scared of any dark thing that moved. They were afraid that all that they had accumulated and stored inside the hearth would be snatched away and returned to the unrestful spirits they belonged to.

The house itself was built on top of bones. She could hear them rattling every once in a while because the shacks, too, were essentially tombstones for the land's First People, often unengraved. Somehow she knew they meant her no harm but also that she might, like anyone else, get caught between the warring parties and die for being trapped in the wrong place at the wrong time.

Puah walked to the front of the house. She took the handful of willow leaves with Ruth watching her from a chair on the porch, holding a bouquet. Ruth smiled at her briefly, which startled Puah. Then Ruth stood suddenly, dropping some of the flowers. Puah thought she raised Ruth's ire. But Ruth looked toward the barn before sitting down in the chair again. She bent forward to pick up the stray petals and placed them in her lap. For a moment, Puah thought she detected something in Ruth.

Regret? **Nah.** Regret was a high thing, out of reach for most. And there Ruth was: bending, stooping, **sitting her behind down.** Puah thought that perhaps what made Ruth what she was had something to do with her **own** beaches—where the tides sung **her** name gently—being snatched away upon tilting her **own** head the wrong way. Still, it couldn't be entirely the same. Ruth's place had to have had the common sun-bleached sands. And surely the daylight shined forever.

Maybe it was true that the barn was safer despite its proximity to the Big House. It might be better for Samuel and Isaiah if they didn't insist upon being themselves. The individual always has to give something up for the group. Puah knew what women gave up, time after time, except for maybe Sarah, who created her own difficulties standing in her own spot. So it wouldn't be completely unreasonable for Samuel and Isaiah to give something up, too, sacrifice whatever force locked them in embrace to appease voracious godlings that saw everything but knew less.

Puah walked slowly to avoid Ruth's suspicion and headed west toward the river. She made her way down. The water rush soothed her. She stared at it for a moment before turning toward the brush. The huckleberries were right where Maggie said they would be, fat and juicy.

Now, Puah had to head south, past the Big House that she didn't want to be near again, toward the cotton field and beyond it. She went behind the house this time lest she inspire Ruth's curiosity. When she reached the edge of the field, she stopped, overwhelmed by the vastness before her, which she had never allowed herself to take in. That was reflex. She knew to never be too open because anything was liable to fly in. And once inside, well . . .

The expanse terrified her. She nearly choked on her breath. She watched birds dive in and out of the blinding sea before her and she wondered how she did it, day after day, back arched and knees bent, bowing against windless skies. And now, all she had to do was walk across it and into the dangerous land just beyond it for a peculiar plant that grew in an inconvenient place.

With grace, she moved. She never before realized how vulnerable being in the field made her. A span of puffy white heads and there she was: black flesh, easy to spot, easy to target, easy to strike. If this wasn't for Samuel, she wouldn't have answered the call. Everybody had their scars, so that was no special reason. But his eyes teased welcome and she couldn't bear them shut forever. Nor could she endure the slit of Maggie's disappointment. So she went.

Shoulders deep in it. Only she and her people knew that cotton had a smell. Not pungent or insulting, but something remotely sweet like a whispered song. But how something so soft could wreck the fingers she knew all too well.

She came to the southern end where the field gave

way to high weeds. Surrounded now by pale green and dry yellow, she felt less conspicuous, but still exposed. This wasn't a place she came to very often. Sometimes, she picked over here, but it was mostly the older people who did their work—not **their** work because it wasn't voluntary and it wasn't on their behalf—this close to the overseers' shacks because they were old enough to recognize the futility of running and how could they anyway on feet already walked down to the nubs?

How many shacks here? About a dozen, maybe a few more, each as ramshackle as her people's, if a bit larger. Some of them sat leaning, like they were built by unsteady hands. In any event, they formed a crooked line that led off to goodness knows where. Perhaps a forgotten sea or a forest that held captive the flying remains of the ones defeated in order to have a plantation in the first place.

She stepped out of the weeds and onto the dusty ground, worn by the trampling of dozens of feet, which created a kind of border between the plantation and the shacks. **That was where they felt it,** she thought. Separate from their deeds. Parted from the effects of their own havoc, which they refused to admit was their own doing, so it would, in some future time, long after she was dead she was certain, also be their undoing.

She was lucky. Most of the adults were at church or in their cabins asleep, or in some corner hiding from a sun that seemed to be plotting against them. Some of the older children were there, left behind to watch the younger ones, and they, too, watched Puah with something between contempt and longing. They scowled, yes. But their hands were also loose, not gripped into fists, which meant that she had a moment to do what she came to do before they remembered who they were.

She held her dress up, just above her ankles, and walked up to the closest shack, which, as Maggie said, had a patch of comfrey right at its base. It was beautiful, too. Deep green stalks and leaves accented with flowers that looked like tiny purple bells. The kids on the porch stopped playing their little game and jumped down near her.

"Beatrice, there's a nigger over here! Is niggers supposed to be over here?" the tiniest one said. His face was dirty and he kept pushing his long blond bangs away from his face.

"No they ain't!" Beatrice said. She was older, maybe fourteen, and the boy favored her, so Puah thought she might be his older sister.

"I beg your pardon, Missy and Massa." Puah kept her head down as she spoke. "Massa Paul send me over here to collect some of that there flower. Missy Ruth is having one of her belly spells and they need it to settle her discomfort."

Beatrice looked at Puah from head to toe, then toe to head. "And who you be?"

"Puah, ma'am."

"What kinda name that is?"

"I don't know, Missy. Massa Paul give it to me."

"Don't let her take our flowers!" the little boy shouted. "They's our'n!"

"Hush now, Michael. She ain't taking nothing." Beatrice's eyes narrowed.

Puah wanted to grab her own dress up the middle, ball up her fist, and punch Beatrice dead in the center of her face. She took a step back with her right leg and then caught herself.

"Yes, Missy. I leave you be. I let Massa Paul know you say no. Thank you kindly, ma'am."

Puah turned to walk away.

"Wait!" Beatrice shouted.

Puah turned toward her. "Yes'm?"

Beatrice sighed. She looked down at Michael and then over to the patch of comfrey. "Go on and get what you need. And be quick about it!"

Puah bowed, which pinpricked her inner self, and ran over to the patch. Carefully, she plucked stems full of blooms and added them to her elephant-ear pouch. She stood up and then headed for the field's edge.

"Hey! Maybe you can teach me how to make a carry-pouch like that one you got," Beatrice called at Puah's back.

Puah turned and nodded. "Yes'm." That was what her mouth said. But the stiffness of her back, the squareness of her shoulders, the tight grip of her jaw, and the rhythm of her step all said in unison: **Never!**

Then she dashed into the field.

"WHY YOU HATE MEN, Sarah?" Be Auntie walked up next to her with a slight, tender smile bending her lips. Her eyes said that it was a legitimate question and not Be Auntie being Be Auntie, trying to give known enemies the same consideration as proven friends.

Sarah looked at her briefly, then returned her gaze to the direction Puah would be returning from. "I don't hate men. I hate y'all making me have to consider them." She turned her neck a little to look at Maggie and Essie out of the corner of her eye. "And if'n I did hate them, I reckon I be well within my right." Her gaze returned to direction of the morning sun. Her face was alive with light in the way only darkness could catch it and do with it what it would. She placed a hand delicately upon a cocked hip. "And I don't love men, either. More like neither-way with them. They just—there, like a tree or a sky, until they natures do what it do. I don't bother with them." She sighed. "Only reason I here is 'cause Maggie call for me. And maybe 'cause The Two of Them . . . maybe they not **men**-men. Least one of them ain't. Might be something else altogether."

"Like Massa Timothy?" Essie said from inside.

"Ooh, girl!" Sarah laughed.

Be Auntie shrugged her shoulders.

"Hunk them shoulders if you wanna. You gon' learn," Sarah shot back.

"You forget your people," Be Auntie said before she turned to walk away.

"You talking 'bout me or you?" Sarah let fly.

"One thing to feel your own pain. Right another thing to feel somebody else's," Maggie said aloud, only looking at Samuel and Isaiah. "And selflessly. Not because you feel like they your'n—like a child or a chosen lover. But just because they breathing. I seen a hare once not leave the side of another one caught in a snare. That thing hopped around like it was in the same kind of pain as the trapped one. If a animal can do that and we can't? Well, what that say 'bout what they are and what we are? Like we might've gotten the names mixed up, ain't it?"

"I choosy with who pain I feel," Sarah said. "Some people pain is eternal. Some people worship they pain. Don't know who they are without it. Hold on to it like they gon' die if they let it go. I reckon some people want their pain to end, true. But most? It's the thing that make they heart work. And they want **you** to feel it beat."

"How 'bout these two here?" Maggie asked.

Sarah glanced at Isaiah and Samuel. Her brows furrowed. "Nah. They ain't deserve what they got." She let out a breath and shook her head. "But I ain't do it to them. I was the only one I see who outright refuse to get up in that rickety-ass wagon. So, I ain't carrying that burden, no. I got my own weight."

"You ain't get in that wagon and you ain't do nothing to help neither. Some of that weight your'n to bear whether you heave it or not," Essie said.

"So you claim."

"What is, is what is."

"Essie, I seen you up in that wagon. Holding that baby of your'n, too. Your eyes was closed, but mine won't. I risk a whipping standing there on them weeds, but I ain't go. What you risk, honey? You tell me that."

"How you can fix your mouth to say that to me, Sarah, I don't even know."

Sarah exhaled. "You right. I ain't wanna be led to this, which is why I ain't wanna come in the first place."

"Yes, enough of this fussing. The air foul enough," Be Auntie added.

"I say let me be loose!" Sarah said.

"You be what you need to be, but be careful, too." Maggie looked at Sarah. "Remember, the chopping up starts before they have the ax in they hand. They begin with the eyes. You know what I mean?"

Sarah was going to say yes, but she caught the sight of Puah the minute she made it out of the field. She walked past the Big House and then sped up when she got nearer to the barn. Sarah smiled and nodded her head.

"You quick, girl," she said as Puah approached.

Puah returned the smile and entered the barn. Sarah followed her inside. Puah handed the soft green pouch to Maggie.

"You made this for carry?" Maggie asked Puah.

"Yes'm."

"Ooh wee! This fine. Fine indeed!" Maggie held up the pouch and eyed it. "You got everything?"

"Yes, ma'am. All we need now is that stuff you said. The marrow."

"Heh! Yarrow, honey chile. Come on over here with me. Let me show you what I mean."

Maggie led Puah toward the back of the barn. They stopped for a moment near Samuel and Isaiah. Puah saw that they were still breathing and even heard Samuel moan slightly, and then she and Maggie continued.

Maggie brought her past the horse pens far to the corner of the barn. There, in the darkest spot, yarrow bloomed bright red.

"I ain't never seen no flower bloom in the dark," Puah said.

"Not many can. Specially not this one. But look-a-there. Go on. Pick it. Then hand it to me."

"BRING ME THAT ROOSTER. No worries. I cook it to-night for the toubab."

They formed a broken circle around Isaiah and Samuel. Each one of them wore a different face, a solitary sin: Maggie: solemnity; Essie: sorrow; Be

Auntie: elation; Puah: dreaming; Sarah: indifference. Maggie noticed it and hoped none of it would keep walls up where there should be windows.

"We leave room for you to enter," Maggie said.

"Because we call on you," Be Auntie said.

"To give us memory of how to lay hands," Essie said.

"And to ease and restore and protect," Sarah said.

And then they looked to Puah.

"You remember?" Sarah asked.

". . . and to love in the dark places that nobody sees," Puah said finally.

"Great ones, we come to see the waters sing!" Maggie nodded and sat down next to Samuel and Isaiah. She whispered to them.

"This not gon' be easy at first, you understand? There's something you also gotta do. It seem unfair, but there something you gotta give in exchange. The ancestors, they be a little fickle sometimes. Demanding. Or better, we do it wrong, misunderstand what they ask, and get mighty upset at the result. But one thing we know for true is that you gotta yell loud enough for them to hear you. Because, you see, we don't have the drums no more and your voice gotta carry. Not just across the distance, back to over there from where we was took. Your shout gotta pierce the barrier. It gotta get through the thick divide between us here in the light and them there in the dark. For this, you gone need each other. The strong one and the seeing one. The hard one and the mellow one. The laughing one and the crying one.

The double night. The good two. The guardians at the gate."

Maggie never understood all of the words she spoke. She knew they came from sometime else and she let them come through her because that was the only way the circle would be potent. She stood up. Her eyes rolled back in her head. She bent and grabbed the rooster by its feet and moved it in a circular motion. She broke its neck and spilled its blood. Puah gasped, but Sarah touched her shoulder.

"Shh. Stay inside the circle," Sarah whispered to Puah.

Each of the women dipped her left hand into the pail where Maggie had mixed just the right amount of everything collected so that the water had become a loose paste the color of swamp. In unison, they held their wet hands up to the sky and then, as gently as each of them knew how, they placed their hands on the leaking trail of scars on Samuel and Isaiah's backs.

Isaiah let out a cry so piercing that it made Samuel flinch. Maggie saw it even with her eyes looking elsewhere.

"Yes. Call on them. Call them in her name," she said softly.

Samuel whimpered and squeezed his eyes shut. Sarah dipped her hand into the pail again and rubbed his back, following the trail of cruelty etched there by fools. She pressed ever so slightly and a blister popped. Its juice ran down Samuel's side and he finally let out the sound he had held back with all of his might.

"This ain't your disgrace," Maggie assured him. "This belong to someone else."

Their backs were shiny now, thick with the swamp paste, and it stung like it was supposed to. The women laid down the dress strips on their wounds. It hurt to move, so Samuel and Isaiah lay there calling for mercy in the name, but not yet receiving it. Isaiah placed his hand on Samuel's, who wanted to move his but couldn't. The circle understood that as their time.

The hands were laid upon them again, and in unison they called her by her name. It was then that the clouds began to form, interrupting the sun while it was in the middle of a crime. After a moment, the mossy air announced the storm that was on its way. And little by little, the droplets formed and came down first with care upon the parched earth.

"They're here," Maggie said softly and all the women turned to see.

Inside the barn, the dust swirled; Essie saw it. It came up from the ground as though it were alive. And it had form and grace. She knew then that what she saw wasn't just some random breeze troubling the dirt. It was them, showing themselves in a way she could understand and not be frightened by, but she didn't think she would be scared of their true form either, which is what she longed for.

"Rejoice," Maggie said. "For we have reason."

And all the women jerked their shoulders and laughed.

PUAH LOOKED OUT to the darkening sky. "What time is it?"

"What difference do it make? We close our eyes and then we open them. And here we are. Still here," Sarah said.

"But the toubab be back soon," Puah said wearily.

"Don't worry 'bout them. They expect us to be here. How else these boys finna get back to work if not for our hands?" Maggie said to her.

Puah held herself a little closer. She touched her lips as though a thought had come to her only to be lost again. The sides of her head had become hot and impatience was crawling up her back. She stood up and went to the door. She held her hand out to touch the rain. She rubbed her wet hand on her face and came back to the circle.

"What now?" she asked.

"Now, we wait," Maggie replied.

The women all fell silent as Sarah sucked her teeth, got up, walked over to the entrance, and pressed her back against the barn door frame. The rain was easing. It never got to be the storm she had hoped it would be. She didn't know why, but she needed to see lightning streak across the heavens. She needed to feel thunder rumble her to the gut. Give her a rhythm to undo her hair and replait it by. But no, none of that came for her. Not even a cool mist.

Be Auntie rose and walked toward Sarah until she was shoulder to shoulder with her. She looked out into the dusk. How golden it was, momentarily, before it turned itself inside out to show its lovely bruises, mauve blending into a blush. She would allow herself to regard it as beauty, even in such a grotesque place, even when her own had been abused. No, nothing could be ugly ever again. Not a sky, not a stream, not even two silky people lying on the ground in need of healing.

Maggie stood and joined them. She could unhook herself from the need to believe beauty might have a place that wasn't subject to anyone's unwanted hands and sour breath. Wasn't no way this place was going to keep thinking she was its prime fool. Not at all. Not as long as she had fists. And even if they took those, the stubs.

Essie looked toward the three women standing at the doorway. She didn't understand why she wasn't already dead. Maggie had told Essie that she came from the line of those who built the great angles, but Essie's angle came first, time not being straight. Living, as she was, in the crest of her creases, turned upside down for her own pleasure no matter who dared it without being beckoned, but even then, the truth of it pointing toward the brightest star in the sky. For all the men, women, and others who had used her as their shitting pot, she should have been broke down, should have already surrendered to the worms. And maybe she was a little bit broke down, but in hidden places like the edge of her elbows and in between her toes, where memory slipped in and wouldn't be loosed, not even after a mud ritual. No, the images pressed themselves in, and every so often, when she bent in the field or when she had to kick an attacker in the groin, they would sing out: **Here we are, darling! Let us fellowship.**

Puah got up and then sat down next to Essie. She wondered, too, how she still had breath, how she hadn't yet been ripped up, with so many toubab around needing nary a reason—and she knew they had plenty. **The cow was always useful for something. Milk, if not labor. Labor, if not meat. Meat, if not milk. Rape.** But this wasn't the time to ponder such things. She knew Maggie would tell her that she had to give the circle its time.

The women, one by one, turned and came to sit back down. They were a semicircle, all facing one another. In the distance, thunder finally let itself roll. Sarah lifted her head and inhaled as though searching for something in the air that she almost found, but didn't. She lowered her chin. Maggie touched her shoulder. They looked at each other.

"I know, chile. We all know."

Be Auntie and Puah shook their heads. Essie held her hand against her neck. Maggie looked at her.

"Sang a little, Essie," she said, attempting to bring the women back from the breach.

Essie nodded. Sitting in the old style, she straightened up her back and gripped her knees. She began to rock back and forth. She closed her eyes and tilted her head to the side. And when her lips parted, all the women, chins high, eyes wide, mouths breathless, clutched themselves in preparation.

ROMANS

We do not wish to mislead you into thinking you are all of royal blood.

You are not.

Yet, do not imagine that royal blood is of any significant import.

It is not.

Often, it is the **most** impure, arriving at its creation through vanity and more than a little cruelty.

You are of the common folk. By common we mean dancing, singing, weaving, speaking: the ones who could have held their heads high but chose to hold their hands high instead. For they knew that all the universe wanted was their reverence, not their pride.

Pride is what leads people onto ships, across seas, into forbidden lands. It is what allows them to desecrate forbidden bodies and stamp them with the names of reckless gods. Pride is at once haunted and unbothered by the disgrace it has built from turning people into nothing.

Common.

Ordinary.

Fine and ordinary.

The weaver no less vital than the king.

We do not mean to give you the impression of an untroubled period in which cruelty was unthinkable. That is, unfortunately, not what nature is. Nature is rugged simply—with not a single favored One to be found anywhere. But we are here to draw the distinction between this place and that one.

It requires that we go back further than we are capable of taking you without great sacrifice to our shape and number—which we are willing to do if necessary. It is, after all, our responsibility. Certain promises were made. Certain mistakes bear our names. If we can avoid it, however, if we can rely on your best sense, which lies so dormant in you that we are not sure it can be woke, the undoing of time would neither be called upon nor necessary.

To begin, we just need you to do one thing:

Remember.

But memory is not enough.

II KINGS

The council gathered at the royal hut. No one had the time to put on ceremonial robes of fine fabrics, skins, and furs. They came as they were: the women with heads that weren't completely shaven, the men with their penises dangling behind skirts instead of tubed and tied firm against their navels.

They all sat on pieces of cloth that formed a circle around a large pot of palm wine. King Akusa's six wives darted back and forth between pouring the wine into small bowls and handing them to council members, twelve in all. B'Dula spoke out of turn.

"We should kill them all."

The king shot a damning glance his way as the others shifted uncomfortably on their behinds.

"You never fail to insult the ancestors, B'Dula. Nor

yourself." King Akusa rubbed her hands together and took a breath. "I called this meeting and you did not even think to give me the respect of speaking first. Surely, your saltiness from so long ago does not still cloud your reason. You could not possibly have forgotten your lessons so completely. Kill a visitor and bring down the ancestors' wrath. Kill a neighbor and start an unnecessary war. This is a time for careful contemplation, not childish rage. You will be silent or be gone."

B'Dula sank into himself. He considered the fact that he had been bested by the king in battle and so would not test her resolve.

"Now," she continued. "The Gussu broke with tradition and brought strangers into our midst without proper notification, it is true. But the penalty for this is not death, but expulsion."

Some of the council members nodded. Those who agreed with B'Dula made no gesture at all. Semjula, one of the eldest of the Kosongo, and also a seer, took a sip of wine.

"With your permission, King."

King Akusa nodded. Semjula stood. Her frame was bent. She was the color of the soil just after a downpour. Her breasts hung down as a testament to her life and the lives she nourished. Her red jewelry, not nearly as dark as blood, rattled as she used a stick with the head of a snake for balance.

"Death is the wrong answer," she said in a heavy voice. She wiped her free hand on the green skirt wrapped neatly around her hips. "But I have a very bad feeling about sending them away, too. The voices tell me that we are in an impossible position. Whatever we decide to do, it should wait until after Elewa and Kosii's ceremony. That will give us a few days to think about how to proceed."

"Thank you, Mama Semjula. I wonder, too, if I should send word to the Sewteri and warn them," the king pondered. "Maybe send a messenger."

All nodded.

"Where are the . . . visitors now?" King Akusa asked.

"Still in the guard's hut, my king," Semjula answered.

The king turned to Ketwa. "Did we feed them?"

"No, my king," he answered.

"Well, let us not be inhospitable and cause fire to rain down upon us. Fix them some fish and banana. And bring them some palm wine."

KOSII GATHERED THE LEOPARD-SKIN cape made from a recent hunt that he had traveled far to wash in the river. After, he had set it to dry, pounded it until it was smooth, and all with the skill of his mother, Yendi, who taught him how, he draped it about his shoulders. He arranged the peacock feathers carefully in a circle. He decided to wear the jewelry crafted by his eldest sister's expert hands because Yendi was fond of turquoise and paid close attention to detail. His medicine stick belonged to his father, Tagundu, passed down from his own father. Kosii would be expected to pass it to his firstborn child when the time came.

On his face, Kosii spread the red clay of the earth: a line across his forehead, horizon; two dots on each cheek, sun setting, moon rising; and a short vertical line on his chin, foundation. All of this was to express not just his sincerity but his willingness to protect his betrothed. He smiled. Elewa's aunts were the most difficult to convince. Seven women, but one giant mind that was as immovable as a boulder and brighter than any light in the sky. Kosii knew that he was not the fastest runner, nor were his hunting skills as sharp as some other members of the tribe. But he was a great strategist and the key was in assuring them of the benefits of such an asset in the kinship circle. Furthermore, there was nary another Kosongo who had his proud, young heart. Nor could they be as tender, and certainly the aunts would want that quality to be present in anyone who even dreamed of holding their nephew Elewa.

The village was decorated in blue. Berry-dyed cloth hung from the thatched roofs of surrounding huts. Lobelia was gathered in bunches and spread along the perimeter of the village square. Everyone in the village was there, all dressed in red, except Akusa, who, as king, wore bright yellow.

Handsome Elewa sat on a lavishly woven rug with his mother, Dashi, on his left and his father, Takumbo, on his right. The rug told the story not of battle—though, at first glance, the woven images of raised spears in the hands of those holding them seemed to indicate such. However, the direction in which the spears were pointed, to the left, specified both protection and supplication. Behind the spear holders was a giant orange sun, setting, not rising. And this was what the spear holders were both guarding and worshipping. Elewa looked down at the rug and touched it, hoping it would transfer some of its strength, prepare him for the responsibilities he and Kosii were about to take on.

They were born guardians, Takumbo had told him. The whole village knew it from the moment he and Kosii met as barely-walkers. The way they took to each other and remained as inseparable as a tortoise and its shell. Only with great violence could they be split, which all of nature would frown upon. It was providence, their connection, for the last guardians had transitioned a few seasons before, valiantly, during the mountain war, and there was no one in the village to guard the gates, not just the formidable ones here, but also the ones between here and the invisible place where the ancestors sing, dance, and drink palm wine for all eternity.

Elewa looked at his father, whose eyes were glassy from tears that welled but did not fall. Takumbo smiled.

"You make us proud," he said.

Dashi patted Elewa's hand and then fixed a stray dreadlock that escaped from its place behind Elewa's ear. She checked his face paint, licked her thumb, and then used the moist part of it to wipe away an imperfection in the line on his chin. Takumbo inspected his medicine stick, looked at Dashi, and nodded. Dashi leaned back to get a better look at her son.

"There," she said. "You are ready now."

Elewa stood up and helped his parents to stand. The three of them were as sturdy as trees when they rose. Kosii arrived, walking through the gathered crowd, flanked by Elewa's seven aunts, with Kosii's family bringing up the rear. Just as he reached where Elewa and his parents were standing, Semjula made her way to the front of the audience. She had a hollow medicine stick in one hand and her cane helping her to walk in the other. She balanced herself and then held her stick high and ululated. The crowd returned her cry. And then the ceremony began.

Elewa and Kosii danced toward each other as the rest of the crowd stepped back and formed a wide circle around them. Elewa and Kosii shook their sticks, which, filled with dried beans, rattled like snakes. The tribe provided a hand-clapping rhythm. Elewa smiled. Kosii bit his bottom lip. They circled each other, never losing the beat. Elewa kicked his foot, casting dirt in Kosii's direction. Kosii stomped and kicked dirt back toward Elewa. Then they approached each other.

They placed their rattling sticks on the ground, lined up so that they were parallel. Then Kosii grabbed Elewa and they tussled. The crowd was elated; they clapped rapidly, creating a staccato rhythm. Kosii was on top, then Elewa. They rolled around on the ground, one unable to best the other. And just when the frenzy had reached its pinnacle, the clapping stopped. Kosii and Elewa stood up. Dirt stuck to their bodies; they looked celestial, like human-shaped pieces of night. Panting and smiling, they turned to each other and laughed. The whole village laughed with them.

Semjula stepped forward, this time with a thick vine rope in her hand. She made her way toward them and stopped where their medicine sticks lay on the ground before them. She placed her cane down on the ground parallel to theirs.

"Give me your hands," she said in her strongest voice.

Kosii held out his right hand, Elewa his left. Semjula held up the vines and displayed them to the village. Many nodded. Dashi and Takumbo clung to each other.

"So that you may never be cleaved," Semjula said and she wrapped the rope round and round their wrists until they were securely joined. She took a step back. She placed her medicine stick on the ground so that it lined up with the three sticks already there.

"Now," she said, signaling with her wrinkled hand. "Come."

Elewa and Kosii took deep, simultaneous breaths, and then they leaped, clearing all four sticks. The entire village erupted in ululation. Elewa and Kosii beamed. They turned to each other and embraced, seemingly for this life and for the next.

King Akusa raised her fist in the air and the drummers in the rear of the crowd began drumming. The crowd split in two, clearing a path for Kosii and Elewa. They danced down the opening, followed by their families, then the king, and then the rest of the village. They all danced and danced and danced until they were wet with celebration. Then they headed toward the king's hut.

It was bad fortune to keep the intruders captive in the guard's hut as the rest of the village celebrated. King Akusa found it harmless to allow them to partake in the bounty and merriment. She thought it would, in fact, illustrate just how charitable her people were and please the ancestors. Fierceness should always be tempered with kindness; that was wisdom. An unwise king was the mark of shame and this she would not be.

She offered her own hut for the celebration, for it was the largest and it would, after all, please Ketwa because Kosii was his favored nephew. The ground before them was covered with unfurled banana leaves, stretched out for the length of the more than one hundred Kosongo who sat cross-legged at either side. Others stood just behind. There was not a space on top of the leaves that was not taken up by some dish. Ketwa and Dashi made sure that each was impeccably prepared. Fish, quail, stewed coconut, banana, wild rice, mango, ackee, bread, mashed yam, honey pudding, and lots of palm wine. The king sat at the head and Elewa and Kosii—newly bonded, still roped by the wrist, each feeding the other with his free hand—sat at the tail.

Each member of the tribe took a moment to walk over to Elewa and Kosii and leave a gift with them: colorful feathers; headdresses made of dried, braided, and studded palm leaves; tall spears with elegantly pounded heads. A great pile formed around them and had to be moved in order for them to continue eating. King Akusa's wives laughed as they cleared away the gifts and placed them near the entrance. They would help them take the gifts to their new dwelling in the morning.

The king, meanwhile, kept the three ghosts and their guide to her right, her spear-throwing arm, where she could keep close watch on them. The one called Brother Gabriel was talkative. He constantly turned to the Gussu chattering in an insufferable language that grated on her ears. How the Gussu could tolerate or decipher it she did not understand.

The Gussu—who said one of his names was Obosye, as the Gussu had many names for many different uses—seemed exasperated at one point.

"Enough," King Akusa said to Obosye. "He will now direct all questions about my tribe to me. You will translate."

Brother Gabriel spoke to her in very soft tones. Each word did not seem so much spoken as smiled. And although she did not immediately admit it to herself—and, later, would judge herself harshly for having missed it—his smiling frightened her.

"Queen Akusa," Gabriel said, but Obosye had sense enough to change the title back to its appropriate form. "A lovely village you have here. And this ceremony—thank you for allowing us to partake."

The king nodded.

"If I may be so bold as to ask: What is the nature of it?" he asked. He gestured toward Elewa and Kosii. "Are these two being initiated into manhood? Is this a warrior's ritual?"

King Akusa nearly spit out her wine. She put down her cup and chuckled.

"How could it not be obvious even to a stranger? Does your own land lack even the most basic of traditions? Their courtship has been witnessed and approved by generations of ancestors. They are bonded."

Gabriel's eyes widened.

"Bonded? Does she mean wedded?" Gabriel looked to Obosye to clarify the translation. Obosye merely nodded.

"But they are two men," Gabriel protested. "These are the seeds of Sodom."

The dead are silly, the king thought. **Silly, foolish, and reckless,** which was perhaps why they intruded here now. Cast out from wisdom, they wandered, confusing everyone they encountered, like the Gussu who had forgotten who he was and stumbled his bare behind into the village without announcement and brought the skinless with him. She took a gulp of wine. She then pinched off a piece of fish and dipped it into some of the mashed yam. She put it in her mouth and then looked at Brother Gabriel. She chewed for a long while, so long that Obosye, Brother Gabriel, and the other two grew visibly uncomfortable.

"I do not know this word, **Sodom.** But I can tell by how it leaves your tongue that I do not like it. They are Elewa and Kosii as they have always been. Do you not see their bond? You will humble yourself before that."

"But respectfully, Queen, they are two men."

King Akusa would have regarded this as insolence had she not understood that this pale, pale man was evidently ignorant and knew nothing of the world as it actually existed. His vision was limited to this realm. "Two men?" These colorless people had the strangest system of grouping things together by what they did not understand rather than by what they did. He could see bodies, but it was clear that he could not see spirits. It was humorous to observe someone who did not know the terrain but refused to admit it, stumbling around, bumping into trees, then asking who put them in their path so suddenly.

"Impossible," she said with a laugh. "They are bonded. Do you not see?"

"I think your people would benefit from our religion," Brother Gabriel said.

The king was not bothered by this, for she believed she understood her own fortitude and that of her people. This Brother Gabriel, who called himself

Portuguese—with his imprecise, bland, gibberish language—was a fool, a charlatan, and no number of his clan would move any Kosongo from their position. Besides, the wine had put her in an inquisitive, playful mood. She called to Ketwa and Nbinga and asked them to sit with her as she made room for them on either side. She held both of them by a hand and stared at Brother Gabriel.

"Who shall keep guard of the gates?" the king asked him, smiling. "You say Elewa and Kosii are some kind of problem. Who guards your gods' gates, then?"

"The gates of Heaven? They don't open upon blasphemy."

"Heaven? What an unusual name. And what an unusual place that does not open its gates for its own guard."

"Be that as it may—"

"Is that what happened to your skin," King Akusa interrupted. "Did your gods snatch it away for treating the gates as a trivial matter?"

"Your Highness, I don't think—"

"Enough."

The king laughed and lay back into Ketwa's full embrace and pulled Nbinga's hand to her mouth and kissed it. King Akusa's chuckle filled the room. She asked two other wives to prepare another round of food and drink for the visitors, who had already eaten what was previously placed before them. They would need to find a space for them to sleep in one of the greeting huts and then send them on their way in the morning. She reminded herself to also instruct Obosye to tell the Gussu chief to never allow his people to guide bad spirits to Kosongo land. Ever. Such behavior communicated disrespect and, in light of the long-planned ceremony, even contempt. She would be glad to never set eyes on these ugly-skinned people again.

Here is what she did not know:

She did not know that far beyond the green mountains where the lightning frightens, but does not strike, hundreds more of Brother Gabriel's kind were making their way from the sea, emerging from great hollow beasts whose bellies craved only the darkest of flesh, dredging through seaweed until they met the unwelcoming rock of shore, armed with weapons that pulled the very thunder out of the sky. A journey so long that it was almost forgivable that their appetites were so ravenous and undiscerning.

She did not know that they would devour not just her own people but would wolf down many other tribes as well. Friendly tribe or hostile tribe, these greedy people would not discriminate, could not, in fact, discriminate. To them, her people were all living pieces of ore: fuel for engines of the most ungodly kind but, bafflingly, in the name of a god that they claimed was peaceful. A lamb, they said. She could not know that was merely a costume.

She did not know of what Brother Gabriel's people were capable, nor did she know what had already become of the Gussu village or why Obosye—who was instructed that if the three demons didn't return safe and sound within an allotted time frame, his children, even the newborn baby boy, would endure unimaginable suffering in his names—colluded in this deception. No seer, not even Semjula, could have given her an ominous enough warning. No Kosongo elder magic or ancestral intervention could turn a woman into an animal, but these Portuguese, she would soon discover, had access to all manner of craft that was remarkably tailored for performing just such a feat.

She did not know that she would not even live to see her children stuffed, like parcels, into these ghosts' vessels, nor would she ever know that in their desperation, one would leap and others, chained together, would follow, crashing into the unfathomable gray like a string of ceremonial beads. Her daughter's children, whose skin would be unrecognizable to her, would live to suffer at the hands of beasts: never to be embraced or loved, merely used to satisfy whims or serve as a receptacle for burdens, forever and ever, Àṣẹ. No. She could not foresee that her rage at seeing her firstborn chained, and Kosii and Elewa in a death stance to free her, would cast her spear-first into battle. She would take down so many—so many of the undead would fall prey to her fearsome heart and her uncanny aim—before a coward would creep from behind, so as not to see her eyes, and unleash a thunderclap deep into her spine. Who would ever imagine that the last thing she would see was Kosii and Elewa wresting the chains from the invaders so that the king's eldest daughter could run free, only to have new chains wrapped around their own necks?

She did not know that she would not get to hear the skinless curse one another because they wanted to take her alive, but in all her glory she denied them the chance to desecrate her with future abuses, ones that she would have had to be living—and screaming—for them to gratify. Instead, she, unbeknownst to her, would only give them eternal silence, which was, in its way, victory. In the spite of their defeat, they would ravage her children instead, to whom she could offer no solace. But the not knowing, here, would be a wondrous thing. King or not, what mother should live to see her children spiked and mounted?

A tumult would be born of this, of such force that the land would never recuperate. There would be valiant wars fought on the king's behalf, by the other tribes who respected her honesty and giving, once they discovered the coming plague and the treachery that permitted its spreading. But it would be to no avail. Where peace was once possible, there would be centuries of bloodshed and pestilence, and the earth itself would be robbed of its natural belongings and, thus, continually reject the children it could no longer identify.

She did not know. Could not know. Should not know.

King Akusa nestled next to Ketwa, pulling Nbinga over with her. The last thing these demons should see of her village was what huge adoration looked like, given how apparently puny their own was.

"Where are the children, beloved?" she asked Nbinga.

"There." Nbinga pointed toward the entrance. And there, King Akusa could see her children dancing—two who looked so much like Ketwa that she could not remember if she had given birth to them or if Nbinga had, or both.

She looked at the Gussu and the three demons beside him. Then she looked down at their bowls, empty again so soon. People who liked her food so thoroughly couldn't be **so** horrible. She never considered that perhaps they were only hungry.

"Eat," she said. "There is plenty."

The Gussu reached first and the others followed. King Akusa smiled and raised her cup.

"To guardians," she said loudly.

"To guardians," said everyone except the demons.

Then the king put the cup to her lips and drank.

TIMOTHY

There was too much red in the face. Timothy would have to compensate with yellow and perhaps just a drop of black. But he managed to capture the unusual expression, something between curiosity and—what was that? Disgust? The subtle tilt of the head, the slight curl of the lip. A smile and a snarl. And the hair like a dark and jagged sun rising from behind. Isaiah was the perfect specimen.

Timothy's father, Paul, seemed to understand the need to document them, though he chose other, more private methods. While Paul would show Timothy's paintings to everyone who visited the plantation, beaming with pride at the startling skill displayed in each stroke, he forbade Timothy from hanging them anywhere in the house. "The niggers would get the wrong idea," he said.

And so they cluttered his room: canvases triple stacked against the base of three walls; every unused surface—whether desk or floor—a resting place for scene after scene of slave merriment or contemplation, even though his father assured him that the latter was impossible. And, of course, his most successful works were the most suffocating: the ones that captured the sorrow. He didn't know that grief could have such a multitude of expressions—be resurrected similarly, yet uniquely, in so many different faces—until the first time he made a Negro sit for him. His hand quivered and he had nearly missed it. But there it was: wet in the eyes, trapped on the tongue, broken in the palms.

He handpicked Isaiah from a gaggle of Negroes he gathered by the edge of the river. He called them out in the middle of their bathing and told them to stand in a line. The overseers cut their eyes at the interruption. No matter. This land belonged to his father as did their jobs, so the Negroes did as instructed and yes, the overseers spit out their tobacco, but they were otherwise silent.

The Negroes' feet squished in the mud. Some of them used their hands or leaves to cover their exposed parts. Others looked away. They all glistened in the sun. Timothy scoured the crowd looking for a color that would best match the fruit of the blackberry trees he planned to include in the landscape. He noticed Isaiah's halo first, surrounding his head in all its shadowed glory.

"Finish washing," he said to Isaiah. And afterward, instructed him to get dressed and come to the space where the grounds met the cotton field.

Timothy had brought a chair, but not for himself. Upright and solid, the back of the chair rose to just below a seated Isaiah's shoulders. Timothy positioned the chair so that it faced east and the sun shined on his back and on Isaiah's face. He made Isaiah sit there for hours, demanded that he not move a muscle, not even to wipe the sweat from his brow.

"Don't even blink," Timothy joked, and had to reassure Isaiah that he was kidding.

Some of the other Negroes watched from behind trees or from the entrances of their shacks, straining their vision with wide eyes. But they kept their distance. Timothy saw them. They stayed behind, as if fearful that they would get sucked into the painting and, perhaps, have to contend with two places from which they couldn't escape.

Isaiah's face was drenched. Finally, Timothy moved from behind the easel he had placed just off to the left of where Isaiah was sitting so that he would have the proper perspective and capture almost all that he wanted of Isaiah's nature.

"You are an **excellent** model for my work," he then said to Isaiah with a joyful flourish.

Isaiah's silence followed by his head bowing made

Timothy think Isaiah didn't understand a compliment when one was being given. He shook his head
and asked the Negro behind the closest tree to come
forth and assist him in carrying his equipment back
to the house. At the porch stairs, Timothy stopped.
He turned to see Isaiah still seated in the chair.

"You can go back now," he yelled, not unkindly.

It dawned on him briefly that he had never seen a
Negro in the South seated in a chair. On the ground,
yes. On haystacks. In driver's seats. But never in a
chair. Maybe that was why the Negro continued
to sit: to have a small idea of what it meant to be
fully human, to rest a spell on a comfortable surface
and to have support for your back. But he got up
and Timothy watched him move slowly back to the
river and collapse to his knees at the edge of it before
bending forward to splash his face.

THE TRIP TO BOSTON was more difficult than the
trip coming home. Traveling north felt unnatural.
And the things he had seen along the way: it had
rained continually, which meant the wagon was per-
petually stuck and the rain brought with it a mist
so thick that he couldn't tell where he began and
it ended. They had to travel through patches of
Indian Territory, he and the others heading north
for college because they, too, had to gain the skills
necessary to help their fathers manage the tracts of
land that they conquered, and the North, despite its

festering treachery, was home to the best institutions for business thought. His time at the school that his father said he must attend to be best prepared for his inheritance was interesting for the wrong reasons. Midnight art and powerful sleep would be of no use to Paul. He had been told by jealous men, the men charged with ferrying past the imaginary line that separated the northern and southern parts of an infant country, that the fog wouldn't protect them. Indians didn't need eyes to see them, they said, or, rather, could see them through the eyes of woodland creatures—a snake at their feet or a bird circling their heads. They would kill them while they were asleep and eat their flesh raw as tribute to even more savage gods. He couldn't erase from his mind the image of bloody teeth tearing at him. And the envious men looked at him, specifically, when they told their scare stories, as if they could see the timidity at the beating center of his heart. He had perhaps not been careful enough: stared too long at a passing gentleman; said a male name during his slumber, maybe; or it could have been the gentle way in which his hand would occasionally drape at the end of his wrist. You could never know for sure what it was that inspired their malice, so every part of your inside self had to remain inside.

He had found that Northerners, unlike Southerners, had no idea that they were the descendants of cannibals. They had been sufficiently protected, by a myriad of myths involving hard work and superior intellectual, moral, and physical character, from such unpeaceful knowledge. But there was a chance that some of them knew it. There were some of them who had kept themselves in a perpetual state of dreaming, imbibing morphine mixed with water. Some ate the powder straight out of the package. Others inhaled it. Its effect on them intrigued Timothy. He would ask them many questions. In their sometimes incoherent responses, he felt he had been let in on secrets that might have otherwise gone unheard. Some of them talked of feeling something, anything, for the very first time; **a tingle,** they said, **in the chest.** A feeling that made them want to lie on their backs in the soil and greet the sky and everything else with gratitude. **Even niggers,** they said. And they would only call them by that name when they were feeling this grateful. Otherwise, "Negroes."

There they were, pupils as big as buttons, grinning, rubbing on flaccid genitals, not understanding why the genitals were so limp when they, themselves, were feeling so aroused—and by everything; unlocking every part of themselves freely, and letting Timothy in. Saliva was frothy in the corners of their mouths. Timothy suppressed the urge to offer them a handkerchief because he thought it might break their concentration and be seen as an insult.

When one of his dorm mates confessed to being in love with his own mother, of using his baby grasp to hold on to her pubic hairs so as to avoid leaving her womb, to remain there in the comforts of her canal,

Timothy had heard enough, had, in fact, heard too much and wished that he could unhear it. He never asked another question of them, and when they went into their induced passion-stupor, he would leave the room and walk the grounds, wishing he could be as ignorant and stoic as the trees.

Out into the silvery light of the North he bounded, allowing the rays to wash over him, letting it in, deeply, where it chilled him to the bone. He hoped no one noticed what the frigidity was doing to his body: flexing his muscles, goosebumping his skin, hardening his nipples and his prick. He walked on, smiling at the stones beneath his feet, admiring the weeds that had the courage to peek out from between them, golden at their edges, but still green at their roots.

When the air greeted him, it carried with it the scent of burning logs—birch trees, perhaps, that had never imagined being cut up this way and shoved into some firepit. The flames they, these pitiful trees, had imagined were much grander, engulfing everything, but only so that they could be reborn, mightier than before, at some other time. This wasn't that.

Timothy even smiled, faintly, at some of the other students he passed—until he remembered that unlike the stone, the weed, or the tree, they carried secrets frightening enough to chill you to the bone like a silvery light.

He had learned that horror could be planted like seeds, spring to life if given the right tenderness of soil, water, and shine. Unfurl slowly beneath the earth's skin, burrowing down even as it stretched upward toward an open sky. Hiding, at first, its center, it could be coaxed to reveal its core, exposing colors vibrant enough to make even animals weep, unveiling fragrances that could seduce even the most ferocious of bees. You would never know it was poison until you touched or consumed it, but by then it was already too late. You had already been choked, just like the ones before you. And there was no one left unscathed enough to tell the tale, to warn the next person foolish enough to stop and admire, plucked when they should have just left well enough alone.

He wasn't the first literate person in his family; Paul and Ruth read extensively: novels, contracts, and the religious text that was a combination of both. But he was the first to have taken his education this far, and so far north. He was bound to learn other things, discover in himself what Mississippi wasn't wide enough to let prosper. A conscience, perhaps. And something less confined: a white thing with jagged wings that poked at his thighs at night and made the whole room hot.

His art was a sign to some of the other boys at school that their whispers, stolen glances, and subtle gestures toward one another's groins were just fine and dandy. Timothy had to fan himself and stand behind the easel so as not to make it so obvious that he was receptive to the gazes and wanted more. His yearning went on the canvas before it stretched itself into the real time. He painted feverishly: in the morning before class, after afternoon prayer, doodles during lunch, and sketches by lamplight late into the evening. He had never been so pleased.

But Isaiah . . .

"So you work the barn and the animals. You prefer that to the field?"

"I do what I told to, suh," Isaiah replied.

"I know that." Timothy smiled. "Most of you do. But I mean, is it what you prefer?"

Isaiah said nothing, as though he understood that there could be no right answer but silence. He looked down at his feet.

"Please don't move, Isaiah. Look up at me, please. Hold your head steady."

Isaiah looked up without looking Timothy in the eye.

"Because I can have my father put you wherever I ask. So tell me: Where would you rather be?"

"I like the barn just fine," Isaiah said quickly. "Just fine."

It annoyed Timothy that Isaiah couldn't tell him very much about himself. He didn't know his age, who or where his parents were, what he dreamed about, or even what his favorite color was. Not even when Timothy painted a line of every color from his palette on a canvas and asked Isaiah to choose. Although he stared quite a long time at the blue, and then the red, he made no decision, said he couldn't.

"But everybody has a favorite color, Isaiah," Timothy protested.

"What's your'n, sir?"

"Oh, that's easy: purple. Because purple is two of my favorite colors mixed together."

"Is that so, sir? Which two is that?"

"Blue and red." Timothy smiled and winked.

"Then I like purple too, sir," Isaiah said with startling conviction.

Timothy smiled and patted Isaiah on the head. But he wanted to know more.

Isaiah must have been close to his own age, but Timothy couldn't be certain. His father kept impeccable records of everything. So if Timothy searched, perhaps he could find their names in ledgers. This is how he came to venturing into his father's study one day, spending almost an hour perusing religious texts, bank statements, bound letters, and other things, each arranged in rows on shelves surrounding the room.

He took a second to sit down at Paul's desk. He leaned forward and spread his hands over its surface. No. He couldn't imagine this being his destiny. It hovered too high and made him feel less corporeal—just like a cold sun's silver rays could.

He stood up and was careful to return the chair to its previous position. He walked over to a shelf and discovered that it held precisely what he was seeking: inventory. The first books listed sacks of flour and sugar, hogs and horses, some of the furniture Ruth would allow very few people to sit upon, along with the purchase of some Negroes. When it came to the latter, there was no specificity. He could more readily identify the furniture based on the description than he could any of the slaves.

Timothy imagined, briefly, that Isaiah could have been his playmate at one time if he had been permitted to play with Negro children. Paul frowned upon any contact with Negroes that was not utilitarian, however shifty his definition of that word was. So Timothy endured loneliness, and loneliness never failed to make a child resourceful.

He scoured through stacks of books finally narrowing it down to about 1814, a year after his own birth. There were five births recorded in August alone. If Isaiah was born on the plantation, then it had to be 1814. If not, if Isaiah was purchased from another place, then it might have been in another ledger, the one from 1818 titled "Virgins," in which Paul detailed how twenty slaves, chained together, had been brought in on an uncovered wagon from Virginia, which made stops in South Carolina and Georgia, the youngest among them a child of about three or four years of age. Timothy wondered why Paul titled the ledger so but eventually shrugged his shoulders, certain his father had his reasons.

As he turned through the pages of these documents, Timothy thought his father uncharacteristically sloppy: he didn't write down any of the names of the Negroes he acquired, even though the first thing his father and mother always did was name the slaves upon their arrival. They said they did that to immediately gain mastery over them and erase whatever personality had been brewing on the passage over. In the ledger, Paul opted instead to identify them by ambiguous terms like "scar" or "watch," so oblique as to be useless. How easy would it have been to write "Cephas" or "Dell" or "Essie" or "Freddy"? It didn't matter in the end, Timothy supposed. Perhaps for his father, in the case of the record, the name of the tool was less important than its function.

Did Isaiah have any brothers? Was he born on this plantation? If not, did he remember his life before? Timothy decided he would ask.

On another day, Timothy pulled Isaiah away from his work. He sent Maggie down to retrieve him. When the two arrived at the back of the Big House, Ruth was standing on the porch, her arms crossed in front of her bosom. Timothy was standing behind her.

"Mag, I was calling you. Where were you? And who is this?" she said, sizing up Isaiah.

"I was fetching this here barn hand for Massa Timothy is all."

"And what does Timothy want with this filthy creature?"

"I don't know, ma'am. You best ask the massa himself."

Timothy stepped forward.

"Mother, he's my specimen. You know I paint these Negroes."

Ruth sucked her teeth. "'Negroes.' You mean niggers. Call them as you see them. There's no need for pussyfooting," she said as she looked first at Timothy, then at Isaiah. "Well, don't let him in the house. He's liable to stink up the whole place. Settle any business right out here on this porch."

Ruth stood on the porch eyeing Isaiah. Isaiah's head was bowed and he was wringing his hands.

"Stop all that fidgeting," Ruth said softly. "You're making me—"

Timothy grabbed his mother by the arm.

"Mother, I think it's best if you returned to your room. You need your rest. Maggie, would you take my mother back upstairs?"

"This is still my house, young man." Ruth smiled. "And I will roam it as I please. Thank you kindly." She unfolded her arms. "I wish you'd paint something else. All this beauty surrounding us and you find the ugliest thing in the world to waste paint on."

Timothy's face turned red before he composed himself.

"Mother, why don't you go on inside? It will be dark soon and Maggie is about to serve tea and cookies. I'll join you shortly."

Ruth smiled a smile that told Timothy that she would pretend that he wasn't trying to get rid of her. She patted him on the shoulder and walked slowly over the threshold and into the kitchen. Maggie followed her.

Timothy sighed.

"I apologize for Mother," he said to Isaiah, who hadn't moved an inch the entire time. He was still looking at his feet.

"No such a thing," Isaiah replied, but he didn't lift his head.

Timothy walked down the steps and walked up to Isaiah. He put his finger to his chin and lifted Isaiah's head. Isaiah avoided eye contact, but wherever he would turn his eyes, Timothy would move there until, defeated, Isaiah looked him in the face.

"You don't have to be afraid of me, Isaiah. I'm not like my family."

Isaiah inhaled deeply, held it for a moment, and then let the air out slowly, silently. He scratched his head.

"Well, now. I had you summoned for a reason," Timothy said. "I just have some questions."

Isaiah remained silent.

"Who's that other Negro who works with you in the barn?"

Isaiah grabbed his own thigh and squeezed.

"Samuel, suh."

"Is he your brother?"

"No, suh."

"I'd like to meet him. Will you take me?"

Isaiah walked very slowly to lead the way. Timothy

rushed ahead of him, forcing Isaiah to speed up. Through the wide-open door of the barn, Isaiah could see Samuel's flickering silhouette against the walls, dancing alone to lamplight.

Samuel had been down at the river, too, the day Timothy called all of them forth, had also been pored over by him and thoughtfully rejected. They were bathing, modesty a sliver of a thing among them. It was a rest day, so they could do with their time what they wished, within limits. No one could leave the plantation without a pass, and passes were almost never given. But they could sit with their families and friends at the edge of the river and fish. They could gather around a campfire and roast walnuts. They could come together in the clearing and lift their voices to God. And they could bathe.

And on that particular morning, they bathed en masse. Probably those who wanted to be clean for Amos's service—even though they would only mess themselves again by sitting on the ground, on rotting logs, or on mossy rock as the sun tried to break through tree boughs to give great Amos the glow.

None of it really made any sense to Timothy. He had watched them once, in a circle, beneath trees, listening to what sounded to him like nothing. Yes, certainly there were good Negroes, and maybe even some of them deserved to be free or returned to where they were snatched from, but what heaven would have them sitting side by side with decent Christians? The most they could hope for was an afterlife of shelter and enough food to fuel the toil that would be their lot for all eternity.

He interrupted their bathing, but all appeared forgiven because they seemed so glad to see it was him and not his father or James. So they lined up and Timothy recalled that, among the bunch, it was only Samuel who sulked.

Samuel stood up when he heard their footsteps tramping over the dusty trail from the Big House. He held up the lantern and saw Isaiah and Timothy walking toward the barn. He frowned and looked to the darkening sky. Then he slouched and lowered his head.

Timothy waited for Isaiah to run out in front of him to open the gate. Timothy might have simply climbed it had he not been so tired. He walked inside and stepped on a pile of horse shit.

"Christ Jesus," he exclaimed. "Ugh. Lord have . . . Isaiah, I thought you two were supposed to keep this place . . . Shit. Help me . . ."

Timothy pointed down to his boot. Isaiah dropped to his knees and unlaced it. Then he tugged on it, though it wouldn't budge. Finally, Samuel came out with the lamp. He set it on the ground and helped Isaiah pull. With one great heave, they got it loose, all three of them landing on their asses. Timothy laughed.

"My word." He chuckled at them.

Isaiah got up and ran to retrieve a bucket of water. He left the boot on the ground. Timothy rose and dusted himself off. Then he looked at Samuel, who stared aimlessly in the lamplight.

"Good evening, Samuel," Timothy said. Samuel jumped as if awakened from slumber. "Do you know who I am?"

"Yes, suh," Samuel replied.

"Well?" Timothy rushed.

"You Massa Timothy, suh," Samuel said, and added, "Good to have you back home, Massa."

"Well, thank you, Samuel," Timothy offered and straightened his back. His face brightened. "I wish I could say I was glad to be back. I miss the North so—cold as it is. Alas, here I am."

There was silence between them. Isaiah came back with the bucket and he and Samuel knelt and began to clean the boot. Occasionally, Samuel would steal upward glances. Timothy watched as they worked in tandem, with perfect rhythm, like they had been made that way: arms moving, elbows jutting, hands swishing in water, fingers grasping the bucket's edge, occasionally touching as one silently gave the other a cue in a language only they understood. They were together in a way he hadn't ever witnessed, every separate motion building upon the other to form something that seemed to sway to its own music, back and forth, like the sea. For the first time, since arriving home, he felt like an intruder. He didn't dislike the feeling, but the silence unsettled him.

"I've been painting Isaiah, you know," he offered finally. "Out there, over by the field."

Samuel stopped washing the boot. He took his hands out of the bucket and shook them to get the excess water off. He stood up and wiped his arms.

"Painting him, suh?" Samuel looked at Isaiah. Isaiah stood up and handed the boot back to Timothy. Samuel looked Isaiah up and down and then turned back toward Timothy.

"But I don't see a lick of paint on him, Massa."

"What? No," Timothy said, laughing. "I've been painting **pictures** of him. You know, like paintings that you hang on a wall."

"Oh, I see. That's mighty fine, suh. Yes, indeed." Samuel glanced toward Isaiah, who was giving him a stern look.

"Yes, well, maybe I can paint you, too, one of these days," Timothy added.

"Yes, suh."

"If you'd like."

"Yes, suh."

Suddenly, Timothy found himself disturbed and tried to discover why. He stared at the two Negroes in front of him. Something about them was nagging at him. Samuel was obedient enough, tall even when slouching. But he seemed, still, not to see him, to look past him, the smile on his face strained. Samuel was the color of an eggplant, violet more than black, and sturdy. He was about Timothy's height and had just the whitest teeth. Shocking, those teeth were, because most boys Timothy knew had teeth that were either weed green or pallid yellow.

Timothy had sat in classrooms with those other boys, who talked and talked, and whose talking revealed nothing except that their pasts were invented, no matter how fervently they believed them. But Timothy widened his eyes at their tales anyway, gasped during the dramatic pauses, and applauded vigorously at the conclusions.

Those other boys liked the way Timothy spoke, the slow certainty of his voice, and the drawl that inevitably led into a smile. His dimples, pressed snugly into each cheek, were excess; he had already won them over with his disposition. If the South had taught him anything, it taught him how to hide his flaws, flatter his audience, feign deference even when he was clearly superior in every conceivable way, and be quintessential in the art of courtesy. This while holding vile and impure thoughts, while even suppressing the girth of his manhood behind britches that threatened to burst at the seams. A raindrop at the tip of his being that would never reach fertile ground. Yes, he was a gentleman's gentleman, and they were completely taken with him.

In the North, he was told that Negroes were free, but he hadn't seen any during his entire time there. He imagined that the number must have been small and, therefore, sightings rare. He did, however, meet people who called themselves abolitionists. Curious folk, he thought; wanted to free Negroes from the drudgery of slavery, they said, but what to do after was always murky, always shapeless, always an exercise in inadequacy.

"Maybe send them back to Africa," one of them said at an informal gathering at a tavern in town.

"After so many years?" Timothy retorted. "It would be as foreign to them as it would be to us, I reckon. You wish to solve what you call an act of cruelty by perpetrating another?"

"Well, do you propose that they stay here, walk among us, and lie with us in our beds?"

"Why would their presence here lead to our bedrooms?"

"Their lust would make it inevitable."

Their lust or ours? Timothy thought. After all, he knew what lurked in the loins of men, had witnessed it up close. All it took to unleash it was a paintbrush and a skilled hand. He struggled to determine the difference between North and South and concluded that they were more alike than not, the only discernible difference being that the South had thought all of their options through to their conclusions. The North, meanwhile, still couldn't answer the questions of who would do the work freed slaves would necessarily leave behind and how those unfortunate souls would be paid once the position of slave was abolished. These men were bad at business, though there was every indication that they were just as greedy.

Timothy looked in the direction of the Big House, then back at Isaiah and Samuel.

"Well, I must be going. Isaiah, come to the house in the morning. I'll let Maggie know to let you in. I want to get back to work on your portrait as soon as possible."

"Yessuh. Do you need for one of us to light your way?"

"No. I'll be just fine. Thank you. Good night."

He walked down the dark path toward the house with the feeling that he had not seen all he needed to see of them. He wondered what they were like when he wasn't around. Were they as shy, as quiet? What kind of wobbly, imperfect world did they create out there in the barn? He was determined to see.

It was about three in the morning and even the faint lights from the cabins in the distance were extinguished when he climbed out of bed. He went downstairs and sat in a rocker on the front porch, hoping the night would produce a merciful breeze. He was like his mother in this. Absent all light but moonglow, the plantation was a festival of shadows. Black against black, and yet things managed to distinguish themselves from one another: the curly black of the trees from the pointy black of the cabins; the silky black of the river from the massive black of the barn. Somehow, he had not noticed that before.

He wiped the sweat from his brow. No breeze would bless him. He leaned forward. The searing, sticky night was infecting him with wanderlust. He needed to cool himself off, wash the clamminess from his skin. Perhaps a short splash in the river.

He got up and the rocker continued to rock without him. He walked down the steps and walked around the side of the house, toward the Yazoo.

He began unbuttoning his shirt. He had completely removed it by the time he was near the back of the barn. He noticed a faint light emanating from within. He did now what he didn't do earlier: he climbed the gate and hoped he didn't step in any more manure. He crept over to the barn. He walked along the back, the side closest to the river. There was a knothole big enough to fit his fist through. He pressed his head against the wall and peeped in. He tried to make out the figures. Horses? Yes. He was on the end where the horses' pens were. But beyond them, where the lamplight flickered, glimpses. Breathtaking.

Their heat seemed to blur everything in close proximity. Hay stuck to Samuel's back, or maybe it was Isaiah's. He couldn't tell who was holding whom. That's how close together they were, and the light offered no assistance. Nevertheless, the hay was darted against him like sewing needles, as though some unseen hand were stitching them both into existence, right there, together, in that tight embrace, slumbering, joined. Timothy began to tremble. He didn't imagine that Negroes were this way, could be this way: What, to them, was snuggling with no bed in which to share it? Did toil not prevent the contemplation or even the time for a softer nature? Thomas Jefferson had done extensive research, Timothy learned, and the science made it clear. Yet, without any wind to chill the air, they clung to each other as though it were winter and not summer. The witnessing confused him, but also made him stiff inside his britches.

He would paint Isaiah tomorrow.

And why shouldn't he? It wouldn't be long before he would begin to receive visitors. For surely his parents wanted, needed grandchildren; they weren't shy about making this known. Pestering him about whether he had met any fine ladies during his studies, travels, and such, before deciding, ultimately, that it didn't matter, that what he couldn't find he hadn't the experience to do in any regard. And they, his parents, would be better at selection.

There would come young women, girls really, all with the right breeding—with the right shade of red hair, or blond to match his own; with exceptionally green eyes, or blue like his; and bosoms that had just begun to rise at about the same time that he discovered the sizzling thing that dangled between his legs; girls whose eyes would flutter when he walked into the room; whose private parts would glisten with his grin; who might recoil internally and hold back tears so as not to offend their parents or their hosts. They would be paraded before him as though his choice mattered and, once chosen, he would be forced to marry her for whom he had no desire.

And why not with a Negro? Color stopped neither his mother nor his father. There were blond-haired, blue-eyed Negroes with near-white skin who walked just like him, had the same smile and the same square shoulders as he did, the same knobby knees and the same splotchy birthmark on the chin. Only the tight curls of their tresses—and, sometimes, their thick lips and broad noses—gave Timothy relief when he passed one of them. His parents thought he didn't know about Adam, the coach Negro, but he did. Had always suspected it, but knew for certain on the ride into town to see him off to college. The way his mother snapped at Adam and the way she tried to distract Timothy; it was all so very obvious then. Adam looked too Halifax not to be one. There were probably more. He wasn't an only child after all, but wished he could have been.

He had seen enough. He backed away from the barn and tiptoed off to the river. When he was right about at the spot where he had called all of the Negroes out of the water just days ago, he stooped and splashed his face with water. He took off his pants and attempted to cool the heat between his legs, but it only grew. So he felt himself, over and over again, until he could feel himself no longer.

Drained, he trekked back to the Big House, climbed the stairs slowly, reached his room, and fell face-first into his bed. He hadn't slept that well since he returned home. He dreamed of writhing bodies and drool. Only the sun pouring through his window a short while later, its heat beating down on his head, woke him. Temporarily blinded, he rubbed his eyes.

When his vision adjusted, he surveyed his room. The painting of Isaiah, not quite finished, but finished enough, stared back at him. He blushed and turned his face.

When Isaiah arrived later that morning, Timothy came down to greet him. With Ruth still soundly asleep, Timothy led Isaiah up the stairs and into his room.

"Have you ever been in the house before?" Timothy asked Isaiah.

"No, suh." Isaiah looked around as though he were trying to memorize every detail.

"This is my room. You like it?"

"I never seen nothing like it. Almost as big as the whole barn."

Timothy laughed and then closed the door. There was a skeleton key in the lock. He quietly turned it.

"Do you know how to read, Isaiah?"

"Oh, no, suh. No nigger is allowed to read."

"Do you want to know?"

"No, suh. No use in it."

"Well, I'm going to teach you anyway. Our secret."

"Why, suh?"

"Because I like you, Isaiah. I think you're a good boy."

Timothy walked over to a shelf and pulled the Bible from it.

"Here. Come sit with me on my bed."

"I dirty, Massa. I don't wanna—"

"Never mind that. Just come."

Isaiah took unsure steps toward the bed and hesitantly sat upon it, right at the spot where Timothy was indicating with his beating hand. Timothy looked Isaiah over and reaffirmed for himself that he was a splendid physical specimen. He examined his crotch. Negroes didn't wear undergarments, so it was not difficult to see what was beneath. Timothy rubbed his eyes. **It couldn't be.** But wait: it moved! He was certain. Snaked through his pants leg and came to rest on his right thigh as if contemplating an escape route before daring to venture any farther and becoming lost.

By golly, it moved!

He touched Isaiah's arm and marveled at his skin. Seduced by his dark edges, by the sweet curves of his blacker-than-black. He had an overwhelming desire to fall into himself darkly and be lost.

"Massa?"

"I want to see it. Please take off your clothes."

Isaiah hesitated. Opened his mouth but neglected to speak any words. He unfastened his shirt. He let it fall to the floor. Timothy leaned in close to Isaiah and squinted, examining him until he came to Isaiah's back.

"Did my father do this to you?"

Isaiah said nothing.

"Why would he do something like this?" Timothy asked as he kissed the welts.

Isaiah shivered. "I thought you said you wanted to paint me, Massa."

Timothy kept kissing his back.

"Massa, I thought you was gon'—"

"Shhh. Isn't this better?" Timothy asked, but it was not a question.

Isaiah sat rigidly on the edge of the bed.

"Relax."

Isaiah stood up, which made his erection obvious. Timothy smiled.

"I saw you last night. In the barn. You and Samuel. I saw what you do."

Isaiah turned away.

"Massa, I can't . . ."

"Can't?"

"What I mean is . . . Samuel is . . ."

Timothy stood up. He moved in close to Isaiah, close enough that their breaths mingled. Isaiah's brow sweated profusely.

"You deserve someone to be gentle with you for once," Timothy whispered.

Isaiah shook his head.

"Samuel . . ."

Timothy leaned in and kissed Isaiah on the mouth. Samuel's name still on Isaiah's lips, now trapped between them. Isaiah didn't kiss back. Timothy used his own lips and tongue to pry Isaiah's mouth open. Isaiah grunted.

"I can protect you from my father," Timothy moaned, his body pressed into Isaiah's.

While he didn't wish to have Isaiah come to him out of obligation, it would be a suitable, less violent option should Isaiah choose not to come of his own free will. What he wouldn't do was force him beyond that. Because what would be the point if Isaiah did not submit freely, if Timothy couldn't have every last bit of him, including his will?

Timothy pulled down his trousers and lay ass-up on the bed. Isaiah squeezed his eyes shut, then opened them. He wiped his brow and then lay down on top of Timothy. Beneath, Timothy thought of how he had relinquished himself to Isaiah; he was in his hands now. And something fluttered in his chest. He grabbed hold of it and when he opened his grip, there it was, duller than he imagined, but there: free. If he was to give this to Isaiah, then it could only come back to him, as all things did, manifold. To set another man free was to free yourself. This wasn't just the clamoring of an indecisive North, no. Timothy felt the truth of that way down in his cave, which quivered now after having justly been shaken.

"Together, we can be set free," Timothy whispered as he raised his head and closed his eyes. "Only together."

NEBUCHADNEZZAR

It had never dawned on Isaiah how things so close together could be so far apart. The barn was just yonder, a good stone's throw from the Big House, and yet, when walked by legs, the distance between them felt like a journey. The house seemed to be at the bottom of some enormous mountain, or down, maybe, in some deep valley where the thinnest of rivers hid from the sky and wolves roamed. Down there, where you expected it to be warmer, and yet things were chilled enough to blue the hands and feet, and turn breath to smoke.

And here you were, lost and at a loss for how anyone barefoot and without tools could make his way out of it, climb surfaces that seemed too smooth to cling to or too solid to dig into, with nothing but what might be an errant star to guide you upward, into the place that is only marginally safer than the place you're trying to escape.

What of the ascent itself? Isaiah had a strong mind, and he couldn't figure out if it was at all worth it. A road that was supposed to be level was sloped and its incline became more difficult with each step. There was nothing to stop him from tumbling back down right as he reached the uppermost part of it. You could break your bones and then there would no longer be a point in getting up and trying again. You wouldn't be able to. Couldn't.

Yet, the yearning that pulled him at his center like a rope that had been thrown down from the mountaintop, from the level plains at the top of the ridge, from the places that were supposed to be cold but somehow, maybe because they were closer to the sun, were warm to every touch. The grass took on a different character: dewy and blue green instead of dry and gold. People and animals lived together in what he guessed you could call a kind of harmony, but it came from barest necessity rather than a haunting desire. There was one reason, and one reason only, to make the attempt to, wingless and unsure-footed, try to ascend any old way.

By the time the birds had finished singing, after they had completed their circling of his head, he remembered the pain. His own, yes, because it can only be tragedy to be forced, but doubly so when the body refuses to fail; also Timothy's because he was unprepared. Isaiah hadn't anticipated finding a hint of joy in being the source of it. Besides, whatever joy there was quickly faded once he realized that it was the kind of thing that Timothy had no objection to. It was all so very bizarre, and also very new to Isaiah, to learn that toubab had not only relished giving it out, but secretly—in their quiet places, out of the sight of anyone who might judge it horribly, use it against them, or give to them in a way for which they were truly unprepared—they were intent on receiving it.

Timothy cried, but his eyes also rolled into the back of his head just like Samuel's and Isaiah did everything he knew how to do to ensure those faces, those expressions, Samuel's and Timothy's, didn't merge. Somehow, he knew that once they did, only death would be able to untangle them.

He was halfway up the mountain—or midway out of the valley—when he realized that, outside this between time, he had missed a whole day's work, hadn't seen Samuel the entire day, had left him to do everything on his own, which was difficult because just about everything in the barn was a job for two people. It would be barely possible for Samuel to do it alone. He knew Samuel didn't want to do any of it, period, but they had a system. Everyone knew that.

What they didn't know was that the system had been mapped out, mostly in stars, but also in owl hoot and iris scent, and placed over and under everything long before Samuel had the decency to bring the sweet water and Isaiah the thirst to drink it.

Gone **all day!** Sweat ran down Isaiah's back. He wondered if Samuel would be worried, might think him hurt, dead, or worse. More likely, he might simply be angry. As children, they took to each other—at first, like the best of friends, until both of them got the scent under their arms and the little goat hairs at the southernmost edges of their chins. They went from looking as plain as soil to each other to something that could nourish. Not some**thing,** some**one.** And one Sunday, sixteen seasons ago, one hand not so accidentally placed on top of the other while at the riverbank—neither of them looking the other in the eyes, but gazing off to something on that other side, where the trees formed a wall that only a curious deer could penetrate—was all it took for their evening shadows to later dance.

As he crossed the fence, Isaiah realized that this was the first time he had been away from Samuel this long since memory, which discomforted him. It felt like a small yet jagged piece of flesh hanging from the finger, ripped off too quickly, pulling down the whole side of the digit, leaving a trail of raw burning, blood oozing out of it the same way mushrooms do from the earth: a pain that can't be soothed but can only be coaxed into subsiding with promises.

This is what it would be like?

Isaiah imagined Samuel chained up in the bed

of the wagon as Adam, the lightest-skinned person Isaiah ever did see who could still be considered a person, covered his long Halifax-but-not-Halifax face so as not to see the crumble of bones that Isaiah had become because they had used a hammer and chisel to split a rock from its base. When the image left him and he saw the barn come back into view, just like that, the danger Amos spoke of found its menacing shape. His heart punched his chest from the inside.

He quickened his pace. His breath came in slow, shallow huffs. His legs buzzed with impatience. The day's stench was still on him. He briefly contemplated jumping in the river real quick before the sun dipped, before going into the barn and having to return Samuel's gaze with his own altered one, but Samuel didn't deserve to wait another second.

When he reached the doors, he was afraid to open them. How could he explain leaving his seed where he left it and that, in some small, irresponsible way, it felt like an act of liberation? He tugged at the door, but it was a halfhearted attempt. Samuel heard the noise and got up. He pushed the door open a little too hard and nearly knocked Isaiah down.

"What happened to you?" Samuel whispered as he helped Isaiah regain his balance.

Isaiah placed an arm around Samuel's neck and leaned into him. Side by side, they walked into the barn. Isaiah fell limp into a haystack.

Samuel stood over him.

"Man, talk! What's wrong with you? Where you been?"

Isaiah looked off toward the horse pens.

"We should open up those pens, Sam," he said slowly. "Let the horses out. They look cooped up."

"What?" Samuel walked over to the lamp that sat on the ground by the pens and lit it. He brought it back to where Isaiah lay and then sat down next to it.

"It can't be comfortable, you know? Locked up in such a small space," Isaiah continued.

"Heh. That toubab had you cramped up all day, huh? He paint you, what, sitting on some stool, not even letting you get a break for something cool to drink? Maggie couldn't even sneak you some lemonade, could she? You gotta be meaner, man!" Samuel laughed. He looked at Isaiah to return the laughter, tried to find if the lamplight reflected in his eyes, but couldn't.

"Yessuh. I tired. All-the-way-to-the-bones tired." Isaiah attempted a smile.

Samuel's eyes squinted. "You always asking me to talk. Usually, I can't shut **you** up. Now you only telling me some of it," Samuel said, louder than he intended.

Isaiah got up and walked toward the water bucket they kept against the front wall. He tripped over a shovel left lying in the middle of the barn and landed on his hands. He jumped up, dusted himself off, and felt around for the bucket. He grabbed it and walked back over to Samuel and sat down. He drank from the ladle in large gulps.

"You gon' talk?"

Isaiah took another big swig of water and swallowed it all at once. It went down hard.

"I ain't a animal, but I know. I know that when you trapped in a small space, you start getting used to being small. And people, they know, too, and they start treating you like a small thing. Even if you big like you are, Sam. They still treat you like something small." Isaiah took a breath. "And at the same time they want you small, they want your thang big. You hear what I telling you?"

"I don't understand all that," Samuel said in a huff. "What you saying?"

"I here, Sam. They don't know it, but I am."

"I know it."

"Do you?" Isaiah looked down.

"Did he . . . ?" Samuel moved closer to him.

"They say funny things." Isaiah's brow furrowed and he looked off into the past that had just materialized before him, but faded so that he could still see now. "Feel goodness in the most hateful things, Sam. Nigger, do this to me. Nigger, do that to me. They want you to treat them like an outhouse. And always, always talk about how big. Stretch me, they say. And I can't stand to hear it or to watch them writhe. Giving them pleasure while all they give in return is grief." Isaiah put the ladle back into the bucket. He scooped up another serving of water. "But still . . ."

Samuel straightened his back. He searched Isaiah's face for a reason. Maybe the bump of the chin, a nose twitch, maybe the curl of his lashes would tell him something about why this man had decided, out of nowhere, to crush him and take his time doing it.

"When you went to him, you walk or run?" Samuel said. He looked at Isaiah with sharpened eyes. "And you get on me 'bout Puah?"

Isaiah's mouth opened and his tongue looked for the proper words, but found none. The space in front of him narrowed. His vision, a border, however imaginary. For a moment, there was silence and all either of them could feel was heat emanating from nowhere and from each other. Isaiah decided surrender was a better option than retaliatory action. He went to touch Samuel's knee, but Samuel jerked it away just as Isaiah reached out. Isaiah smiled, shook his head. His eyes blinked slowly, heavily. He yawned. He stood up as though he were about to walk away, but he merely turned his back to Samuel and looked toward the barn door. On each hand, his fingers wiggled quickly, like someone trying to bide his time but who couldn't figure out what to do with his body as he waited. He started to mumble.

"The men got no curve. Not a one. From the back of they necks to the tip of they heels is a straight goddamn line. Strangest thing you ever did see." He chuckled. "They ask a heap of questions. He ask me 'bout you and so I tell him. **Ain't no use in lying,** he say. **Because I seen with my own eyes,** he say. So I tell him: 'Samuel? He touch my shoulder. I open him up. I open him up wide. So he can feel everything. He collapse in on me. And everything feel good.'"

"Why I have to hear this?"

"You asked."

"Not for this."

Samuel turned his head. He scooted over, closer to the bucket of water. He grabbed the ladle and took a gulp of water. Then he dipped it again and took another. Then another. Then another. He could hardly catch his breath. Isaiah turned slightly to see Samuel's face, bronze in the lamplight; beads of sweat spotted his forehead; his nostrils were flaring. Isaiah wondered if he should keep talking.

Samuel looked up at him. He pushed himself back, away from the bucket. He wanted to get up, to grab something and destroy it. Instead, he just sat there, not wanting to look at Isaiah anymore, not even wanting to smell his scent, which wasn't his scent. Isaiah moved back over toward him and got down on his knees.

"You mad at me?" Isaiah said to Samuel, looking into his face as though some blemish on his skin might hold the answer.

Samuel looked toward the doors.

"Don't be mad. Never mind what I say 'bout Puah. I . . . I didn't wanna die. To you, I freely come."

Samuel continued to stare at the doorway. Then, slowly, his eyes moved over to the wall where the tools were hanging, then over to the bales of hay. Finally, he locked eyes with Isaiah.

"Talk to me, Sam. Tell me something good," Isaiah said as he took one of Samuel's hands in both of his.

Samuel bit his bottom lip. He looked at an object hanging on the wall. He let his eyes linger over the ax. He admired its shape, longed to wield the sharp edge of it. He crossed his legs. Isaiah remained on his knees and so he was raised higher than Samuel. Samuel put his hand on Isaiah's thigh.

"This bump right here," Samuel said.

Isaiah smiled and touched Samuel's waist.

"This curve right here," Isaiah replied.

"The way your left arm move."

"How soft your lips is."

"Your pointy elbows."

"Your big forehead."

"Back of your neck where skin meet hair. 'Specially when you walking away."

"When you touch me here."

"The time I were too sick to move and you fetched me sweet water for wildflower tea."

Isaiah threw his arms around Samuel. He held him for a moment before weeping into his shoulder. Samuel held him tight, then he pushed him back so that he could see his face. His hands caressed his chest, then moved down to his navel. Isaiah reclined and Samuel moved forward and then rested his palm against Isaiah's firm belly. With his finger, he traced the boundaries of Isaiah's body.

"What you do to me?" Samuel asked.

He caressed Isaiah's face and Isaiah leaned into the caress. Isaiah smelled Samuel's hands, kissed them, then grabbed them and pressed them into his face.

"I didn't mean . . ." Samuel said.

"Folks never do."

Isaiah rolled over onto Samuel. He paused for a moment, hovered there slightly, enjoying the feeling of being taller for once. He descended a bit, leaned in, then a bit more, wondering if Samuel would let him without demanding that he go to the river and scrub the filth from himself. Finally, their navels touched. Breathing into each other, their bellies fluttered at the same time; sweaty, every time they inhaled, one's flesh would peel from the other's and it tickled. They laughed quietly.

Isaiah dove into Samuel, lips and teeth against his neck, hands gripped around his wrists. Samuel raised his legs and wrapped them around Isaiah's waist. With a heave, he turned them both over so that he was on top again and Isaiah's back was against the ground. Isaiah's foot knocked over the bucket. Samuel turned to watch the water soak into the dirt. Isaiah grabbed him and pulled him down so that their bodies pressed. Samuel writhed gently. He smiled. He looked at Isaiah.

"You gon' have to go to the well now," Isaiah said. He pressed his forehead against Samuel's.

"Now?" Samuel asked.

"When, then?" Isaiah closed his eyes.

"In the morning." Samuel said, his lips pressed against Isaiah's eyelids.

"And what we gon' do if we thirsty before then?" Isaiah opened his eyes, but only partly.

Samuel took a deep breath. "All right, then." He softly moved Isaiah aside. He got up and grabbed the bucket. Isaiah got up, too.

"I go with you."

Isaiah kissed Samuel, then he walked on ahead.

Samuel watched him from behind. He shook his head and continued to walk at a steady pace. As he reached the door, he looked over to the wall. The tools hung on rusty nails, but they were there. Just within reach. He looked at the ground and spit before jogging after Isaiah.

MACCABEES

He called for me," Samuel said, almost mumbling while filling the trough with slop. He shook it thoughtlessly out of the pail. Steam rose off of it. The hogs were squealing and pushing one another out of the way to get to it. The flies gathered around.

Isaiah froze, but only momentarily. Then he returned to shoveling the manure out of the pen and into a pile on the other side of the fence.

"I know you heard me," Samuel said, placing the pail down before picking up another.

Isaiah stopped shoveling.

"Yes. And there ain't nothing for me to say. You ain't got no choice. Just like I ain't have one."

"You wrong 'bout both those things."

Isaiah looked at Samuel as he emptied the last pail.

"Don't say that," Isaiah whispered, wanting to tell Samuel that he had already surrendered. The battle was over. There was no longer a need. Retreat. Retreat.

"There is choices. There is always choices. You just make wrong ones."

Isaiah felt that, just like it had been the fist that Samuel never raised at him, not the palm that had just before caressed his face after some coaxing. The rough-hewn but somehow still delicate hand that led down to the sinewy left arm, which was the protector of that troubled heart. Sometimes capable of such kindness—never forget the water carrier. But also, time had passed and no matter how hard you tried, this place crawled to a safe space inside you, leaving behind not just marks, but hatchlings to be warmed against your will by your own life's blood. And it didn't even give you the respect of telling you when they might hatch or if, when they did, the pain of it might show itself in the way you regarded a lover. Or, rather, in the way you allowed a lover to regard you.

Before Isaiah could protest, in his way, not in the pointed way that was Samuel's, they saw Maggie coming down the path. Despite her limp, Maggie always seemed to walk with purpose. Even if she was just passing by on her way to the river or to go see Essie, she had the stern face and upright character of a woman with a message. They only saw her smile a handful of times, but when she did, it was contagious. She wasn't a woman of big laughter like Be Auntie, but the small sounds that came from her mouth and the way her shoulders jerked when she was amused seemed to magnify the joy of anyone around. When Maggie was happy, all of Empty had reason to be. And when she wasn't? Well.

Isaiah dropped his shovel and ran to open the gate for her. When she walked through the opening, she pinched her dress in her fingers and raised it so its edge fluttered just above her ankles.

"Good morning, Miss Maggie," Isaiah said as he closed the gate behind her.

She nodded. She had a cloth in her hand, undoubtedly some meal she had managed to smuggle out of the Big House. She walked right up to Samuel.

"Good morning, Miss Maggie."

"Here," she said.

Maggie could be like that. She didn't seem to have the time for pleasantries. It was as though something inside of her needed to get to the heart of matters quickly, needed the truth to be laid bare as soon as it was able. Yet, with Samuel, it seemed that the particular truth sought always had some kindness attached. Maggie's kindness was prickly and thorned, but it was also beautiful to see coming from someone who had every reason to bristle at the very idea of kindness and hock-spit on it.

Samuel eyed the bundle suspiciously. He had never done that before.

"I ain't gon' eat no more of they food," he said, trying to dampen his tone so that it didn't come off as disrespectful to Maggie.

She laughed. "So you telling me you gon' starve to death? Ain't not a lick of nothing on this here plantation not they's—whether I hand it to you or not. Might as well take the best of it."

"Oh, I finna do just that, Miss Maggie."

"What now?"

"Miss Maggie, don't pay him no mind," Isaiah said with a frown.

"What's the matter?" Maggie raised an eyebrow as though she could sense that there was too much heat—or rather, not enough—coming off both of them. "Is this got to do with Amos's foolishness? Essie told me he sent her to bring a peace."

Neither of them replied.

"I know I just asked y'all a question."

"We can handle Amos," Samuel said.

"My foot," Maggie said and gave Samuel a suspicious look.

Samuel reminded her of someone she hadn't seen in a long, long while. Someone she had the good sense to put out of her mind and shut it so they couldn't come back in no matter how politely they asked. But yes, Samuel's face had a forgotten character: shiny skin whose source was its own light, eyelashes like a doe or something, eyes as big and oval as almonds, and heavy lips because the bottom one drooped like a studying infant taking in all of nature because it was all still new.

Yet his demeanor reminded her of someone else. The way his face welcomed but snatched itself away without a moment's notice felt quite familiar to her. And here she was—with an apology, wrapped in white cloth, on behalf of people who were beyond forgiveness—ready to be snatched up.

"Are you gon' take this or am I gon' have to eat it myself? I come all the way down here for you to stand beside yourself? Boy!"

Samuel glanced at Isaiah and then took the parcel from Maggie.

"Thank you, Miss Maggie," he said, head bowed.

"Mm-hmm," Maggie replied as she turned.

As she started to limp away, something black flashed across her back that made Samuel flinch, though he would deny it if anyone said they saw him. It flickered quickly, the blackness, like how light can sometimes do as it passes from sky to tree bough to ground. And he told himself that is exactly what happened, that it was light he saw and not shadow—even though no light he ever saw looked like the absence of it and there were no trees close enough to make light dance like that. But he was certain (but not really) that it wasn't the shadow returning to point its crooked finger at him for something he didn't do, denying the accusation without even knowing what the accusation was. Nah. It wasn't that. Couldn't be.

Isaiah moved ahead to open the gate anew for Maggie. "Thank you kindly for your trouble. Let me get this here gate for you again," Isaiah said. His soft eyes regarded her as one would royalty. Keen Maggie saw it there, sparkling in him. She appreciated the sentiment but knew that it was misapprehended and the young had to understand deeper things than pageantry.

"Don't put that on me," she said very seriously. "Unless you want harm to come."

Isaiah was confused and didn't understand what he'd done wrong, unsure of what he showed other than the awe he had for her, but he nodded as he closed the gate and watched her walk slowly back to the Big House.

Whatever Maggie brought with her wasn't just in the wrapped piece of cloth. Isaiah felt it, but Samuel felt it more. Maybe because he was the one holding on to her gift or because he was the one who didn't see (**No I didn't!** he kept telling himself) the not-a-shadow-can't-be streak across her back. Either way, whatever fight had been building in them seemed to be of secondary concern now.

"Timothy called for me," Samuel mumbled again.

Isaiah took a deep breath and held it. He let it out. Then, because what else could he do, he shrugged. Silently, grief shook his body.

"Don't," Samuel said, standing still in the same spot, holding the cloth in his left hand.

Don't what, cry or shrug? Isaiah didn't know and he was too tired to ask. But he did think about the ways in which his body wasn't his own and how that condition showed up uniquely for everyone whose personhood wasn't just disputed but denied. Swirling beneath him were the ways in which not having lawful claim to yourself diminished you, yes, but in another way, condemned those who invented the disconnection. He hoped. Maybe not in this realm, but absolutely in others—if there were others. Matching hard for hard did nothing but create wreckage. But being soft, while beautiful, was subject to being torn asunder by the harder thing. What other answer was there then but to be some kind of flexible? Stretch further so that there was too much difficulty in trying to pull you apart?

Samuel was a hard thing. There was no use in trying to make him anything other than that. And he had every right, even if sometimes he didn't understand how his rigidity, that impenetrable door that Puah was perhaps the first one to notice, was built up in the wrong direction. But some people thought hard was the answer and believed that rather than bend, you had to try to snap them in half because they were confident that you couldn't.

Isaiah, however, knew of the sporadic but attendant softness inside Samuel. Ground cover rocky, yes, but soil giving.

And Samuel only half trusted him with that knowledge—preferred, actually, if Isaiah didn't know at all. So some things he kept to himself. The shadow with the pointing hand would be one of them. It was in the barn, he could admit to that, but it wasn't in the woods or riding Maggie's back like a strapped babe.

A mutual sigh released them from having to

continue the argument. No one had to willingly re-
lent or gloat over a victory. The inhalation then ex-
halation of breath provided enough room for them
both to hold on to a little bit of dignity even in the
middle of desecration.

Samuel looked down at the bundle in his hand.
He looked up and motioned with his head for Isaiah
to follow him as he walked around to the back of the
barn. Isaiah walked behind him, tracing Samuel's
steps, walking in them sometimes and sometimes
making his own path through the chicory and
spurge. When they came to the rear center of the
barn, where the sun was bright with anger and the
knothole that betrayed them was a kind of memo-
rial, Samuel stopped. Isaiah walked a bit farther, to
where there was a little bit of shade because a yellow
pine, not thirty years old yet, was in the process of
spreading itself there, and he found its scent reassuring because of the way it hid his own.

He turned to look at Samuel. Moving against his
nature because there was the possibility of accusa-
tory shadow, he walked over to where Isaiah was
and sat down at the base of the tree. Isaiah sat down
next to him. Samuel flattened his lap and unfastened
Maggie's cloth. And what did they have here? A veri-
table feast of boiled eggs, fried ham, blackberry jelly
on thick slices of bread, two whole nectarines, and a
big ol' hunk of brown cake.

"Mercy," Isaiah said.

Samuel didn't want to remember the shadow he

didn't see. He picked up a nectarine and gestured for Isaiah to take one for himself. Almost at the same time, they bit into them. The juices ran down their faces. Isaiah wiped the juice away but Samuel didn't. He stared ahead at the rear of the barn.

Neither of them spoke, but they each continued to eat, picking things from the cloth, slowly, carefully, one with grateful hands, the other with discerning ones, like ritual, but without prayer because they didn't need one, and respect was freely given.

But still, it was solemn-like, holy, as unto a last-last supper.

The Revelation of Judas

Sometimes, in Mississippi, maybe in the whole world, except one other place lost to memory, the sky was heavy. It was thick with something unseen but surely felt. Maggie looked up to it as she swept the porch and had the feeling that something was looking back at her. It was smiling, whatever it was. But the smile wasn't the kind to bring comfort. It was the same smile a man had sometimes, the wrong kind of man, the kind whose curling lips were a warning that he was prone to unpredictable acts, that he thought he was entitled to touch what he wanted to touch, take what he wanted to take, spoil what he wanted to spoil, and all of that was his birthright for merely existing. She didn't know where men got that idea from. But it was one they shared with whoever was willing to follow.

Perhaps the heaviness was just a rain on its way. Maggie sniffed the air and yes, it had the whiff of moisture and dirt that preceded storm. But there was something else there, too: a bright and pointy smell, like a star plucked from the nighttime and brought low before it dimmed forever. No one could touch it, though, for it was hot enough to singe hairs. There was something coming. Maggie put the broom up against the Big House and dug in her apron pocket. She pulled out a handful of pig bones. She descended the stairs. She cleared a path of dirt using her foot to brush aside pebbles and dead leaves. She stooped down as low as she could before the hip caused her to wince. Then she threw the bones and closed her eyes. When she opened them, she blinked. Then she blinked again. And again and again. Finally, her eyes widened.

No, it can't be! Lies! He wouldn't dare.

INSIDE HIS SHACK, Amos awoke with a dull ache bumping inside his head. It was from all the rattling that he heard in his dream. No sights, no colors, just the sound of a rattling, like bones, which was off rhythm with his breath, but he wouldn't read that as a sign, not a bad one at least. He rolled in his pallet, away from Essie and Solomon, and the stiffness between his legs made him think briefly about Be

Auntie and if he should go to her this early in the morning, which he had never done because night had been their portion. And it was strange to him that Essie hadn't said a word, didn't ask a single question about where he roamed in the dark, out into a night where James and his fellow jackals were poised to invent a reason, any reason, to choke, whip, or shoot.

"They tried to run, Paul," they would say of a people whose legs were so mangled from the field that they could barely drag, much less head for the North. And Paul would take them at their word not because he believed them but because the alternative was to believe the mangled people, and both God and law, as well as ownership of land, prevented him from doing that.

Amos wasn't a fool. He realized the god he now served wasn't the will of his people. But he knew it could be convinced to be. More than worshipped, all gods wanted to be adored, and his people had that in them more than Paul's: to abide more, rejoice more, revere more, surrender more; climb on top of a golden pyre and burn more. He had seen it in the circle of trees. The way his people swayed, the way they rocked, the way they offered themselves up willingly to the cloudy sky above, and the way they sang together in a harmony that wasn't rehearsed because people who shared the same bitter lot connected in ways unseen by nature.

He covered his nakedness not out of shame but out of obligation. Massa Paul would think it savagery and Missy Ruth, perhaps, an invitation. He cloaked himself in ratty clothes, but at least they were clean. He had beaten them against the rocks himself and soaked them in a bucket of lavender water. He couldn't ask Essie to do that **and** be kind to the burden that nursed at her breast; that would be too much.

He dressed quietly as Essie and Solomon snored and wheezed asleep, unmoved by his waking. He walked to the door, pushed aside the covering, and stepped out into the cloudy, humid morning. **The rain will take care of this,** he thought, feeling the stickiness that sapped strength and beaded in droplets on his forehead. He looked to the right, squinting, to see the big red thing that was the barn. It cast a looming shadow in the light of the rising sun behind him. He shook his head. Had they only listened. Had they only heeded. Had they only put the people above themselves, just a little; given up what everyone worth their weight in cotton had to give up in order to survive relatively unscathed—even though "unscathed" was a wholesome and comforting lie.

They felt like sons to him, particularly Isaiah, who was his charge, given to him by a mother who didn't tell Amos what her name was, but did manage to whisper to him the child's name, which Amos thought sounded like a howling. He was, however, emboldened by the fact that this woman had managed to hang on to her old ways even in the blue ridges of Georgia and had entrusted him to ensure her child would carry those ways with him if only in name.

He was waiting until Isaiah had become a man, or if he had the inkling that either one of them was going to be sold away, before Amos revealed Isaiah to himself. **You know your name is Kayode? Haha! No, not kie-oh-TEE. Kuh-yo-DAY. Your mam tell me it mean "he brings joy" in the old tongue of her mother's mother. Must be that in her misery-misery world, you one of the only things that ever make her smile truly. Yes suh. Oh, what's that? Where was she? In Georgia, sure 'nough. Yes, your pappy was there too, but it be best if'n I don't say what I saw of him that wet and greedy day other than I remember this: your face is his face.**

It would have been their own quiet celebration, something Isaiah could have taken back with him into that barn and shared with Samuel, something Amos himself could have brought back to Essie, helping all of them to endure the breeding that had to be done so that they could **live** live, even if just in short bursts in the dark, rather than just survive.

He didn't mean to use it as extortion. He saw the look on Isaiah's face when he wouldn't reveal it. There, then, he remembered Isaiah's father's face: all twisted up in the way it does when the soul is trying to leave the body. The difference between grief and sorrow lay there, a cavern in the face that threatened

heartbreak for all witnesses, or, in Amos's new language, the threat of being turned to living salt, to be
like an upright but unmoving sea.

In the brand-new tongue of his master's people, he
had contemplated a different trinity. If Samuel and
Isaiah's natures rose only in each other's company,
then why not allow them each other and the pleasure
of one more? Samuel and Isaiah, father and son; he
wasn't sure what the order was there. Samuel was
bigger, but one could never know with twisted shadows. Puah could be the Holy Ghost. Three to make
one. One out of three. This might have been the way,
the truth, the light.

But, no. His gut, which is to say, his god, told him
that this would have been even more obscene than
what was already happening in the lair of the golden
calf, would open up caverns that led to no one knows
where. Besides that, Amos knew not near none of
them would have it. Shame was a sturdy master with
strong legs and clinging embrace.

He was almost primed to accept failure—until he
dreamed that he saw Essie in their shack, turned to
the side, staring at the wall, Solomon crawling at her
feet and pulling at the edge of her dress.

"Paul saw me," she muttered. "He **saw** me."

That was it. Samuel and Isaiah left him no choice.
They had rebuked all entreaties, no matter how reasonable. The stubbornness of youth had left them
incapable of compromise. If they were determined to
make this a war, then this was Amos's only strategy:

always, always, the many must have its safety over the few.

This would be his final act, he believed. Yes, that was what rumbled inside him. His mouth began to bend into the cavern he hoped never to see again. Eyes misty, he held it all back. He wiped his face with his hands and, surprisingly, took on the weight of clouds above. In them, though, he saw a dark something, waiting for him, ready, it seemed, to raise its sword in battle if it had to.

MAGGIE HELD HER HAND up before her, almost expecting it, alone, to stop Amos in his tracks. She had briefly forgotten how powerful Paul's god was. And she was, after all, standing on the land that was now his, the very land that his god waged war on, defeating the gods that used to reign here on their own sacred territory, which Maggie didn't even know was possible. With all of the force that sustained them right beneath their feet, how was it that these old gods, who weren't so unfamiliar to her people's gods, succumbed to the vigor of the newer and less wise? What chance did she have against that kind of power, removed as she was from the land where she should have been born and the people she should have been born to?

What she didn't understand was how Amos had been able to find this god's favor. He who had militarized his people—armed them with icy glares,

boom-cannons, ships that could survive the tumultu-
ous gray waters, and His leather-bound instruction—
and led them to bounty. And what bounty meant to
them was everything: not just the land, but the trees,
the animals, the voices, the children. This god had
expressed nothing but disdain for them and yet, here
it was, fully shining on Amos in such a way that he
paid her hand, which was held there by the voices
and the shadows, no heed.

"Don't cross these bones!" Maggie said loudly, not
caring, for the moment, who heard her.

Amos continued to walk toward the Big House.
Maggie's mouth dropped. She moved back some.
Quickly, she picked up a stick and drew a circle with
an X inside it, then spit. Amos continued right past
it. Stunned, she scuttled back even more. She reached
into her apron pocket and pulled out a pouch. Inside
it was rock salt. She threw it on the ground in front
of Amos and finally, he stopped. He looked down at
the pouch in front of his feet.

"Cross that and not near none of us can stop what
happens next," Maggie said.

"I shoulda known you was the dark cloud," Amos
said calmly. "This a mistake, Mag. I ain't got no
quarrel with you."

"What you finna do—I got a **quarrel** with **that.**"
She put her hands on her hips.

"I been patient. I tried to . . ."

"'Patient'? You talking they words now; talk ours."

Amos swatted away a fly, or maybe it was Maggie's words. In either event, his hand went up by his face in a flurry. When he finally came to a stop, Maggie eyed him up and down.

"You won't like this before. I had seen you, so tender with Essie, up full in your manness, not a stitch of harm to you. But now," Maggie shook her head. "It's a bone-chilly that freeze all inside things. Your eyes starting to turn blue; I see it. Blue, you hear me?"

"How 'bout your'n circle, Maggie? You would see that expand or broke?"

No, Be Auntie ain't tell this man! For us only! Those the rules. Oh, that girl something else! That was all right. Maggie had some private knowledge of her own.

"Were you in the dark or in the light?" Maggie said, speaking of the particular anointing hovering over Amos like a horde of gnats. "Did you fall forward or backward?"

Amos didn't answer but his silence told Maggie what she needed to know.

"And you still took heed? You know better."

Amos sighed and turned around, looking past the willow tree, past the cotton field, and into the woods, toward the circle of trees. Maggie knew what he was doing. He was gathering strength to get past the salt that his god knew the sting of all too well. She reached out and touched Amos's shoulder. She heard something. It was Amos's voice but not coming from his mouth. It was coming from the sky—no, from the clouds themselves. And this is what happened when Amos of the sky spoke:

Hearts pounded then stopped then pounded again. There were sharp intakes of breath and then long, wet exhalations. People stood up with the speed of lightning bolts and shouted louder than they were allowed. And then they looked to the sky and closed their eyes. Some of them swayed. Some of them wept. All of this was nothing but reprieve. A moment away while still there and, therefore, necessary, priceless.

Maggie snatched her hand away. She stood there shaking with fury when Amos turned back to face her.

"You see?" he asked. "You see?"

She slapped him. Dead in the face. She slapped him hard enough that spit flew from his mouth and she saw exactly where it landed and she was glad because it would be of some use. Her upturned chin told him that whatever she saw, rather heard, from the clouds, mattered less than what she could perceive on the ground. She would show him.

This was their impasse: each responding to a slight the one claims the other invoked. The truth lost both to time and to people who never understand the point of ritual. Or who understood it all too well.

Amos, tired of wielding what they knew against each other, decided it was time for risk. He looked Maggie directly in the eye, then he looked down. He

stepped right on the salt pouch before kicking it full
force across the weeds. Maggie jerked in disbelief.

"You . . . you would save the right-this-instant and
forfeit the long-tomorrow?"

Amos held his head up and his lips formed defiance, though there was a tiny bit of fear in it. He
moved Maggie aside as gently as he could and she
swung at him, hitting him on his back. He stumbled, but he didn't stray. He walked straight ahead.
Maggie grabbed at his shirt and he pulled her off. She
came back at him and he swung her around and she
hit the ground, landing on her bad hip. She balled
up her fists and cussed Amos deep in her throat. He
returned some cusses of his own. She looked back to
see if she could see where his landed.

She couldn't.

Meanwhile, Amos walked up the stairs to the Big
House and Maggie crawled on the ground. The first
drops of rain began to fall.

Maggie grabbed her chest. **He was gon' walk in
through the front door! He had the gumption (he
called it "the blood") to walk right in through
the front like a toubab.** This simply confirmed
what Maggie's spirit had told her all along. Peace
was tricky. There was a matter of sacrifice involved,
but rarely did the peacemaker sacrifice themselves
as much as they were willing to sacrifice some other,
lead them up to the stake to get burned, comforting them as they were about to be lit up so that

everything on earth and in the heavens could see, telling them, **Don't worry; glory's next.**

Fuck glory! Give us what's ours by right, and what's ours by right is our skin tint, skin, our breath scent, breath, our eye blink, our feet steps! Who broke the covenant with creation such that a person could be a cow or a carriage? Release yourself from that low-down place where another's pain is your fortune. Get up, you hear me? Cleanse your outhouse spirit and set yourself to leave us be! Otherwise, you leave us no choice.

Those words were in her head, but they came from somewhere else. Voices, yes; more than six.

As Amos prepared to walk through the door, Maggie struggled to her feet. She looked over at the barn. The pig bones were still on the ground, but in her tussle with Amos, they had been rearranged. She limped over to them and took a deep breath. There was a new portent. She nodded and then turned to walk toward the barn as fast as her hurt could take her.

In her head, the voices continued: **Don't fret, Maggie. You know you hung on as mightily as you could.**

Amos was framed by the doorway. And what was it to walk in through the front door and march proudly, chest out, but head ready at any moment to bow? They allowed Maggie to do it as keeper of the house, so there had been a precedent. And after he was gone to the far-off somewhere, where weary bones lay in rest and the tired soul was welcomed with open arms into the peaceful bosom of Abraham, some other who would come after him would have a path through treacherous terrain. And Amos, from the majesty of what he and he alone called the Upper Room, would smile like God did because he, too, would see what he did was good.

He opened the door and walked in. Slow, steady steps, and tracking no dirt on the floor; Amos was careful. Upon reaching the oak door of Paul's study, beyond which he heard the rustling of papers, Amos noticed a marking. It was small enough to be nearly imperceptible. The scythe and lightning symbol no bigger than a boll weevil carved in the dead center of the door. Amos knew it immediately to be a rune of some kind, perhaps symbolizing the Lord, but hadn't the Lord asked not for graven images that weren't of His hand or word? To place no other before Him meant that all old gods, all of them, had to die, whether in who-really-named-it Africa, or Europe, or even in this here place falsely called America.

Hm. Maybe one day he might muster up the courage to ask Massa Paul about it himself. Maybe when Massa Paul was in one of his more somber moods, after having tasted the dazzling warmth of the spirits he took kindly to after a long hard day of telling people to work harder. Yes, that was the best time to find out, when Paul was fine and mellow and a nigger's inquiry wouldn't be seen as heresy.

Paul saw me.

A Holy Trinity.

Amos raised his hands in prayer.

Go 'head, Amos, knock on that door. Long ago, Moses also led his people through the furious waters. And they all made it out, cleansed, right on the other side.

CHRONICLES

The first mistake you made was in trying to reason with it.

Do you hear us?

You attempted to understand the source, hear the beat, find the rhythm for something that sprang from chaos (never, never look into the heart of that which has no heart to speak of). Foolish.

You sought the nature of something that occurred by accident so has no nature at all. Things without a nature always seek one, you see, and can only obtain one through plunder and then consumption. They have a name. They all have a name: Separation.

You have been warned.

In this, there is only so much we can tell you given our purposeful isolation. This is why it is there, you know, the bush: to insulate, to protect. Though as you have already surmised it is no match for curiosity. They tumbled down from the great mountains and they washed up from the wide sea. We were assaulted from both sides. We were doomed.

There are many stories. These stories are far older than we are. We cannot tell you for certain which of them is true. What we can verify is the outcome. The outcome is always the same: in the end, death. But before death, the unspeakable.

There are many stories to tell. Here is one:

He was forbidden from engaging in the practices that drew him away from his people and into the lair of his demise, but he was arrogant and refused to heed the warnings. He took women and subjected them to things without their consent. These were among the very first rapes. Born of these colossal blasphemies were children without our marks upon them. This was not their fault, but the blight was undeniable. As horrific as all of that was, that was not even the difficult part.

The difficult part was in realizing that all abandoned children seek vengeance.

And most will have it.

BEL AND THE DRAGON

The ship rocked and made everyone sick, but then the whole thing smelled of sickness already. Birds were confused. The rot had made them believe there was a feast to be had when there wasn't. Driven wild, they sat perched on masts and pecked at the scent, beaks snapping at nothing at first, then at one another before they finally dove into the ocean and sometimes came back up, their mouths filled with something other than salt water. Happy, then, to fly away, but still confused about the seductive odor of death lingering.

It was coming from the stomach of the ship where not even birds' eyes were keen enough to penetrate. Hidden, but not a secret to those with other kinds of appetites. The crew, pissy and gruff, sang rough-hewn songs and even those could only reach the bottom by great force. Grief's melody, in the strange tongue of a ravenous people. Laughter that stung dripped through the boards down onto the chains and onto the flesh not fully digested in the belly. Where is hope? Trapped in the ribs, which held them in place when they longed to be shat out—yes, even shat out would be better than the suffocation that allowed them yet to breathe.

Someone screamed out in the dark, a voice that Kosii couldn't understand, but its rhythms were familiar, spoke to his blackest parts in the midst of incomprehension. The flashes of light that barged in—when one of the skinless fools came down to check on the chains, and to bring not enough water and inedible slop—allowed him the opportunity to snatch glimpses of his surroundings: other bodies chained to him and around him. Between inhaling and vomiting up the funk, and eyelids squeezed shut from the effort, he opened his and the light hurt, too, but he looked around to see if there were any people marked like him with the Kosongo symbol of eternity: the snake kissing its tail and the woman at the center. But there were too many shadows. There were too many wails and too many men crying and too many women screaming and too many people silent from death. He couldn't hold on to who he knew he was. There was a puddle of blood on the floor, after all, and the woman next to him, big with child, had her legs spread as far as she could get them, which was not far enough, and the baby's feet were coming first. If there were midwives among them, they were likewise chained. His mother caught babies and he watched. He could have done it, but he couldn't lift his hands. So the baby would die and he would watch and wouldn't even be able to tell the woman that he was sorry for her loss because he couldn't speak her language and by the time he was able to find a way to lay a hand on her ankle after tugging and tugging at the chains, she would have bled out and he would be touching an uncovered, unoiled corpse, and only elders were allowed to do so. He could only moan his mourning and hoped that in her last moments, she knew that it was for her and her baby.

He slept a sleepless sleep, eyes never fully shut, body never truly at rest. He couldn't unprepare himself for the turmoil that could, at any moment, lie down next to him and everyone else like a dutiful lover.

"Elewa," he whispered.

He lost track of him at the shore. They, the ghost cannibals, had burned everything: Semjula's canes, Mother's drums, Father's blankets. The royal jewels and metals from the tips of spears they stole: adorned themselves in profane ways with them, carried them in their mouths, intended to melt pieces down to use as teeth. Gaudy displays of ignorance, no respect for the age of the items, how they had been passed down for hundreds of years from mother to son, father to daughter, each holding a piece of those who held them, blue, red, gentle, strong, shimmering once, but now stripped of their luster, debased in the grimy hands of thieves, victorious criminals who had crafted great vessels, traveled from the distant universe, but didn't have the good sense to wash their hands before they ate. Shameless.

Kosii and Elewa had just stumbled, exhausted, out of the forest and were already separated by ten people between, in the line of joined iron collars. The skinless men had even put the craven devices on Semjula, whose neck was designed only for turquoise, shells, and a child's embrace. People had to hold her up and **still** the cuts were deep.

Of his people, he saw only Semjula and, down the line, Elewa, who was battered and bruised. He committed to memory each place Elewa was marked for he would repay his captors in kind. He looked frantically for his family, for King Akusa, but saw only faces of neighboring villagers and others who must have been from remote and distant lands, stolen also. It didn't matter. They were each leaving footprints on a shore he knew none of them would ever see again, and the womb water wouldn't even give them the decency to leave their footprints untouched so that the land would always remember the shape of its children.

Every time he turned to look at Elewa to reassure him, one of the strange skins would yell or strike Kosii. They were fortunate that they had chained him. But all chains were loosed eventually. Though he thought himself a forgiving man who sought solutions and camaraderie, these walking blights, these dead risen had done nothing to deserve his gentle nature. With each step he took, they earned only additional parts of his ire—and they seemed giddy at the prospect, as if they couldn't imagine his ever being a threat, not so long as they kept a firm grasp on the armaments that clapped like the heavens.

One by one, they were loaded onto one of the ships, larger than anything Kosii had ever seen in his life, somehow able to float atop the womb like they had no weight, some kind of powerful spell. They were led down into the dankness of the spell-cast behemoth where rodents chattered and ran about, and where it smelled of soul death. They would be eaten, he was certain. These revived dead had captured them as a food source, would replenish themselves and regain their spirit, vigor, and perhaps their color, by ingesting them. Maybe they wouldn't even give them the honor of killing them first but would eat them alive as they watched themselves being consumed.

He thought his eyes were accustomed to darkness, but this was a different kind entirely. This dark had nothing to do with inky night or ancestral shadows or the ebony of playmates and lovers. No, this dark lived inside the captors like a chasm that nothing could ever fill no matter what was tossed into it. But that didn't stop them from trying, from inventing things to try. Not a bridge, though. They had decided at some point never to be so creative, that the tug downward was too strong, had caressed secret parts of them too flagrantly to give it up. So into the hole they pushed everything, sometimes even their own children, anticipating the sound that would indicate that a bottom had been achieved and they could rejoice in the fact that the dark did indeed have its limits, too. But that sound never came. What came instead was the whistling of things still falling, forever, without end.

This was the kind of dark that engulfed Kosii now as he lay foot to head with the other captives, chained together, trapped in spaces where there wasn't even room to raise their heads or excuse themselves to pass waste. To bend a knee meant knocking into the wood slats above or the person adjacent. Prostrate was the only answer; stillness the sole misery. The insects and rodents occasionally breaking the periods of thirst and hunger.

Kosii thanked the ancestors that he couldn't see himself. No lake or river to peer into to see his face reflected back. The things that made him smile now were too foreign to his nature to be talked about, much less gazed upon. People brought so low should at least have the privilege of distraction. Who could watch themselves being gobbled up and live to tell the children? All of the witnesses were dead; the testimony would end here.

Why hadn't word of the life-snatchers reached his village in time for them to mount a suitable defense? Perhaps it was because some of the other villages despised King Akusa. The Kosongo people had been one of the few to maintain the original order, and it vexed some of the other kings that a woman should call herself such. These men had been stripped of their memories as surely as if someone cut into their heads with malice and allowed them to be drained of all that had been passed to them, for millennia, through blood. And the shame of it was how easy it could have been retrieved if any of them had been willing to reclaim the stained sand just beneath their feet. But they were belligerent, which gave spite its sustenance.

So it was spitefulness, Kosii concluded, that allowed them to be left wide open for anything to swoop in and grab them up, claws digging into their innards.

He wished he could curse in all languages so that both the life-snatchers and the traitors who shared his chains would feel the universe's wrath. He hadn't even enough moisture in his mouth to spit.

"Elewa," he said as loud as he could with a parched throat.

The silence that responded pierced him in odd places: the palms of his hands, the back of his neck, his temples. There was no point in licking his lips. Saliva ran dry. If only there was enough moisture for tears.

"Why?" was the thing that needled its way into the small of his back and ensured his discomfort. He couldn't think of a single treachery they committed that could explain this predicament. Why hadn't the ancestors warned them? The skinless's god was mighty, then, even in his solitary status. Kosii shuddered before the might of their three-headed god, who had managed to block out the ancestors as simply as a cloud could sit in front of the sun, eat up rays, and cast a shadow over everything. He took a little bit of comfort in knowing that clouds pass and the sun eventually regains reign. But he also knew that that took time and the plane on which this battle was being held moved at its own pace. What felt like generation after generation to him and his people was, to the ancestors, merely a blink. His certainty wavered. By the time they defeated the three-headed thing, would the ancestors even recognize the people they engaged in battle with Triple-Head to save?

These risen-from-dead people; their lack of skin and their peculiar appetites scared Kosii. He never heard of such a people.

No.

Wait.

That was a lie.

As a child, his father told him of the Great War when the people came down from the distant mountains with torches, and bows and arrows.

"They had skulls around their necks," Tagundu said. "Human. No bigger than your own."

Tagundu tapped Kosii on top of the head when he said that. It sent a chill through him.

"Their king was against it, so they killed her.

Stabbed her with her own spear and burned her alive."
Tagundu looked away from his son. "They wanted
to kill some of us, the men mostly. They wanted to
make the women . . . tools."

"Why?" Kosii asked then. Tagundu looked at him.
The upward arch of Tagundu's eyebrows displayed
his inadequacy to the task of explaining, revealed the
guilt stemming from what he would leave out.

"My son, some people's hearts, they just . . ." He
pressed Kosii's hands against his chest. "They just
beat the wrong way."

Kosii just stared at his father, unsatisfied, unable
to make out the shape of things, even when they
were right at his fingertips. He had never seen the
mountain people, never heard the clank of the skulls
around their necks, wasn't pierced by their weapons,
so he could afford to bury what his father told him,
unfinished as it was. He was, after all, surrounded
by people who had only loved and protected him.
The only weapons he had ever held were for hunting or ceremony. The only fights he participated in
were practice, playful. All of it misleading. His father knew better and tried to tell him, but he had
left out the whole and thus the ends of Kosii's small
circle couldn't touch. Inside it, there was no room for
mountain people and skull necklaces, just joy.

He wondered now if the people who built vessels
big enough to swallow entire villages conspired with
the mountains to destroy everything in between. The
chains were proof.

"Does anyone here speak my tongue?" he croaked.

A man turned toward him but had no tongue in his mouth with which to speak.

Kosii's eyes widened. He lost his breath and tried desperately to find it. His chest heaved quickly and he closed his eyes tightly. After a moment, when his breathing became normal again, he opened his eyes and saw the man again.

"I see you," Kosii said, quivering. "I see you. I see you."

The man closed his eyes, lips mouthing what might have been his village's prayer. Or maybe he was a mountain man double-crossed. There was no way to tell, no one to trust.

Across Kosii's mind ran images of his mother and father, and King Akusa raised her spear and chastised him for not letting the lion in him roam freely. And there was Semjula caressing him and telling him to pay the king no mind; her spirit was set for war and the ancestors had other plans for him. **Beat your drum,** Semjula said to him enough times that it had stretched itself over every hollowness like skin and clamored to be handled for its rhythm. He would need to be the keeper of memory so that everything Kosongo, down to the dust of the ground, would live on. Whatever far-off place they would be taken to, of skinless cannibals and land that despised all those to whom it didn't give birth. Wherever King Akusa was now, if she had been cursed to survive the cannibal's good aim, he hoped that some Kosongo were with her, too, and when she was removed from the vessel, they had sense enough to adorn her with red feathers and not let her feet touch the ground.

In the early hours, the skinless had descended once more into the bowels, bringing with them salt and light, and also laughter and wilderness. They had the nervous, itchy hands of people who had no control over their passions, spitting into their palms and rubbing them together. That didn't get rid of the dirt but merely moved it around, thinned it out, gave only the appearance of cleanliness, and the smell made that plain. But they walked about like men who believed their hands unsoiled nonetheless. Smiling even as they coughed, they turned up their noses and held their breath. This funk was of their own making, so their gagging garnered no sympathy.

Slowly, they went down the line of chained people trapped in the rib cage, moaning and gasping for air. One of them banged on a person's foot and then held it. The other one with the jangling metal in his hands came behind him and unlocked the shackles from the ankles, the hands, and the neck. They pulled the lifeless body from its unrestful place. They were mean about it, not handling the woman's remains with any delicacy whatsoever. Ruffians about their task, they seemed to revel and complain at once about what they had been charged with doing. They carried her, uncovered, up into the light. One kicked the door closed behind him.

The ship bellowed before it dipped down and then

back up again, and things rolled from one side to the other. Kosii listened to the cycle. Something, maybe a cup, clinking then rumbling to the opposite wall and clinking again. Perhaps in another place, at another time, the noise would soothe him, be some sort of nighttime song into which he could dream. And in the dreaming, he and Elewa led the hunt, capturing grand and succulent pheasant, which they cleaned and made into stew. Uncle Ketwa had taught him how to season and so every bit of meat was sucked from the bones and there wasn't a drop of stock left. They fed each other roasted banana, which Elewa liked smashed and mixed with mango and coconut water. They were too tired to clean up, so they left the mess for tomorrow and gazed at each other lazily, smiling like drunkards, until the darkness and the smell of impending rain had pushed them into each other's arms.

"What shall we do with the feathers?" Elewa asked.

"Let us make you a crown."

But it was daytime and the light once again barged into the room and the two skinless men stomped down the stairs and surveyed the captives. They walked all the way over to the far end, holding their noses, walking uncarefully, not paying attention to whom they climbed over or stepped on. One of them moved ahead, into the far corner where the light couldn't reach, where rats played, where there was human silence and the air of rot.

Body after body hefted and carried out to be tossed

aside like food gone sour. Not even the dignity of a pyre. He counted the bodies. Three. Eight. Twelve.

Then number seventeen.

And the words couldn't leave his lips. Stuck in the crevices of his mouth and tying his tongue. He wanted to scream, but a lump lodged itself in his throat and the air couldn't flow. He coughed until the tears, finally, from somewhere, somehow, ran and the saliva, too, leaked, and his face pulled itself into foolishness.

Elewa's body had managed to maintain its beauty. Aside from some bruises and his half-open eyes, he looked like he was enjoying a princely slumber. Had he been carried higher, above their heads, it would have taken on the character of a celebration—reaching puberty, the first hunt, the calling of the ancestors, the crowning of a king. Kosii stretched out his arms as far as the chains would allow before the rusty metal dug into his wrists and droplets of blood hit the floor. It was almost intentional, the arc the spilling blood formed. The perfect circles themselves forming a larger circle. Almost a head. Almost a tail. Almost infinity closing in on itself, just right there at the bottom, beneath all notice.

They were jumbled when they came out, his words. Mixed in with his dribble, they were only clear to him.

"A curse. A curse upon you and all of your progeny. May you writhe in ever-pain. May you never find satisfaction. May your children eat themselves alive."

But it was too late and the curse held no meaning because it was redundant. Kosii's hands fell to his sides. **Disaster,** he thought. **A pure, plain disaster.** Not only because of what he had already lost, but also because of what he would have to lose.

He had, after all, made Elewa's seven aunts a promise.

PAUL

Paul was just a boy, no more than seven or eight, when his father, Jonah, led him into the middle of everything and exhaled. Jonah made a full spin and spread his arms open wide. Then he laughed. He laughed and laughed and then patted Paul on the back before resting his hand on Paul's shoulder.

"See, boy? Look," Jonah said, pointing.

Pointing to what? Treetops? Tall grass? A deer that stood frozen in his gaze? All of it, Paul figured. Yes, Paul saw those things. But what he saw most readily was his father's hand on his shoulder. It was warm and firm and sent a charge through him. Had his father forgotten himself? This was their first intimacy, and Paul had, for the first time, felt like the blood of his father's blood: his living, breathing offspring: his son. Paul looked at his father and his father looked back at him and smiled.

"This is everything," Jonah said, looking out at the land that was his because—because God willed it.

And Paul had watched as the very land turned Jonah from a miserable man—who barely spoke, who was spiteful and covetous, not even softened by the forgiveness of his wife, Paul's mother, Elizabeth— into the father Paul had always hoped would show up. How, then, could it **not** be worshipped? In their joined grasp, not unlike hands pressed together for morning grace, it had been razed. Yes, raised up in their very hands, together. The most important thing now, his father told him: Grow. Gather. Keep. Because then, in the echoing halls, and even in future whispers, they will build monuments in your honor and you will be remembered not for your failures— not for your stumbles or your transgressions or your kills—but for only your greatest triumphs.

Paul didn't doubt that this was true, but it was Elizabeth whom he watched till the fields until her body could take no more. When she took ill, laid up in her bed, almost motionless if not for the smile that rose across her face whenever he came in to see her, Paul had never before lost anything, and the thought that he could lose his most precious thing—the one who had given him everything: life, milk, and a name that was her father's—made something inside him crumble.

By the time Elizabeth began to tremor and bleed,

not respond to Paul's or his father's voice, and soon, not respond at all, both boy and man silently agreed that the only way to honor her was to name everything that belonged to them after her, which was another kind of immortality. Jonah called it the Elizabeth Plantation. He committed himself to it—accumulating slaves, hiring hands, raising animals, and planting cotton damn near to the horizon—as though the "plantation" part of the name was merely a formality.

Then, when Jonah became as tired as Elizabeth had, when his hands wouldn't stop twitching and fevers had left him parched and drained, he, too, offered himself up in tribute to the land that was his by legal right, if not by the blood fact that it had already claimed his wife.

Paul liked to think that his mother and father were both looking down on him, protecting him, magnifying his favor in the eyes of God, because look at what he had done: he had built upon the foundation they left to him and had gathered the enormous wealth that they had twisted their bodies seeking. His parents were **comfortable;** they had provided him a decent life and he couldn't remember a single hungry day. But they were never **this,** not even with full access to the law of the land—and beyond the law, the very **ethos** of it—that said, **No one can stop you; take as much as you damn well please!**

As God had passed destiny down to his father, and his father down to him, Paul saw it as his duty to ensure that Timothy also received this Word. For in the beginning, before all else, there was the Word and the Word wasn't merely with God: the Word **was** God. The first utterance, the primary incantation, the initial spell that willed itself into being from nowhere, turned nothing into everything, and had, itself, always been there in its potential, needing only to express itself through action for existence to exist. A power so grand that all it took was a breath to make the unreal real and pull the seen from the unseen.

When Timothy first came back home, Paul had brought him out to the same spot his father took him to, pointed to the same treetops, smiled at the same horizon, spun with the same openness. And when his hand landed on Timothy's shoulder, Paul felt the same unexpected giddiness that he was certain was the thing that took Jonah from choke to laughter. But when Timothy looked up at him, the boy's eyes were blue with worry and there was no awe. There were no jolts of joy reverberating between them. There was only the distinct scent of cotton blossom heavy in the air and the wind blowing at the tops of both of their heads.

Looking to the dark clouds in the distance, before looking back up at his father, Timothy asked, "Rain?"

Rain. Paul sat at the dinner table later that night staring at Timothy. As evening surrounded them, he looked at his son with the candles giving off only enough light to see him, and so shadows swayed on all of their faces, and the eyes of the servants glowed. Would it have been astute to point out that the expanse of the land itself—which stretched from river to woods, from sunup to sundown—was living proof of his righteousness? That ownership was assuredly confirmation?

Of what?

Of things being precisely the way they were supposed to be.

Timothy ate delicately as Paul watched. Maybe Ruth was right. Maybe his education should have been here, in the bosom, if not of Abraham, then of Elizabeth, where his hands, like Paul's hands, could know the soil so that they need not ever touch it again. Timothy, instead, spoke of bitter winters the likes of which Mississippi couldn't imagine; of righteous men who spoke eloquently of liberty; and of niggers unchained, of which he had heard, but hadn't seen.

He had cultivated the most curious art form, and Paul was, in spite of himself, impressed by the divine hand his son showed. But that was just it: there was no mention of God. And there was no veil upon him that might have evinced contemplation of such matters. The North had done its job, perhaps too well.

As everyone had left the table and the slaves had cleaned it, Paul sat in his chair. Something had kept him there and he tried to determine what it was. He hadn't, this time, remarked on where Maggie placed the cutlery. He paid no special attention to the tablecloth or its rigid corners. He said nothing when, while chewing, he bit into something hard—like a bone, but burned and circular, in the fowl that Maggie and Essie had jointly placed before him. He had carved it himself, so he had no one but himself to blame.

And yet, he didn't want to move. He sat there as candlelight had become dimmer and dimmer still. He rubbed his eyes. He pulled his watch out of his pocket. It was attached to his waistband by a gold chain. It was only eight o'clock. He wasn't tired but had no desire to get up.

When it came, it came from somewhere unexpected. It started not in the cave of his chest, as he imagined it would, but in the pit of his stomach. A rumbling had just begun to form as he clutched himself. The feeling was familiar. He wondered if he would make it to the outhouse in time or if he would have to call Maggie in with a bedpan. How unseemly to have to unfasten one's britches in one's dining place, ass exposed in the same room where one feasts, the two scents mixing in unfriendly ways such that one might be unable to separate them ever again. No, he couldn't do that.

He managed to get up from the table. He rushed into the kitchen, past Maggie—who didn't look at him, but bent her head as she was supposed to—and past Essie, whose back was facing him, taking the lantern they lit so that they could make quicker work of cleaning, making his way to the back of the house. He burst through the door, bounded down the steps and rushed to the left of Ruth's garden, to the soli-tary red outhouse in the cusp of trees.

It was thin and shocking set against the backdrop of the wilderness. He had it built there, far enough away from the house that the odor didn't overwhelm. Not too far from the flowers so that they, too, could be the arbitration between what stank and what bloomed. He burst into it and closed the door be-hind him. He put the lantern down. The smell in that summer air, the insects that buzzed and clicked; he didn't bother to check for snakes because there was no time. He couldn't get his trousers down fast enough as the suspenders took too long to unfasten. When he felt the warmth begin to slide down his leg, he nearly took the Lord's name in vain. Though he was sure vanity had nothing to do with it.

"Maggie! Maggie!" Paul cried.

She arrived not as quick as he would have it. She knocked on the red door.

"Massa? You call for me?" she asked, holding an-other lantern up.

"Did you bring a cloth?"

"No, suh. You need a cloth, suh?"

"I wouldn't have called you if . . . never mind. Hurry and get one. Send Essie if you can't move quickly. Go!"

After a moment, Essie knocked on the door.

"Massa, I has the cloth Maggie sent . . ."

Paul opened the door and saw her lantern first. "Yes, yes. Now give it here."

Paul grabbed the cloth and it was dry.

"Where . . . this . . . no water. You didn't wet this? Where is my bowl with water?"

"Oh, you wanted water, too, Massa?" Essie put her hand to her mouth. "Maggie said you only asked for a cloth. So that's what I did. I hurried and brought you this cloth."

"Blasted!" Paul exclaimed. "Maggie! Call Maggie. Maggie!"

"Maggie!" Essie joined in.

Maggie returned.

"Maggie, get me a bowl of water immediately. And another pair of britches. And be hasty about it. "Essie, here." Paul took off his pants, suspenders dangling from them. "Go and tend to these. Make sure you wash them thoroughly."

Maggie looked back. She and Essie glanced at each other. "Yessuh," Essie said, as she walked off holding the pants out, away from her.

Maggie returned shortly.

"Here, suh," she said, as she placed the bowl and her lantern down on the ground.

Paul handed her the cloth and she dipped in the warm water and handed it back to him. He looked at her with narrowed eyes and a crumpled brow.

"You don't expect me . . ."

He stood up, turned around, his ass now at the level of Maggie's face.

"Clean me."

He cupped himself in front as Maggie, in upward strokes, like one would with a baby, wiped his bottom, and the muddy stream down his leg, shiny in the lantern light. When she was done, she threw the soiled rag into the bowl and handed Paul the trousers.

"Where are my suspenders?" he asked, as he pulled the pants up, which were spacious around his waist and wouldn't remain up.

"Massa, suh, I reckon you gave them to Essie for cleaning?"

"Dang it!" Paul shouted. "Move," he continued as he pushed past Maggie and stomped his way back into the house, holding his pants by their uppermost edge so they wouldn't fall down around his ankles.

He wanted to blame them. So he had them stand there in the kitchen as he walked back and forth, looking at them as though it were they, not he, whose words weren't clear and thus left open to interpretation. He would have the doctor to visit and give him something for his stomach—a soothing tea, a healing rub perhaps. He had run out of both since the last time. He looked at Maggie and Essie. Their heads were bent, but they were holding hands.

"Stop that," Paul snapped, pointing to where their hands were cupped. They released. "Heh," he spat. "I like to beat you both where you stand," he said as he paced. He looked them up and down in their twin white dresses, in their twin black skins, though one taller and thicker than the other, one whose body was more familiar. "Maggie: No more cranberry sauce with dinner," he said finally. "Or maybe it was those blasted greens; the way you spice them . . ."

Maggie nodded. "Yes, Massa," she said, looking over at Essie quickly before returning her gaze to the floor. Then: "Oh, Massa, so sorry! Your shoe," she continued, pointing downward.

At the tip of Paul's black boot, a brown splotch.

"Give those to me, suh. I shine them for you," Essie said and knelt down to take them from his feet. Maggie joined her.

Paul held on to a nearby wall as they unfastened and removed his shoes. Three lanterns lined up on the floor gave them all a warm glow. He liked Maggie and Essie there, stooped, crawling around at his feet. But there was something odd: They were both kneeling, clearly. But briefly, for just a blink, he could have sworn it was they who were standing.

And that it was he who was on his knees.

"YES, COUSIN. I **do** need a drink," Paul said after James asked.

He and James left the cotton sacks to James's men, walked over to the barn, climbed atop the horses, led to them by one of the niggers who had performed all of his duties well, save one. And just a moment before, Jesus was offered as a possible solution for that by another nigger, the lot of whom was so low and insignificant beneath Jesus's consideration that it made even James laugh. But it made Paul think.

They rode on down the rigid and dusty trail. Evening sounds of birds, and cicada, which had claimed the gloaming as theirs, emanated from either side of them and also above. That's what the trees were for, Paul thought, to shelter and to fortify. They were the breathing borders between man himself and the natural everything that Jehovah gifted to him to survey. Either could cross with some peril involved, but man, above all other creatures, had shown himself most adept at survival.

It was unusually cool, so Paul didn't mind riding close to his cousin. Had, in fact, in that lessening light of sky and honey glow of lamp, seen the family between them. He had been told that his mother and aunt bore a striking resemblance. In this place, when all of creation was in between light and dark, Paul saw that James carried that matrilineal weight much more than he did. Despite the cranky brow, James looked like their mothers: Elizabeth and Margaret. That was why he didn't have to do too much to verify James's story. Kinship was clear on a subliminal level if not, at first, on an obvious one. Paul felt glad that his spiritual senses were, then, intact and led him not to turn away his flesh and blood, since all of his other relations, outside of the family he created himself, had passed—or were as good as.

Sometimes, he thought that his created family

might pass, too. Ruth's womb couldn't catch hold at first. Might have had something to do with her youth. But soon, she gave him a son with shocking hair and piercing eyes that everyone all over town had come to see for themselves. Paul could detect the envy hidden in their voices even when he carried on about how Timothy hadn't come into the world all shriveled up like most babes, no. He came into the world not unlike Christ, with ringed blessings above his head and the cornflower vision to see into the very souls of those who would ensure his passage was safe. He let out a deep and lasting cry, and Paul and Ruth laughed because all of those who came before him had only whimpered before they eventually, and too quickly, returned to the dust.

Downtown Vicksburg soon appeared before them. Women in petticoats and men in wide-brimmed hats hurried about, on horses and in wagons. Store owners stood out on the porches of their businesses—the tailor, the butcher, the apothecary, the haberdasher—saying so long to their customers as they prepared to close up shop.

Paul and James rode up to the saloon. It had a gentleman in front of it. Unlike the purveyors of clothes, meat, medicine, or hats, this man was greeting his clientele; he wouldn't be saying so long until the morning sun peeked over the eastern trees. They dismounted, Paul and James, and fastened the reins of the horses to the hitching rail. They exchanged hellos with the greeter on their way in. When they entered, they moved through a number of people, nodding their respects. They sat down at a small table near the back. When the barmaid came to them, wearing a long black dress and white apron, James smiled and ordered a dark ale; Paul a whiskey. They were silent, taking in the energy of the place, until the waitress returned with their drinks, James's in a mug, Paul's in a shot glass.

"So you thinking of giving him what he ask for, that nigger?" James asked, taking a swig.

Paul sniffed the whiskey. Smooth and a hint too sweet. He placed the glass back down in front of him.

"The whole question, you know, is whether a nigger can minister," Paul said.

"Or be ministered to," James added.

"That's not really a question," Paul said, recognizing that James wasn't the biblical devotee that he was. "Even the waters curve to the word of God." Paul shook his head. "No. But can a nigger speak honor to that word, give it its just due via the auspices of his mind?"

"I say no." James curled his hands into fists at either side of the mug.

Paul added, "I suppose the fundamental question is does a nigger have a soul?"

James grinned. "Men greater than us been debating that since the first settlers came to this hunk o' land. Doubt we find the answer at this table or at the bottom of these here glasses."

James held his glass up nearer to Paul and nodded.

Paul picked up his own glass, and briefly the two of them clinked their glasses together—James with a "heh" and Paul trying to find the answer in the glass James said it wasn't in.

On the ride back, James was singing some old ship song he said he learned on his voyage over. It was a briny tune that made Paul shake his head and consider how much James, himself, needed Jesus, never mind niggers. But it also made him chuckle, which made him think about how much he still needed Him, too.

"You never really talk much about your trip. Or England. Or my aunt and uncle, for that matter," Paul quietly noted.

James inhaled. He blew the air out through his mouth. "There's so little I remember about my mother and father. Those paintings of Aunt Elizabeth you have in the house help me a little, though," James looked ahead of him, lulled by the rhythm of the horse beneath him. "And what's to say about England or the ship? All I can recall is the filth."

Paul looked at James a moment before nodding. "I reckon so," he said. "I reckon so."

They reached the gates of Elizabeth. They both, still on their horses, lifted their lamps up to each other in lieu of verbalizing their good nights. Then Paul went one way and James the other. Paul dismounted and tied up his horse in front of his home rather than lead it back to the barn and have Samuel or Isaiah tend to it. Tired and a little bit dizzy from the whiskey, Paul climbed the steps, walked into the house, then up the stairs, and into his bed. He longed for Ruth, but he didn't have the strength to take off his boots, much less venture into her room, wake her by lamplight, and wonder, in the midst of it, if she were still young enough to give Timothy a sister. Not that Timothy didn't already have sisters, but he meant one whom he and Ruth could claim; whose skin was not tainted, not even a little; who sprang out of love, not economy.

He closed his eyes because that was the sweetest thought he could find slumber to. He smiled before the drool gathered at a corner of his mouth, the air lumbered through his nostrils, and the darkness, that he didn't know was living, entered his room and consumed everything, even the lamplight itself.

When he coughed himself awake, golden arrows were piercing his windows because he hadn't drawn the curtains upon stumbling in. He had one thought, above all others, on his mind: **Give God His glory.** Yes, then. He would share His teachings with Amos. Paul wiped his face with the back of his hand. He sat up and swung his legs around to the edge of the bed and faced the window. The brightness caused him to squint and his head pounded just a little. Despite the sting and the thumping, he smiled. **James wasn't completely right,** he thought. Maybe the answer wasn't at the bottom of one glass, or two, or three.

But it could be shook loose from the mind when the ambrosia was sweet enough, by which he meant kind enough.

A few months into their study, Paul believed that it was right to provide Amos this opportunity to demonstrate, on behalf of his lot, that niggers could be more than animals. Amos's sermons out in the tree circle had the necessary tone and tenor, and Paul had to admit that there was music in the way Amos repeated the words Paul taught him that wasn't present even in Paul's own pastor. But was there a hint of original thought anywhere to be found?

When Amos came to Paul crying one afternoon, right after Essie had finally given birth to the child, proving Paul right, Amos told him of white-hot dreams and spiraling. Paul immediately recognized this as communion with the Holy Spirit. He didn't understand how, after just those months and months, God decided to press his lithe and probing hand against the forehead of a nigger—and yet, even in the ecstasy of his own midnight prayers, down, down on the abiding floor, and reciting the proverbs and the psalms and the Ecclesiastes, he felt not even the slightest touch: not on the spot on the shoulder that forever gleamed with his father's prints, and not at the center of his head. He had no choice but to nod his understanding. He wouldn't question God's will, for it was almighty; anyone who knew Him knew that. And there was a crown for anyone who let that knowledge be his portion.

Yes, then, he conceded. Niggers had souls. Which, in itself, introduced new troubles. If slaves had souls, if they were more than beasts over which he and every other man had godly claim, then what did it mean to punish them, and often so severely? Was their toil in the cotton fields on Paul's behalf also the wages of his visited sin? He returned to the Word and was comforted. For God had said, plain and clear, render unto Caesar, first, and, also, slaves shall be obedient in order to one day find reparation in that exquisite cotton plantation in the sky. The clouds were evidence.

To bring things forth from the abyss was no easy task. The land had its own mind. So did niggers. Only by wresting the control either believed they had from their hands with yours—and more than hands, will—could you claim ownership over things that imagined themselves free.

From the indistinguishable masses of black-black niggerdom, Isaiah and Samuel had grown to the peak state of brawn, which is what Paul had intended, from the start, by placing them both in the toil of the barn. It wasn't too much to impose upon them the weight of a bale of hay, which, just like cotton pick-ing, required the back to be strong. Besides, darkie children weren't actually children at all; niggers-in-waiting, maybe, but not children.

The plan was to multiply them through the strate-gic use of their seed. Matched with the right wench, every single one of the offspring would be perfectly suited for field or farm, fucking or fuel. Niggers with purpose.

Paul watched this plan crumble one morning—just to the right of him, in the lazy corner of his library where the sun refused to shine, so the best books could be placed there without worry of them being bleached by yellow rays. Right there, a pile of ash as Amos quoted chapter and verse of the destruction of Sodom and claimed that the barn had become exactly that.

"Their blood upon them. Their blood upon them," Amos said barely above a whisper as he quivered, head bowed, hands clasped in prayer formation.

Niggers never had any loyalty to one another. That was what saved them from threat. No way would it have been possible to yoke them and drag them across widest oceans, then stretch after stretch of green meadow and forest, hill behind hill, to sugarcane, to indigo, to tobacco, to cotton and more, without the kin-treachery of which only they seemed capable.

A moment, please: Untrue.

The European, too, had a penchant for drawing the sword for the sole purpose of raising it to their sibling's neck. But they had long since determined that sometimes, such causes for grievance could be set aside, at least temporarily: a ceasefire for the greater good. Niggers hadn't yet learned that. Everywhere, everywhere, white folk let out a sigh of relief.

"I taught you the Word, for you to bring it to me like this?"

Paul was seated behind his desk, Amos on his knees before it.

"All this time," Paul continued. "And you forgot your purpose was to bring the Good News?"

Amos was silent but had a feverish look upon him. Like one who had seen things and called to be heeded, though fools laughed even unto the warning. Still, Paul couldn't see defeat where it was and insisted upon victory.

"This is a trick. You have failed at what you were to deliver. Shall I take you back to the day you interrupted my cousin and me?" Paul asked as he stood up and pointed out the window, in the direction of the cotton field. "You seek to blame God for what lies at your feet."

"Massa, no such a thing. I only speak truth to you. Only."

Paul leaned over his desk, his hands firmly planted on top of it.

"Then I ask: What proof have you?"

Amos wiped his brow. "Massa, suh, I say that I humbly submit to your gracious hand. My first testimony is that neither boy has given themselves completely to woman. Both can't be barren. That seem too outside the nature the God you, in your mercy, show me. That the first thing revealed to me."

Paul tilted his head. "And what was the second?"

Amos cleared his throat and swallowed. "The second: I seen they shadows touch in the nighttime."

Paul sighed and then shook his head. What did

it mean for shadows to touch, and what did it matter if it was daytime or night? The shadows of pails
touched. The shadows of trees touched. Hell, Paul's
shadow touched James's when they were standing together and the sun was good. Of **course** their shadows **touched**! They were cooped up in that barn and
were each other's company. It was the same kind of
closeness that Paul had heard about in war, where
soldiers became something like brothers, but more.
There wasn't any reason to bring Sodom or Gomorrah
into any of this, least of all on the very land covered
by the will of his father and his mother's very name.

Paul sat down. He leaned back in his chair and
folded his hands before his lips. He couldn't decide
which would be the greater sin: if Amos spoke true
or if Amos spoke false. This matter could only be
settled through prayer, deep and heavy prayer that
would end with foreheads weary and clothing stained
by sweat. This was what they thrashed for, the witnesses who had made the longest journey through
the desert and didn't dry up from thirst. Instead,
they fell to their knees before, during, and after, and
cast up gratitude to He who'd been their stone, their
bread, and their water. Oh, yes, praise should come
before anguish, for this is what God had said: **Put no
other before Me and ye shall have the abundance
of Heaven.**

Paul got up and moved around his desk and stood
over Amos. Paul raised his hand and brought it down

thunderous against Amos's face. Amos cowered and pleaded.

"The blood of Jesus, Massa! The blood of Jesus!"

Indeed, Paul thought, Jesus's blood was precisely what this occasion called for.

At the saloon, James had laughed.

"I'm stunned that you're stunned, Cousin," James said between gulps. "You expected niggers to behave in a way that makes sense?" James laughed. "That's why they're niggers, for Christ's sake!"

"No need to take the Name in vain," Paul said, nursing his whiskey. "I'm not certain Amos even understands what he saw. The Word overwhelms him. It's a lot for a nigger's mind to handle."

"I don't never put nothing past no nigger," James said. "Whether that be to lie or to lay."

"Still, there is a natural order," Paul replied.

"And when did you not know a nigger to act outside of it? I had to punish them not too long ago for looking at Ruth wrong. They're low things; you said so yourself. But you think they capable of higher things just because you command them to be so?"

"They looked at Ruth wrong?"

"That's what she said."

Paul touched his bottom lip. "Why didn't she tell me? Why didn't you?"

"You pay me to do a job, not to worry you with it. I imagine Ruth knows that, too."

That answer delighted Paul unexpectedly. But

when that faded, he returned to Isaiah and Samuel. "I don't tolerate paganism."

"I don't understand the hand-wringing then. Get rid of them and get your money for it."

"I don't like to waste the things I cultivated. You already know this."

"Your pride will be your end, Cousin."

NEITHER OF THESE BARN STUDS were of Paul's line. Perhaps that was where the error lay. He rid them of their previous names and renamed them with the calls of righteous men, but it seemed that did nothing to surrender them unto decent passions. Somehow, through some unseen wickedness, Samuel and Isaiah, two witless niggers, couldn't discern the difference between entries. The two bucks had natures that caused them to resist.

Paul had heard of such unnatural goings-on in antiquity: the Greeks and the Romans, for example, who were great men otherwise, had given themselves over to obscene intimacies. This, which was nothing more than the very workings of paganism itself, was what, to his mind, led to their destruction. It was inevitable that Zeus and the like would crumble before Jehovah because chaos must always give way to order.

The very thought of two men giving in to each other in this way sent a shiver down Paul's spine and made him queasy. He couldn't much longer allow them to risk incurring the divine wrath that would certainly be aimed squarely at them, but might also destroy innocent bystanders. Like all old men, God could sometimes be puzzlingly haphazard; His aim not always true. So many dead Halifax babies had been denied the ability to testify, but fortunately dipped in the baptismal waters, they held on to the right to do so.

Isaiah and Samuel were fine specimens that responded better to instruction than punishment. He put them to work in the barn just before either of them had reached puberty. They were stunning in their leanness and musculature. He thought that giving them this specific kind of farm labor wouldn't only build their bodies, but would also build their character. Caring for living things could do that. With this act, and their transformation and readiness, he would then breed them, hoping to create from their stock gentle but strong niggers who would take production on the plantation to an all-new high. Wouldn't his mother and father be so pleased?

He observed them out by the barn. Young, fit, black and blue, they moved with an efficiency and expertise of which he didn't imagine niggers capable. They seemed to have some sort of system, one they devised themselves, which sometimes made it possible for them to accomplish all manner of work in time to go out into the fields and help the other niggers pick the last bit of cotton before quitting time. They would pick almost as much as the others in less than half the time.

The key, it seemed, was in their proximity to each other. They seemed to energize each other, perhaps even inspire each other in a way that not even the couples he didn't have to force together did. If they were his sons, he would have been proud.

When Paul finally decided to cross the gate with specific intention, it was early morning—so early that the sun had not yet overpowered all else and drenched land and people in hot light. He held a whip in his left hand, let it dangle at his side and its tip drag against the ground. In his right hand, he held the Bible, the same one that civilized Amos. His hat was pulled low, just at the edge of his eyebrows, but the top two buttons of his shirt were undone, enough for his chest hair to protrude. He unhooked the gate and crossed the barrier surrounding the barn. He didn't bother to close the gate behind him. It hadn't occurred to him to bring someone with him, James or one of the other dullards, in case the two niggers had become untenable.

The air could choke with either the scent of dandelions or manure, and the two together overwhelmed. Paul wafted through the stench toward the barn where Isaiah and Samuel busied themselves. They came to attention when they saw him. Their heads downward and their bodies erect, they stood close to each other, but they didn't touch.

Momentarily, Paul felt something like a breeze blow past him, something that tickled the hairs on his chest and forced him to close his eyes. It was something like a caress, unseen and gentle.

"Samuel," he said softly. "Fetch me a drink of water." What he really wanted, though, was whiskey.

Paul observed the troubled manner with which Samuel held the ladle, but careful still to ensure no drop might spill. For a moment, Paul believed that it might be fear that guided those actions, but also there was no quiver in his step and his hands didn't tremble; downward-cast eyes evinced no supplication. Before him stood a creature who, under all the grime and drenched in the smell of grudge work, imagined itself possessing a glimmer of worthiness. This was vanity and it explained so many things.

Paul sat on a bench and motioned for Isaiah and Samuel to stand before him. He opened the Bible, the whip still in his hand.

"There's trouble here," he said without lifting his head, flipping through the pages, seeming, occasionally, to have lost his place, before closing the book with a loud thud that startled Isaiah.

"James says that the nature of the nigger is debased, but I imagine that even nature can be changed. I watched my father do it with his own hands. Wrest it and redirect the course of rivers. Bend trees. Put flowers where **he** wanted them to be. Catch fish and fowl to nourish. Erect his home in the middle of what his work had rightfully claimed. His birthright that God Himself ordained as dominion."

At that moment, the sun revealed itself and, inch by inch, began to shine down on the standing Isaiah and Samuel, touched their crowns as though they were actually so consecrated, bright in a way that didn't hinder sight but did make the face pinch just a little. Inside, Paul begged for a stray cloud, something that would dim the glowing and perhaps act as a sure sign that the divine wasn't singling out the wretched before him for blessing. And then he realized that the light itself was the message, giving him the insight, guiding his wisdom, confirming his authority, God showing him the way with the first thing He had ever created. This wasn't Isaiah and Samuel being bestowed with some sort of majesty; impossible. Rather, this was merely the dawn. God had finally touched his forehead, too!

He took the ladle from Samuel and sipped, secure in the knowledge he held in both hands. He wasn't thirsty, but it was necessary for them to see how elementary his power was, that there was no need to raise voices or hands and yet, with only a few words, reality had knelt to his bidding, and so simply, illustrating the only order under which it could function. He smiled.

"Their blood upon them," Paul said, finally settling on a direct approach. He sighed. "Bleeding is so easy. The body gives up its secrets at the slightest provocation. Man is only separated from the rest of nature by his mind, his ability to know, even if that knowing was born in sin," he said, taking a deep breath and looking dead into their closed faces. "Fruitful!" he said a little louder than he had intended. "Multiply," he continued, raising his hand quickly and dropping the ladle, which fell to the ground and landed at Samuel's feet.

"Pick it up," Paul said calmly as he balanced the Bible on his lap.

Both of them rushed to do so, banging heads as they stooped. **Had they not been standing so close together,** Paul thought. The sun shone against the ladle and stung his eyes. He pointed to the ground, gesturing for Isaiah or Samuel to hurry and pick it up. He turned toward the sun's direction to avoid the reflecting light and was confronted with another.

There, off in the distance, Paul saw her first as a flash, then in full form. Standing, he could be sure, at the edge of the cotton field. Actually, she was a few rows in. The cotton laced her belly like a soft belt and colorful birds flew over her head. Elizabeth held court in the morning, not in the past but here, waving at him feverishly, or was she signaling for him to come closer? Paul stood up. No, Elizabeth was telling him to go. But go where? She stopped waving. Her hands returned to her sides. Paul rubbed his eyes. He looked to the field again. Elizabeth was gone in a blink and took meaning with her.

When Paul returned to himself and saw Samuel and Isaiah standing, looking wide-eyed at him, like he was the one in danger, he wanted to laugh, but he scowled instead. The mercy in him was walking away, no less stunned by his actions than they were, needing, maybe more than ever before, the bitterness of spirits.

It was the first time in a long time that he had felt anything resembling doubt. Unclear of what his mother appearing on the white bluff had portended or why her calm face belied her frantic manner, he walked away, nevertheless, confident in his stride lest everyone else imagine him unsure, to their own peril.

Why turn back and see those two boys—whom he now knew, in just that short time with them, he had to sell, not because he wouldn't be able to in-crease their stock with children from their seed, but because acts of defiance were always, unequivocally, contagious. He told himself that his sadness, which had mysteriously bubbled up out of nowhere and sat heavy in the pit of his chest, rested in the trouble-some arrangements that now had to be made on be-half of two insolent niggers, and not in the fact that being in their presence had almost convinced him that they belonged together, leaned up against each other in their confusion.

He had been a disruption, but not the kind he had hoped. He, maybe, strengthened their bond, gave them the sense that together they could make a way out of no way, which was what the nature of their work had been if Paul wanted to be honest with himself. His plans worked **too** well. It was he who encouraged them to work in tandem, in uni-son, and they had but followed his instruction. It was his own fault that he neglected to recall how they lacked nuance or the depth of knowledge that allowed for a measured existence. He only had to see it for himself, witness . . .

No! Coming here—to witness what? Niggers behaving as such; low-to-the-ground things, after all, acted lowly—was an error. The whole enterprise had conveyed to them, however slightly, that they were of some value. This was a mistake.

There couldn't be peace. Paul couldn't let there be. There was something in his center, a jagged thing, that stuck him at the very thought. He would never admit to this, but there was something wild coating him, not so much an armor as a balm. And it drove him frantically toward his home. His steps, however, were unsure, the ground wavy. He felt a heaviness of limbs that made him stumble. The Bible, wet with his perspiration, slipped from his grasp. His knees hit the dirt, and before all things darkened, he saw Timothy sprint toward him.

What was he doing on the ground? Ah, yes. He must have passed out from the heat. He told himself that it wasn't his proximity to the glow of either Isaiah or Samuel that had done it. And was there even a glow, or had he imagined it? Slaves sometimes rubbed themselves with oils from vegetation so that the sun would light them up. That had to be it.

The sun was doubly at fault, then. Yes, it was the scorching sun that hit him in the head with its rays, and he just needed the sweetness of well water to bring him back to himself. Paul looked around, weary. Some of the slaves had gathered, surrounding him, crying, asking if he was all right, taking away all of the air he needed to return to power. He shooed them away, told them to git, and rose too quickly to his feet. He took a wobbly first step and fell down to his knees. Timothy helped him stand up again. Paul dusted himself off and took another step. He asked Timothy to pick up his Bible and then slowly and even-keeled, he walked back to the house, Timothy following behind.

PAUL RODE SILENTLY in the coach later that night, almost obscured by the shadows that came from the cover of trees. Adam drove the horses at a slow, steady pace, their hooves stepping to whatever rhythm he indulged. Paul stared at the back of Adam's head through the coach opening. He noticed that Adam had begun to lose his hair at the crown. Had he really been born that long ago? Despite impeccable records, Paul began to doubt that he had been employed at this business for so long. But Adam was indisputable evidence.

There was a faint light coming from the town; the glow of lanterns and candles made things seem softer than they actually were and this brought Paul unexpected calm. In this calm, he paid attention to the town in a way he never bothered to before. It was still bustling, even though the shops were closed for a while now. But horses and slaves were still tied to some posts, and night ladies and rugged men with wide-brim hats and holsters, some of which were empty, casually walked the wide dirt road that split downtown in half. They were headed for the one place that had just begun to open up.

The saloon doors swung back and forth and body after body made their way into the space. Smoke and laughter escaped and reached Paul as Adam pulled the coach up to the post outside. Adam jumped down from his seat and tied the reins to the post before quick-stepping over to the coach to open the door for Paul. Paul stepped down slowly. He tugged on his collar and pulled down the brim of his hat so that his nose and mouth could be readily seen, but one had to do a bit of work to make eye contact.

"Mind the coach," he said to Adam. "And you have your papers."

"Yessuh," Adam said as he nodded his head and then let his chin rest on his chest.

Paul passed a few fellows saddling up horses, friends of James, who were all cheerful enough.

"Mr. Halifax," they said.

Paul turned to acknowledge them but made no other overture. The men read this as disrespect. But since they weren't courageous enough to confront Paul directly about their grievance, they turned, instead, to Adam.

"You would almost think that nigger was a white man, but just out in the sun a little too long," one said to the others.

Paul smiled and hopped up onto the boardwalk leading to the saloon.

He pushed through the saloon doors, and they creaked back and forth several times before they were still. Inside, it was cooler than he had expected it to be and a shiver shook him before dissipating at the back of his neck. Something sweet scented the air and mixed with the blunt aroma of cigars. People passed in front of him, not recognizing him at first, too caught up in the mood, which, if it could be given a color, would be crimson because it was almost as if the lanterns had been covered in some careless woman's frock and the caress between the two would dim the whole world, recast it in the light of a fast-pumping heart, or even the blood that shot through veins with such force that one could hear the rush. This, of course, before the heat was too much and everything caught fire, but people were too rapt to notice the world burning around them, ashes mistaken for confetti.

Paul carried that crimson inside him against his will. He promised himself not to let it escape or taint his thoughts. Looking at the women in dresses buttoned to their necks, some with smiles that he didn't recognize as strained, and the men with jugs in their hands, raising them, occasionally, in the air,

awkwardly spilling some of their contents onto giggling bodies as a prelude to what will happen when
they leave and step behind the saloon, behind water
barrels, hidden by the starlight that couldn't reach
them. Dresses raised up and pants pulled down, and
then the gyrations that don't last very long at all before both parties feel a bit of shame as they don't look
at each other when they part. This was Vicksburg,
yes, but it was also the whole world. James didn't
share much about England, Paul thought, but there
was so much revealed in his silence and eyes that refused to be looked into. Paul was sure that not even
an ocean between them could eliminate the ways and
means that connected them.

He found his way to a back corner of the saloon
and sat at a small table closest to the wall. Since he
had chosen to come without James, who was often
the buffer between him and the nosy Vicksburg
denizens, he wanted to be as tucked into a corner as
he possibly could. He preferred that James remain
at Elizabeth this time, ensuring safety because he
would be out late as he needed to be. He wanted to
contemplate his next move without interference and
arrive at his decision without James's judgments or
simplifications. That was his right as a man.

The barmaid made her way through the crowd
toward him. He barely acknowledged her beyond
a quick dissection that attempted to see, foolishly,
what she didn't uncover, even when she asked what

he wanted to drink and even when she returned with a bottle of whiskey and a glass whose cleanliness was suspect.

"I know you," Paul heard someone say at a distance too close for anyone with the proper manners. "You own that cotton farm over yonder. Halifax, ain't it?"

Paul turned only slightly to see the skinny man in a hat with a jug of ale in his hand. "Elizabeth Plantation." He nodded, simply to acknowledge him, hoping he would leave.

"We never see you 'round here without your cousin. Where's James, too drunk to drink?"

Paul snickered and poured himself a little bit of whiskey and took a gulp.

"Jake. Jake Davis," the man said, extending his hand to Paul, which Paul sized up and took a moment too long to finally shake. "Can I join you?"

Paul grunted and poured more whiskey into the glass. He shrugged his shoulders. Jake raised a finger and mouthed words for the bartender to send over a bottle of gin.

"Your cousin tells me that you're looking to sell a couple of studs," Jake said. "As it turns out, I know a buyer ready to pay you top dollar. Much more than you would get at auction."

Paul looked at Jake with narrowed eyes. "Hm. And if that's the case, I wonder why this buyer can't just attend the auction like anyone else." He took a swig of whiskey. "And I also wonder what you might want in exchange for introducing me to this buyer."

Someone had sat down behind the piano, a man with large eyes and a mustache that grew over his mouth. His grin was too big for his face, Paul thought, and made him seem more like a painting of a man that an artist had gotten wrong. The man banged his fingers down on the keys and the first couple of notes had missed their mark. He was drunk, surely, but soon the melody made sense and the pitch was pleasurable. The man sat as upright as he could and barely looked down. Instead, he looked out at the people who had begun to clap and dance.

Paul tapped his foot because the rhythm reminded him of something his mother's attendants used to sing to lull her and make her forget about the pain that came with wasting away. In one of the moments when she was lucid, she had described it to him, the pain. She said it was like someone was trying to pull her out of the world by folding her lengthwise until there was nothing left. And each fold, she said, felt like a red-hot poker being laid upon her soul.

"It burns," she said.

Paul gave her water, but it didn't matter, she said. It would just cloud everything in steam and she needed him to see what happened to her so it wouldn't happen to him. He didn't understand what she meant then and he still didn't understand. The piano notes brought him back and his foot tapped a little faster now. He took another gulp and he started to feel the numbing, the buzzing, the light-headedness that he was looking for to help him forget—no, to help him remember that it was a not a loss that brought him here and there was no use in grieving. James had made it plain and only Paul's pride had prevented him from seeing that this was merely the price of doing business. And what was a win if it wasn't a strategy that ended in profit?

"He's a private man," Jake said. "Not much for public things like auctions. And before you ask, he likes to conduct business directly so he doesn't send men in lieu of him."

"And yet, here you are," Paul replied.

The saloon shook as the men rose in song, something Paul had never heard before. They were slurring and off-key, but that almost seemed to be the point. Merriment had its own way, and the messiness of it all, under the red-red light, in the fuzziness of Paul's inebriated senses, wasn't just a **kind** of beauty, but beauty itself. He felt loose enough to stand and raise his glass.

"He didn't really send me," Jake said. "I sort of volunteered. As a favor to James."

Paul looked down at Jake, who was still seated. "James said nothing to me."

"I told him not to. Not unless I could be sure. But then you walked in here tonight and that was . . ."

"Providence," Paul said.

He turned back to the table and grabbed the bottle and, this time, drank straight from it. Some of the whiskey missed his mouth and dribbled down his chin. His condition made it so that he didn't care.

Come to think of it, right now, he didn't care about a lot of things. Not Isaiah and Samuel, not Ruth, not Timothy, not the plantation, not nothing. And the load that was loosened from him made him feel like he might well float right up to the ceiling with no earthly idea on how to get back down. And he didn't care about that, either.

"So when can I meet this mysterious gentleman?" Paul said to Jake.

"As a matter of fact, he's here. He's out back. As I said before, he's not much of a people person and prefers his privacy."

"If he prefers his privacy, what is he doing in the back of a saloon?"

"He has other business to attend to. Otherwise, he'd be home."

"And where is home? In fact, what is this man's name?"

"You should save all of these questions for him. You won't be disappointed. Follow me, Halifax. Right this way."

So Paul followed Jake as he led him to the back, where the music could still be heard through the open door. The red-red light had followed them, too, but fainter now, confoundedly absorbed by the night as they strayed farther and farther away from the tumult that he strangely, but unmistakably, craved. Bottle still in hand, he took another swig before they made it out the back door of the saloon.

The bottle was all but dry and he threw it and lost

his footing and fell down laughing. Jake helped him back up. When he got to his feet, he saw three men standing beside Jake.

"All right. So which one of these men is . . . Mr. Privacy?"

Jake said nothing as the three men charged Paul. They knocked him to the ground. Paul kicked one of them in the face and the man fell back, but the other two kept on him.

"His pockets!" Jake yelled and the two men began to tug at Paul's pants. Paul went for his holster and one of the men grabbed his arm, trying to prevent him from pulling out his gun. Then the man whom Paul kicked returned to the fray and began to help the one who was trying to wrestle the gun from Paul. The third man, meanwhile, had managed to take the banknotes from Paul's pocket and also pulled the gold watch from the chain attached to Paul's waistband. He held it up to Jake.

"I got it!" he exclaimed.

"Good! Let's go!"

One man grabbed a handful of dirt and threw it in Paul's eyes. Paul covered his face and the men took off running. Blinking and trying to rub the dirt away, Paul fired off a shot in the direction he thought they were running. He couldn't really see if he had hit his target. He tapped his shirt pocket and pulled out a handkerchief and began to wipe his face. He slumped against the rear wall of the saloon, looked up to the starry sky, and shook his head.

"Auction it is," he whispered.

He slid down the wall until his ass hit the ground. He looked at his shoes a moment before he stood up. **At least they didn't take my shoes.** Then he laughed. Then he laughed full belly. Then, finally, he fell backward onto the ground, unable to control the laughter that rocked his whole body. He had never before felt so light. He wished he could keep falling backward, relishing the flutter in the pit of his stomach, the tickle at the bottom of his sack. But he got up again because he thought he could float. When he was no closer to the stars than he had ever been, he swatted the thought away with his hand.

He stumbled toward the front of the saloon. He turned the corner and he saw his horse and coach, and Adam in the driver's seat nodding off, head jerking before he caught himself and returned to the upright position. Paul straightened himself, but his mind still belonged to the whiskey.

"Where's my boy?" he said with a smile on his face. "I need my boy."

Adam, still dozing, didn't hear him.

Paul got closer and repeated himself but louder. Adam shook and turned to see Paul standing there, disheveled. Forgetting himself, he recoiled at the sight of a smiling Paul. Realizing what this might earn him, he quickly resparked the dying light in the lantern at his side. He jumped down from his seat, lantern in hand, and bowed his head before Paul.

"Massa," he said in a voice that had traces of

interrupted sleep all up in it. "Is everything all right, suh?"

"Yes, my boy. Everything is perfect." He touched Adam's face and lifted it. He was dirtying Adam's face with his scuffed and dusty hands. Adam's eyes widened. "I need you, Adam." Paul smiled with woozy eyes. "I need you to get me home right now. You hear me? Ready the horse for home. You know why?" Paul moved his face a little closer to Adam's. "Because God has blessed us."

"Us, Massa?" Adam interrupted before he caught himself.

"Has blessed us with the answer to my prayers. Isn't He amazing, Adam? Doesn't He give so much to His children, His blessed children who He has charged with stewardship of all things earthly?" Paul finally removed his hands from Adam's face and they slipped to his chest. "Oh, sometimes I can shout, Adam," he said. "Sometimes, I feel that I could just stand in the middle of everything, like your grandfather did, and shout to the whole entire world that there is no greater gift than to be in God's favor. No matter how low you may fall. No matter how many times you stumble, there is no greater knowledge than knowing that everything you do is in service to God Almighty and is, therefore, righteous. That's why your grandfather did it. I never did tell you how he spun 'round with arms extended and laughed into the sky. That's how I know God. That's how I know He will make a way. Just when you think there is no portion, He will come to move mountains and reveal treasures for your chest only. You may half know this. But I hope at least some of it is getting through. You aren't us, but you aren't them, either. So maybe I'm not wasting my time by telling you this. And if I am, no one would believe you, anyway. So it doesn't matter."

They stared at each other in the lantern light, two faces that were reflections of each other to even the least discerning eye. Paul saw it clearest now. In another life, they might have been actual father and son rather than the hush-hush kind. Paul swallowed the notion that Adam made a more suitable offspring than Timothy. He would shit it out later.

The light between them had started to dim and the shadows had weakened. The dark had begun to claim them.

"I think the lantern need more oil, Massa," Adam said quietly.

"More," Paul replied, just as quietly, just before the light went out completely and the two of them breathed heavily in the dark.

THE MOON, sliced in half by the encroaching darkness, was nevertheless suspended high up in the night. It could be seen through the boughs of trees, threaded against it, as Adam steered the horses slowly up the trail to the Halifax property. Adam sat erect and cautious in the driver's seat as Paul lay back in the coach, looking straight up into the sky through its opening.

He was in and out of consciousness. His head was pounding, but he ignored it. Instead, he looked at the half-moon. He raised his palm to the sky and blotted it out, then put his hand back down. It was easier than he thought to pull the moon out of the sky. He looked at his dirty hands and then down at his torn clothing. Empty pockets. No pocket watch. To find one's self the winner even when life had designated you the loser. If his trip to the saloon taught him anything, it taught him that. Slumber finally caught up to him. The moon he saw now was inside his head, still half, but less bright.

The horses moved slowly by Adam's hand. The road was gentle and rocked Paul and the half-moon that was now inside him. Other than the half-eaten moon that had now left him, Paul didn't remember much about the ride other than how comforting it was, and he was startled not just by what seemed too quick a journey (and whiskey-induced slumber was always the best kind), but by Adam, who was now leaning in near his face. Too close.

"What are you doing?" Paul asked.

He sat up, finally. Adam moved back a bit, faced the ground, and said something Paul had no interest in hearing. They remained like that—ground-seeker and gazer—until discomfort set in. Paul then told Adam to take him to the house. Adam walked to the horses, grabbed their reins, and led them through the gate he had obviously opened while Paul slept. They approached the house. Adam helped Paul out of the coach.

"You need me for anything else, Massa?" he asked.

Paul shook his head because he didn't have the patience for words and moreover didn't wish to waste them. He stumbled less and walked slowly toward the house.

"You all right?" Adam asked.

Paul just waved him off. Adam led the horses by their reins, coach still attached, over toward the barn.

Paul continued walking, now more steadily, toward the house. All of the lights were out, except for a warm, dim glow coming from Timothy's room. He hated that Timothy stayed up so late and painted by such low light. **The quickest way to harm the eyes,** he thought. Then he saw tussling shadows in the window just as the light went out completely. Pigs squealed and he perhaps heard hooves and cowbells.

His heart became a fist in his chest, trying very hard to batter its way out. He removed his pistol from its holster at his hip and ran to the house, moving quicker than his body would normally allow. He tripped on the first porch stair and banged his knee. He crawled up the next four stairs and stood, finally, at the top and stumbled into the entrance door, pushing it open with such force that it hit its adjoining wall and swung back into Paul's face. Annoyed, he pushed it out of his way, but gentler this time, and started for the inside staircase. He called for Maggie but didn't wait around for her to show up. He took the stairs two at a time and stumbled, again, at the top for being unable to see in such thick darkness. He called for Maggie again, this time waiting for her to arrive with a candle or lantern, which he would snatch from her the moment she appeared. But she didn't. He would remember that come sunrise. He took off down the hall toward Timothy's room, calling for him and for Ruth as he sped down the long stretch of it. Where was Ruth?

He was breathing heavily now but didn't let that prevent him from reaching Timothy's door, which he kicked open. The room was dark, there wasn't even a bit of moonlight coming in through the window for him to see the outline of things. He walked quickly into the room and bumped into the bed. He ran his hands across the bed but felt nothing. He climbed on the bed and crept across it quickly; too quickly, and his foot got caught in the blanket and he twisted and turned and fell off the side. He landed on something, something soft and wet. He felt around; it was a body and it was sticky. He got on his knees and looked close.

It was Timothy.

He tried to pick him up, but he was heavy, so he only got the top half of the body onto his lap. He touched Timothy's face and felt a deep, soggy gash in it. It took his breath away. He jumped up, dropping the body to the floor.

He looked up, his lips quivered like a cowardly

man's, and he shook his head slowly, disbelief grabbing him soundly. He screamed.

For the first time, he cursed God, over and over
again. Then he stopped midcurse, because that was
when he saw it.

From the corner of his eye. Some sparkling thing.
A twinkle. A spark. A sudden flash. An elusive memory. A silver fish in a stream. Sunlight at the edge of
a wave. A thunderbolt in a passing cloud. The last
note in a song.

He raised his gun just as he caught, briefly, the
night. Yes, unbelievable, but true: the night was
coming at him and it had teeth, gleaming teeth that
had apparently kept their brightness from a steady
diet of white flesh.

ADAM

There was a line that ran down the middle of Adam. It was so thin that no one could see it, not even Adam. But since he could feel it, like a wire that had been held over the fire until orange and then laid upon his most sensitive spaces in the center of him, from his forehead to his crotch, he knew it was there.

It ached. Sometimes, it throbbed. Even though he appeared whole in everything he did, whether he was cleaning the coach or driving it, the line split him in two. Inside him, it erected a border, a wall, that separated his lungs, which had longed for each other but were trapped on either side of it, making breath short always. It cut off his heart from the right side of thinking, so the left side often made decisions without it. Acts without compassion to balance them were the genesis of cruelty.

Right eye knew not what left could see, left being so prone to releasing a tear when it saw the Sunday people and left ear heard the Sunday songs. Right didn't understand. Saw only a blank space, heard only blue, and found, in fact, that these things provided no clarity, which meant in no uncertain terms that it was primarily a waste of time.

The left hand was reckless. Adam had fought for it not to be the dominant force when he practiced, in lamplight, the forbidden arts. It was bad enough that he could spell his name and write it in the most elegant script—every loop, hump, and slanted line a masterpiece, which meant that no matter who owned him, whether it was his father or not, there would always be a piece of him unchained, and a piece was enough. But to allow it all to flow through the left hand, which was the portal through which the devil himself made his way from flames to dry land: this magnified the danger, but also the thrill.

Nevertheless, it took Adam great effort to hold himself together because there was no place where he wasn't pulled apart. He could only ever hear the Sunday songs from a distance because the Sunday people—well, they never told him that he **couldn't** sit with them among the spotted shadows and creeping moss, but the circle seemed to close in front of him whenever he came near, and their skittering eyes seemed to suggest that he hadn't gained their trust. He could sing too, if only they would let him sing.

He was one of the few people allowed in the Big House, but he wished he hadn't been. Ruth laid elegant traps. Once, she hid silverware and claimed he had stolen it. Had Maggie not interrupted, holding the spoon high, talking about, "Missy Ruth, it right here. Funniest thing, too: it, plain out in the garden. Beats me how something this fine get out there," it would have certainly cost him in lashes.

He chose the coach. The coach, too, was in the middle. Between the house and the field, but also, frequently, on the road.

He couldn't be sure that he was the first. It was possible that there was a girl before him whom Ruth got to before the little thing even had the chance to play and prosper. Before she even had been given a name. So he thought of her as Lilith, his older sister who died so that next time, his mother would be wiser. His mother, whom he didn't remember. Where she was now, he couldn't say. Maybe she bore the brunt of it so that he would be spared. That could have been the trade: her life for his. And then perhaps she was taken to auction, breasts still filled with baby's milk made specifically for him, which leaked when she heard the crowd jeer because it sounded so much like an infant crying. No dress to stain, the milk dripped down her ribs, then her thighs before hitting the wood planks of the block to be absorbed by heat and dead trees.

And perhaps she felt dead herself, cleaved from her baby—if he was her only one. Or she could have felt very alive once she saw his coloring and realized that he would never be as dark as she, and would always only ever remind her of her torment and tormentor.

Could she have escaped? Gone north through some kind of brilliant subterfuge that covered her trail and disguised her scent from dogs? Mint leaves and onion root used to stunning effect to confuse and repel. Nights inside the deepest caves with God knows what or high up in trees where biting ants were only the beginning.

Either she was free or worse. It was futile to contemplate, but then Adam's entire existence was futile, so he continued. And he could do that in relative peace as he sat in the coach, directing the horses to whichever place the Halifaxes wanted him to go. He, by birth if not by law, was a Halifax too. But still: he had to be careful. Eyes always ahead. Face always front. He couldn't give even the slightest impression that he was glancing to the left toward the wild and creamy hydrangeas that lined parts of the dusty path, or toward the right, where the cyrilla gathered like family with forgiving yellow fingers that pointed casually toward the ground. Least of all could he reveal that he, indeed, saw the sun rise and set, and noticed that what each did to the sky differed in ways that entire volumes could be written about and he could write them. Not to mention what a tender blanket nighttime was.

The horses provided a kind of shelter. Their rhythm remained steady and so the coach rocked and it made Paul, Ruth, Timothy, and, sometimes, James, prone to napping. Paul snuggled into himself with a frown. Ruth, a dreary smile. Timothy had always a sketch pad about to fall from his lap. And James, even in slumber, maintained the tightest grip upon his rifle.

When they returned to Empty, they each seemed angry that the ride had come to an end, as though the plantation had somehow made them feel that no rest could be had. This struck Adam as arrogant. How could they dare think of anything they did as work, or that they were entitled to rest because of it? Meanwhile, niggers—sometimes he liked that word and sometimes he didn't—worked their (our?) fingers into knots such that even a welcome embrace was painful.

He, like everyone else, had that weight to carry and nowhere to put it down except in bittersweet repetition. So he would just unfasten the horses and stroke them gently on the nose. Always he would ask them the same question: "You ready to eat?"

Then he would lead them back to the barn and steal a moment to drink sweet water with Isaiah and Samuel.

He couldn't understand the fuss, the whispers that had grown and threatened to be heard by the wrong Halifax. **So what if in the silent dark they intertwined? What difference do that make?**

Don't people gotta do what they gotta do to make it another day? You can't expect all this work to get done and misery be the only massa to oversee it. Even a nigger need a reprieve. Otherwise . . .

Otherwise what? Even Adam knew that had to remain unspoken until it didn't. That was the only chance at triumph.

All three of them drinking from the same pail with the same ladle, passing the sweetness between them, one behind the other, interrupted only when nibbling on the corn bread Maggie snuck them earlier, and they were anxious to share. She would always treat those boys like they were her own, sneaking them things she thought no one else knew about. Adam guessed it only went unpunished because it was seen as no different from fattening hogs. Since Isaiah and Samuel were better fed, their bodies were better defined. Between the food and the work, they were sinewy and slick with sweat. Only by their faces could you tell that they were still just boys.

"What it feel like," Adam asked quietly, knowing full well the answer would never satisfy. "To have each other?"

Samuel winced, but Isaiah broadened his chest.

"Like it supposed to," Isaiah said. Samuel shifted his foot back and forth on the ground, creating an arc in the dust.

"But you not afraid they might tear you apart?" Adam could find no more delicate way to say it and thought they might appreciate his direct approach because it acknowledged their bond as a fact rather than a problem.

Samuel looked at him. "Afraid? No. Not afraid. Other stuff, but not afraid."

"What other stuff?"

Samuel only grunted. Adam knew that to mean that it didn't matter. They had enough. Good God: it was enough! But how? How could they not need more of everything: more love, more life, more time?

It didn't go unnoticed by Adam the stark contrast between himself and Isaiah and Samuel. It began with the skin. Of theirs, one was a deep cavern without lamplight to guide, the other a midnight sky, but without any stars. He saw his own as a starry night without any sky. All three were impossible, but there they were, connected by terrain and grievance, and also by the thickness of lips that outlined the mouth in a most peculiar way. Adam's were pinker and, too, the dead giveaway.

When he wet his hair and pushed it back, there were moments that toubab women had looked at him as though he had potential, until, upon closer inspection, his lips revealed the crime in such an as- sessment. There was nothing he could do about the lips unless he tucked them inside. But he eventually had to talk and they would reveal themselves again. If women could discern, so could a catcher or lynch mob. The lips were the sole betrayer since birth.

He knew then, at least, that his mother had a

mouth shaped like truth because his was too. But truth called attention to itself in ways that were usually detrimental for the teller. His admiration for Isaiah and Samuel magnified because there they were in that barn, dim in the shadows of a truth that openly vexed anyone accustomed to lies. They were in the midst of each other and that hurt Adam as much as it pleased him.

Would he find someone with whom he could bide? It wasn't as if he hadn't been with women before, maybe even loved one or two of them. He just couldn't get past not having the choice. It was always there on the women's faces, too. Unwillingness wore a woman in a way that made him want to weep. And sometimes he did. Though none of that altered his actions—threat of whip or not.

He envied Isaiah and Samuel. Willingness radiated off of them in heat. It caressed their words, even the harsh ones. It adorned their hands, especially when they touched. They looked into each other's eyes and, despite all of Samuel's efforts to the contrary, something opened. How blessed Adam felt to be a witness to pure intention! He could carry this with him everywhere, even to his grave when it was time. No matter where they buried him—if they buried him: chances were that he would probably die at the end of a noose and swung from a tree before being lit aflame and foraged for parts—he would be aglow with the possibility he was shown, not the residual embers of an unkind torch.

He had it there with him, Isaiah and Samuel's gift, in front of the saloon, where he waited patiently for Paul. Watching the people come to and fro, through the swinging, creaking doors. They were laughing or stumbling. They were by themselves and they were in groups. Or they were arms-locked with lovers who were most likely only embraced for that solitary evening. All of this—the noise, the swinging, the high-stepping—was so different from Empty. Full, maybe.

Adam hoped that when Paul finally emerged from this lively place, he didn't come out too drunk. Toubab were unpredictable by nature and even more so after they had spirits. Adam reckoned that was probably because the spirits had such a cavern to fill that they had to work extra hard inside of them, and that additional inner labor is what made toubab outwardly meaner.

He had to be especially careful now in the bustling center of Vicksburg. The town kept its energy into the wee morning hours thanks mostly to the saloon, which drew toubab from neighboring towns and even from as far as Alabama. Usually, Paul would be leaving, finishing up whatever business just as things began to become merry. Adam only knew of the town's unrelenting character because he would, in the dead of night, drive James there, when James would pretend the coach was his, and he would spend his meager wages on liquor and women, which seemed to make him feel like a better man.

Things were most lively on Saturday evenings. That was strange given that these were the same people filling the churches the next morning. Then again, they said Jesus turned water into wine for just such frivolity and commanded the Sabbath for rest. So what were they doing in church anyway? Ah, yes: they were asleep.

A stranger approached. Adam quickly looked down.

"Excussse me. Can you point me in the direction of the nearessst outhoussse, pleasse?" the man slurred at Adam.

Lips safely tucked into the moisture of his mouth, Adam pointed toward the road, going back in the direction of Empty. It was a dark stretch of road that seemed, at a point, to be swallowed up by the woods. The man looked out at the path. He shivered and then smiled. He turned to Adam.

"Blacker than a nigger's pussy down there. And where exactly you say the outhouse is? I don't see it."

Adam raised his head and glanced at the man. He had already wet his pants, so an outhouse wouldn't be any good to him.

"Down the road and just 'round the bend on the right, suh."

"'Suh'?" the man said as he stumbled back a little. "What you call me?"

"I think you best head on now," Adam said, his chin tucked into his chest. He made a movement toward his hip as though he were packing something that he didn't have. He settled his shoulders, squared his chest, and lifted his face, finally, and looked the man in the eyes.

"Go on now."

The man looked on with blurry eyes. He moved a step closer to the coach and squinted. His lips parted as though he were about to ask Adam a question, a question that Adam knew before it could be uttered. The man snarled a bit, then eventually waved Adam off. He turned and looked at the darkness, then walked wobbly toward it.

Adam exhaled deeply and wiped the sweat from above his lip with the back of his hand. The motion angered him. He held his moist hand up before his face. He gazed at it. It didn't make any sense. Even at night, it was the same color as any toubab, and yet he wasn't one. He was only what could be seen in the shape of his mouth. He covered his mouth with his hand. Now what was he? Well, what he looked like was a fool aghast or a fool with a secret. But either way, a fool.

He noticed how the noise worked here. It was localized, coming not from every direction, but only from the saloon. Meanwhile, they were surrounded by a circle of quiet. Not that the woods were devoid of sound, but simply that the sound wasn't an intrusion. It moved with the pulse of everything, including Adam's heartbeat. It was like all of creation was inhaling and exhaling. Even the darkness seemed to move, but he knew this to be a mere trick of the eyes. He saw them back on Empty, in the dark of his shack, which wasn't filled with children, though he had them. They were elsewhere now, if they were still alive. He had only ever seen one of them. A girl. A color in between his and the mother's, whose name was lost now to memory. And that didn't matter because the name was chosen by Paul anyway and she likely never had her own name in the tongue of her mother, who was likely dead. A blessing.

In the dark of his shack, he had seen the movement of shadows that should have been still. The swaying imitating the dark rhythms of trees; that made sense. But why should the dark refrains of the door or the squares cut out of the wall for ventilation also be moving when what they were representing were stone-still? A game of the mind. That's all it was. Loneliness could do that to you. In the solitary moments, reality became undone and the physical laws ceased to abide by their promises, especially in that time between woke and slumber, which is when the boundary between here and there was at its thinnest. It was sly the way owls seemed to speak human tongues and figures long gone appeared out of nowhere to visit for a spell. Yet by the time you blinked or wiped the crust from eyelashes, everything returned to boredom. Adam sighed and learned to ignore the temptation that would lead him to believe that this was anything more than cruel teasing.

He thought that all this pretend movement would have given him the desire to move himself, but it just made him tired. He simply wanted to close his eyes even if there was danger in it. In slumber, there was . . .

What?

Rest for the body maybe, but nothing for the weary. His head nodded forward and then jerked back up. His eyes were dreary. He worried about how he might look to the festive toubab, even as they were distracted, for a night, by the smoke and spirits. He feared the thing hidden somewhere in the bowels of their laughter, that thing that made them say to niggers what they would say to themselves if they had any courage, what they used to say to one another before niggers became an unfortunate disruption. If they noticed him now, barely able to hold his head up straight because the night struck him, they would say niggers were lazy, but they would be incorrect. Niggers weren't lazy; niggers were tired. Bone tired. And when they finally weren't anymore: fire.

He let his eyes close. The last thing he saw was the red light creeping out of the saloon, shifting shape, blending with the night to give everything its dull glow.

"Bloody," Adam said, grinning.

When he finally fell asleep, head lolling, and snoring, he dreamt of nothing but words.

WHEN ADAM SAW PAUL, raggedy, in front of him it was as though disparate pieces of his reality snapped

immediately into place. Adam wasn't pleased with
the picture that formed. Paul reeked of spirits, and
his clothes were wrinkled, shirt untucked, and pants
unfastened. He was dirty. He had lost his balance
and swayed in order to keep it. And his hat was missing. Adam felt a twinge in the pit of his stomach.

"Massa. Is everything all right, suh?" he said with
a genuine look of concern wearing him like it was the
true face and his was the mask.

Paul slurred a response that Adam couldn't understand. He hopped down from the coach and got
a little closer. He caught Paul as Paul leaned a little
too much into him and breathed hell straight into
his nostrils, which made him hold his breath. This
was the closest he had ever been to his father. Maybe
father was too strong a word. Nevertheless, he had
an urge to be in his embrace irrespective of the odor
and the weight. Paul, in attempting to regain his
composure, put his hands on Adam's face.

"I need you . . ."

Adam stood, holding him, losing himself and forgetting where he was by looking into his face. He
was amazed by the question because it seemed to
be laced with tenderness. Paul's hand on his cheeks,
feeling the pulse of his body, and sweat forming right
where the palm covered. Is this what it felt like to be
someone's child? He had never before felt so close
to calling any man Pa, but there it was, rising in his
throat, lodged on the back of the tongue, silky.

"God has blessed us."

"Us, Massa?"

Paul looked at Adam and now his hands went from Adam's cheeks to Adam's chest. Adam's eyes widened as a smile crept upon Paul's lips. Unseemly, but maybe Paul had finally seen it, too—the identical bridge of nose and the same muscular forehead that was unmistakably Halifax. Not that he didn't already know, but seeing it all this close made him a firsthand witness. He didn't have to say. He didn't have to say anything. Adam understood. Truth could be known as long as it wasn't spoken. Given form, truth laid waste to even the most elaborate and fortified of walls. Not even the rubble was safe. Paul began to cough and Adam patted him on his back before grabbing the lantern sitting in the coach and holding it up to Paul's face, almost as if he wanted to make sure he wasn't dying.

Adam's face went blank. Here he was holding this man who was shivering even though the heat had not let up because the sun had gone down, so it must have been the spirits and whatever else had messed his hair and clothing. Adam cleared his throat.

He felt a stirring in his stomach that was likely to push right through his spine and leave a hole there that his soul could use to crawl out of the body. To go somewhere, to do something that was worthy of him being here. Not the basic drudgery that only unimaginative people with the lowest of minds could conjure up. But something that would give him the time to contemplate whether darkness could, in fact, move on its own like it was indeed living. And despite what any toubab had said, he had a soul, and not because of the toubab who interfered and caused his creation.

Since Paul had said "us" like they were actually kin, perhaps a sliver could be made into a gap. Had he the courage, Adam would have asked him about his mother. What did she think about giving birth to this special child? (He had only thought of himself as special because of how he could go from fitting into to not fitting into so many of the spaces he inhabited.) This special child who came out of the womb of the blackest of women, bright as a sunbeam, and could have damn near been a toubab if not for the tattletale mouth.

Maybe Paul treated her special, too. But what could that mean on the condition of death or worse? Adam liked to make room for the possibilities. That is what the line that sliced him as surely as the prime meridian allowed: to dance on both sides, to think a thing in theory, to measure it, observe it, to let it wander the mind for no reason other than because that was the only private place for someone like him. At the end, he had a choice to make: either give it back to its proper owner or slide it into his own britches to be used at some later time, if he was still there to use it.

Paul stumbled again and Adam held on to him and lifted him back to his feet. He realized how even his dead weight wasn't as heavy as he imagined it would be. Paul had been talking, mumbling some strange things about God that Adam could scarcely understand because Paul's tongue was tied by the spirits. But that was less strange than how Paul had previously held Adam's face between both of his hands and looked him in the eye and didn't ask for Adam to look away. This was the first time Adam saw, unflinchingly, his father's eyes, the same eyes that looked at his mother, or more honestly, looked away from her, and whatever was the thinnest line between the two.

He wanted to believe that the cold stare was a mis-interpretation. But even as Paul had tried to be gentle and use his momentary scene as the drunkard as the excuse to do so, his eyes kept telling the truth. Hard they were. Tearing, but still a golden menace.

These were the eyes his mother was also warned never to look into, not even when she was down on the ground in some older Fucking Place that rested layers beneath the one he knew so well. He wasn't sure if Paul looked at her or looked away, but he was positive that his mother looked away. He could feel it now. He searched deep in Paul's eyes for her face and it wasn't there, which meant he had only her body, but not ever her mind. Surely, afterward she may have lost that herself. It wasn't her fault.

But why would Paul treat her special? Given his color, whiter than pure black would permit, he wondered if his grandmother or grandfather were also raped. More likely, his grandmother since if it was his grandfather, his mother would have been a free woman by law, thus making him a free man. Not that they honored law above skin. Their commandments—haphazard, arbitrary, and utterly provisional—shattered sense to pieces. Father could also be uncle. Adam thought his entire life a gamble. His freedom or captivity reliant upon something as fragile as which toubab parent was shameless.

It was no longer safe to remember his mother. Doing so might bring her back to the same place and in the same condition in which she left. He didn't want to be cruel. But most of all, he thought that the woe she would bring with her, which could, he was sure, level the ground they stood upon, wouldn't only be a danger to Paul. He was tempted, though, to take the risk even if it meant ruin. Just to see her and see if he could see his face in hers. The mouth, he already knew.

"All right now, Massa," he said to a still-smiling Paul. "You want I should take you back to the Big House?"

The lantern went out and Paul buried his head in Adam's chest, and before Adam could ask again, he heard the snoring. He lifted Paul and placed him into the coach, plopping him down with more force than he intended. He looked at him for a moment. This man, this one man wielded power by his say-so alone. Outnumbered, but by the sheer force of his will had bent not only the land but the countless people under his control. How could the many be terrified of the one? The niggers back at the clearing were right: the toubab god must be the right one.

Adam shut the coach door and climbed back up to his seat. He pulled on the reins and the horses turned the coach slowly back in the direction of Empty.

If some posse had met them on their way, Paul was too deep in slumber to be of any assistance. They could snatch Adam right from under Paul's nose and sell him down the river to some salty-minded fools who would find his skin curious and his lips even more so. Ones like him went for a bit more on the block because they were thought to be more capable of intelligence, therefore less frustrating to instruct. But they had to be watched closely to ensure they didn't blend. Nothing a hot-iron brand on the chest couldn't solve.

Adam hoped that the thick of the woods on either side of them and the kindness of sleeping blooms would be the fence between him and thieves. The alternative was just as dangerous. He might have to kill a toubab, which was another way of saying he would have to die by suicide. There were never any real choices for chained people in this world, but for the strong . . .

It won't that people loved the strong. No. The strong were only to be feared, placated, lied to in the hopes of acquiring favor, a comfort, even if for a moment. It was that they despised the weak. They despised weakness because there was none

of the pomp and fervor erected to disguise its essential nature like there was with the strong. In the frail mercy that is weakness, deception's weight cannot be borne. Everything collapses, leaving only the debris, the casualties, and a fine layer of dust coating the air. This becomes trapped in the lungs and chokes all who inhale, and all must rightfully inhale; nature commands it. That is to say that weakness is but a stark reflection of the faces most wish to hide. The sad face, the mourning face, the weeping face that has stared into the abyss and discovered that there is nothing staring back. Empty. There was only us: Empty's children, every single one a cannibal. Weakness revealing how miserable it be that there ain't no such a thing as grace.

Adam stopped the horses. The night was thick, the air was heavy, and everything was still. Crickets chirped, the wheels on the wagon creaked, and Paul's roar remained, but otherwise, there was silence. No footfalls. No bushes rustling more than they should. No human-shaped shadows casting human-shaped darkness onto that of nature's, which was already dark enough. There was no need to rush and Adam enjoyed the free air, the scent of pine, and a sky full of stars, looking to the left and to the right as he pleased because he imagined Paul was sleeping. He heard insects whizzing past, some knocked up against his face harmlessly. Tiny as it was, this was peace.

He jerked the reins and the horses moved again.

They rode slowly. Adam's leg shook softly to the beat of his own making. The horses' hooves clicked. The leaves of trees rustled in the small but welcome breeze that the night was sometimes courteous enough to give after the day had been as tightfisted as it wanted to be. Adam allowed himself to slouch. He felt it then: how burdensome it was to remain straight-backed. It held the spine in a vise grip; perhaps he was more sensitive to it because the spine was part of the natural border that held one side of him from greeting the other civilly.

As they turned the bend up toward the edges of Empty, he couldn't see a single shack in the distance; the people were asleep. But there was a small glowing coming from somewhere. Dead tired, surely, from the fields and anxious for Sunday to be here already so that they could rest on their pallets until just before noon and wander lazily to the clearing to praise something in the sky that refused to see anything beneath it. In the distance, the shacks were erased and neither the moon nor the starlight could make it right.

Adam reached the gate. Before he jumped down from the coach to open it, he sniffed the air. Beyond the blooms, the weeds, and the animals, there was something in it that he couldn't exactly catch or name, but even the nameless took up room. He slid out of his seat and pulled open the gate. A part of it dragged against the ground, deepening, just a little, the curved route that had already been etched beneath it.

He went over to the coach, then opened the door to find Paul still snoring—laid back, drooling, and looking helpless. Adam leaned in close. Faintly, he could see the pulse throbbing in Paul's neck. Gently, Paul's chest heaved and caved to a rhythm that wasn't altogether predictable. It was off, and Adam's furrowed brow might have read as concern if his eyes weren't looking askance. **It would be so easy,** he said to himself. He got closer to Paul's face, noticing for the first time the creases that his hat normally hid. Worry wore the face like that sometimes, right across the forehead, for everyone to see, three of them, to tell the story. A warning.

Adam reached his hand out to touch them and, maybe more. Just as he did, Paul's eyes opened. Paul lifted his chin and narrowed his eyes.

"What are you doing?" he said as he lifted himself to an upright position.

"Trying to wake you, Massa. We home."

The both of them were motionless, Adam looking downward, Paul looking at Adam. They remained that way for a moment, allowing the silence to fill in the gaps, words sitting just on the inside of their mouths, pressing against the softer side of their lips, both on the verge of something sharp cutting the interior before striking the target. **What it would be like to call him "Pa,"** Adam thought. Then he reasoned that it wouldn't be worth the risk to find out.

"Well. Go on then. Take me back to the house," Paul said, though Adam sensed he wanted to say something else.

He left the coach and grabbed the horses by their reins and pulled. They followed him through the gate and up to the front of the Big House, where they stopped. Adam helped Paul out of the coach. Paul stumbled a bit, like a man who had not used his legs for a while and could no longer feel them. But he quickly found his footing. He looked upward and his expression changed from one of indifference to one of angst. From somewhere, he had regained himself, and the Paul of Vicksburg disappeared to be replaced by the Paul of Empty.

He didn't need Adam, so Adam didn't follow. The price of carrying out a favor that wasn't asked for was costly. Sticking to the routine was the safest option. So Adam pulled the horses over toward the barn. He stopped at the fence and opened it before taking the horses, still attached to the coach, through.

He moved around to the space between the horses and the coach and undid the connection. He then unbuckled and unfastened all of the leather straps holding the horses in place, whether ones that limited their motion or ones that blocked their sight lines. But he left the reins because that was how he would bring them back to Isaiah and Samuel, who would remove them after they were placed back in their pens. Then, if they weren't too tired, they would offer Adam some sweet water and maybe chat a bit before he walked back to his shack, alone, quiet, square, empty.

Usually, Isaiah and Samuel were up. But if they weren't, he wouldn't wake them. It was Sunday now and all niggers had was Sunday. He would unrein the horses and lead them into the pens himself.

He heard movement. They were up. Good. He wondered if they would mind him telling them about Paul using the word "us" even if it was during a drunken stupor. And would they also understand if he told them about the line? Surely they would if no one else did. Didn't they, both of them, also have a line shooting down their middle?

Closer and closer to the barn and the noise coming from inside was getting louder than the sounds any two people could possibly make.

SAMUEL

I cradled you because you was the only one who knew I won't no block of wood.

They stood quietly in the dark, perfectly still. They raised their voices no higher than the night sounds around them. Paul had come to them—and made a damn fool of himself, too. But his visit was a clear signal that it was time. Timothy, too, was waiting, would likely walk right into the barn now if Samuel didn't go to him, endure a travesty, and then be rushed out so Timothy's secret could be better kept than theirs.

There would be no argument. There would be no pleading. **Just do it. Now. Then run. Just like Maggie said.**

They stared at each other, but neither of them moved.

"But if you go . . ." Isaiah pleaded.

"I know." Samuel sighed.

"They sure to be after us if you . . ."

"They sure to be after us either way."

Earlier, between slopping the pigs and feeding the chickens, they had drawn it in the dirt: the bank, the river, the trees. Beyond that, they didn't know. They studied it carefully before Samuel wiped it away with a bare foot. Between the patrols (be sure to wait for the beat; even toubab have a particular rhythm) free the animals, head for the river. Food would be a problem. There was nothing to protect it from the water. So they would have to forage once they got over, where they would remain in the wilderness until passage north—past the grinding teeth of Tennessee, through the gripping claws of Kentucky, to the uncertain arms of Illinois—into free land was possible. The Choctaw had been known to give shelter despite the rumors Paul and the others had spread about cannibalism and the peculiar sweetness of black flesh, projecting their sins onto strangers.

Isaiah moved slowly toward Samuel and put an arm around his waist. He pushed against him. Samuel threw an arm around Isaiah's neck. They pressed their faces together. For long moments, they breathed heavily into each other. One of them coughed. The other choked. A sob and its refusal. They rubbed

their foreheads together. Finally, Isaiah put his hand
on Samuel's jaw and they looked each other in the
eyes. They kissed. It was neither gentle nor rough,
but it was full. Something had been exchanged.

When they released each other, Samuel wiped
Isaiah's face. Isaiah moved away. He bent down, feeling around for the lantern. He touched the top of
it and grabbed it. He walked over to the tool wall,
retrieved a flint, and lit it. He handed the lantern
to Samuel.

"Across the river," Isaiah said.

"Just keep swimming. Even if we can't see each
other in the water. We meet on the other side, deep
in the trees. Climb up them if we have to," Samuel
said. "If I ain't right behind you . . ."

"Maybe another way . . ."

"Need something sharp," Samuel insisted.

Isaiah sighed. "I got my wits."

"How you outwit a gun?"

"Ax no better."

Samuel felt it then, stiff against his back, not unlike a lover, unyielding, too close, obliging or deadly
depending on the wielder's intention. He stowed it
away when Isaiah was elsewhere in preparation, but
somehow Isaiah still knew. Knew **him,** more like it. It
was things like this that endeared Isaiah to him: the
knowing, the touching, the seeing. They were different, though, but somehow it was okay. It felt natural.

**Fine, then. Take nothing. Not a single thing
from this place. Not even a memory. Too heavy, I**

guess. Might as well shoulder the burden for the both of us. Always been like that anyway.

Isaiah stopped. He leaned back a bit, sizing Samuel up. "You fixing to be vex even now?"

"Good a time as any," Samuel said. He turned from Isaiah and looked out of the barn. It vexed him, indeed, how lush the plantation could be: a deep green where reds, yellows, or even purples could pop up any and everywhere without warning. The birds would fly about, swoop and dart in arcs and circles, dodging or crashing into the rays of sunlight, singing songs from the treetops that no one had the right to hear. How dare nature continue on as though his suffering didn't even make a dent, like the bloodshed and the bodies laid were ordinary, to be reduced to fertilizer by insects and sucked up by crops. No more than cow dung in the grand scheme. Same color, too.

The rain also came down, regardless, right upon the face only to obscure tears, mingle with them, wash them away, yet leave, still, the pain untouched; if anything, it ensured that the pain continued to gleam. The universe would have to pay for its indifference. Or somebody would.

It was creeping up inside him, the thought that peace might have lasted a bit longer had they listened to Amos. Maybe not, though, because you never knew with toubab. They made a lot of ceremony about their treaties, but those pieces of parchment meant nothing other than **Be careful.** Amos had abandoned them too quickly, yes, but Samuel also felt like Isaiah had been too resolute and forced Samuel to also be that way. What could it have hurt to be a comfort to Puah just once? Isaiah should have known, as he had given Essie hers. Why didn't Isaiah tell him about that? He talked and talked, and asked and asked, but never word one about what went on with Essie.

Maybe we not nothing better than the people, Samuel thought. **Who we to think that because when we lie together it feel like water and moonbeam that we far away from danger? And who come close we put in danger, too. Where this courage come from that we choose beat over quiet? Look at where we at now. Now we might be dead. Yeah. We might be dead.**

Samuel headed for the door. He turned back to look at Isaiah. The dead he felt inside didn't move in Isaiah's direction. No, there he felt something move and kick. There he felt something tremble and yawn. He had tried to look away from it, but it called to him. It called his name and he was anxious, stumbling over himself to say, "Yes, I'm here!"

It was almost happening. Almost happening in his eyes. **Go away, mist! Don't descend yourself here.**

"I don't wanna," Isaiah said. He walked up to Samuel and grabbed his hand.

Samuel looked down at their clasp of fingers. He squeezed tightly. "Run," he said, looking deep into Isaiah, this time without fear. Then he darted into the night, his lantern the only evidence that he was there.

EMPTY WAS ALL Samuel had ever known. His first memory was lying on a blanket, being surrounded by cotton plants, and hearing voices moan out a song. Suddenly, he was at someone's breast and she was smiling. Then he was among a bunch of children and they took some of the other children away and he was left there with a few to carry water back and forth from the well to the field. Soon, he would carry the food—first for people, then for animals. And all the days ran together, weren't worth delineating until that boy came, the one with the dry lips and skin as black as the sun could make it. Samuel gave him some water and Isaiah peeked into his soul. It shocked Samuel's eyes wide open to feel something touch him from the inside, like a song unfolding in his gut. It tickled. He figured that was the day he was truly born, that was his birthday if he ever had one.

How many midnights had they between them? An audience of animals, kinder than toubab, who could keep what they knew to themselves. He and Isaiah had stumbled into something he had never exactly seen before. There was someone called Henry once who would only answer to Emma, but that was different. She wasn't a man and everybody except toubab knew it. But that wasn't the same. No one cared much about Isaiah and Samuel, either, until a person thought he could also be a toubab and the two simply couldn't coexist.

During his endless chatter, Isaiah whined and whined about chains and who held what, but that was nothing but a coward's deal. Scared men always had silver tongues, and that was Isaiah's flaw. Still, Samuel would curl into himself only for Isaiah. He had the marks on the inside to prove it. When they were finally beyond this place and out in the world, some place far away where animals were said to run like thunder, he would teach Isaiah how to speak not in metals, but in flesh.

"You don't never get tired, 'Zay? Tired of begging for your life? Everything you do—the way you smile, the way you walk, where you look and don't look—just another way of begging for your life. You don't **never** get tired?"

He had meant to convey that just with his eyes, but the mouth would have its say.

Isaiah sat down on a pile of hay. He leaned back and then immediately sat up again. He brought his knees up to his chest and hugged them. Then he rubbed his head.

"I get tired. But I wanna live," he said.

See? That was where Isaiah had faltered. To survive in this place, you had to want to die. That was the way of the world as remade by toubab, and Samuel's list of grievances was long: They pushed people into the mud and then called them filthy. They forbade people from accessing any knowledge of the world and then called them simple. They worked people until their empty hands were twisted, bleeding, and could do no more, then called them lazy. They forced people to eat innards from troughs and then called them uncivilized. They kidnapped babies and shattered families and then called them incapable of love. They raped and lynched and cut up people into parts, and then called the pieces savage. They stepped on people's throats with all their might and asked why the people couldn't breathe. And then, when people made an attempt to break the foot, or cut it off one, they screamed "CHAOS!" and claimed that mass murder was the only way to restore order.

They praised every daisy and then called every blackberry a stain. They bled the color from God's face, gave it a dangle between its legs, and called it holy. Then, when they were done breaking things, they pointed at the sky and called the color of the universe itself a sin. And the whole world believed them, even some of Samuel's people. Especially some of Samuel's people. This was untoward and made it hard to open your heart, to feel a sense of loyalty that wasn't a strategy. It was easier to just seal yourself up and rock yourself to sleep.

But Isaiah.

Isaiah had widened him, given him another body to rely upon, made him dream that a dance wasn't merely possible, but something they could do together, would do together, the minute they were free.

A dreadful thing to get a man's hopes up that way. Hope made him feel chest-open, unsheltered in a way that could let anything, including failure, make its home inside, become seed and take root, curl its vines around that which is vital and squeeze until the only option was to spit up your innards before choking on them. Foolish Isaiah.

But how tender his affection.

When Samuel reached the Big House, it was dark. There wasn't even a single candle lit. The back porch door was open just like Timothy said it would be. Maggie was on a pallet in a small side room just off the porch. Her fists were tightly balled and pressed against her chest like she was ready for something.

"He told me leave this door open. Why I ain't lock it I don't know," she whispered.

Samuel was only half surprised that she was still awake. He moved closer to her with his lantern held up in front of him. Her face was screwed into distrust. Samuel loved her for it. She would be the one he missed most.

"You warm," Samuel said, which made Maggie smile. "I go this-a-way?" he asked, pointing toward the kitchen.

"You need to go that-a-way," Maggie replied, pointing outside, toward the river.

"You sound like Isaiah," he grunted.

"Sound like Isaiah got sense. Where your'n?"

"I got sense, Miss Maggie. Just this one last thing and then I heed you."

"You listen to me, now," Maggie said softly. She held on to a nearby wall and lifted herself up. Samuel extended a hand to help her, but she refused it. "You in this place, but you ain't of it. You hear what I telling you? Neither you or Isaiah—what you call him, 'Zay?—ain't neither one of you belong here in this place. Now, I ain't saying that you ain't welcome. No. What I saying is there be a whole better place for you, maybe not somewhere, but some**time.** Whether that particular time is in front or behind, I ain't got the power no more to tell. When you don't use a thing, you lose a thing, you know. But I know for true it ain't **this** time. So you gotta make a place to find the time where you belong. That's what they tell me."

"That what who tell you?"

Maggie pointed outside, and Samuel saw a shadow flash.

"Uh huh. You seen it, too. I can tell by your eyes," she said. "That mean you got it."

Samuel was still looking outside, but that shadow had already passed. "Got what?"

"The favor. It something that get passed down. Sometimes skip a generation, but you got it anyhow."

Samuel looked at Maggie. "Where I get it from?"

Maggie looked outside. "From them, I reckon."

Samuel didn't understand. His gaze returned to the outdoors. He had hoped that by now Isaiah was halfway across the river. There was only a beat in between patrols.

"Miss Maggie, I gotta . . ."

"I know." Maggie smiled. "A shame, but you gotta."

She took a couple of broken steps over to him and she threw her arms around him. Samuel stiffened up. He was afraid that the shadow might ride her back again and grab him along with her arms that were holding him now. But he didn't see it, which gave him the room he needed to bend a bit into Maggie's embrace. She patted the top of his head.

"Foolish," she said softly. "But if you finna go this-a-away . . ." She pointed toward the kitchen and the doorway on its right. Then she stopped. "You know something, you remind me of somebody. Man called Ayo Itself, but toubab called him Daniel."

Samuel smiled at that first name because it sounded like it meant something important. He looked at her. "You warm, Miss Maggie. Always been."

Then he walked off the porch.

He walked through the house slowly, straining to see the rooms filled with stuff—lots of things he couldn't imagine the use for. And so many look-ing glasses, which didn't surprise him in the least. He looked into one and thought he saw two faces. Maybe that other one was his mother's?

He climbed the stairs and the shadows flickered and faded, grew and shrank as he ascended and made his way down the second-floor hallway. When he reached Timothy's room, which was right where Timothy said it would be, Timothy was standing there, not far from the door, naked as day one, in the dark. Samuel nearly dropped the lantern.

"I'm not certain when my father will return, but I imagine it will be soon." Timothy smiled. "He didn't take James with him, so I don't know if he'll stay out as long."

He pulled Samuel close to him and planted a kiss squarely on his mouth. Samuel jerked a little, revolted by how catfish it felt. Timothy, noticing his shock, slowly pulled away.

"I imagine you've never been in a bed like this before," he said, pointing at it. He moved closer to Samuel again now that he could see that the ice had been broken and perhaps the bulge in Samuel's pants wasn't a trick of shadows. "Have you?" Timothy whispered in Samuel's ear.

Samuel shook his head.

"Come."

Timothy walked him over to the bed.

"You can put the lantern down over there," he said, pointing to a desk in front of the windows.

Samuel looked out at the moon, a bright white half circle in the dark. He hadn't realized before that Timothy was the same frosty color, and he wondered if that was where all toubab came from, if they fell here by accident or punishment, and that was why they were all so troubled: they were merely homesick.

Samuel looked in the mirror that stood in a corner of Timothy's room. Isaiah once told him that he might find his mother's face in his own. So when he would go to the river, he would look at his reflection to see. There was his face, only slightly distorted on the water's skin. When he smiled, he thought that maybe the dimples that appeared on his cheeks were where he could see her. Locked in a grin, he found her where he had never before thought to look. And perhaps in the way his nose flared and spread across his face with that knowing, perhaps that signaled his father, from whom he was certain he received his impatience and stubborn clinging to love.

In the mirror, the image was much clearer than that of the river. He looked closely. Something tumbled from his eyes that was not tears. War maybe, the wild. There was a time and place for wild, but it mostly had to be curbed, reserved, set aside to keep from interfering in the moments when he had to be tender. Or wily.

He thought about what his father must have been like, whether he was forced upon his mother in some other Fucking Place. Some of them forced, anyway. He wondered if they had, instead, stumbled upon each other, clumsily, but of their own free will, pulled together in an awkward movement and slightly averted gazes, but smiles nonetheless. Free as will could be under the circumstances. Like him and Isaiah.

What Samuel didn't know, he invented. His father's name, then, was Stuart, a name he had heard Paul call a friend of his once. Samuel liked it immediately because it reminded him of hock-spitting, something he imagined his father to have done in the face of his own master, which explained his absence. He probably got his strength from Stu, Samuel figured, though he imagined it was his mother who survived.

"I know you're not as shy as you seem," Timothy said to him, breaking Samuel's concentration. "I've seen you and Isaiah, you know. At night, I've seen you."

Samuel shifted uncomfortably. The blade dug into his back.

"Take off your clothes, Samuel. Or should I call you Sam? Come lie with me."

Slowly, Samuel removed his shirt. Timothy shuddered.

"You're a different color than Isaiah." Timothy's eyes softened and he stroked his own cheek. "He said purple was the one he liked most. I thought he was just repeating my words back to me." He rose from the bed and moved toward Samuel.

"In the North, it snows in the wintertime. You know what snow is? Have you ever seen it? No, probably not. Doesn't happen here much." He touched Samuel's chest. "It's what happens when it rains, but it's so cold outside, the rain freezes and comes out of the sky like tiny pieces of cotton. It's a beautiful sight. The ground gets coated with it and somehow, things get so quiet. Children love it. They play and laugh and throw it at one another. Makes it hard to walk around, though. Wagons can't even come down the road. You can't even see the road actually because it's all covered in snow. The whole world, it seems, turns white. It's so peaceful." He traced his finger down to Samuel's navel. "But after a few days, after people have trampled through it and it has started to melt, everything gets so messy. And it musses your clothes and you tramp the mess into your room and all you start to do is long for the spring again. I swear, you'd sell your soul just to see a flower bloom somewhere. That's what made me miss home. Up in Massachusetts, the winters are so long and brutal you start to think you'll never see a flower again. That's not true, of course. But for a little while, you think that the color won't come back ever. Maybe one day you'll get to see the North in the winter."

Samuel didn't want to be anywhere where the white fell out of the sky cold and frozen, laying its claim over everything.

"When my father dies, I inherit all of this." Timothy looked around the room and seemed disappointed. "All of it. The house, the land, the Negroes, everything." He stared at Samuel as if expecting a response. Samuel stood unmoved. "You know the first thing I'm going to do when it's all mine? I'm going to set every single slave free. Well, maybe not every single. I will still need some to do the housework and harvest cotton, but I know I don't need as many as my father has now. He's overcautious."

Samuel made no gesture.

"Manumission, Sam. That means I'll set you and Isaiah free—that is, if you want to leave. I imagine it will be much harder out there than it will be on the plantation with me in charge. I don't want the responsibility, to tell you the truth. I'd much rather be somewhere earning a commission for my artwork. But my father is depending on me, you understand."

Man-u-mission. The word echoed in Samuel's head, rang bells, and made him vibrate within. In the tolling, Samuel allowed himself to think about how weeds feel between the toes of a free man. He might rip them up out of the ground or leave them be on a whim, all without having to worry about whether his choice would disturb the already tenuous balance and incite some fool to violence for something as simple as consideration. Color would be different, too, mainly because he would finally have a chance at figuring it out, detecting the tiny differences in shades moving one into the other. He would have the gumption to pick a favorite since there would be a reason to, might walk into a tailor's store and buy a pair of britches for his trouble. **Pardon me, kind sir, I take this pair right here. Nah, I won't need no box for them. Do you mind if I wore them right now? And those shoes—yes, I take those, too.**

Shoes on his feet!

Freedom, he imagined, could be some fancy thing if done correctly, papers in hand, watching, quietly, in deference, the disappointment on the faces of the catchers after he told them that his massa had **let** him be a person, finally. Joy was never meant to be boxed in. It was supposed to stretch out all over creation, like the snow Timothy had just finished talking about. Just like that.

A burning sensation shot through him. He was unsure how the word **let** had slipped its way into his most private of places, places even Isaiah had only glimpsed. He was too close; that was the problem. For too long, the edge had rubbed right up against him, grabbed his stuff, and licked his cheek for salt. These were the channels for contamination, and he wasn't sure that a split could reverse the ailment. He had already been exposed. There was no one to tell him how to cleanse the body or gather the right herbs for a healing ritual, no one to show him how not to be a danger to himself or those he loved. It wasn't his fault, though. He didn't choose this. It chose his mother, so his selection was umbilical. And he didn't even have the pleasure of knowing her name. So he gave her one, too: Olivia.

Yes.

He liked that.

Timothy kissed his neck and, for a moment, Samuel thought it was Isaiah. He almost allowed his head to fall back and his eyes to roll to the whites. At the corner of his mouth, dribble had just begun to glisten, his arms nearly ready to embrace. Isaiah would do that very thing: start softly, coaxing. Maybe that's who Timothy learned it from.

Everything was similar except the smell. No matter how long Isaiah shoveled manure or turned hay or lugged pails of slop, beneath all of that, he always smelled like a coming rain, the kind that would make you lift your head in anticipation. Open your mouth and wait. Because of that, Samuel could roam free in those meanwhiles, touch the veins of leaves, build pillows out of moss, drink dew from the palms of his hands. This, too, was a kind of freedom, for it sought to nourish rather than make the act of living a crime. **Who built this?** Samuel asked Isaiah as they flew through the woods and smiled at robins as they passed by. **We did,** Isaiah said. Then the sunset let loose purple and hummed its way into the ground.

Isaiah's breath smelled like milk and his body curled snugly into Samuel's. Moonlight did all the talking. It just happened. Neither of them chased the other and yet each was surrounded by the other. Samuel liked Isaiah's company, which had its own space and form. Samuel knew for sure because he had touched its face and smiled, licked every bit of calm from its fingers and giggled. Then, without either of them realizing what had happened, it snuck up on them—the pain. They could be broken at any time. They had seen it happen so often. A woman carted off. Tied to a wagon screaming at the top of her lungs and her One risking the whip to chase after her, knowing damn well she couldn't save him, but if she could just stay near him for a few more seconds, his image wouldn't fade as quickly as it would have had she not challenged death.

No one was the same after the Snap. Some sat in corners smiling at voices. Others pulled out their eyelashes one by one, making their eyes seem to open wider. The rest worked until they collapsed, not just collapsed in the field, but collapsed in on themselves until there was nothing left but a pile of dust waiting to be blown away by the wind.

This is why Isaiah and Samuel didn't care, why they clung to each other even when it was offensive to the people who had once shown them a kindness: it had to be known. And why would this be offensive? How could they hate the tiny bursts of light that shot through Isaiah's body every time he saw Samuel? Didn't everybody want somebody to glow like that? Even if it could only last for never, it had to be known. That way, it could be mourned by somebody, thus remembered—and maybe, someday, repeated.

Well, shit. If their fate was to be found in two piles of dust that would be swept up and scattered, then damn it, let there be a storm beforehand. Let the blood run down and the heat, too. If the Snap was to come, at least they would have known what it was like to be each other, be really in each other, before the brokenness was brought to bear.

This was the balm. And this was the thing that made the ax necessary even though silly ol' Isaiah didn't wish to carry his own. Everything was worth it for just a few more seconds of Isaiah's singing, so it wouldn't fade so quickly when they parted.

Timothy smelled wrong. Not exactly like whips and chains, although that was there, too, underneath the softness and assurances. Mostly, he smelled like hound dog, fresh out of the river, splashing against fish, wagging its way back onto shore.

"Did you hear me, Sam? I said that once my father is dead, I will set you and Isaiah free."

But this was a trick of surrender and Samuel refused to buckle. What would they have to wait, forty, eighty seasons? Hope that they survived, intact, the hours; weren't sold off, maimed, or murdered, whimsically, beforehand? Worst of all, trust a toubab to keep his word—in exchange for what? How many times must they lie with him, endure his affections, however sweet, rise with the smell of hound upon them for a time that might be mirage or fleeting? Whoa, then, man. Whoa!

"I admit," Timothy whispered to him, "I have much to learn still. But I know this: You **are** a people. Love **is** possible."

Never ask a man his thoughts before he has had an opportunity to come. He's liable to say whatever is expedient, whatever shall remove obstacles to his orgasm. Speak to him after, when he has been released from the throes, after the spasms have subsided, and his breathing has returned to normal. Wait until he has rested and wishes to scour the previous act from his body and mind. Ask him then, when calm has crept back into his lungs, for that's when it's most likely that the truth will prevail. Samuel, however, refused to shoulder such risk. The heat rose up in his back and spread like wings. Malice couldn't be found anywhere except in the faint smile curling upon his lips. **Do it, man! Go on and do it!**

"You can look at me, Sam. It's okay."

Samuel knew there were two things you never looked in the eye: dogs and toubab. Both will bite, and only from one of those wounds is there a chance to heal. He had never wanted to be with Isaiah more than now. He and Isaiah shared each other. He thought Timothy should know.

"They said we was something dirty, but it won't nothing like that at all. It was easy, really. He the only one who understand me without me saying a word. Can tell what I thinking just by where I looking—or not looking. So when he look in on my inside . . . the first time anybody or anything ever touch me so, everything in my head wanna say nah, but nothing in my body let me."

Timothy stepped back and looked at Samuel.

"I understand. If nobody else understands, I do," Timothy said.

He touched Samuel's face. Timothy's smile was telling. It confirmed for Samuel everything that his intuition had already revealed: he didn't have to be able to read to know that toubab were blank pages in a book bound, but unruly. They needed his people for one thing and one thing only: To be the words. Ink-black and scribbled unto the forever, for they knew that there was no story without them, no audience to gasp at the drama, rejoice at the happy ending, to applaud, no matter how unskillfully their blood was used. The first word was power, but Samuel planned to change that. He bent his fingers to tell a tale that would make the audience scramble for cover.

"Maybe tomorrow you and Isaiah come and visit me together?" Timothy asked softly.

Samuel snapped.

It was as though the room had become untenably wide, like he had all the room in the world to move, to spread limbs, to jump, to hold his chest in glee. From the first time since walking into that house— they called it big, but it, too, was empty, which made its crimes easy to discover.

In this wideness, Timothy shrank in his view, but his pitiful entreaties stretched to meet the size of the room blow for blow. This made Samuel catch a fever that ignited his forehead. The shape of his fury, because that is what his face became, was a scythe: curved, sharp enough to slit the throat, its edge pointing mercilessly back at its wielder. But that didn't matter. It never does.

He reared back and his fist came quicker than he thought it could. He knocked Timothy to the floor and the thud tipped the lantern over. Timothy let out a small whimper. Samuel reached behind his back, snatched the ax from its hiding place, and with one quick swipe, he put it deep into Timothy's temple.

He watched as the blood sputtered and ran down Timothy's face. It began to form a puddle on the floor. There was no scream, not even a whisper, but the face contorted and the mouth moved, tried to form, maybe, a question. Samuel turned away. He knew that Timothy, in his last moments, was confused, needed to have an answer, and Samuel would ensure that he would never get one. In that small way, this charming young man who fancied himself blameless would know a fraction of what it felt like. Haints did. Countless people whose voices could be heard even if their bodies were nowhere to be found, who followed them all around and would give them no rest because they, themselves, couldn't rest. The tiny word left on their lips made rest impossible and so they pecked at them not realizing that they had the same question, too.

The body jerked for much longer than Samuel anticipated. Finally, there was a sound that came out of Timothy's mouth, not words, not the question that Samuel would certainly ignore, but more like rainwater spilling into a hole. Then, suddenly, his body stopped moving altogether and the expression of agony was gone and he looked more peaceful, like someone sleeping with his eyes open.

Samuel stooped down. He had never looked this closely into Timothy's face. It was the first time he had the chance to study a toubab's face without having to worry about the chaos such a prideful move could bring. Everyone made such a big deal about those eyes, blue as noon sky. Samuel didn't understand it. They just looked empty to him, bottomless and liable to suck up anything that waded into them. He couldn't see himself in them. Isaiah had said the same thing, but never with the conviction that Samuel thought it should have.

He left the ax where it was embedded and he stood up finally, rose himself off of his first kill, astonished by how hard he imagined it would be, but how simple it actually was. He thought that he would be plagued by guilt and shame, but he actually felt like he had, in the tiniest of ways, righted a wrong. He would need to claim more bodies before he could feel proud about his actions, though, and there were more bodies to be had. But he was satisfied that if he had died that very moment, he would have forced them to pay at least a portion of the debt owed. They would have imagined that this made them square.

What ain't nearly enough to us, he thought, **more than enough to them. But they gon' be fixed.**

He looked down at his blood-soaked chest and let out a sound that was somewhere between a sigh and amusement. He imagined that he would smile a little bit, but only a tear could come. He didn't bother to wipe it away. Wiping it away would be to admit that it was there in the first place. So he withheld and it tickled his cheek but didn't make him chuckle. It ran all the way down to his chin and quivered there before disappearing into the blood on the floor.

There was still so much to know. Like where did Isaiah learn how to cornrow? And why? The singing. How far back in Isaiah's family did it go? Was the kink in his hair proof that his mother was a warrior?

He would have to creep now, low to the ground like a night mist, not hugging the eager weeds but teasing them with the promise of his moisture, perhaps leaving behind a thin layer, enough for them to get by.

He put his foot on Timothy's lifeless neck, grabbed the ax by the handle, and pulled it out. Timothy's head made a tiny clunk, which was followed by the drumbeat of footsteps headed for Timothy's room.

LAMENTATIONS

A separation from your suffering requires a separation from yourself. The blood has been maligned, which means that conflict courses through your very veins.

It was a matter of survival. But time does not function the way you think it does. We knew this before and we know it now. So judgment must come soon because you have made the conflict, which is now your blood, a matter of honor, and this mostly leads to arrogance. This is the thing that pumps through your heart. Or will. Or has. Sometimes, we must remember that you perceive time as three separate occasions, when for us, it is only one. It **will** be the thing that pumps through your heart, if you are not careful, if you do not heed. Do you understand?

Given over to this raging war inside, you will not be able to attend to your liberation in the manner that will most certainly set you free. You will make something else, something impossible, the priority. In the interest of preserving your reputation among the children of your conqueror—who are also, oh!, your siblings—you will compromise your living and consider half-life better than death when they are truly the same.

We weep for you.

You are the children we had fought for and lost.

You are the offspring betrayed and bemoaned.

The regret, however, is not on your behalf. It is because of what we unleashed. In damning you, we doomed ourselves.

First the external war, then the internal one. The latter much more bloody.

But there is hope.

We have brought storms with us. Followed you across mighty waters and distant lands to a series of stolen places where we owe other peoples another great debt, all of which rests on their forgiveness. And yours.

These are forces created in your name that will be renamed beyond our ability to control. Forgive us.

It is the only magic we have left.

SONG OF SONGS

The sun was burning high when they were walked above onto the ship's deck. A strange rotation around the ship, and some of its crew spat on them, laughed, and downed libations. They seemed unaware of their own filth as they pinched their noses and frowned. Some of them held on to guns, others had knives. Kosii looked into their faces. He wanted to understand what they were, see if he could retrieve something from them that could explain all this. He saw pits with hands reaching out of them. He saw little skinless girls lined up to sing. He saw boys running into sea-foam and when they turned to wave goodbye to their families standing on the shore, they had everything except faces. Suffocation was their birthright.

Chains rattled as Kosii and the two others he was linked to shuffled around the deck to the jeers of all. Then he saw him, nearby and partially hidden by the glint of the sunlight and the mask of shadow, but recognizable by the tone of his grievances. It was Elewa. In the pit of his stomach, Kosii felt spikes jut out from a sphere. There was a vibration then, which summoned forth the tremors in his entire body, bringing up everything and taking him down to his knees.

One of the skinless said something to Kosii in their jackal language in which everything landed like an insult. But there was another voice coming from that corner of the ship where the sun couldn't all the way reach. It sounded so near, the voice, and yet he couldn't pinpoint its direction. It didn't matter. He recognized its clicks and timbre, its highs and lows, and on them he could climb, reach the frightening heights generally hidden in the mist and shrouded in treetops. A hand. All he needed was a hand, a signal of some kind, a call, permission. In the silence, seven women, linked by the crooks of their elbows, heads newly shaven and breasts firm—the one in the middle ululated. It had begun.

Then Elewa moved closer, through the crowd, and Kosii saw that it wasn't Elewa risen after all. It was a boy. He was pale but not hard, looked younger than Kosii even, perhaps had just reached puberty himself, walking in footsteps twice as large as his own feet. Admirable. Dirty, but it was clear that he was a boy denied the playfulness that all boys enjoyed, to give chase and smile mischievous but harmless things into existence. To pick fruit from trees and stain their hands with the juices. Stick a toe in a river and get pushed in by a friend, but only outside of the presence of the hippos that ruled the water. Watching peacocks bow and preen and walk in circles to impress their betrothed. Someone had denied this boy all of that, had interrupted his flow, dammed it, and replaced it with thorn and dry weed. And it was apparent in the moisture of his eyes, which he wiped away before it had the chance to be a sign of life.

Kosii held on to the boy's budding sympathy with both hands, marveled at its shape, rubbed its smooth edges, and let its sweetness dance on his tongue. It was alive, curled into its own warmth and only unfurled slowly like a fist opening unto peace. This was kind, but too late. Kosii had already spotted the pulse of life throbbing in the boy's neck and this, too, had its calling. Loud and rambunctious, wide open and seductive. It asked for him and he obliged.

He shot up and roped his chains around the skinless boy's neck, then snatched his wrists apart. The boy kicked and struggled and thrashed. Kosii didn't let go. The others began to charge him, but Kosii had already managed to pull himself back, up against the half wall of the deck. He took a deep breath and shouted.

"This triumph is for Elewa in the name of King Akusa!"

Then he fell backward, over the wall of the ship, the boy in his grasp. With them, the two other people chained to Kosii crashed down into the waves, shocked then comforted by the cold embrace of the water, soothed by the sea-foam and then absorbed.

Kosii wouldn't swim. He held on to the skinless boy until his body was still then he let out his own breath and together they began to sink.

Such a shame, but he had to do it. Had to. Pressed into this corner, there was no way he was going to die alone. It had already been determined: they shall die together. For this was glory.

Elewa.

As they descended, Kosii prayed for forgiveness from the woman and the man who were chained to him. He didn't ask them if they had wanted to drown but took it upon himself to drag them into the deep. Way down, lower now than the bottom of the beast they had dropped from. Maybe that was the sin his father left out of the story, the part about how, in order to survive the mountain people, they had come down from a mountain of their own, had to wear the remains of some other people's children around their own necks. Victors gave themselves the right to rename murder "triumph" and adorn themselves with jewelry made from the bones of the vanquished.

So this is what it looks like, Kosii said to himself as the shifty, watery light began to fade. **The view from the mountaintop; it hurts.**

Then, as the blackness took everything:

Good.

JAMES

James wandered the perimeter, kept himself at
the edges, surveyed the middle spaces by walking around the entire border of the land, first alone,
then with a few of his hands, like Zeke, Malachi, and
Jonathan. There was no way to fortify what was already keeping the niggers at bay: the fence, the river,
the woods rigged with traps and assassins, fear. Well,
the last was the one exception. He could always em-
ploy indulgences that allowed them to ratchet the
last up high.

"When is Paul due back?" Malachi asked.

"Not sure," James answered. He slung his rifle over
his shoulder and made more determined steps. He
couldn't locate the moon. Perhaps it was behind the
trees preparing for its descent, leaving the inkiness

of the sky for the sun to obliterate. He yawned and held his lantern out in front of him. Its corona wasn't bright enough to do anything except show him how impenetrable the night could be. He kept it moving.

His clothes were a bit more raggedy than he would have liked, but he had no means, not enough means to dress better. Like Paul, for example. He had no wife to stitch something together for him, no children to wash and fold his belongings as a part of their daily chores. No children that he would claim anyway, which was probably for the best since he had nothing to give them except hard hands and aching feet, which were useless. He didn't even have his cabin to turn over to them; that belonged to Paul. He couldn't even afford slaves.

If James hadn't looked so much like his mother and, therefore, like Paul's mother, he was certain that Paul would have turned him away, accused him of fraud, and maybe called for the sheriff to lock him up for trespassing or vagrancy. But his face saved him.

"You walk that-a-way," he said to Zeke, pointing over toward a row of slave cabins, which sat ramshackle and simple, just beyond the weeds. "Holler if you see anything out of order."

He realized as soon as he said it the futility of the command. To be a nigger was to exist in a constant state of disorder, a darkness that could only be righted by light, a jungle that could only be untangled by machete, a chaos that could only be overruled by a slow hand and swift authority. **Blood,** James thought. Sometimes, he hungered for blood.

And blood was plentiful among the slaves, flowed through them like passion—singing and dancing, beating in their tongues, pulsing through their lips, stretched into wide smiles. He could smell it. They had changed very little from the ships and he had to admit to himself how much that surprised him. He had expected that they would pull themselves up like he did, find possibility in the flourishing impossible, break chains like he broke out of the orphanage. But no. They had merely brought the belly of the vessel with them everywhere they went. It assailed the senses. Then again, who were they lucky enough to be kin to?

They were of raggedy dress (his anger was fueled by the similarity of their attire and his) and little intelligence. They lived on top of one another, packed into dwellings by their own will as much as Paul's. They were belligerent and smelled of a toil that couldn't be washed away. They ate refuse and their skin bore the curse of wild. It was easier to think of them as animals, not so different from cows and horses, apes of great mimicry that managed to speak the language of humans. That they could sometimes inspire erections was no ill reflection on the bearer of such hardness. The fact of the matter was that they could pass for human and, therefore, trick the loins, if not always the mind.

After a long while, Zeke returned to the fold.

"Everything looks all right. Niggers accounted for," he said.

"All right, then. You three can wait for the next shift and then go," James said.

"Oh. You might wanna go see 'bout Miss Ruth," Zeke said. "She out there. Wandering for no good reason."

James scratched his chin.

"What she doing out there?"

Zeke shrugged his shoulders.

"Well, where is she?"

"Over by the river, just past the barn."

James shook his head. "Goddamnit. Keep watch. I'll see to Ruth."

She was the one woman on the entire plantation worth her salt and that would make things difficult. Her pale skin, red hair, and tight bosom hurt his feelings so deeply that masturbation only picked at the wound. She did nothing to hide her offense, not even the decency of a shawl on cool evenings in autumn.

He remembered how it was back then. It was a year of debilitating heat that emanated from everywhere, of him crossing his legs or squatting to contain it or keep it away. He pulled his hat down low over his eyes whenever Ruth would pass. He stuffed his face with any food that was near so as to occupy his tongue. He was barely able to resist smearing manure under his nose to prevent the smell of verbena from reaching him. He thought he would collapse from longing if he didn't do **something.**

One sticky twilight, a nigger was bathing down by the edge of the swamp when she should have been in the kitchen. She stood in the path of the setting sun as it reflected off the water's skin and caused a bright beam of light to obscure her body. She thus appeared not-nigger, was revealed as a figure he was able to hold in his mind until the deed was done. In that crimson light, her nigger tangles became golden locks, her black face, a coy blush—just like the women back home in Merry Old.

And she proved just as feisty. She bit him. She scratched his neck, leaving a mark that was still raised there. For that, he punched her timid face repeatedly until the blood ran down her mouth and covered the lower part of her face like a veil.

When he pushed himself inside of her—when he pumped and twisted and jabbed, bringing to already scarred spaces new contusions—he discovered that what he heard about these wenches wasn't true after all: there were no teeth on the inside of their cunts, no hooks that would hold the cock inside, bleeding it dry while the man hooted and howled in pain. He didn't feel his soul being sucked from him. No, sir. It was just as smooth and proper as all the prim white pussies that escaped England just like he did.

But she was spirited, and not even his massive slugs to her top lip or to the edge of her chin could stop her stark raving. So, after he released his thick spray, he, with his pants trapped around his ankles, clutched her throat and smashed her head under the water. And she kicked and kicked, bruising his jewels and darkening his inner thigh. She kicked for what seemed longer than any human being could feasibly hold her breath. Then he remembered that he wasn't dealing with a human being and that perhaps those things—her hell-fury and her gumption, her animated arms and legs—were the teeth and hooks of which they spoke. One final blow to her hip to keep her legs at bay and he heard something snap. He let her go.

Drenched, he stumbled back to drier shore. And up she rose: bent to the side from where he struck her, soaked in blood and river water, staring at him with black, glowing eyes. Then suddenly, she looked past him and he swore that he felt a razor slice his shoulder as her eyes moved over it toward the distance. He felt himself loosening. It started in the pit of his stomach and worked itself outward. He lost control of his bowels. Urine trickled down his legs, to the ground, and toward the river; shit dropped into his pants. His breathing slowed. He felt light and empty. It was as if his body was turning to air. Was he dead? He looked at his feet and he seemed to be floating, like a haint. It made him laugh. The one magical nigger in the whole place and he had the misfortune of choosing her.

Ain't that just dandy?

The next thing he remembered, he was back in his shack, facedown on his bed. For a moment, he felt well rested. Afterward, however, he could sleep only in fits, and his walk was suddenly bowlegged. There wasn't a nigger on the plantation who didn't make him want to vomit—especially the females. The resolve it took for him to overcome the sudden bout of nausea he would experience when one of them came near and, perhaps, stood too close, or when one of them would speak his name and drag it out a few seconds too long as the slow-witted were wont to do. And if James tried to say her name, the name of the one had he desecrated, tried to pronounce even the first letter, **M** . . . mm . . . mm, he found himself, again, coming undone, like at the river. So he kept his mouth closed and avoided her. No more dinners at Paul's, not even when a place was set for him. **No, I'll eat in my cabin. It's fine. I can keep my eye on the niggers better from there. Just in case.** His rifle became a crucial border. And from the safety of that demarcation, he learned a great deal more about them than those who ignored the line.

Trying to find where Ruth could be, he walked through the darkness as rock and weed crunched beneath his boots. The only song was the click of crickets backed by the river's rush. He was listening for other footsteps, looking for other imprints, sniffing for perfume, but detected nothing. He slipped on the mud of the bank and caught a glimpse of a figure in the periphery. He turned quickly only to see the frilled edge of a gown pass by a tree. He followed it.

He walked along the bank and then through the

trees. His lantern flickered and then from behind him, a voice.

"Late for a swim."

He couldn't see her face even when he held up the lantern because she wore the shadows like something given to her by an old friend.

"Impolite not to speak."

He wanted to, but she had caught him by surprise.

"You must be the one who stole the moon, eh?" he said finally.

She smiled. He intentionally denied himself the opportunity to.

They walked across the plantation, neither of them speaking. He was amazed by her ability to go out in the darkness without stumbling, without uncertainty, without a lantern. He tried to provide her the benefit of his light, but she refused it, retreated into the thickness, laughed at the mere suggestion. And he wanted so badly to see her face.

"What you creeping around for, Ruth?" he asked, hoping to draw her out.

She twirled in her nightgown, praising the coolness that rushed underneath it, and hummed a melody. By the time they reached the fence, she was already under it and skipping up the stairs to his cabin.

He thought her a puzzle missing more than a few pieces. But maybe those were the best kind. Those were the ones that required a bit more from those putting them together: a bit more time, a bit more patience, a bit more imagination. The last was the most fertile of grounds, where mastery was sown, and he had planned to patiently await what might grow.

She walked into the cabin and danced around it.

"This place is a mess," she finally said. "Nobody ever taught you to keep house? You need to get hitched, maybe."

He smiled. He thought she might have, too. He put the lantern down on a small table with only one chair tucked under it. It was the first time he had ever even given that any consideration—**Me? A wife? Who would? My manner ain't exactly roomy for another.** He was distracted, though, because her hair was fire.

Ruth turned and went toward the door. He didn't want her to leave.

"I hope your cousin comes home soon. He's going to sell those niggers that looked at me, you know."

"I know."

He looked at her as she walked past him. "Ruth, ain't safe for you to be wandering the plantation at night. You should get back home, you hear?"

"Why should I be scared of what's mine?" She looked at him, puzzled.

He removed his hat for the first time in her presence. As he had said before, his manner wasn't roomy. He leaned his head to the side. "If only it **was** yours." He held his hat to his chest to express respect and sincerity.

Ruth chuckled and then she left. When he went to the door to see which direction she was traveling, she was already gone, swallowed up by a night she felt comfort in, which he didn't understand. He saw four overseers off in the distance, talking to Zeke, Malachi, and Jonathan as the shift exchange began.

James went back into his cabin. He sat down on his bed but didn't remove his shoes. Eaten through as they were, it really didn't matter if they were on or off. He threw his hat onto the floor. He reclined. He put his rifle next to him, in the place where his wife would have slept had he the inclination or the space. He put both of his hands behind his head and looked up at the ceiling. The lantern glowed and the flame made things in the dark move, but it also made James not want to. Heavy as his eyelids had gotten, he just let them do what they were asking.

When he entered the dreaming, he was in the field and the niggers were picking cotton. But the cotton was alive and shrieked with every pluck. Then suddenly, the slaves stopped, all of them, at once. Like a flock of birds, they turned in unison. They raised themselves from their prostrate positions. Old and young, they all faced him. None of them had eyes, but somehow they could still see. And there was a noise coming from in between their legs: the sound of something moving, buzzing; listen closer: voices: beating. And the niggers started toward him and he had his gun, but there were too many of them and each of them had a pitchfork in his hands. He opened his eyes just as the first points were coming toward his forehead.

He swung his legs around to the side of his bed and kicked over the spittoon.

"Goddamnit."

He got up and surveyed the room for a rag. He avoided the mirror. The plank wood walls closed in on him. Four walls, blank, darker at the tops and at the bottoms, dyed black by mildew and fungus. The low ceiling sloped upward but granted no room to breathe, stretch, or stand tall. Just one room and very little furniture: a bed, a small table, and, yes, only one chair; atop the table the lantern still alight. Over in the corner: a washbasin, and next to it an extinguished fireplace with a small black pot hanging within.

He found a used rag on the floor by the window. The glass reflected the flickering flame of the lantern. Outside was blackness, but still, shapes: the trees, the Big House, the barn, the nigger shacks on one side, and twelve or so others on the other side of the field. His own cabin was only a smidgen larger. How dare they do that. Give him a cabin that small. Let the niggers build ones almost as large. And on the other side of the fence. The fence that he couldn't even see the shape of because it was so close. The fuckers. All of them: the propertied, their niggers, and the chasers.

He wiped his saliva from the floor. In it, lumps of

chewed tobacco that made him frown. He threw the
rag into the fireplace, underneath the pot, into the
ash. There was a stain on the floor where the spittoon
had spilled. The brownness of its contents seeped into
the wood grain. It would always be there now.

He patted the pocket of his overalls. There was
still half a plug of tobacco left. He pulled it out of
the pouch, broke off a piece, and shoved it into his
mouth. He sat in the only chair in the room and
stared at the dying light in the lantern: how it shrank
and dimmed but still made the whole room jump,
inhale and exhale in its light, casting shadowy auras
around everything. It made him long for evenings
on the London plains, as foggy as they were, but not
for its people.

The promise of riches, he thought, **was a damn
lie.** It had rendered his journey—his long, ardu-
ous journey on ships with gaunt, diseased men—a
mockery. But he didn't have the resources to return,
not that things were much better in England. There,
he would have the same sallow face and necessity for
chewing tobacco. At least here his pockets were not
as empty. But they were still not full enough, and
that wasn't what his cousin Paul had promised him.

Paul didn't tell him how disagreeable this land
would prove to be, how it would harden him further,
that even his voice would change. No one told him
that the women here would scoff at him and that, as
a result, his beauty—the one thing he could count
on across the sea—would fade from disuse. Paul

had called him vain and he thought Paul gluttonous. Linked by sins, he realized that they were family not merely because the same blood ran through their veins, but because the same blood stained their hands.

James's father died first; his mother, moaning and coughing up something dark, shortly afterward. He was four and he had not yet learned how to bathe himself. So when two tall men finally came to the broken-down house of festering and insects, claimed him, and brought him, on horse, to some place where the mist hid everything, they scrunched their noses, and James blended into the mass of messy-faced, disheveled orphans forever dressed in gray.

As he chewed on the tobacco, he thought, **Dirty children should remain dirty for as long as they can. Clean ones attract too much attention.** At the orphanage, busy hands were as much a workshop for the devil as idle ones. And because he was such a good student, he learned to do interesting things with his own. Picking locks and pockets, and sometimes women, was what he resigned himself to until he reached the age of nineteen and learned that his mother had a sister.

There was no other way across the ocean than to rent himself out to the slavers. He was astounded by how many niggers they managed to squeeze onto the ship. They were filed away in the hull like documents, carefully stacked upon one another, barely enough room to wiggle their toes. Hot and funky, they were jammed into the space, chained together in a prostrate position, weeping and moaning, praying in their gibberish languages, surely begging their black-ass godlings to grant them the gift of being able to stretch their arms and breathe.

Every day, James had the task of entering the space to feed them whatever slop was in the pot he was carrying. The food smelled almost as bad as the niggers. Each day, he entered and each day he left wishing he never had to see any of that ever again.

Sometimes, the niggers died. Spoiled, the slavers called it. And he, with a few other men no older than he was, had to unchain the dead, carry their decomposing, vacating bodies up to the deck, and hurl them over the side of the ship for the sea beasts or the ocean itself to dispose of. He wondered how many niggers had met a similar fate, if, in death, they had begun to assemble in the deep, designing the shape of their vengeance, which would come in the form of some infinitely black whirlpool or gigantic, crashing tidal wave that would wipe clean the face of the earth like it did in Noah's time.

No. If James learned nothing else in the gray orphanage, he learned that God's heartlessness would never again include mass murder by drowning. The rainbow was His promise that He would be more creative the next time His sadistic impulses got the better of Him. The priests had assured James of this,

but only as a confession after they had already unleashed themselves on him and could no longer stand
his sorrowful eyes.

Weeks sailing across the gray ocean and then they
finally reached land in some place called Hispaniola.
He stumbled from the ship with wobbly legs that
were, after such a relatively short period, no longer
accustomed to solid ground. It would take him a few
months to make it to Mississippi, where his mother's
sister's son owned a plantation. He had to make his
way across untamed land where people scowled because of the heat and were suspicious of every new
face. Hungry and exhausted, he arrived, on foot, at
the Halifax plantation just as the sun was sinking.
He could barely even stretch his arm to greet his
newfound cousin, but he had strength enough for
a smile.

He didn't even allow himself the time to be overwhelmed by the sheer vastness of the land on which
he stood, or the house that seemed large enough to
hold everyone he ever knew. After downing bowl
after bowl of possum stew, and lazy conversation
with his cousin, in whom he remembered what he
thought he had lost of his mother, he was escorted to
a bedroom by some young darkie, and he slept until
it was night again. He didn't know what to make of
Paul's offer that he oversee the plantation and watch-
dog the slaves. He would get his own piece of land,
right near the northern edge of the property, and he
would have help with his duties, of course. Paul had

befriended some poor wretches from town who were rough but malleable. He let them, too, set up their shacks just on the other side of the cotton field, a parcel of land on which they could raise their families in exchange for becoming nigger barriers. Still, they were outnumbered. They would need an equalizer.

Out of his mind and back to himself, James got up from the table and walked over to the spittoon he had left lying on the floor. He picked it up and spit a huge wad into it. It was still slippery from the spill. He placed it down on the table and the clank against the wood almost disguised the sound of barking coming from over the fence.

The bloodhounds' noise meant that stirring somewhere in the thick void was a quail or an unfortunate nigger. James grabbed the lantern and retrieved the rifle from his bed. His heart beat vigorously. He spit the rest of the tobacco juice onto the ground as his boots trod the last step of his porch. The woofing continued, and it was coming from somewhere over by the barn.

The barn was a source of vexation and an interest to almost everyone on the plantation, but James wasn't even the smallest bit stunned by what went on between those two young niggers, Samuel and Isaiah. He couldn't tell which was which, but the orphanage taught him to recognize animals when he saw them.

For this particular purpose, the whippings would only make them devious, deceitful, he told Paul. It wasn't like a fit of laziness or an eye that dared to lay itself upon the face of a white woman. No, it was a blood mark and one that was relatively harmless. It was best to just let them be. All that mattered was that the work get done. And, by all accounts, the work wasn't done better by any other niggers in the state of Mississippi.

"It's ungodly, James. If I allow that here, without punishment . . ."

"Silly to be concerned with that when you have this," James said as he looked around the plantation. He had finally paid attention to the vastness upon which they stood.

"Have this even longer if I breed them," Paul responded.

"Greed is a pitfall, Cousin."

"Ability, Cousin. A man does what he is able to."

James shook his head. He could see his cabin in the distance.

He quieted himself. For all Paul was doing to sabotage those two animals, did he know that he had one living right in his own house? Paul and Ruth had so protected their only surviving child that they softened him and had the audacity not to notice. Had they let his strength develop unhindered by their fear and sadness, perhaps he would have had the chance to be a man. Instead, he followed after one of the barn animals, grinned insufferably, painted nature's nonsense, and had the same desperate eyes as all malnourished people.

He didn't envy Timothy's fascinations. He wanted terribly to be as far away from niggers as he could—except when they sang. For when niggers sang, it was something that no white person could imitate, not even the ones like him, who suffered and were miserable. What the folks in Paul's church did were birdcalls compared to what the niggers did in the tree circle. One hundred wolves howling at the moon in perfect pitch. A fleet of ships creaking simultaneously at sea. He gladly stood in the trees and listened, occasionally rocking with the rhythm and humming, keeping his rifle close.

"Sell them, if it makes it any better. I know a few folks who will give you more than they're worth."

But it wasn't singing that James heard now; it was the sound of dogs barking. He put the lantern down, but not the rifle, and climbed the fence. He grabbed the lantern through the post and trod slowly toward the slave cabins. Nothing stirred. But as he got closer to the barn, he saw the horses running free. The pigs were meandering about. Chickens were perched on the fence. The other overseers ran from around the back side of the barn.

"What's going on here?" James demanded. "Get these animals back in their pens. Wake the niggers and have them help you. Get Zeke, Malachi, Jonathan, and the others to come out. Need as many guns as possible."

"They getting paid for coming back out during their sleep time?"

"Don't worry yourself with that now. Do what I tell you to. I'll go check on Ruth."

James ran toward the Big House.

His lantern at his side, he ran into the house and saw Paul. He was covered in blood. The hounds were in the house, woofing and pacing in crooked lines. There was a trail of blood leading down the stairs. On the floor, at Paul's side, a nigger with more blood on him than Paul.

"Why didn't you wake me?" James yelled.

Paul said nothing, didn't so much as twitch a finger. He stared ahead at the tree that could be seen through the doorway behind James.

"What's the matter with you? You hurt?" He looked at Paul, held the lantern up to his face. "Paul? The animals are loose. I got some of my men waking niggers to help round them up."

James took a step toward him and Paul flinched.

"What?" James asked.

Paul mouthed some words.

"Speak up!" James shouted. "What happened to you?"

Paul said nothing. He swatted for James to move out of his way and headed toward the door. He dragged the nigger's body out of it, onto the porch, then down the steps, and toward the willow tree.

"Paul, goddamnit! The animals!" he said, following Paul, reaching the porch and refusing to step on the blood trail that he knew no amount of scrubbing would remove. "What's going on? Paul!"

Paul stopped. He straightened his back and then sank into himself again.

"In the house," he croaked.

"Ruth?" James shouted.

He ran back into the house and up the stairs. He looked around. He heard nothing but saw shadows. He ran down the hall. The floor was wet. There was a light coming from up ahead. Timothy's door was open. He walked inside. The room was ransacked. Ruth was on top of the bed, writhing, weeping to herself, mouth agape, but barely a whisper coming from her.

"Are you hurt? Who hurt you?"

James's face had begun to contort. He ran around the bed and tripped over Timothy's legs. He looked down. Timothy was disgraced. No eyes, just like the niggers in his dream.

"Christ Jesus," he whispered.

He stepped gingerly over Timothy and toward where Ruth lay. He tried to pick her up to carry her to her room and help her clean herself, but each time he got his arms around her, she fought and tried to bite him. He exhaled loudly.

"Ruth. Ain't nothing we can . . ."

It didn't matter. This was how she would mourn. It seemed ancient, what she was doing. Older even than his beliefs. Like it might have come with the land itself. So maybe she was in the grasp of something, wasn't **herself** because she **wasn't** herself. Who was she now, then? He would have to leave her to know, and inside him was something that desperately needed to know.

He flew down the stairs and out to where he had seen Paul. Now there was a group of others who had finally awoken, and what seemed like an endless crowd of niggers being gathered around the fat willow. James ran to the tree where Paul stood. He had dragged the nigger by his hand and held on to it. But the way he held it, like a parent would hold a child's hand, gave James chills.

"Rope," Paul said.

Zeke hooted. Malachi danced. Jonathan howled. James told Jonathan and some of the others to help with the animals despite Paul's command.

"These niggers ain't godly!" Jonathan shouted into James's face.

Zeke started to giggle and James yelled, "Quiet!" but Zeke kept giggling.

James walked over to Paul, pointing to the nigger on the ground beside him. "Who is that?"

"Do it matter?" Malachi shot back.

"Paul?" James turned to look at Paul again.

Paul dropped to his knees and began to weep. He let go of the nigger's hand. James bent down next to him.

"Paul."

Paul looked at James. In his eyes, James saw his mother not on her deathbed, but in a coach riding away from a magnificent sunrise. She held her hands daintily and smiled at the thought of her son, who was now a man, and she didn't even judge how he had lost himself because somewhere, perhaps, there was a piece left, but only a mother had the skill to find it. It was she, after all, who had built it. She wasn't looking at him, no, but she was still smiling and that was enough. There, James and Paul's relation became real, realer even than it was that first day, when he stumbled, could barely keep his eyelids open, and took all of Paul's lies for inevitable truth. James whispered something that only Paul could hear, but it wasn't for Paul. Then Paul said, loud enough for everyone to hear: "String this nigger up. High!"

James blinked, then nodded. He took the listless, dying body from Paul, and he and some of the men noosed then hefted it. All of their rifles lined their backs.

"Be on guard," James said and some of the men stopped tending to the body and raised their weapons toward the crowd of niggers, some of whom wept, some of whom shook, while a few stood resolute in the face of everything.

Paul began to grab at the weeds, pulling them out of the ground by their roots. He started to shove them into his mouth. Dirt still clumped at the bottom, he pushed weeds into his mouth and began to chew. Crying, moaning, and chewing. **It had finally happened,** James thought. Something vital had broken. He helped Paul to his feet and whispered to him, "They can't see you this way."

Paul just stared wordlessly and, for the first time, James put his arm around his cousin's shoulder. Briefly, everything was theirs. They looked at each other and it wasn't an ending, but it **was** something new. It frightened James, and he could tell from his quivering lip that it had frightened Paul, too.

After he had disassembled his lantern so that he might light his makeshift torch, James heard the buzzing. As he made his way toward the swinging body and set it aflame, the buzzing. All guns were pointed toward the niggers and he knew from his dream that was the first mistake. **How many might we get? Twenty? Thirty? What of the other hundred or so?** Then he saw the nigger whose name his tongue was forbidden to curl around, and she made her move, and something in him froze.

That was why the mulatto boy was able to catch him by surprise.

NUMBERS

We are the Seven.
    Sent to you to watch over.
What is required of you is to look up.
And remember the star.
But memory is not enough.
We told you from the beginning. Perhaps not in the way you might have expected, but we told you.

It would not make much difference to explain to you what happened to us. You already have that answer. It is how you wound up here.

Memory is not enough, but know:

Infants cannot be reasoned with, they can only be fed or starved.

To break an incantation, another one of equal or greater power must be evoked.

The cosmos is on your side.

It will be all of you or none of you; this is immutable.

The cure is outside of our knowledge, but that does not mean that there is no cure.

Do not be afraid of the dark.

For that is what you are.

EXODUS

1:1

Samuel's eyes were rolling back in his head, and James had the rope in his hand. He flung it over a branch. The noose dangled. The people—themselves tired, and yet their hearts thumping loud enough to hear—weren't sure where to look. They kept their eyes downward until they were told to do otherwise. That is, except for Maggie. Maggie's face was creased. She shifted the weight from her bad hip to her good one, and she crunched the edges of her dress in her hand. In her other hand, the glint of metal.

The blood dripped from Samuel's chest quicker now. They wrapped the rope around his neck. His head rolled around as though nearly detached. His eyes were swollen, but he could see: animals roaming as far as the cotton field. That was good enough, but the other things he saw—a clenched fist, a call stuck in the throat, low-level eyes that had something written in them that he might coax out momentarily—those things gave him strength for one last smile.

He gurgled when they raised him up, still legs that came to life flailing, an involuntary response as something else took over. His hands pulling at the rope choking him, and the burn even though he wasn't on fire yet. But there was James creating a torch. The only question would be whether he would wait to light the flame or do it right away.

Things were red, but they were becoming purple on their way to blue. Then black. Samuel's choking had taken on the shape of words, one word in particular. A name. Through spittle and lips that had begun to lose their color and swell, up through the bulging veins in the throat, a mystery. Who would be able to understand that his last breath would be marked by the joy that had been given to him strictly by chance and taken from him with grave intention? A name. Just a tiny, simple name.

"'ZAY!"

Samuel's legs had stopped moving as soon as the name erupted out of him, trailed by blood. James doused Samuel with the oil and then held a torch against his leg. The flames raced up his body. And no one made a sound.

Except Puah.

1:2

She collapsed as was the proper way to mourn the dead, especially if they had for you a kind of affection, not exactly as you had hoped but as they were able, with pure heart, to give. So when she fell, she came down with the weight of what could have been, not what was.

Sarah tended to her, wrapped herself around her and spoke a little something into her ear. She knew this as a way to connect them both to the line of women who had come before them, women who had, in some other time, met their fates with the kind of courage that she was looking for in the crowd right now. Who would be the first? Would it have to be her? It seemed that it had always fallen upon the women to be the head or the heart, to throw the first spear, to shoot the first arrow, to clear the first path, to live the first life. It was a thing that took much energy and that was why they needed so much rest now. So ready to put it all down, lay it all by the river and let some greedy tide take it if it wanted to, flow it to some other body to let them fish it out of the water and drape it over themselves if they thought it would do any good.

But no.

Such would never be the case. Woman is the lonely road. It is at the dead of night, crossing through untamed breezes, and off to the side are the deep bushes that separate the road from the wild. In that wild, eyes ever peer, voices ever howl, and what thoughts remain are not fit for articulation. Thus no woman should ever be unarmed. As long as she had teeth, she had a weapon, and the toothless could find a pointy enough stick or sharp enough rock to bear witness.

1:3

Maggie knew this, too, and the calm on her face was the surest sign. She had been holding on to herself, gripping her belly in her two hands, trying to keep the memory housed there in its proper place. There was a specific feeling when a thing went from tiny to big inside yourself, with nothing but you in between it and heartbreak. You prepare for the time, and there will always come a time, when you have to watch them take the thing you yourself created and use it for untoward purposes, defile it and say that it's in accordance with nature, and the only thing you could ever do about it is join it in death.

Well, let there be twin deaths, then!

It wasn't that Samuel reminded her of someone; he was her someone. He was her flesh made real to laugh and tumble outside of her body, and the pain of that was too hard. So she had to move it to a part of her that could shoulder the weight and keep the switch to itself.

My last baby. My onlyest one left to see.

Everything had called on her to remember, but

sometimes, she had to forget in order to make it through. Ayo Itself had told her that. He wouldn't let them do to Maggie what they did to him, not without risking everything to prevent it. Eyes wide and fists raised, he risked his body, which Maggie had willingly touched, knowing it would eventually cost her. There could never be peace, only moments in which war wasn't overwhelming. He had been cut off. All he ever got to see of Samuel was Maggie's out-to-here belly, which he kissed at night and spoke to in the old tongue, which wasn't Maggie's old tongue, but some of the words still held meaning for her.

"I am joy itself!"

Those words flew at her now, circled her head like birds, in his voice. Soon they were drowned out by others, in the language of her mother, and in voices that sounded almost like hers. These words she remembered.

She stretched out her arms and some of the people looked at her, but she only looked ahead. There was Paul, his back to her. He was facing her son, whose body was alight and hung from the tree in a way that was so plain that it seemed normal. She had separated herself from her child even though she loved his father. She gave him to the plantation to raise because she didn't see the point in adoring something that would only, in time, give her the right to hate. And that was what had her in its grip now. The hate had such a sweet smell, and when she took it into her mouth, it delighted her and gave her limbs energy. She felt the pain in her hip still, but that was a good thing. Her motions returned to their even gait, which made her look and feel taller. For the first time in years, she ran. She ran toward Paul.

It had been hidden near her wrist the whole time: the metal object, the knife that Paul had told her was supposed to go on the right and then said, he never said that, it was to go on the left, and then beat her when she put it there. She didn't raise it high, but she held it forward like seven women had told her exactly how to hold it and where it should enter his body. James and his men didn't even see her coming. The glow coming off Samuel had them transfixed, almost as if he were still alive and doing it on purpose. And maybe it was on purpose, not because of him, but because of the beating of the toubab's hearts, which guided them to a place where looking at their chaos brought them a sense of comfort. They had never felt so close, surely. This lit-up body had given them the reason to stand close to one another with the same look on their faces: **I have found it!** They had discovered something about themselves in this, a kinship closer than if they shared the same blood or the same bed. Had they given themselves completely over to the moment, which they might have had the niggers not been standing there, they may even have held one another, not with lust in the heart—well, maybe a **little** lust—but surely with goodwill and generosity of spirit.

Maggie crept not at all carefully around this

euphoria but knew that it wouldn't matter in the end. With bent hands that found new power, she lunged forward. The tip of the knife met Paul at the back of his neck and slid through much more quietly than she had expected. Aside from his head tilting back some, he made no attempt to move or turn. It was as though he had been expecting it and so let it be, or not expecting it at all and so froze in shock. He fell forward with the knife still left in its place, and Maggie breathed heavily as every eye widened and looked first at the body and then at her.

1:4

James picked up his rifle and pointed it at her, but he couldn't look directly at her for reasons that still disturbed him. He would have to rely on memory. But before he could take his shot, he was tackled by Adam, who came up from behind. They wrestled on the ground, tearing at each other. James saw rage streak across Adam's face and then he saw his teeth. When Adam banged his forehead against James's, James thought he might pass out, but he managed to maintain his tight grip on his rifle.

They struggled over James's rifle and when it went off, it was Adam's eyes that got wider before the blood trickled from his lips. The nigger who didn't look like a nigger unless you got up close and tilted your head and squinted.

James let out the breath he didn't even know he was holding as everything around him slowed to a crawl. A body on top of him, he saw over the dead man's shoulder. He saw all of their faces, people and niggers; the cowardly and the courageous; struck by the lightning of their tussle; voices deep, stretched, and unintelligible; hands clawed, each grasping for, and gasping for, the last measure of life left to hold. Surely, as things began to return to their natural speed, he found himself, eyes wide open, caught in the middle of a shout:

"Shoot, fools!"

He was angry that he had to tell his marksmen to move and not stand there in some kind of stupor, but also understanding that this was the end-nigh that each of them had kept buried in his loins in order to pretend that the tingle was sensuous and not apprehensive.

Over in the crowd that had begun to swell, toward the back, there was a moment, just before the firing began, when tearful Essie thought she had been given a vision. She held on to Solomon tightly and began to step farther backward, even though none of the rifles were pointed directly at her.

Then there was thunder.

1:5

A shot rang out and somebody fell. The others, some ran; Zeke, Malachi, and Jonathan took off after them, laughing as though they were playing a child's game. However, some charged, and that was the Good Night that James had feared. Shots fired and all he saw were bodies, and some of the bodies he couldn't see because the night and the smoke from the body conspired. Somehow, though, his aim was still reliable, and if it weren't for the nigger who tackled him, he might have eventually broken the spell.

He got up and his legs carried him past tussle and shout. He stumbled and returned to his feet, turning behind him to see if there was anyone trailing him before returning to his quick step. In the dark, he couldn't be sure how he ended up at the edges. Perhaps it was just his legs hurrying him to the spaces they knew best. But there he was: at the farthest reaches of Elizabeth, where the tumult and flame and blood were now a reasonably safe distance from him. There was nothing he could do. He didn't feel ill or cowardly standing there, masked by the unblessed woods that surrounded him, his rifle still in his hands, and a massacre left behind. He had seen far too many of them, had almost been swept under the might of them, to care.

He had touched women as he had been touched. They fought as he had fought. They surrendered as he had surrendered. This, he figured, was the way things were. Everyone got a turn, at some point, to be on top or on bottom. It didn't matter how good you were or how evil you were. All that mattered was that you were alive and, therefore, unsafe. Subject to His will in the here and, likely, the hereafter. And His will was as brutal as it was arbitrary.

James's legs had finally grown tired. The ache was both unbearable and deserved. He knew that now. There was no escape, but he could retreat. His one regret: abandoning Ruth. He slung his rifle over his shoulder, the barrel pointed toward the sky. Under the half-moonlight, there were many shadows, though not as vibrant as the ones seen in the daylight. His own shadow pointed eastward, so he walked that way, swatting away insects, tripping over raised stones, until he had reached where the forest was so thick that no man could pass it. He climbed into it as best he could, getting scratched on his face and on his hands. There were now more shadows in front of him. These shadows were bigger than his. Elongated and moving wildly, like they were fighting—or preparing to. One of them made a noise, but that was impossible because shadows didn't make noise.

Trapped in the confines of thorny and twisted roots, he snatched his rifle down and took a shot. **CRACK.**

The shadows froze. And then, as if they were only momentarily shocked by the sound, they merged. Big as a tree now, but wider. It hovered over James, blotting out the stars and making it seem as though everything in the universe was black. The darkness engulfed him completely. He held tight to his rifle as he spun the best he could and let off three shots. The dark closed in on him. It felt like an embrace: warm, close. He almost extended his arms to return the sentiment, but that was when he heard the noises that took his breath: buzzing. And what was that: voices underwater?

1:6

Before, Beulah never dared dream. But Be Auntie's dreams were silver and hot. In this place where metal was brilliant from heat, the men were lined up and obedient, even if they were toubab. They licked every part of her, but only when she commanded. Otherwise, they kept their eyes, hands, tongues, and things to themselves. Quivering, yes; anxious even; but nevertheless tucked away. She wanted to call them soldiers, but that would be wrong. The men in real life were soldiers. They were continually starting wars for any little difference of opinion and causing bloodshed that they insisted was necessary if they were to have their way. These real-life men expected her, and all women, to forget that women were always the first casualties of their lusts, claiming that Eve had made this the order of things when, truly, if you gave it even a second of thought, you would know God planned it like this from the start no matter what Amos said. In her dreams, the men were what men were supposed to be: secondary like they were in the beginning before imbalance. Useful for their strength and humor, sure, but they knew to leave the women alone to think. Therefore, finally, worthy of her worship.

Amos had come closer to this than all the men she ever knew. He left her mornings without a "good" and nights without an "evening," but he lay next to her all the same. He raised no hands, but he did touch her in the way she liked to be touched: with her permission, always with her permission. Not silver just yet, but hot.

She was smiling in her sleep, touching her lips, when the toubab came to get them. The boys leaped up from around her and dashed outside when they heard a noise. Their thundering startled her awake. She was groggy, and her vision still blurred, but she saw the rifles.

"Sons?"

Be Auntie's heart beat in her throat. Her tongue was dry, which told her that death would be walking the plantation for a while, snatching up the bluest of berries, even the ones that didn't know that what was wrong with them all along was that they were blue.

"But it's okay. I know my boys is gon' protect me. I raised them rightly. If not them, Amos," Be Auntie said just before the toubab entered her shack. She sat down and smiled a big smile right into those pale-as-hail faces. Slowly, slowly, so slowly that the toubab didn't even see, the smile faded when she noticed that none of her boys came running in after them. Not even Dug.

They couldn't all be dead. All six of them? So quick? Nah. And none of them tapped her, woke her from her pretty sleep to tell her to run even? Can't be. Not after what she gave. Not after what she saved, turned over, made room for, and squirted out of her nipples to keep them whole.

Amos, too?

Did he pick Essie over her?

Can't be.

With rifles trained on her and toubab yelling for her to get on out of the place she failed to make home, which was not her fault, Be Auntie plopped down on the floor. The toubab laughed because they thought she fell by accident. She looked out front where the grassy cushion was. Toubab legs were obstructing her view so she tried to see through them. That was the easy part. It was their laughter that split her. That allowed what she thought she had digested to rise herself up out of the bowels and into her center. Ooh, it was cold, gray, and funky; vines crept and the mist stuck close to the ground. Then **she** burst through, hands first, holding red carnations. Not even the courtesy of a hug. Got her nerve!

Yes. Beulah began to climb out, partly by mouth, partly by ear. While exiting the latter, she whispered, harmonizing with herself: "I tried to tell you."

1:7

Bodies fell, but Essie held on to Solomon, and beside his head, she could see that some of the people had stormed the toubab, Sarah leading them. There, in the middle of Empty, the writhing crowd of bodies must have looked like a festering wound from above, but nothing had ever before been so beautiful. Essie continued to step back, in awe of that beauty and seeking her own, until she was behind the barn and hidden by the trees that bordered the riverbank.

She held Solomon tighter. He trembled momentarily but didn't cry. He kept trying to turn around, to see where the noise was coming from, like he was drawn to it, like conquest was his birthright and this had to be seen to be understood so it could never happen again. Essie looked down at his chubbiness. He looked like his father.

She bit her lip, almost hard enough to draw blood, but it didn't prevent memory from choking her from the inside. Only one thing had been denied her. Well, not only one thing, but this was the thing from which all other denials had sprung: No. Her No had no weight and no bearing, and so how could it ever have any mercy?

This, then, was her No. A little late, perhaps. A little too late, but here it was, nonetheless, bright and difficult, but tangible.

They had made a terrible mistake. They had given the child to the wrong woman. They should have let Be Auntie take it. For she, above all, loved these kinds of children. Instead, they had given it to the woman who thought splitting it through the middle and sharing the halves with whomever wanted them was reasonable recompense. They knew who she was (clearly, they didn't) and she was obliged to be her. She hadn't lived up to herself, but that was over and she would disappoint them no further.

The crickets warned her in screeching song, but she ignored them. The moon shot down half-light, but still bright enough that she could see the child's round face, gentle especially when he looked away.

She reached the bank and looked into the black waters before her. She smiled at how calm they were and felt shame at being the one who would disturb them. She held the child close to her, tighter, and tighter still, until he began to squirm and fight. She was surprised by the strength in his tiny body, but she held on, used all of her strength until she heard a snap and the body fell limp. She raised Solomon's body high above her head. It was as though she were showing someone in the sky the evidence for which he would be convicted. Then, in one quick motion, she threw him into the river.

It swallowed him with barely a gulp.

1:8

Puah's grief laid her out on a field in the middle of a war. Every part of her wanted to lie right there, close her eyes, and wait for the wolves to do what nature created them to do. And after her bones had been picked clean, after her flesh had been digested and shat out, maybe a bouquet of poppies would sprout wherever her remains had nourished the soil. Maybe nature would remember her long after everyone had forgotten.

She closed her eyes to prepare when a hand grabbed her.

"Get up, girl!"

It was Sarah.

Puah ignored her because there was no reason to get up only to be shot back down. Puah closed her eyes again.

"Mercy, gal! I don't wanna be the one to say, sister. I don't wanna have to be the one to say," Sarah said. She got to her knees and looked deeply at Puah. "But you gon' have to put down hard things and get yourself up."

Puah smiled at the indignant tone in Sarah's voice. Perhaps she thought it a gentle, warm correction that lifted her up between the shoulder blades and offered **There, there now, sweet child.**

"They did this," Puah replied.

Sarah nodded her head. "I know it. Couldn't be nobody but what they is. But you gon' have to put him away. Now. Because all you can do for him now is run."

Puah didn't move.

"This is me and you know it, Puah. Let troubled things keep they distance," Sarah said.

Puah continued to curl and linger.

"What I tell you 'bout this, Puah? Get on up. We gotta go."

"Where?" Puah asked.

Sarah looked into Puah's eyes. "Do you see me?"

"I see circles. They wobbly like. And you look blue, but soft."

"Up, chile, up."

"But where we . . ."

"Any damn where but here!"

"Sarah," Puah said, and her words were slurred. "Samuel."

"Get up. I done told you from the start: Hold your things! Tie them up in a place where only you can reach it. And reach for them only when you ain't got no other choice. When the beasts threaten to stampede you. When the hole get so big you 'bout to fall in it. When you look in the river and the thang looking back at you, you ain't never seen before. Ain't that what I been telling you? Ain't I been plaiting that right into that big ol' head of your'n? You done let it go carelessly and now look. It spread out right here on the ground waiting for the hooves to come stomping on it. Get up, gal. I said: Get. Your. Ass. Up!"

Finally, Puah raised her shaking fingers. Sarah

grabbed them. She pulled Puah up and Puah leaned her weight into her. They began first to walk, then, holding hands, they began to sprint. Gunshots startled them and they kept moving through the trees and made their way to the river. What they couldn't see, they felt around for. Nothing. There was nothing except rocks and twigs, and two bodies.

"Can you see who it is?" Puah asked.

Sarah squinted. "Naw."

Puah grabbed her chest. She stood for a moment and looked back through the trees. She took a breath and then stepped forward toward the river. She looked at Sarah.

"We could swim."

"My big ass can't swim. Never could. But look—you gotta do it."

"What?"

"Save yourself. Go on. I find another way."

"Sarah, they might kill you."

"They had plenty chances already."

"But . . ."

"On the other side of that river, you finally have a chance."

"For what?"

Sarah grabbed Puah by both of her hands and kissed her on the cheek.

"To **see** yourself."

Puah shook her head.

"Fool chile. If you can make it 'cross the river,

when you come up on that other side, you ain't gon' have no other choice."

"I can't."

"You can. Go. Swim, sister," she said to Puah, pushing her gently forward. "Swim."

Puah pulled off her dress and tied it around her waist. She crept lightly, sinking slowly beneath the water's skin. A dragonfly zipped past her and she turned toward the sound. She was neck-deep, then she disappeared.

1:9

Sarah held her breath, waiting to see Puah's head or a braid or a stroking arm—anything. She waited. Not even a bubble came up to glide on the surface and burst quietly. Did the down-deep catch hold of her legs? Some errant spirit mistake her body for its own? Fingers pulling every which way and down-ward for company?

She had sent Puah to her death. How needless. How sloppy of her to push when she should have pulled. Then she heard a splash. And then another. And an-other. In the darkness, silver flashed and she caught sight of an arm, graceful, shimmering. She was glid-ing. Puah was gliding across the river as though the forever mamas had laid hands to buoy her. Sarah panted her excitement quietly, to herself. Too bad she couldn't stay longer to watch her friend-girl fly. But there were jaws everywhere, and flicking tongues.

Puah had asked Sarah where she would go, and Sarah had no idea. **I find my way,** she had said. She had long given up on safe space but would settle for a living one, where at least a small piece of her soul could sparkle without having mud kicked at it.

Sarah remembered climbing on top once, up where there might have been safety if the world was right sided, and she saw, off in the distance, women as black as caves raising their hands to acknowledge her, beckoning her, telling her that she had **an infinite number of mothers who, themselves, were the mothers of infinity. They were the first to give birth to the last, to give life to the woman who is also a man who is also neither, who will gather all of creation, tree and wolf alike, in perfect submission to peace. What had no start would have no finish. And this was the congress of dreams. It is a circle, you see, a wheel in the sky, spinning; bubbles in the sea-foam; a ring of hands joined in the deep, holding mercies in the middle and witnesses on the perimeter, laughing, knowing. These are those of the land that does not eat its young. Ask your blood. For it will tell you.**

"You know where I ain't never been?" she said aloud to all of creation.

She ran over to the cotton field. Between the loosed cows, she went near the edges, until she made it to the other side. She emerged to see the rows of abandoned shacks, lit faintly by Samuel's light. She walked past them slowly, delighted by the colors they became under scrutiny. She looked to the woods just beyond.

"I ain't never been this-a-way," she said out loud.

She meant south. She had never been south because Paul and others had spoken of the Choctaw as though they were the living vengeance anxious to gobble up lost black flesh. But hadn't they also said that about the infinity mothers, likewise slandered their grace as though they were no longer around to lay waste to those deceits? Nah, if the Choctaw were monsters to Paul and them, they could only be reprieve to her. Whatever lay over there, beyond these new woods, in that other darkness—well, shit. Nightmares walked **here.** Gobbled up was better than having another set of pasty hands try to pry her knees apart.

"Ain't that right, Mary?" she asked the darkness in front of her.

But beating behind her heart was the most recent in a long line of women who kept razor blades hidden in the warmth of their mouths. Let toubab try if they wanted to. She tucked in the loose end of her head wrap and grabbed her dress between her legs so that it clung to her thighs like pants. She stomped into the woods, brushing aside branches and bushes with her free hand. Just as she got to a clear spot, there they were, standing in her way: a posse. Some of them ragged and toothless. Some of them tall and thin. All of them lined up like spikes on a pitchfork, waiting to make their jaggedness known.

When they approached, she had figured out something that had been like a splinter in her foot: the easy thing to believe was that toubab were monsters, their crimes exceptional. Harder, however, and even more frightening was the truth: there was no such thing as monsters. Every travesty that had ever been committed had been committed by plain people and every person had it in them, that fetching, bejeweled thing just beneath the breast that could be removed at will and smashed over another's head before it was returned to its beating place. The splinter pushed out, she could walk evenly, though cautiously, whether the ground was level or not.

She smirked at them. They had already removed her name from all of the monuments and replaced it with the titles of men, thoughtless, violent, cowardly men who were at once afraid of and captivated by the womb that gestated creation—in other words, the cosmos. They had already pulled the goddesses out of the sky and buried them in the deep, hidden away from all but the most gracious. Now what they wanted to do was wipe her face from the record, scatter her remains so that they would never be found again.

She balled her right hand into a fist and with her left, she reached into her jaw and pulled her weapon from where it rested against the interior of her cheek.

It didn't matter what fires were started or how much timber had fueled them. Nah. She wasn't going to be anyone's sacrifice but her own.

She swayed with the cotton plants in the distance behind her. The wind danced between her legs. She held a fist out in front of her and her other hand pulled back like a viper before the strike, a fang glistening in its mouth. Delighted by the potential shock that would overcome their faces as she took at least two of them down with her into the places her people thrived—hot places, thick with ruin—she braced herself:

"Come on with it, then!"

1:10

Amos walked to the very center and raised his hands.

"Be calm! This is the dawning of the Lord's day!" he shouted, his voice mixing with the tumult but not rising above it.

What they didn't know was that out yonder, tragedy would be plentiful beyond any that could be imagined here at Empty. They knew of course what that fence, long and wide, had confined them to; there was no need to enumerate what was already plain on the flesh. But what it protected them from was what they couldn't reckon with. Amos knew, though. There was nothing more frightening than patrolling toubab boys, whom some toubab woman's tears had nourished, gussying themselves up for a ride into the woods to find a gaggle of niggers hidden in some quiet cove or tucked in the branches of a solemn tree.

They had known what it was to be hungry, but what they didn't know were the miles between that and starvation because they hadn't yet seen a man poison himself, picking the wrong leaf to chew and satiate the pain that tore at the gut after five days when not even raccoon meat was forthcoming.

To be without a working well was the worst. The river water was full of salt and upset the belly. And rain couldn't be counted on because this land was fickle like that. And at most, you could catch a handful before the pouring stopped for no reason other than spite. Never mind the wolves and the snakes and the gators, all teeth and all waiting for a fool to stumble. And what about the babies? How can you bring along a baby into this and muffle its cries when the milk runs dry because the mother's belly is empty?

No, Empty wasn't in no ways safe, but it was reliable. And what all could a people who had nothing—and would never have nothing so long as toubab remade the world in their own lonesome image—hope for except to know the who, what, when, why, where, and how of their misery?

I ain't rotten fruit; I a man.

"Come, be safe in my arms."

No need to fear, no need, he thought to say to

the bodies living and dead. Some of the living would respond to his call because if in the untoward night someone held up a light, however dim, evincing arms open for embrace, where if those arms could not protect, they could at least offer that you wouldn't die alone, there was, at last, a direction. But neither Essie nor Be Auntie was among them and that pierced him in places hidden and in plain sight.

Amos stood next to Paul's body, and the people gathered there, encircling them both. That was the safest place to be: weeping around the body of the master of land, while all the others ran wild and free. When the cavalry arrived—and trust: they would be a-coming—he would give them all of their names. Starting with hers.

"All we wanted was a little quiet, huh. Massa, can you manage that for us? A little quiet, and maybe . . . some peace?" When he received no answer: "We stay here with you. We stay."

He was certain the shots wouldn't come near because he had seen and already been touched by the Blood. He looked up and saw Maggie. He stood there, in the middle of everything, looking downcast at Maggie, though she herself seemed to be rising up the slope from the tree to the Big House, but he still chose to look at her downward. Their eyes met. Only he had tears in his. He raised his hand slowly, pointing at her. Accusing her. Of what? She would understand and only she. That was why she smiled and turned her back to him. Still, he needed to say it aloud, for the benefit of witnesses. It didn't matter that it would simply land at her heels.

"They was putting us in danger. All I was trying to do was keep us safe."

1:11

In the middle of nothing, there was music.

Maggie stood above everything, facing east; the light from far off couldn't reach her yet, but she knew it was coming. She bent and snatched up the torch that James used to cook her baby, the only one who remained and who she thought was better off not knowing, but she saw, with her own eyes, that he had found something good in this life that would make his short time here bearable. She gathered up the torch and limped quickly back to the Big House.

It was dark inside, and even if the torch had not lit her way, she knew every inch of the house better than she knew the slim curves of her body. This was the place where she was damned, so its contours and boundaries, even its most secret crevices, were all known to her, known and committed viciously to memory. Each spot had a story. The cotton-filled chair was where she was made to stand for hours on a bad hip as the Halifaxes entertained their guests. The fireplace that almost consumed her when Paul pushed her too close. She could have fell down the fucking stairs—and she called them that for good

reason—if not for her quick reflexes. And those bitter mirrors. Oh! The house was lawless.

She walked through it anyway because what choice
did she have? Up the stairs and into Massa Paul's
room to start at the core, as fire should cleanse from
the inside out. She held the torch to the bed and only
looked long enough to see it ignite. Then she went
back outside, torch in hand, and headed to the fields.

How she despised those rows! Each so very neat in
their appearance, all of them methodical and rigid,
but also offering up the kind of softness that claimed
lives. She walked up and down, quicker even than
her injury would allow, possessed as she felt by something very old beside her, running in unison, spears
pointed forward. She thought, **What it look like if
it were them, for once? If** they **had been split from
their children; if** they **had to toil for no wages
and meager sustenance; if** they **backs had been
mangled for the slightest offense or none at all; if**
they **fingers were stripped to the bone picking and
picking and, damn it, picking; if it was** they **heads
that had been placed haphazardly on spikes for a
stretch of miles. How it feel if** they **were under?
They might not know soon, but eventually, they
would know. And they knew, too. That was why
they cradled guns like offspring.**

With a gentle motion, she began to burn the plants
as she walked by them. The sizzle filled the air, and
hearing it gave her over to herself, made her feel that
her body was, finally, her own. As each bush became

a torch, she looked back at the Big House, and in an upper window, inside an upper room, she saw a figure just . . . standing there. Standing there looking, maybe at her, maybe at the people in the distance as they swarmed and reclaimed their dignity with the swiftness that comes when it's long overdue. But the figure didn't move. It became just another window dressing, and that was how she knew it was Missy Ruth.

They could have been sisters if Missy Ruth didn't believe the same deception that men did. Oh, but the deceit was so alluring, sweet on the tongue like cane. There weren't many who could spit it out.

Nothing compelled Maggie to shout to her or signal that the flames would soon reach her, giving her the chance to flee. Where would she go? Out in the woods like she always did, probably. Or into town. Or find some place of worship to give shelter. There were traps everywhere, sure, but, too, there was no shortage of people who would spring them and endanger themselves to spare a toubab woman grief.

Maggie just stared at her, remembering the dress. Then she held up the torch and for whatever reason, a tear streamed down her face. Maggie decided not to question where it came from or why it came, but was certain that it, alone, was enough.

She wasn't standing on a hill, but that's what it seemed like. It was as if the smoke were, instead, clouds, and the ashes—some of the flakes could have very well been her own child's, mixed in with how far Empty was about to fall thanks to her, yes **her,** it should be known and remembered, but it won't be— the ashes could have been the starry heavens because they, too, were remnants of dead things.

No one would remember her name, but she had become a larger spirit now: head bigger, hips wider, and whatever the hurt. All of the ones who had come before her simply pumping through her heart and they had found a place to be in the caverns of her throat. There, she recalled her voice.

With both her hands in the air, she cast her last spell:

"Look! We lined up in a row, stretched damn near across the whole place." The people, crying some of them, looked over toward Maggie and scurried nearer. "Make a circle. We need a circle because both ends need to be closed up. A snake. A snake eating its own damn tail. Don't that just beat all? What matter do it make if you are **seen**? You are **here**!"

She took a moment to look at each of them. "All you done seen. All you done touched. And you let something as small as a ocean part you? Ain't you shamed?"

As the knowing rose upon their faces, Maggie smiled. Finally: "A wisdom!"

Only one question: What to do when the cavalry arrives? Only one thing to do:

With every drop of blood:

Rebel!

ISAIAH

Be a stone. Please be a stone.
That was what some rocks said to some feathers, to the dandelion-wishes that floated about minding their own business before coming down slowly to land in some meadow and, after a time, take root. They wanted soft things to harden, for their **own** good, for **their** own good. But that left no consideration for the traveler who had to walk barefoot over the terrain, left them no comfortable place to step. And Isaiah wanted to be that for Samuel.

But comfort for travelers wasn't the point. Because wonderful for them that they had some place to rest their feet, weary as they might be, but what about all the soft things beneath them?

Yes, I know. But I can't be what I can't be.

Open fields, then, where the blues were heartbreak and the black-eyed Susans were high in their conceit. Isaiah laid down both sword and shield way before he even got to the river. Whatever was ahead would be the hell toubab feared, unless it also came with a promise: the tip of Samuel's trembling tongue at the edge of Isaiah's impatient nipple. That was the thing to make the head roll back and the face worship sky. That was the thing to unfurl itself, a delicate bloom holding on to dew like joy. That was the thing to cause the many waters to rush toward calm and therefore to harbor. Yes. That was the thing.

And all the while he babbled in their covered intimacies, making Samuel ask him why he liked to talk so much; where was the quiet and could they have it for themselves, if just for a time? "Sleep is quiet enough," Isaiah had told him. "When we awake, I wanna make sure you hear me. Inside you, I want you to hear me." Samuel looked away. He understood it, but he couldn't hold it. Elusive, like trying to catch a wish when a stone was easier to grasp.

But Isaiah couldn't be a stone, especially not now, unless he wanted to sink to the bottom deep.

I be your stone for you.

How would Samuel get across the river with that weight on him? He, too, had nearly succumbed. No one would ever know how close he came to betraying everything, even himself in exchange for a tender name.

"Why they hate us?"

"The answer plum right in front you, 'Zay. Because Amos told them to. And Massa told Amos to."

They could deal with stares and whispers. But the cleaving? That was what pushed Isaiah into the night waters, where who knows what was liable to have at him. No, he couldn't be a sinking stone, for he needed, now, to float. Nameless because Isaiah wasn't the name given to him by those he truly belonged to. Thus he walked about wearing an insult like castoffs. He answered to disrespect every time he was called, whether the caller adored him or not. Yes indeed, nearly a stone.

He took all of that, every single piece of that, and carried it on his back when he shot into the dark river water not knowing what abyss could be below. They had said that his people were afraid of water and couldn't swim. He had heard the stories of the elders who leaped into the sea rather than make it to these bitter shores and how easy they went down. He thought maybe it was true then, that his people were made of stones, and the minute he thought he could make it across, he would sink to the bottom and drown.

He took a deep breath before he disappeared below the surface. Sound became muffled, bubbles bursting and water rushing into his every space. His eyes were squeezed shut. He opened them and it made no difference. Everything was black and maybe that was a good thing.

He kicked his legs and shot forward. Forward and forward, legs and arms and breath. All of the things that the river seemed to be taking from him, pushing against him as he swam through its flow, but not letting it carry him. Samuel had told him that they would be safe on other shores. Isaiah didn't know for sure. There was what he was told and what he felt in his core, but he wasn't sure which could be trusted. He had no way to measure, no sign to read, no mother and no father to correct him because they had already erred and could assure him that all the traps had already been tripped so it was safe to gallivant in that other direction. There was, however, a thing in the center of him that said, **Better than where you are.** So he swam underneath, almost like he was beneath the world itself, and he wondered if he would ever make it back on top.

He saw something flash in waters too dark to see in. Quick, fleeting things that looked like watchful eyes. He told himself that those were products of his exhaustion. His limbs had weakened, and it didn't at all matter how many piles of hay and shit he had shoveled that allowed his biceps to swell and caused toubab to think that there wasn't any load he couldn't carry. Confused sometimes, he had taken such regard as a measure of his strength: the more he could take, the stronger it made him feel. Then he realized that he, the cow, the horse, and the hogs— even the chickens—served the same purpose.

His head came up and there was the night sky in all of its stardom and finally, before nearly giving up, there was suddenly ground beneath his feet.

He dragged himself on hands and knees across the muddy bank of driftwood and moss. Then he turned over and lay flat on his back, panting into the murky place he was now in. Some of the rocks he lay upon cut into him. He knew that he didn't have much time. Instinct told him to run, but his legs disobeyed the summoning. He sat up. He tried to avoid looking across the river, back toward what he had escaped. He knew that he wouldn't hear his dream: Samuel in the river, taking massive strokes, head beneath and then above the water, getting closer and closer until finally reaching dry land and collapsing into his embrace, free.

But he looked anyway and he could see the flames burning in the night and the figures at war. And from so far away, he couldn't master his eyes enough to search for the shape of the nightness he knew better than his own.

There was no sign of Samuel in the water, but across the river, nearer to the Big House, rocking from the hated tree, head cocked to the side as though curious, lit up like a lantern, there was somebody. He would have been surer of the form before the fire began to ravage it. But who else could it be?

He vomited, and the river wasted no time in lapping up his offering and dragging it off to sea. Isaiah tried to stand, but fell to his knees. He stared at the fire. He imagined he had a part in it, too. Living in the world as designed by toubab had given that gift to him: regret and, with his left hand, pointing a finger at his own chest when there were plenty remaining to point elsewhere. Circling his head was his present: he could have left Timothy's calls unanswered, recoiled from his touch, refused to remove his britches, and refrained from stroking himself to life. What if he had failed to lean into him, push a laugh loose, gaze too long into his eyes like he might have, by chance, found something there? Worse, he had almost let out a sigh, and there was no doubt that he enjoyed the softness of the bed. Was survival worth this? Was Samuel right to think it treason?

During the betrayal times Isaiah had pushed the thoughts away from him, into the corners of Timothy's room, behind triple-stacked canvases, where they remained like things you never wanted people to see. He didn't look into any of the mirrors, which helped. For he knew now that these were cowardly acts as good as any noose. Samuel had told him before that he would have to risk something and stop trading body for comfort. Wounded, Isaiah wanted to tell him to think of cotton to see how some comforts can draw blood.

He had to go. They would be coming for him soon. They would cross the river on a raft or perhaps a small boat. They would bring the hounds and weapons of death whose noises would echo into forever. They would come and try to extract from him all he had to give even though everything he had wasn't enough to fill a palm. His knowledge no bigger than a stone.

He looked at the stars. Maybe those flashing eyes at the bottom of the river were just a reflection of the sky brought low. That would explain why people drowned, being unable to determine up from down because they looked the same. But there was still the sense that they weren't just **eyes,** but they were **watching.** Stars don't do that.

Isaiah exhaled. He wondered what he and Samuel could have been, would have been, if they hadn't come of age in chains. There was no need for tears. Not when the feelings were still fresh and tucked inside his folds, moist and safe beneath the foreskin, accessible by memory and caress. This could only be destroyed if he, too, was destroyed. And even then, the destruction would only serve to bring them closer, hand in hand in that next place, wherever it was, where his parents and theirs found permanent escape from the people whose bodies were covered with nothing. Not Heaven, certainly not that dreadful place. But somewhere else, where the first songs could be sung without interruption.

Swam the whole way underwater, only coming up for gulps of air when his lungs threatened to burst. He saw not stars, he figured, but people down there: faces in the mud, smiling or maybe screaming, hands joined in a circle, feet tapping to the rhythm of the river's ebb. He recognized them, but didn't know them.

"Women in the water. They defend you," Maggie had once told them at the river's edge, looking at the unmoving forest on the other side.

"Don't know what you mean, ma'am," Isaiah said.

She smiled. "They black." She laughed and slapped her knee. "Well, of course they black."

Samuel wasn't paying much attention. He seemed lost in his own mind, fist tightening, mouth pressing. Isaiah, on the other hand, was listening intently, but he was still confused. Maggie thought she had cleared up his confusion by saying, "No, not women **in** the water. Women **is** the water."

Had she somehow seen? Did she somehow know? Wordlessly and in the mind, and thought to offer up the only protection she could give for their journey? An invocation ancient as the water itself? Was that what Sarah was teaching him by the river that afternoon?

He knelt there in the muddiness, the river's rush drowning out most other sounds. He prepared to get up and make his way into the forest behind him. But a hand grabbed his ankle.

How did they creep up on him so soundless? Had he been so distracted that he'd become willing prey? Bless his contemplating heart.

He didn't have the strength to fight none of them now—not James, Jonathan, Zeke, Malachi, none of them. He let his breath come as it might and didn't even try to kick them off. He remained there on his knees hoping that they would kill him before they dragged him back across the river. He closed his eyes and awaited the bullet to his face.

Then a familiar voice panted his name.

"'Zay!"

He opened his eyes and was sure that he was dreaming.

"Samuel?" Isaiah's eyes opened wide as he saw Samuel standing before him, dripping wet.

Samuel smiled. "Here," he said.

Isaiah jumped up and squeezed him as though he were trying to be one part of him. He shook his head. He looked at him and touched him all over his face with both hands, searching for the truth of things, using his fingers to confirm belief.

"Man, what you doing? You gon' poke my eye out!"

"I beg your pardon." Isaiah gasped between sobs. "You here."

"I told you I be right behind."

Isaiah grabbed him again and held on to him. "You hate me?"

Samuel pulled his head back and looked Isaiah square in the eyes. "Hate you? Man, after all this you ask me such a fool question?"

They held on. Samuel kissed Isaiah's ear. "I gotta go," he whispered.

"What you say?" Isaiah looked at Samuel, not sure he had heard what he did over the water's rush.

"We gotta go."

Isaiah nodded, squeezed both of Samuel's hands in both of his. They released each other and headed into the forest.

There was no trail to follow. The bush was overgrown and took up all space, uninterrupted as it was by human hands. There was no break in the canopy, not a single bit of starlight could penetrate the dense woods. Isaiah and Samuel broke their way in, moving as swiftly as they could as tired as they were, tearing at branches and vines, stepping on rocks and worms. The hissing of snakes caused them to pick up their pace. They listened for the owls; that would give them some inkling of direction until they could once again see sky.

After what seemed like hours of breaking, falling, pushing, and stepping, they came to a clearing. The ground was soft and wet beneath them and the air was heavy with the scent of cedar. Animals were howling and mosquitoes whizzed about. Leaves rustled in the breeze and an owl hooted. With the night sky once again exposed, Isaiah and Samuel could see the outlines of each other, which was enough. They stood there facing each other, ebony and midnight blue in the faint light of the moon and stars. Their breath came hard and their chests heaved in unison. They were too tired, scared, and hungry to smile, but their lips curled in that direction anyway.

"You think we far enough in?" Isaiah exhaled.

"I don't know, but I gotta rest. Just a minute."

Samuel lay against a sycamore tree whose trunk was covered with moss.

"They say moss grows on the north side of trees," he said softly.

"So then we should head that-a-way," Isaiah said, pointing to the other side of the clearing.

Samuel didn't reply. He just breathed in deeply and exhaled for a long time. Almost too long. His breath became labored. Isaiah came over to the tree, stood in front of Samuel, and leaned in.

"You all right?"

Samuel smiled between heavy breaths. "Think so. Just tired. Thirsty. Hungry, too."

Isaiah sniffed around for anything edible. He couldn't find chicory, cattail, or clovers, but he did find some fireweed, its bright color making it a little easier to spot. He walked quickly back over to the sycamore tree.

"This was all I could find for now, but when day breaks I can find something else . . ."

Samuel was curled up on the ground.

"Sam!"

Isaiah knelt over him. Samuel's face was tight. He squeezed his eyes and a little light grazed his cheek.

"I feel funny," Samuel said as he tried, with Isaiah's help, to stand, sliding across the surface of the tree, landing at its roots again, halting his fall with an outstretched arm. "Something ain't right," he said as he began to rub his hands across his chest and on his forearms. "I don't feel right."

"You sick?" Isaiah asked, grabbing at the same areas. Samuel felt hot.

"No!" Samuel shouted suddenly. He pulled himself up and leaned his back against the tree. "Don't touch there. I don't wanna hurt you."

"You scaring me. Tell me what's wrong!"

Samuel's eyes opened wide. They began to glow like lamplight. At the edges of his body, a halo orange as a sunset and red at the rim appeared. His breathing changed from quick panicked spurts to a labored rattling. His glowing lit up the night. Isaiah stumbled backward. He hit the ground as though he were pushed by something. In the night around them, Isaiah could see what looked like faces, so many faces. Some of them his.

The light grew brighter and brighter and Samuel screamed.

"KAYODE!"

The name spun and echoed, sped by Isaiah, and left a burn streak across his chest, marking him. He put his hand there. He looked down at the scar, then back to see Samuel reaching his hand out to him. Isaiah crawled forward, pressing against the invisible thing pushing him in the other direction. Closer, closer, humming, from everywhere, humming, like voices, five? Six? No! More! A proper circle. He heard it. Pushing, pressing, away, away. And Samuel right there. Isaiah getting closer. Almost. Their fingers trembled and nearly touched. Then it was too late.

The last sound was fluttering. Samuel burst into

fireflies. Or was it embers? On his knees, shaking his head, mouth open and quivering, with his eyes still dazed from the light, it was hard for Isaiah to tell.

The tiny bits of light that were once Samuel, maybe still Samuel, swirled upward, into the night, with no regard for who or what they were leaving behind, blinking, twinkling.

"No!" Isaiah yelled and tried to catch them, but they floated in the air, too high to reach. And soon, they disappeared into the darkness. Isaiah stopped. He fell face forward to the ground. Slowly, he turned on his back. He closed his eyes and it was, he thought, as if a light rain had fallen on him, dew trembling at his tips. He opened his eyes. **I witless,** he thought, allowing himself, finally, to be calmed by his own slowing breath.

But he had touched Samuel's face, so it couldn't have been a dream. He had felt his breath, his wet skin, stared into his eyes and seen the virgin soil of them. It was real. Had to be. He looked at his own chest. Mark right there. But people don't turn into fireflies, do they? He had seen eyes at the bottom of the river, his own face in a light. Dead, then. Maybe he, too, was dead.

His heart cracked. As each piece fell, it made it increasingly difficult for him to move. He couldn't get up and he didn't want to. He would wait right there for Paul and them. Whatever they decided to do with his hide was all right. However they decided to skin, stretch, and wear him was now destiny. So he sat there, trembling, weeping into the palms of his hands.

Then someone whispered a name.

He looked up and saw, in the north direction, a tiny orange light.

"You here?"

He got up and ran in the direction of the light, not looking back, not stopping. It could have been a piece of Samuel, lingering, drawn, sent to fetch him. Isaiah followed it, panting and reaching out for it. It led him deeper into the forest, where he stumbled over bumpy roots and felled branches, got up, and leaned on pecan trees whose fruit hadn't yet husked. And still the light, like a tiny, dimming star, hovered, danced, and whispered a name. When it did, Isaiah lunged forward, allowed himself to be pulled along and led to the source of everything.

He leaped and bounded into patches of dirt, pieces of earth that seemed scorched and not yet reborn. It was hard to tell in the dark. He fell over and over again, scratching his legs on jagged rocks. But he kept going, running until his chest burned right where he was marked, and begged for all motion to cease. He collapsed onto his hands and knees at a place of great darkness. He looked behind him and it was as if the world had sealed itself off, a barrier never to be breached. All that was there was the speck of light he knew had to be Samuel, bouncing gently in the air, holding within itself the dawn.

He heard a sound coming from that place, too—a

hissing, maybe a growling?—and thought that meeting his end by way of copperhead or cougar was unfair given the lashes he took from other animals; his
back was proof. Besides, something else had already
begun to eat him: desolation. No more Samuel.
No Maggie. No Essie. No Sarah. No Puah. No Be
Auntie. This was the purest damning. Even Amos's
company would do now, as long as he wore the name
somewhere on him for Isaiah to see.

Deadly thing this kind of solitude. When unwanted, it was a tingling, then a burn. At least that
was what it felt like to Isaiah, starting right at the
gash on his chest. It was growing, spreading like
fingers that might at any moment become a fist or
curl in an attempt to choke. He knew that the pain
would become harder and harder to bear. And he
knew that it would always be with him, whether he
was alive or dead. This was the burden of the soft
ones: to suffer in all but silence because the whimpering that slipped through the lips was inevitable.
Samuel must have been right. Surely, he cussed the
heart that knew not how to protect itself from the
rift. For shame.

There was nothing else to do, then, but wait. In
those last moments, the least Isaiah could do was
honor Samuel by giving stone a try. It wouldn't be
long. Just time enough to receive his blessing though
no one was there to see it. He looked ahead to face
it, whatever it was, in the same manner he was sure
Samuel faced it: eyes open. The darkness before him

wasn't still. It convulsed like a living thing with seven tentacles, attached to figures maybe, twin dark-nesses. Holding sticks. Voices that sounded more like pebbles than humans. He had no choice. He reached out to them, fingers unsteady in the moist air, and felt something touch him. He jerked away and then, in the following quiet, reached his hand out again. Whatever it was, it was smooth, silky, fa-miliar. He crawled toward it, plunging his hand in farther and farther.

"That you, Samuel?"

Finally, something caressed him. Not just caressed him, but coiled itself around his arm and pulled. He screamed, finally, the one word he could never utter.

Then, to his surprise, in ululation, the darkness screamed it back.

NEW COVENANT

You know who **we** are now.

So now you know who **you** are.

We are seven and we do not absolve ourselves of blame.

So you must not absolve yourself of it either, blameless though you think you are.

Listen:

Heed:
We are calling for a witness!
Ay!

We are only telling you what we know.

You have to be willing to come forth when the hands are open widest.

Why do you think we are in this clearing instead of in that other one?

We heard you sing:

Come see about us, Lord!
And that is not your song.

That is why you try to make home a paradise instead of a place where life can take root.

Yes, well.
Home is not frozen.
It is not some insect trapped in amber.
Neither is it soft like clay for you to mold to whatever shape suits you.
It is bigger than you.
Do you understand?
Home is the beginning of every possibility and here you are trying to ruin it with your limitations.
There are mountains here, **too.**

Do not look away.

This is not who you were supposed to be.
You disrespect artisans.
You throw stones at guardians of the gates.

You ravage the spirits too grand for the body.
You imagine your own rituals savage.
You forget the circle.
Living so far from the existence you were snatched
from—

a half-truth.
Also given over to.
Becoming ever more like your captors, you cannot
even look your lover in the eye.
This is the mark you leave upon each other:
separation.

Well, let us gather you. Come: let us gather you all.

Where you are, it used to have a name.
They found the name and hung it from trees.
Someone should call this place by its real name.
O, ordinary!
How fine and ordinary.

Hear us:

There is a darkness that moves.
It is the beginning of all things and the end of
all things.
It is eternal, drawing with such great force that
even light bends to its whims.
It is hands covered in oil, wiping lines across faces,

pulled outward, spread like fingers, and waiting for the dawn.

It is cosmos dangling at the ends of braids, children dancing a thousand nighttimes, elders dressed in blue garments giddy to be submerged in new waters and to shed old skins.

This to the unseen.

This to the unheard.

This to the periphery people swimming between the glint of light and the bend of shadow.

In the midnight.

In the sanctity of caves.

In the private moments between lovers who have, for the first time, touched each other's faces.

The waves crashing against the shore?

That is a language, too.

The horrible secret, children, is this:

It is not you who are chained.

Remember this, for it is the key to tongue-speak.

But memory is not enough.

We are complete.

We are, all by ourselves, complete.

Do not look away.

There is a child, now, wandering in unknown woods.

Inside him, there is a wound, which you placed there, that may or may not blossom.

It may be uprooted.

Or it may be visited upon you: a kind of return, the way things often return to the hands that unleashed them.

The others, they are here with us, guarding the gates as always, pleased that a piece of them is still with you.

Would you like to feel it?

Close your eyes.

See:

The shape of suffering is not jagged.

It is not bumpy; it is not flat.

It is not even sharp.

It is round as eyes and smooth as skin.

It fits perfectly in the crook of the tongue and falls from the lips like a seeing stone.

Leave it where it lies.

Do not worry.

Hips will sway.

Heads will spin.

Arms will swing.

Oh, our bloodlings, beds will rock and it will be as close to good as our natures allow.

You will walk upright in your mother's house!

You are trembling.

Do not be ashamed.
Tremble freely, but do not sleep.
And. Do. Not. Look. Away!

There is a sound when darkness withers.

It is a whimper, much like a slumbering baby's, but
gentler, quieter, softer in its own way, and much more
tragic because unlike a baby's, it always goes unheard.
Like the last thing they—**they**—said to us:

L
O
V
E.

That is the living word.

But you refused it.
Spat on it when it was shown.
Gave it the wrong cheek to kiss.
No different from the field you became, you
are changed.

It is difficult

to withstand the touch
of a people who only
bring their hands together

to sow suffering
who treat
the menace that they create
like it is not their creation.

It is difficult

to be among these trees
that have been complicit in the destruction
of so many people;
every leaf, every crack in the bark, every drop of
sap, every twisted root:
guilty.
But don't they stand anyway,
tall and thick in denial
blocking out the sky?

Blessèd be the ones who gaze upon the night and
holy are the ones who remember.

And memory is not enough!

Kosii!

To know from beneath:

That is a story only a prophet can tell.
But with the world being what it is
and the world being what it forever will be
never without a grieving heart.

Àṣẹ!

Here is the fire now:

> dancing, destroying.
> But honestly
> only wanting to be sung to
> softly
> sweetly.
> It is a dying flame
> shrinking
> flickering
> waiting to be extinguished
> finally
> by a lullaby.

But there are no singers left.

> For the noose has already been hung.
> The bond has already been broken.
> The seen has already been foresaw.
> The then is arriving now.

And nothing in creation able to stop the coming.

Nothing

except You.

Acknowledgments

Please forgive me if I forget to mention your name.

James Baldwin: It is in your name that I found the justice that my heart craves, the fairness that my mind seeks, the peace that my soul remembers, and the triumph that my body has been waiting for. You asked that we find you in the wreckage. We did that, "Pop." Now we shall gather the pieces and build a fine altar to your intellect, light candles, and love you the way you loved us: with gratitude.

Jandel Benjamin: Auntie, I write because you were the first in our family to write. I saw your poems and it made me know that writing didn't have to be an intangible dream. It didn't have to be a hobby. It could be real. Thank you for that gift.

Sherise Bright: Your friendship/sisterhood is an entire blessing and I'm so grateful that the universe saw fit to bring us together. You are a constant source of optimism, faith, humor, and intuition. You predicted this moment and I thank you for your insight into things that cannot be seen, but only felt.

Victoria Cruz: You are a living legend. What a blessing it was for me to bask in the glory of one of our greatest foremothers. Thank you for your advocacy, grace, humor, fierceness, and love.

Valerie Complex: Your genius amazes me. I'm not sure I've ever met anyone so effortlessly and endlessly creative, funny, beautiful, and kind. I can't wait for the rest of the world to know what I know: that your gifts are inspiring and life-changing. Love you, sis.

George Cunningham: It was you who gave me all that the American education complex denied by showing me the truth they never intended for me to see. It was in your course, "Reading Race," that I learned that my perspective and purpose was not some aberration, but was actually the latest in a long tradition of resistance. I don't know how to repay you.

Ava DuVernay: I don't know how you find the time to do it: create an endless stream of magnificence and also embrace us and laugh with us and break bread with us and dance with us and keep us ever so close. That is nothing short of miraculous and you are nothing short of a miracle. Thank you for giving of yourself so that we all might hold our heads a little higher. I ride or die for you, sis.

Janet Jackson: You have left an indelible mark on me, not just with your angelic voice, impeccable dancing, bright smile, sauntering stage work, and fierce music, but also with your seething intelligence and unyielding social consciousness. I broke my mother's dining room chair practicing "The Pleasure Principle" back in 1987, but it was all worth it because "Rhythm Nation" showed me, in ways accessible to an eighteen-year-old mind, that

I had a responsibility to help make the world a better place for not just myself, but all those who are oppressed. Thank you.

Joan Jones: Ma, you always say, "He raised hisself," but what you don't know is that your courage, liberty, take-no-shit-from-nobody stance, rejection of patriarchy, skepticism of all belief, requirement of hard facts and tons of evidence, acceptance of violence as a defensive option when necessary, and insistence on being precisely who the fuck you are irrespective of who did or didn't approve was the example that I needed to survive and thrive. You are an outlaw and a free woman. And I thank you for it.

Tron Jones: My blood brother. Thank you for your sacrifices. Thank you for your laughter. Thank you for holding on despite the things holding you back. Please—share your writing with the world.

Sally Kim: My vision board foretold of our meeting and of our melding. Thank you for your knowing eye and discerning heart, undying support, respecting what I am attempting to do and say, and for helping me to focus and fine-tune so that others might likewise respect those things. Thank you, also, for understanding my superstitions.

Kiese Laymon: Brother. You are such a tremendous source of love and light that English isn't suitable enough to describe you. Your belief in my ability carried me high when I was extremely low. Your writing—your deep, rigorous writing—gave me permission to say what I feel I have to say. Thanks are not enough, but thank you.

PJ Mark: I have never had someone believe in my work so fiercely, fight for it with such diligence, and defend it with this level of tenacity. I heard that in the agent industry, they call you "The Pitbull," but I think James Bond is more accurate. Thank you so much for your guidance, kindness, expertise, and no-nonsense approach to my work and my career.

Calvis McLaurin: One day, brother, it will be impossible for you to ignore your calling and you will get to work. More than politicians, pastors, priests, police, and pimps, the world needs its painters. Your brush is then pen; your pad your canvas. Go make a masterpiece. For our sake.

Ernesto Mestre-Reed: When very few others saw value in my writing, had, in fact, diminished it with their thoughts and words, had cautioned me about the "danger of becoming a Black writer," you saw what they refused to: that the danger was present not how they imagined, but how they feared. You encouraged me to continue writing and showed me that there was inherent worth in my work. Your mentorship was invaluable. Thank you.

Toni Morrison: It was my dream for you to read this book, believe that it has merit, offer your blessing, and perhaps invite me for a cup of tea at your house so that I could tell you how without you, this book could not have been because it was your holy scripture, your complete indictment and rearrangement of the English language that inspired me to write it. You said if I couldn't find the book I wanted to read, then I must write it. So I did. Wherever you are in the universe, it is my sincerest hope that you are pleased.

Roni Natov: "Intake of breath . . ." You have been a tremendous advocate of not just my academic success, but of my overall success. If not for your boundless kindness, support, and belief in my abilities, I'm not sure where I'd be right now. You are a joy. Thank you.

Osvaldo Oyola: You saw this work at its earliest, clumsiest stages and still thought it was worth something. Thank you for your keen set of eyes, indelible mind, and brotherhood. Started from the Cyborg, now we here!

Samora Pinderhughes: Bruh-Bruh, from the moment we met, we became family. Thank you for listening, wishing only good things for me, cooking healthy foods, letting me get sneak peeks of your music, being one of the most brilliant musicians on this planet, having a big-ass heart, and having an incredible conscience.

Robert Scott: As I wandered the halls of Brooklyn College lost, you found me, as you have found generations of others, and put me on the right track. Thank you for your careful mentorship.

Arlene Solá-Vargas: For over forty years we have shared joys and pains, triumphs and tragedies, and look at us! We made it. We made it in spite the circumstances, maybe even because of the circumstances. Thank you so much for your encouragement and for welcoming me into the family.

Adrian Techeira: My husssband. LOL! Never did I imagine that your Virgo-ness would come in handy. Thank you for your critical eye, your legal expertise, your support when I can't operate at one hundred, the house that is now a home, and the love that is now bonded and witnessed. Thank you.

Charles, Marcus, and Victoria Thompson: One realist. One learner. One dreamer. Thank you for your undying encouragement, trusted friendship, and for choosing me to be part of your family. I'm eternally grateful.

Crystal Waterton: You, whose diapers I changed. And now you are a grown woman and creating the most brilliant of art. I can't wait until the world learns what I already know: you are one of the most brilliant film-makers around. Make. Your. Art. Sis!

David Wells: You have been like a true brother to me, helping me feel whole when I feel like I could fall apart, checking on me when the days are too long and the nights are troubled. I know now what they mean when they say "brother's keeper." Thank you.

To the Janklow & Nesbit Associates team, Ian Bonaparte and Zoe Nelson, and **the G. P. Putnam's Sons/Penguin Books USA team,** Joel Breuklander, Brennin J. Cummins, Ivan Held, Christopher Lin, Ashley McClay, Katie McKee, Emily Mlynek, Gabriella Mongelli, Vi-An Nguyen, Nishtha Patel, Anthony Ramondo, Amy Ryan, Alexis Welby, and the entire Putnam sales team: You helped me pull a lifelong fantasy out of the ether and into the material world. Your commitment and teamwork is inspiring. My gratitude is never ending. Thank you.

To my blood and chosen family, who have seen me at the beginning, through my tribulations, and into my triumphs—you have been my solid ground and I love you deeply: Khadeem D. Wilson, Khadijah I. Wilson, Sandra Benjamin, Alfred Benjamin, Jr., Shahaira Davy, Justin O. Christopher, Orlando J. Davy, Jr., Sheronda Benjamin, Lenice Smith, Kayin Davy, Errol Waterton, Orlando Davy,

Sr., Melissa Barnaby Hernandez, Christian Alcazar, Chastity Hernandez, Angel Bright, LaFawn Davis, Hilda and David Sola, Sr.; Eduardo Sr., Eduardo Jr., Isabella, and Daniel Vargas; David Jr., Laurie, and Olivia Sola; Tron Jr., Taina, Destiny, and Terrence Jones-Bosse, Julian and Milagros DeJesus, Dorothy, Simon, Nneka, Nya, and Jordyn Spence; Tiffany, Lole Sr., Lole Jr., Rowan, and Ivan Techeira, Jennifer Jacinto, and Tina Honeycutt; Beth, Tara, and Matthew Benjamin-Botas; Dawn Benjamin and Anthony Purge, Darlene Horton, Dawn Horton and family, Jimmie Horton and family, LaMont Horton and family, Renee, Cameron Jr., and Cameron Kelly, Dondria, Gary, and Ty Gadsden; Elena, Raquel "Mama Rock," and Howard "Pop" Pinderhughes; my Jones aunts: Angela, Laverne, Mallie, Mary, and Rita; My Jones cousins: Cheryl, Christine, Christopher, Daniel, Eric, Ebony, Elijah, Isiah, Jacob, Jamal, Jason, Jordan, Joshua, Justin, Kelly, Lashawn, Michael, Monae, Sean, Shauna, Stephanie; Lester Wint, Shannette Duncan-Wilson and family, Nicole Wilson, Starr Lester and family, Keesha Peets and family, James Peets and family, Scooner, Glenn, and Deena McCray and family, Willie "DJ Ill Will (Your Wifey's Favorite DJ)" White, Daniella "DAN-NELA" White, Octavia "Tay" Davison, William "Goddy" White, Jr., Rashawn "Red" White, Quincy "Penguin" White, Kimora "Whoop De Whoop" Simon, Summer "Zibba Zobba" Simon, Ashley "Ash Cash" Saint Louis, Reina Monserate, Scorpio Simon, and the entire Davison and White families, Michelle and Dream Holder, Tanya Edwards; Songhai, Glenn, Caleb, Kendi, Eli, and Taylor Deveaux; Karen and Joe McCord, Lori Petty, Anaya McLaurin,

Stephanie Acevedo-McCardle-Blunk, Miles Law, Paula Bryant (Brion), Margaret Prescod, Chanda and Kevin Hsu Prescod-Weinstein, Mary, Cheryl, Wanda, Felicia Diane, and Dawn Carpenter; Baldwin the cat, all the Benjamins, Betheas, Denmarks, Gaineses, Hines, Joneses, and Wilsons. Thank you.

Your unfathomable creativity, artistic achievements, and shining genius made it possible for me to imagine a reality where I had a chance: Wallace Thurman, Gloria Naylor, Alice Walker, Octavia Butler, Zora Neale Hurston, Chinua Achebe, Michelle Alexander, Maya Angelou, Kola Boof, Ta-Nehisi Coates, Edwidge Danticat, Debra Dickerson, Tananarive Due, Nikki Giovanni, Max S. Gordon, Joseph Illidge, Lorraine Hansberry, Ernest Hardy, James Earl Hardy, E. Lynn Harris, N. K. Jemisin, Jamaica Kincaid, Gabriel García Márquez, Ayana Mathis, James McBride, Herman Melville, Nell Irvin Painter, Gabby Rivera, Sonia Sanchez, Ntozake Shange, Danyel Smith, Brandon Thomas, Jean Toomer, and Isabel Wilkerson.

When I was lost, your voice and your song guided me home: Aaliyah, Marsha Ambrosius, Ashford & Simpson, Bobby and IZ Avila, Bahamadia, Anita Baker, Big Freedia, Black Stax, Radha Blank, Mary J. Blige, Boyz II Men, Brandy, Dennis Brown, Foxy Brown, Bry'Nt, B.Slade, Cakes Da Killa, Tevin Campbell, Mariah Carey, Chika, Sam Cooke, Bernadette Cooper, D'Angelo, Frenchie Davis, Deadlee, Smoke E. Digglera, Johnathan Douglass; Earth, Wind & Fire; Missy "Misdemeanor" Elliot, En Vogue, Rachelle Farrell, Aretha Franklin, Rah Rah Gabor, Kenneth

Gamble and Leon A. Huff, Medino Green, "Cat" Harris-White, Donny Hathaway, Lalah Hathaway, Lauryn Hill, Whitney Houston, Phyllis Hyman, Stasia "Stas" Irons, Freddie Jackson, Mahalia Jackson, Millie Jackson, Luke James, Jidenna, Syleena Johnson, Jimmy Jam and Terry Lewis, Kevin Kaoz, Chaka Khan, Patti LaBelle, Ledisi, Lady Leshurr, Le1f, Ari Lennox, Lil' Kim, Enongo "Sammus" Lumumba-Kasongo, Cheryl Lynn, Janelle Monae, Stephanie Mills, Laura Mvula, Meshell Ndegeocello, Mr. Strange, New Edition, Kimberly Nichole, Gene Noble, Jessye Norman, Sinead O'Connor, Rahsaan Patterson, Leontyne Price, Prince, Rapsody, Della Reese, Rihanna, Amber Riley, Minnie Ripperton, Diana Ross, Sade, Salt-N-Pepa, Bobby Short, Nina Simone, Bessie Smith, The Staple Singers, Sandra St. Victor, Donna Summer, Sylvester, Tank and the Bangas, Sister Rosetta Tharpe, Monifah and Terez Thorpe, Tina Turner, Tweet, Usher, Dionne Warwick, Jody Watley, Vesta Williams, Angela Winbush, Stevie Wonder, and Nicole "Lady" Wray.

Seeing you on screens and stages, as well as behind them, gave me self-esteem and the gift of daring to follow a dream: Yahya Abdul-Mateen II, Adepero Adoye, Kofi Agyemang, Erika Alexander, Alana Arenas, Nicholas L. Ashe, Reginald L. Barnes, Angela Bassett, Nicole Behari, Asante Blackk, Nahum Bromfield, Yvette Nicole Brown, Roscoe Lee Browne, Jade Bryan, Dyllón Burnside, LeVar Burton, Rosalind Cash, Diahann Carroll, Rashan Castro, Rodney Chester, Denzel Chisholm, Stanley Bennett Clay, Michaela Coel, Ryan Coogler, Emayatzy Corinealdi, Laverne Cox, Julie Dash, Loretta Devine, Aunjanue Ellis, Yance Ford, Dawn

Lyen Gardner, Marla Gibbs, Rashad E. Greene, Danai Gurira, Lisa Gay Hamiton, dream hampton, Winnie Harlow, Jackeé Harry, Brian Tyree Henry, Monique Angela Hicks, José Hollywood, Gwen Ifill, Dominique Jackson, Michael R. Jackson, Barry Jenkins, Jharrel Jerome, Christopher Jirau, Mustapha Khan, Regina King, Eartha Kitt, Kasi Lemmons, Deondray & Quincy LeNear-Gossett, Donja Love, Moms Mabley, Tina Mabry, Rajendra R. Maharaj, Sara'o Maozac, Sonequa Martin-Green, Sampson McCormick, Tarell Alvin McCraney, Akili McDowell, Edgar Mendez, S. Epatha Merkerson, Janet Mock, Indya Moore, Stacey Muhammad, Terrence Nance, Niecy Nash, Adaora Nwandu, Lupita Nyong'o, LaWanda Page, Keke Palmer, Tammy Peay, Numa Perrier, Tonya Pinkins, Patrik-Ian Polk, Billy Porter, Aamer Rahman, Naima Ramos-Chapman, Dee Rees, Della Reese, Shonda Rhimes, Beah Richards, J. August Richard, Bobby Rivers, MJ Rodriguez, Anika Noni Rose, Angelica Ross, Shaun Ross, Aston Sanders, Narubi Selah, Gabourey Sidibe, Justin Simien, Madge Sinclair, Brian Michael Smith, Justice Smith, Jussie Smollett, Doug Spearman, Darryl Stephens, Tika Sumpter, Ryan Jamaal Swain, Andre Leon Talley, Regina Taylor, Lorraine Toussaint, Cicely Tyson, Leslie Uggams, Gabrielle Union, Alok Vaid-Menon, Pernell Walker, Kerry Washington, Benjamin Charles Watson, Jr., Alek Wek, Rutina Wesley, Emile Wilbekin, Paul Winfield, Oprah Winfrey, George C. Wolfe, Charlayne Woodard, Tyquane Wright, and Bradford Young.

Your unmatchable skill and enviable diligence are wonders to behold. Thank you:

Simone Biles, DeWanna Bonner, Elena Delle Donne, Gabby Douglas, Candice Dupree, Chelsea Gray, Brittney Griner, Natasha Howard, Mae Jemison, Allie Quigley, Caster Semenya, Courtney Vandersloot, Dwyane Wade, Serena Williams, and Venus Williams.

Thank you for the beauty of aesthetic truth: Derrick Adams, Jean-Michel Basquiat, Jamal Campbell, Olivier Coipel, Njideka Akunyili Crosby, Jermaine Curtis Dickerson, Bilquis Evely, Tatyana Fazlalizadeh, Ramona Fradon, Paul Gagner, Vashti Harrison, Phil Jiménez, Kerry James Marshall, Jamie McKelvie, Kadir Nelson, Mikael Owunna, Jennifer Packer, Gordon Parks, Aaron Radney, Khary Randolph, Trina Robbins, Roger Robinson, Will Rosado, Jacolby Satterwhite, Augusta Savage, Ashleigh Shackelford, Liam Sharp, Alma Thomas, Hank Willis Thomas, Alberto Vargas, Kara Walker, Kara Mae Weems, Kehinde Wiley, and Ashley A. Woods.

Your vision helps me to navigate unkind terrain. Thank you: Gloria E. Anzaldúa, Ella Baker, Joseph Beam, Derrick Bell, Charles M. Blow, Tarana Burke, Kimberlé Crenshaw, Angela Davis, Joy DeGruy, Mona Eltahawy, bell hooks, Barbara Jordan, Barbara Lee, Audre Lorde, Manning Marable, Marlon Riggs, Assata Shakur, Harriet Tubman, Desmond Tutu, and Malcolm X.

Your courage is a balm, but also a shield. Thank you for service and sacrifices: Mumia Abu-Jamal, Phillip Agnew, John Amaechi, Robert Bailey, Dee Barnes, Jesse Ray Beard, Mychal Bell, Richard Blanco, Lanisha Bratcher, Robyn Crawford, Wade Davis II, Anita Hill, Rachel Jeantel, Marsha P. Johnson, Carwin

Jones, Gia Marie Love, Erica Malunguinho da Silva, Erica Malunguinho da Silva, Antron McCray, Michel'le, Wes Moore, Bree Newsome, Stella Nyanzi, Bryant Purvis, Raz-B, Kevin Richardson, Sylvia Rivera, Yusef Salaam, Karol Sanchez, Raymond Santana, Theo Shaw, Bryan Stevenson, William Dorsey Swann, Ciara Taylor, Zaya Wade, Jewel Thais-Williams, Korey Wise.

I learned at the altar of your boundless wisdom. Thank you for being my teachers: Moustafa Bayoumi, Prudence Cumberbatch, Michael Cunningham, Stacy D'Erasmo, Wendy Fairey, Howard Firestone, Pamela Grace, Irene Horowitz, Rosamond King, Jerome Krase, Laura Mattiga, Jenny Offil, Laurie Pea, Alexis Emilia Pierre-Louis, Madelon Rand (RIP), Joan Reale, Dorothy Rompalske, Ramsey Scott, Robyn C. Spencer, Ellen Tremper, Brooke Watkins, Salim Washington, and Kee Yong.

Thank you for your gifts, and your commitments to the word and the truth: Ashley Akunna, Zaheer Ali, Michael Arcenaux, Eroc Arroyo-Montano, Kenyette Barnes, Regina N. Bradley, Yaba Blay, Richard Brookshire, Jericho Brown, Clay Cane, Jasmyne Cannick, Maisy Card, Rebecca Carroll, Cody K. Charles, Roger Cipo, Hillary, Lemu, and King Kinti Crosley-Coker, Brittney Cooper, Timothy DuWhite, Chana Ginelle Ewing, Ayesha K. Faines, Kimberly N. Foster, Donte Gibson, Kieron Gillen, Jenn Jackson, Fatima Jamal, George M. Johnson, Myles E. Johnson, Kimberly Jones, Sarah Karim, Ibram X. Kendi, R.O. Kwon, Angel Laws, Creighton Lee, Inigo Leguda, Jamilah Lemieux, Felice León, Maurice Lucas, Tamika Mallory, Shane McCrae, Tiq Milan, Darnell L.

Moore, Isabelle Mosado, Frank Mugisha, Eddie Ndopu, Mark Anthony Neal, Tambay Obenson, Oronike Odeleye, Josh Odom, Nnedi Okorafor, Daniel Jose Older, José Guadalupe Olivarez, LaSha Patterson-Verona, Brontez Purnell, Imani Perry, Tony Puryear, Helen Phillips, Ayanna Pressley, Donovan X. Ramsey, Franchesca Ramsey, Kiley Reid, Sonya Renee, Maurice Carlos Ruffin, Namwali Serpell, Aishah Shahidah Simmons, Danez Smith, Kaila Adia Story, Rebecca Theodore-Vachon, Steven Thrasher, Ezinne Ukoha, Ocean Vuong, Imani J. Walker, Lawrence Ware, Kirsten West-Savali, G. Willow Wilson, De'Shawn Charles Winslow, Ravyn Wngz, Ashley Yates, Damon Young, and Hari Ziyad.

Thank you, squad, for lifting me up, having my back, and "holding me down": Clinton Adams, Irva Adams, Robert Agyemang, Trey Alexander, Yasmin Ali, Henry Anderson, Keisha-Gaye Anderson, Torrese Arquee, John Avelluto, Ivan Baptiste, Monique Baylor-McCall and family, Marie-Helene Bertino, Lemmie Blakemore, Karen Blitz, Jonathan Lee Bowles (you got next!), D'Ambrose Boyd, Jason Boston, Beqi Brinkhorst, Daniela Brown, Zedrick Brown, Aishah Bruno, Quonnetta Calhoun, Horace & Bryant Campbell-Coleman and family, Tyrone H. Cannon, Bernadette Canty, Ray Caspio, Seve Chambers, Madonna Charles, Sandra Clarke, Don "DJ" Davis, Kiev Davis and family, Camille DeBose, Lisa Del Sol, Gwen Devoe, Gerado "Gee" DiFeo, Robert Finley, Jr., Zinga A. Fraser, Erika Frierson, Steven G. Fullwood, Stephen Funches, Tungi Fussell, Alyssa Gargiulo, Tanisha Green, Natalia Guarin-Klein, Feargal Halligan, Justin LaRocca Hansen, Mobina

Hasmi, Addie Hopes, Reginald Idlett, Lacy D. Jamison, Loretta Jenkins, James W. Jennings, Tasha Jones, Vondia "Peaches" Jones, Thomas Jordan, Greg Jurick-Blackshear, Meghan Keane, Jennifer Kikoler, David Kim, Amy Klopert, Kevel C. Lindsay, Katy Maslow, Dina Maugeri, Shayne McGregor, Kristen Meinzer, Kamela Mohabeer, Cristina Moracho, Cynthia Naughton-Goodman and family, Doreen Naughton, Michelle Naughton and family, Natalie Naughton and family, Nicole Naughton-Lincoln and family, Pamela Naughton-Allen and family, Barry Nelson, Kevin Dwayne Nelson, Karen Parker, Bernadette Parker-Canty, Lucille Pascall, Bones Patterson, Audrey Peterson, Anthonine Pierre, Alexzia Plummer, Temika Polk, Cory Provost, Anthony Punt, Rhea Rahman, Shais Rison, Carrie Roberts (RIP), Maya Rock, Marlene Saez, Michael Santana, Crystal Schloss, Jeffrey Severe, Nichole Simon, Mark Simpson, Jared Shuler, Kevin Smith, Moraima Smith, Nicole St. Clair, Tyrone "Flyronee" Stevens, Aimee Stevland, Renee Straker and family, Bernard Tarver; Mammen, Betsy, Saramma and Suma Thomas; Lealand Thompson, Randi Vegh (RIP), Melissa Velez, Stanley Walker, Raina Washington, Darryl "The Griot" Watson, Zora Wells, Jackie Williams, Trina Yearwood, and Keith Zackowitz. **To the entire Son of Baldwin community:** Thank you for the discussions, the disagreements, the laughs, the tears, the love, and the pain. You have elevated me and provided sanctuary. You educated and enlightened me. Y'all are so, so dope. Thank you so very much. **To my JanFam, my Rhythm Nation:** You are all black diamonds: Shawn Arnold, Vincent Bernard,

Roger Brown, Elgin "Emperor" Charles, Michaela Harrison, Lamont Hicks, Harold Jacobs, Gray Lappin, Jordan Listenbee, J. C. and Mike Litherland-Neilson, Ify "Angie" Olie, Denise P. Oliver, Ralphie Scarborough, Robert Snowden, and Thomas "Trey" Simpson.

To my Marlboro Projects family: Through all the ups and all the downs—and those downs were ROUGH!—we found community. Thank you.

To the booksellers, libraries, readers, and all makers and lovers of books: Thank you. A special thank you to Sarah McGrath at Riverhead, Peter Blackstock at Grove, Kate Medina at Random House, Alison Lorentzen at Viking, Erin Wicks at HarperCollins, and Barbara Jones at Henry Holt.

To oppressed peoples caught up in the prison industrial complex: May true justice, rehabilitation, and reconciliation prevail.

Shout out to sex workers and to every House of every Ball. May you all be Safe.

Halsey Street: You are forever in my heart.

We speak your names: Tanisha Anderson, Ahmaud Arbery, Ricky Beeks, Sean Bell, Sandra Bland, Muhlaysia Booker, Rekia Boyd, Rashawn Brazell, Kalief Browder, Venida Browder, Michael Brown, Eleanor Bumpurs, Philando Castile, Stephon Clark, Coobah, John Crawford III, Kaladaa Crowell, Michelle Cusseaux, Amadou Diallo, Jamie Doxtator, Henry Dumas, George Floyd, Janisha Fonville, Ezell Ford, Korryn Gaines, Eric Garner, Erica Garner, Pearlie Golden, Ramarley Graham, Oscar Grant, Freddie Gray, the Grenfell Fire victims, Sakia Gunn, Akai Gurley, Latasha Harlins; Markis, Hannah, Jeremiah, Devonte, Abigail, and Ciera

Hart; Yusuf Hawkins, Stephen Hicks, Tony Hughes, Kyra Inglett, Malik Jackson, Botham Jean, Atatiana Jefferson, Marquis Jefferson, Duanna Johnson, Kendrick Johnson, Kathryn Johnston, Bettie Jones, India Kager, Oliver Lacy, Stephen Lawrence, Errol Lindsey, Renisha McBride, Tony McDade, Laquan McDonald, Natasha McKenna, Brandi Mells, Ernest Miller, Margaret LaVerne Mitchell, Kayla Moore, Shanta, Jeremiah, and Shanise Myers, Yahira Nesby, Islan Nettles, the New Cross house fire victims, Sean Reed, Bailey Reeves, Tamir Rice, Aura Rosser, Relisha Rudd, Walter Scott, Anthony Sears, Konerak Sinthasomphone, Eddie Smith, Raymond Smith, Aiyana Stanley-Jones, Curtis Straughter, Breonna Taylor, David Thomas, Emmett Till, Tituba, Mary Turner, Matt Turner, Nia Wilson, and too, too many others.

To the Native, Indigenous, First Nation People whose land I was born and natured on: Thank you.

To the entire African diaspora and all marginalized peoples everywhere: Together we can create a movement. Together we can smash injustice. Love makes us capable of both things.

About the Author

ROBERT JONES, JR. was born and raised in New York City. He received his BFA in creative writing with honors and MFA in fiction from Brooklyn College. He has written for numerous publications including **The New York Times, The Paris Review, Essence, OkayAfrica, The Feminist Wire,** and **The Grio.** He is the creator of the social justice community Son of Baldwin, and was featured in **T Magazine**'s cover story "Black Male Writers of Our Time." **The Prophets** is his debut novel.